Kate Forster lives in Melbourne, Australia with her husband, two children and two dogs, and can be found nursing a laptop, surrounded by magazines and watching trash TV or French fil

The Last Will and Testament of Daphné Le Marche

KATE FORSTER

First Published in Great Britain 2016
By Harlequin Mira, an imprint of HarperCollins*Publishers*
1 London Bridge Street, London, SE1 9GF

The Last Will and Testament of Daphné Le Marche © 2016 Kate Forster

ISBN 978-1-848-45449-1

58-0916

For my mother Joan, the ultimate Francophile.

Prologue

The ornate marble fireplace glowed from the fire that hissed and danced within it, as though in celebration of what was to come for Daphné Le Marche and, as she watched the flames, she imagined her final descent into hell.

Was it Mark Twain who said that you should go to heaven for the climate and hell for the company?

Daphné would always take the excellent company over a sunny day; besides, the state of the weather had never bothered her. She lived so much in her head that she often failed to notice the black clouds building on the horizon.

That was often the problem in her eighty years on Earth, she mused, as she watched the cremation dance in the distance of her bedroom.

The nurse had said it was too warm for a fire in this mild July summer, and the doctor said the smoke wasn't good for her heart, but he had said it half-heartedly, she thought, and she smiled at her own pun.

What did they know about her frozen bones and broken heart? What did they know about being housed in an eighty-year-old body with a thirty-year-old mind?

Of course, the fire was lit as requested, and a new nurse was employed; one who didn't sigh, and blow her fringe up with her breath when she entered Daphné's bedroom.

She looked around her bedroom with her tired eyes. It was splendid; everything in her world was splendid. Her bedroom was perfectly appointed in every way, from the pale apricot silk curtains to the antique furniture, but the only items that gave her pleasure at that moment were her mother's linen sheets which she lay upon, given to her on her wedding day sixty years ago.

How she wished for her mother now, tears burning her tired eyes, as the heavy oak door to her bedroom opened.

Edward Badger entered the room, standing awkwardly in the entrance, holding a leather satchel and an iPad.

'Madame Le Marche,' he said in a deferential yet somewhat embarrassed tone. He had probably never seen her so vulnerable and looking so old, she thought, and she took a little pleasure in still making those around her feel uncomfortable. She liked people to not feel too familiar with her. Just because they knew the stories, they didn't know the woman, she often told those nearby, a boastful warning of who they were dealing with.

For twelve years, Edward had worked for Daphné Le Marche as her personal solicitor, starting as a junior and then working his way to her side. He was the most loyal person she had ever known, or the most stupid—she could never quite decide—but at least he stayed when everyone else had left.

'Edward, please, sit.' She motioned to the uncomfortable Queen Anne style chair, placed by her bedside for visitors. She had deliberately asked for this chair to be used, discouraging long stays.

Not that any of the visitors who had sat by her failing side had offered her any comfort. Who could offer her comfort now, besides the doctor and his heavy leather bag of medicines?

Edward looked handsome with the fire behind him, and Daphné wondered if he had left a woman's bed to be in another woman's bedroom at nearly midnight. Edward never spoke of his love life, although she was sure he wasn't gay. Perhaps if she were younger, she might have helped him in some way to find his lover or she might have kept him for herself. She smiled to herself at the thought of her younger self in seduction mode.

'I have decided,' she said finally, feeling her heart beat in random triplets.

Edward nodded and sat down as she instructed. He then opened the satchel and took out a thick sheaf of papers.

'Do you believe in heaven and hell?' she asked.

To his credit, Edward didn't seem perturbed by her question even though Madame Le Marche had never really engaged in small talk with him, but then again conversations about the afterlife could not be construed as small talk.

'No,' he answered as he shuffled the papers, finding the one page he needed to record her final wishes.

'You seem so sure, have you already had a preview of what's to come?' She laughed a little.

He looked up at the old woman and smiled. 'I deal in facts and there isn't any evidence to suggest that such places exist outside this life.'

His eyes were kind and his voice steady and she wondered if he was as good to his own mother as he was to her.

'Are you suggesting there exists a place within this life? That heaven is here on earth?'

Edward raised his broad shoulders and shrugged. 'Perhaps.'

Daphné felt a rare stir of interest. Age makes you not only weary but also bored, she often said.

'Go on,' she demanded.

Edward smiled, almost to himself, she noticed. 'Do you know those days that are perfect? Where everything makes sense and who you are with, or your own company, feels like destiny, when everything is flowing your way, that is heavenly, isn't it?'

'Perhaps,' she said, slightly imitating him.

He went on, ignoring her dusting of scorn. 'And those days or nights, yes it's usually night-time, when you wonder how it all could have gone so incredibly wrong, why the person you love is in pain, or how can a baby have cancer? How can people suffer so much? I think that is hell. It's usually between the hours of two and four in the morning that the worst of those thoughts occur.'

'Hell has a schedule? A timetable?' She laughed again, but it sounded hollow to her ears.

She knew those hours. She knew that hell.

Edward was silent, as though he had said too much, but she didn't have time for his guilt. She had her own to deal with.

She paused, as her long, thin fingers clutched the edge of the sheets.

She remembered her mother tucking her into bed when she was sick, the smell of lavender on the sheets, the sound of a fire in the bedroom lulling her to sleep.

When I die, I will go downstairs and my mother will be

upstairs, she thought, and at that moment Daphné regretted the choices she had made in life, for only her mother was enough to cause a woman like Daphné Le Marche penitence.

Edward waited patiently for her decision to be revealed.

'Is the formula safe?' she asked, and Edward nodded.

'It's in the bank vault,' he said.

'And the journals?'

'Locked in the drawer in London,' he answered.

Daphné sighed. There was no point postponing it any longer. She knew what she had to do.

'The girls, I leave it all to the girls,' she said finally.

Edward blinked a few times, as though trying to process her ruling.

'And Robert?' He asked of her only surviving child.

'He made his decision years ago,' she said and Edward was silent.

The Le Marche family history was enough to fill scandal sheets for years to come, but he knew her decision to overlook her only son and heir was not made lightly.

'They must be here in London; they must work at Le Marche for a year before they can sell and they must always have two signatures on every decision. They are each other's conscience.'

Edward wrote notes on the iPad as she spoke, her hands now running along the edging of the top sheet. Back and forth, like practising scales on the piano as a child.

She thought of her business and she wished she could stay. Nothing was as good as working, she once told her sons. What a shame neither of them had her work ethic.

'And the formula?' he asked.

'They receive it after they have worked together for one year and one day.'

Edward made a note and snapped the cover on the iPad closed as though it was an audible full stop on the moment.

'Where are the girls now?' she asked, tiredness creeping up on her.

'Celeste is mostly in Paris, but is sometimes with her mother in Nice, and Sibylla is in Melbourne—she lives alone but spends a lot of time with Elisabeth.'

Daphné felt her eyes hurt again at the thought of lovely Elisabeth. How she had suffered, in some ways more than Daphné, at the loss of Henri.

'Mothering isn't easy, that's why I worked,' she said almost to herself.

Edward was silent.

He was understanding company, she thought, wishing he would come again, but she knew she wouldn't see him again after tonight.

'A year. I give them a year to work together, and one cannot sell without the other. If one sells, they both sell.'

'They can't buy each other out?' Edward's face was now frowning.

'Don't frown, it gives you lines,' said Daphné automatically.

Edward tried to smooth his face but failed.

'They can't sell the company to each other?' he asked again.

'No,' said Daphné. 'I want this family to rest its quarrels. The only chance we have now is with the girls.'

'But they haven't seen each other since they were children,' Edward said.

'You're frowning again,' she reminded him.

The fire spat in annoyance, and he glanced at it and then back to Daphné who was speaking again.

'I am not concerned about petty reasons of an obstacle, such as separation. They're family, they don't need reintroductions. They have more in common than they think.'

Edward wrote quickly and then handed the papers to Daphné, who lifted her hand.

'Where do I sign?' she asked with a tired sigh. Dying was exhausting, she thought. No wonder people only did it once in their lifetime.

Edward picked up a book from her bedside table for her rest the paper on.

'*The Book of Perfumes*,' he said with a wry smile. 'Still working, are you?'

'I am always working,' she said tiredly, as the door opened and the nurse came into the room. 'Even on my deathbed, I am working.'

'Can you witness this, please?' Edward asked the woman, in a tone Daphné admired. He had grown into a confident man and she trusted him, which was as rare in business as it was in love.

The nurse watched as Daphné signed her hand and then Edward and the nurse added their signatures to the document.

'It is done,' said Edward, in a deferential tone, after the nurse left the room.

'I don't envy you,' she said, a small smile creeping onto her face.

'Why is that?' he asked, as he packed his papers into his satchel.

'What is about to come, I am sure I don't pay you enough.' She laughed a little, happy at the thought she could still create waves, even after her death.

'I am capable of handling anything, I've been taught by the best,' said Edward, reaching down and touching her hand.

Her skin was cold, but her grasp firm, as she held his hand.

'Thank you,' she said, meaning it deeply. Edward had been her greatest support over the last years and she hoped he could be the same for the girls.

'Look after my *petites-filles*,' she said, so tired now.

'I will, and I will be back to see you again,' he said, his thumb stroking the back of her hand.

She nodded, but she knew he wouldn't be back while she was alive. If there was one thing Daphné Le Marche knew how to keep it was a schedule.

After Edward had gone, and the fire was dying in the grate, she saw the colour she had been chasing her entire life.

Dernières lueurs—the perfect afterglow.

And she cursed God that she could never replicate it in her lifetime. All she had ever wanted was to create a product that gave women the glow as though they had just fallen in love or made love or even both. She touched her own cheek with her hand and tried to remember when she last had that glow.

It was too long ago, she thought sadly, and she closed her eyes and slept, and between the hours of two and four, just as she had suspected she always would, Daphné Hélène Le Marche née Amyx died. She had never been late to a meeting before, and she sure as hell wasn't going to be late for this one.

Part 1

Spring

Chapter 1

Celeste

Sometimes Celeste Le Marche wondered if she should have died instead of Camille.

If she had gone to the dance lesson with Camille instead of having a tantrum at home because she didn't get new ballet shoes like her sister, then they would have argued over who got the front seat, and Celeste, being the more aggressive of the sisters, even though she was younger, would have won.

Camille would have been relegated to the back seat behind Papa, because that was the only seat belt in the back of the Audi that worked and it would have been Celeste that died instantly when the truck hit the car.

Then Camille would have gone to the hellhole school that was Allemagne and Celeste would have gone to heaven with Uncle Henri and Pépère, and everything would be as it should be.

She used to wonder what it was like in heaven. Every imagining changed according to her age. One year it was bowls filled with sweets on pretty little tables and talking goldfish that swam in ponds, then it was filled with every fabulous item of clothing she could imagine, and then it was champagne and cocaine and dancing without ever needing to sleep.

Now, as she wandered through the dark villa belonging to her mother, she wondered if heaven was actually being able to sleep through the night.

She could hear the sounds of the waves on the rocks below and she wondered about her uncle for a moment, and then pushed the thoughts from her head.

Why did the darkest thoughts always come when there was so little light?

She checked her phone and saw the missed messages from Paul in Paris.

Instead, there were over twenty messages from the press. News of her affair with the Minister of Trade had just been leaked by someone, probably that little shit who worked for him, she thought. He was always flouncing around wearing too much cologne and his pants too tight. Now it would be in the news tomorrow, unless Paul tried to put a stop to it by offering something in return.

A text came through from him as she peered at her phone.

Celeste, we need to talk. Now!

She snorted at her phone. He had a night free from the confines of the family home and he thought her worthy enough to give her his company, except she was in Nice and he wasn't happy about it all, judging by the tone of his text.

He could wait for a change, she thought, as she sat on the cane chaise and covered her long legs with the cotton blanket her mother had left at the end of the lounge. The sun must be nearly up, she thought, as she peered into the darkness. On the horizon, a light glimmered, and Celeste was thankful the night was nearly over.

Matilde was so thoughtful to her guests, thought Celeste, as she straightened out the blanket. It was just her daughter she forgot about. The only time she had been nurtured by Matilde was when she had her tonsils out when she was six, the year before Camille died. Matilde had put her daughter into clean sheets and rubbed lavender onto her temples when she had a headache. Camille had sat at the end of the bed and had read her *Babar*, and Papa had bought her little honey sweets to soothe her throat.

Her mother certainly hadn't been in this mood when Celeste arrived unannounced from Paris the day before.

'Celeste, what are you doing here?' she had asked, surprise showing in her blue eyes. At fifty-five years old, Matilde Le Marche had retained her figure, her married name, and her love of socialising.

'I needed to get away from Paris,' was all Celeste had said, pushing through the door of the villa.

'Married men make women crazy and women make married men crazy. It is better to be single,' said Matilde as she'd picked up her tennis racquet, which was next to the front door. 'Look at me.'

Celeste knew better than to open the door to the conversation that would start if she commented on her mother's statement. The only thing Matilde liked to do more than gossip was to complain about the affairs her father had had while they were still married.

Of course, Matilde had learned of Celeste's affair with Paul

Le Brun from the nephew of a friend, whose ex-boyfriend was in love with Paul.

Too many visits under the guise of decorating his office had brought attention to their relationship, and since then Paul had been retreating from seeing Celeste as often.

Was it just her, or was the sex a little less intense also, or was that because he was nearing fifty?

What if he died while they were making love? She had heard of such stories, and the idea of Paul dead on top of her while still inside her made her shudder.

Celeste tried to shake her morbidity and closed her eyes, the cool air caressing her face. Her phone chimed again and she rushed to turn it down and saw a text message from her father.

Grand-Mère passed last night

So much death in this family, she thought, as she read the message.

Her father Robert was not one for extreme displays of emotion and the news of Grand-Mère Daphné's passing was handled in his usual taciturn way.

She thought about messaging him back, but what could she say to ease her father's relationship with his mother?

She had enough problems with Matilde. The idea of her mother was far nicer than the reality. It was the same with Grand-Mère Daphné. She was always frightening to her as a child and she hadn't seen her in a year, not since Daphné's heart went into failure and she had gone into hiding.

'I'm surprised she has a heart to fail,' her father had quipped over their quarterly lunch at La Tour d'Argent, which Celeste loathed but knew it was vital to attend if she were to keep her measly allowance from Papa.

Daphné Le Marche was never a warm person to Celeste or anyone else, but she had rescued her granddaughter from her time at the Allemagne school and that alone was worth a moment's silence for the old woman.

She would organise the funeral, she thought. It would be an elegant event, like Daphné. God knows what it would turn into if her father was left to manage the details. If he had his way, her grandmother would be shipped out to sea in a cardboard coffin, and not even a prayer offered.

Perhaps she should have said more to her grandmother over the years, especially after that telephone call from Allemagne, made to Daphné when she was sixteen, which saved her life. Robert and Matilde were so immersed in their own grief and self-destruction that they didn't see their surviving daughter was dying at boarding school.

It was the only time in her childhood that Celeste had had a champion. It was Daphné who had told Robert that Celeste was anorexic, and a victim of extreme bullying and that she had tried to overdose on painkillers. It was Daphné who had told Matilde to step up and be a mother or she would lose both children. It was Daphné who had organised Celeste to attend hospital and finish her final classes at home with a tutor.

And it was Daphné who had ruined the school's reputation with Europe's elite when it refused to acknowledge any wrongdoing and turned a blind eye to the beatings of Celeste, the urine-soaked bed, courtesy of the girls in her dormitory, which Celeste was forced to sleep in most nights, and the ostracising of her from every meal and every social event.

What were once rumours of a culture of bullying at the school soon became absolute truth once Daphné made calls to certain important families. Soon there was a removal of some of the most elite students by their families and the school never quite regained its footing among the upper classes again.

Celeste never knew why it was her who had been chosen as the victim of the bullying. Was she too tall? Too thin? Too blonde? Too something?

The only time it had been discussed was when Matilde had called her on the telephone as Celeste was being put on a drip for dehydration and a low heart rate.

'They don't like you because you're too beautiful, like me. Women don't like women like us, we're a threat,' Matilde had slurred down the phone.

So Celeste grew to view all women as the enemy, even her own mother.

She opened her eyes, as she heard the sound of birds stirring in the bougainvillea, scratching and fighting to wake first. I envy them, she thought, it must be easy being a bird. She looked out at the growing light in the distance, colours of sherbet orange filling the sky and, for a moment, her eyes pricked with tears for Grand-Mère. She said a little prayer for Camille to look after her when she arrived in the afterlife.

She was under no illusions though that her grandmother would have thought of her on her deathbed. The woman barely had time for Robert, let alone his daughter. All she cared about was her business.

Now Le Marche would belong to Robert, and he would sell it to the Japanese as soon as he could. She pulled the cotton blanket up to her chest and wondered about Sibylla.

Did she know? Who would tell her? Would she come to the funeral?

But Celeste had no idea how to contact her cousin in Australia.

God, that was so far away, she thought. She struggled even travelling to London. Everything she needed was in Paris, Paul was in Paris. With his family, playing the perfect husband and father. That would be all over tomorrow if the news got out about their affair.

But if that were true, she thought, why had she run to Nice?

There were too many thoughts to try to put into order, so, instead, she watched the sun rise like fire in the distance.

But her thoughts came back like the waves below the villa, crashing into the cliff.

Was Paul at home in his bed with his wife, while their children slept peacefully in their little beds? Was he watching the sunrise from his balcony? Would he think of her as he showered? Would he think of her undressing as he dressed?

Did he sip on his coffee and wonder if she was thinking of him also?

Did he love her like she loved him?

Tears burned so harshly, she squeezed her eyes shut, even though Grand-Mère had always told her to never line her face with anything other than a smile.

A half sun sat on the horizon now, and Celeste felt more at peace in the glow.

Darkness was her worst time. Nights like this were hard to bear alone.

Thirty years old and the mistress of a politician. Thirty years old with no discernible career, except as an occasional interior designer and stylist. Thirty years old and still taking an allowance from her father.

What a joke she was. She lived off her father's meagre allowance and her lover's gifts, and was given her mother's apartment in Paris because Matilde didn't know how to love her only surviving child properly, and the apartment went some way to absolving her guilt.

For a moment, she was envious of her father and his inheritance. He could do anything he wanted with Le Marche, but she knew he would sell it, as much to spite Daphné as to live off the proceeds.

As the sun rose, Celeste thought of Daphné and her life.

At twenty-one, her grandmother had had two children and, within ten years, she had turned a family business into a cosmetics empire.

Self-esteem hadn't ever been a mantle that draped Celeste's shoulders, and now, when she thought of her brilliant grandmother, her self-sufficient mother and even her estranged cousin, Sibylla, who was a scientist or something similar, according to her research online, she felt hopeless.

She kicked off the blanket, stood up and stretched, then walked to the edge of the balcony.

The waves crashed below her and she could see the white foam greedily lapping the edges of the rocks.

She put her hands on the edge of the iron balcony and peered down further, trying to hear the sounds of the sea, seeing how far down the rocks were, or how far up she was.

What was below? she wondered. She thought of Uncle Henri. Is this what he felt? Did he hear *l'appel du vide*? The call of the void?

That's what her mother once said when she had asked how he had died.

Was it calling her now?

She couldn't be sure, as she saw a gull dive into the foam and pull a writhing silver treasure from the water.

'Well done,' she said with a smile to the bird.

Tiredness draped its heavy arms around her now, and she let go of the iron railing and nodded to the sea below.

'Not today,' she said, and went inside to finally sleep.

* * *

When she woke, dusk was settling in the sky. She walked out of her room and saw her mother had left her a note on the wooden table.

Gone to drink with the Michels. Come and join us if you want.

Celeste had no idea who the Michels were, but she knew her mother would be drinking too much with people who saw too much sun, regaling them of stories and gossip of her ex-mother-in-law, as no doubt the news of Daphné's death would be out now.

Celeste sighed and picked up a peach from the mosaic bowl her mother had made during one of her artistic retreats. Matilde was a frustrated artist with no particular talent, but she had tried every mode possible in which to express herself.

It seems the peach doesn't fall far from the tree, Celeste mused, as she bit into the soft flesh of the fruit. As the skin brushed her tongue, she missed Paul's touch and so she picked up her phone from the table and dialled his number.

He answered on the first ring. 'Darling, where are you? What's happened? Are you with your *grand-mère*?'

Hearing his voice, Celeste relaxed. She walked out onto the balcony.

'No, I'm with my mother,' she said. 'I'm sorry I didn't call you back, I've had some things in my head I needed to think about.'

She took another bite of the peach and then threw the rest over the edge, down into the void.

'But I'm coming back to you now,' she said and everything was back to how it was before, except it all felt so different and she couldn't explain why.

* * *

Back in Paris, Paul was late, as usual. Celeste, feeling less restless than usual, thanks to a glass of wine and a few puffs on a cigarette, leafed through a copy of French *Vogue*.

Her phone rang.

'Darling, I can't get away,' Paul complained.

Celeste took a gulp of wine.

'But I came back from Nice for you,' she said, hating that she sounded so whiny.

'I know, but there is a meeting I must attend,' he said. She could hear laughing in the background. 'I will come to the funeral. Has your father told you the details yet?'

'No,' snapped Celeste. She had tried to call her father numerous times to learn of the funeral plans, but Robert wasn't answering his phone.

'You will let me know?' Paul asked, sounding very formal, and Celeste hated him for a moment.

'Perhaps,' she said and ended the call.

She then scrolled through her phone until she found a number that made her smile.

After dialling, she waited. He would always answer her calls.

'Hello.' His voice sounded wary.

'It's Celeste,' she said in her most seductive tone.

'I know, your number came up on my phone.'

This wasn't quite the greeting she had hoped for. She had left Charles for Paul and had ignored his calls and heartache for a year. Surely he wasn't over her yet? She needed to let Paul know she also had a life outside of her bed.

'Did you want to get a drink?' she asked, running her finger over the rim of the wine glass.

'No thank you, I have plans,' Charles said.

Celeste believed him. She knew he wasn't playing games; that was her job.

'Are you seeing someone?' she asked softly.

'I'm engaged,' came the reply.

Celeste sighed. Charles was a good man, which was why she had left him for Paul. She had terrible taste in men, Matilde had once said, not that she was the greatest connoisseur either.

'Felicitations,' she said and then ended the call with no further promises.

She leaned back in the chair and lifted up her long blonde hair so it spilled over the black leather.

She had dressed for Paul just the way he liked, in a black chiffon cocktail dress and no lingerie. The dress was short enough to show off her endless legs and plunged to take advantage of her décolletage.

God, men were so easy to amuse, she thought, as she

kicked off her heels and then stood up, and peeled off her dress and walked naked to her room.

Pulling on sweatpants and an old T-shirt that was fraying at the edges but softer than what she imagined clouds would feel like, she went back to her chair, collecting the bottle of wine on her way through. Celeste could have been a model if she had been prepared to work hard enough, attending the castings and doing prestigious jobs for little money to build up her portfolio, but she didn't want to work that hard, and her first two years after leaving Allemagne were spent in Amsterdam, where she got stoned every day and worked in a café, trying to recover from her schooling experience.

Her head began to hurt, so she took two of her extra strong painkillers and put her music player into speakers. Soon the soft sounds of Marvin Gaye singing accompanied her as she poured herself more wine.

She needed to do something about Paul, but she didn't have the energy for it now.

Marvin was asking her to dance and Celeste needed to move. She felt her feet tapping and then her head bob and soon her hips moved with the rhythm. Closing her eyes, she turned up the music, put down her wine and gave her evening to Marvin, the only man who had never let her down.

Tomorrow could wait, she decided and she wondered what, if anything, was going to change now that Grand-Mère was gone.

Chapter 2

Billie, Melbourne

The laboratory was empty when Billie March arrived at work. She turned on the lights and breathed in the cleanliness, and then put her bag away. After donning her white coat, she shoved her phone into her pocket and placed ear buds into her ears and turned on the music.

This was her favourite time of day—when her co-workers were exhausted at the end of the week and they struggled into work one by one, talking about their plans for the weekend.

Billie wouldn't have a weekend if she could help it, but this weekend she had promised to help her mother and stepfather move into their new house.

Marvin Gaye sang about his Inner City Blues, which had seemed appropriate on the tram ride to the university, but now she needed something other than her father's favourite singer and she settled on Florence and the Machine.

She moved through the scheduled work, testing new deodorants, and then onto a brand of soap powder that claimed to reduce all stains.

The sound of the door clicked and Nick Miller walked into the laboratory.

'Morning, Billie,' he said cheerfully. He was still wearing his bicycle helmet and had one leg of his jeans tucked into an unevenly pink-coloured sock, but neither of these facts took away from his happy face.

Billie smiled at him. 'You look cheerful,' she said. Nick was her work crush. He was what made it lovely to come in every day. With his good looks and his pleasant banter, she couldn't wait to see him each day.

'I got every green light on the ride to work today, do you know the odds of that happening?'

'I have no idea but I'm sure you can work it out,' she said, as she went back to her soap powder paste, which she was smearing on lipstick-stained cloth.

Nick had put away his knapsack and taken off his helmet and was walking back to Billie when she pointed down at his sock.

'Untuck,' she said.

'Gee, thanks, Bill,' he said gratefully.

When Nick had first starting working at the lab, his forgetfulness became an office joke and once, when Billie had taken a rare sick day, Nick had worn his helmet all morning, including in a meeting, and no one had told him because they thought it was so hilarious.

Nick had said it was funny also, but Billie saw the flash of shame on his face when he was teased and she took it upon herself to socialise him, or at least remind him to take off his helmet and untuck his jeans from his socks. Then they began to know each other more and Billie's friendliness turned into friendship, and then a crush.

Not that she would do anything about it. Billie was as

awkward around men as she was around make-up and fashion.

'You're in early,' he said glancing up at the clock. 'I wouldn't have got here so fast if it weren't for the green lights.'

'I need to leave early to help my mum move house,' said Billie, 'so I thought I'd get a head start. God knows it's going to be a bloody disaster with the amount of stuff Mum has hoarded over the years. The woman finds it impossible to throw out anything.'

'I'm the same,' said Nick with a sigh. 'Thankfully, I live alone, so I don't have to worry about anyone throwing anything out.'

At thirty-three, Nick was the epitome of a nerd bachelor, living in his little house in Northcote, where he would heat up something frozen for dinner and watch documentaries and reruns of *QI* for a little light relief—he liked to regale Billie with the highlights of Stephen Fry's humour.

She knew some people in the lab thought him odd, even weird, but Billie saw through that and noticed his handsome face, and his patience in explaining things to others or when they teased him.

Billie often wondered if he even thought about women, but he hadn't even tried to ask her out on a date, so she presumed it was safe to say he just wasn't interested in women at all.

Not that Billie had pretentions about herself, but as a rare female in a science laboratory, who was pretty and had a slight resemblance to a popular character from *Game of Thrones*, she was nerd candy. Everyone, from the lab technicians to the top scientists, had asked her out, and even some of the married ones gave her the eye. It was exhausting, but slowly they realised she wasn't there to play, she was there to work.

She glanced at Nick as he pulled on his white coat. He had a slim, well-built frame from bike riding, and his pants sat extremely well on his hips. She always looked at the way a man's pants sat on his hips. They needed to hang, not cling and for a moment she wondered what was under his pants and then admonished herself for thinking in such a base manner.

'Are you doing the soap powder tests?' he asked, walking towards her.

'Yes, working on lipstick stains,' she said, wishing she had a solution for dissolving blushes.

'What sort of lipstick?' he asked.

'Just lipstick,' said Billie frowning. 'I just went to the pharmacy down the road and bought one.'

Nick rolled his eyes. 'Is it pearl, gloss, matte, long-wearing?'

Billie felt herself redden. 'I don't know, I don't really wear make-up,' she admitted.

'You don't need it,' said Nick casually.

She reached up and touched her face, knowing she was blushing, but Nick was looking at the lipstick.

'This is a Maybelline gloss. This has a lot of lanolin in it, so it will be more greasy than some.'

He smeared the pale pink lipstick over the back of his hand.

'It's a bit sickly, needs more depth,' he said.

Billie watched him with interest. 'How do you know so much about lipstick?'

'I worked in a make-up lab before here, but they went bust,' he said. 'I actually enjoy the different compounds and ancient recipes. Some ingredients stay the same, regardless of the century.'

'Like what?' she asked, noting how excited he looked as he spoke.

'Beeswax. In Victorian times, they used beeswax with spermaceti . . .'

'What's that?' asked Billie, screwing up her nose.

'It's an organ from inside the sperm whale's head,' he said. 'They would mix it with sweet almond oil and rose water and this became known as Crème Céleste or cold cream, as we know it now.'

Billie laughed. 'I have a cousin called Celeste in France. I'm sure she'd love to know she was named after something that came from inside a sperm whale's head.'

Nick shook his head and smiled. 'Are you going to tell her?'

'Oh God, no. I haven't spoken to her in twenty-odd years,' Billie said, as she held the lipstick up to her face. 'I can't even remember her.

'Is it my colour?' she asked, surprised at her coquettish tone.

She wasn't usually a flirt, but something about Nick being so knowledgeable, and his compliment with no expectation attached, had her head in a little whirl. However, she took comfort in knowing she would never do anything about this work crush. Her life was simple, and love would only make it complicated. The surety of science made up for any brief love affair she might have, when she knew it was most likely destined to break her heart.

'No, you'd look better with reds, but with a navy base,'

he said, peering at her. 'It's the dark hair and blue eyes combination, just like Snow White.' He beamed at her. Then he moved and started smearing soap powder over the stains, as the door opened and the rest of the staff arrived for their day's work.

And Billie spent the rest of the day wondering who exactly Nick Miller was and did he have a girlfriend and then Googling pictures of Snow White.

* * *

'Mum?'

Billie stepped over the bubble wrap and packing tape that lay across the doorway of her childhood home in Carlton. It was a long terrace house, with a hallway the length of two cricket pitches, currently lined with boxes, art leaning against the wall, and ephemera from Elisabeth and Gordon's attempt at moving fifteen years of their life.

The problem was that Elisabeth and Gordon found themselves easily distracted. Elisabeth would drop whatever she was doing to write down a poem that swam through her mind, and Gordon would find an old book that he claimed to have been looking for 'since for ever' and would then settle down in that exact spot to read some old volume on the history of an ancient civilisation of a far-flung country. Billie knew the only way she would get her mother and stepfather moved was if she marshalled them and assigned them tasks, overseeing the project with extreme bossiness, something she knew her mother hated.

No reply came to her call and Billie sighed, as she put her bag down on an empty armchair.

Assessing the living room, she saw plastic boxes of

photographs from the shed had managed to make their way inside, but the lid had been lifted and now snapshots of Billie's childhood lay sprawled across the wooden floors. Photos of her and her father, and her mother, photos with her and her mother's parents, family friends, parties, but no one else. She knew nothing of her father's past, or his family, and loyalty to her mother meant she didn't pry into the past.

'Billie.' She heard her mother say her name and she pulled herself away from the photos.

Dropping the photographs back onto the table, she looked up to see her mother standing in the room, phone in hand.

'How's it all going?' she asked, already knowing the answer.

'Henri's mother has died,' came Elisabeth's reply; her face went its usual shade of ivory whenever she mentioned Billie's father's side of the family.

'Oh, shit. I guess she was pretty old,' said Billie casually.

'Don't swear when you learn of someone's death,' admonished Elisabeth.

'Why not? I didn't know the woman,' said Billie with a careless shrug. 'It's not like she made any effort to see us after Papa died.'

Billie never asked about her any more. When she was younger, she had asked a few questions, but Elisabeth's answers were short and angry, using words such as 'toxic' and 'corrupt', and Billie, who grieved her father deeply, needed someone to blame, so her father's family from France seemed a likely reason. She trusted her mother's opinion and so she joined her in hating them and getting on with their lives as a form of revenge.

'I know, but she was still your father's mother. That accounts for some respect,' said Elisabeth. 'That was her lawyer on the phone. A lovely man, very kind and discreet. He didn't ask me about Henri at all; I assume he knows what happened.'

'OK,' she said slowly, trying to read her mother's face. Elisabeth seemed stressed and worried, as though things were all out of place, which they were, thought Billie, but this was more than just moving house.

'He wants you to go to London for the reading of the will,' she said, surprise showing on her face.

'London? Me? You also?' asked Billie, aware she was speaking in staccato but unable to piece together the thoughts jumbling in her mind.

'Just you, not me. He said it's vital,' Elisabeth stated, clearly saddled with the importance of the message.

'I don't want anything of hers,' said Billie, bending over and picking up the photographs and stuffing them back into the plastic box they had escaped from.

'He said it was vital,' her mother repeated, her eyes widening at the last word.

'I doubt it. Probably some old relic she wants to be passed to me,' said Billie. 'I'm not interested in anything they want to give me or you.'

Elisabeth paused as though about to speak and then deciding against it.

'Go on, say what you were thinking,' said Billie, crossing her arms.

The house felt cold, and the dust was making her eyes itchy.

'Billie, the thing is, you father . . .' Her voice trailed away.

'What about him?'

'He was from a good family in France, they have money.'

'I don't need money,' said Billie.

'No, I know, it's just that, well, when your father died, I changed our names to March, to try to take away the legacy of his family.'

'So what is his name?' Now Billie felt that everything was out of place. She was Billie March. All her documents said so, and it was her mother's name. She had just assumed they were Marches.

'Le Marche,' said Elisabeth, looking ashamed.

'OK, Le Marche. And what else do I need to know that you might have omitted from my past?' Billie felt her arms cross and she tried to uncross them, but she felt like everything was coming at her at once.

'The Le Marches own a successful skincare company across Europe.'

Billie stared at her mother, trying to understand.

'They are very, very wealthy, and I think your father would like you to have what Daphné has left to you.'

'You told me my entire life that they were next to evil in terms of family, and now you're telling me to go there and take whatever trinket or cash they have left me? Do you realise what a hypocrite you sound like?'

'I thought it would be good to find out what it is. It might have something to do with Henri,' Elisabeth said in a flat voice.

Billie knew her mother wasn't a manipulative woman, but she was also not without demands. While Elisabeth would never ask Billie to do anything she wasn't comfortable with, there was always something around her husband's death that made her lose all sense of herself.

But she was as selfless as she was generous, which now made Billie now feel terrible.

Since her father's death, Billie had watched Elisabeth try to get on to the best of her ability without her beloved Henri and, to the outsider, she had succeeded. As a well-respected professor of French poetry, and a poet with a few volumes of her work published, a new husband and a daughter who had a degree in chemistry, she had done well as far as the benchmark of success indicated.

What others didn't see was the toll that came from coping with a death she didn't see coming, and one that she wondered every day if she might have prevented. The anniversaries of Henri's death where Elisabeth wouldn't get out of bed. The man missing in the photos at Billie's birthdays and at Christmas that caused Elisabeth to shed a tear in the kitchen, where Billie had found her many times, weeping over the sink.

But now Billie was furious. 'Why didn't you tell me who Dad's family are?'

Elisabeth swallowed a few times. 'I didn't want you to leave me for them,' she said. 'The lure of money can be very enticing.'

'Did you think I would do that? God, Mum, you don't know me at all.'

'I'm sorry, I just hate them,' said Elisabeth passionately, and then she burst into tears.

'Mum, I don't want anything from them, even if it is

Papa's. He's gone, we've all got lives now that are successful away from the Le Marches.'

Elisabeth looked down at the phone in her hand and slowly nodded. 'Of course, you're right, I will let the man know that they can send you anything via mail, or ship it, whatever it is.'

Billie saw the disappointment in her mother's face and she knew the real reason she wanted her daughter to attend the will reading was to see if there was a final clue to Henri's death. Something, anything, to tell her why it ended the way it did.

'It will be an old painting or something, Mum, honestly, they're not going to give me anything valuable. No doubt the family would have got their hands on anything worth money by now.'

Elisabeth raised her dark eyebrows and rolled her eyes a little.

Billie felt better seeing her mother's scorn replacing her bewilderment.

'You're right,' she said, looking relieved.

'Of course I'm right, I'm a realist,' said Billie. 'You can try so many different ways to get a different result but often end up with the same outcome. That family is exactly the same. No matter what you do, they will always be self-interested, selfish and toxic, the best thing you ever did was move us to Australia. I feel sorry for them all stuck in the past. Now let's get you moved, I'm feeling very organised.'

'God help me,' laughed Elisabeth, as Billie picked up a flat carton and started to assemble it.

But, as Billie worked through the rest of the day, packing and sorting, labeling and lifting, she couldn't help but wonder what on earth Grand-Mère had left her and would it be worth something. If it was, she would give the money to her mother; that was the least of what she deserved after what she had been through. Losing a husband so young, starting a new life with a young child.

Her mother was the bravest person Billie knew and there wasn't a chance in hell she was going to let her mother get caught in the Le Marche web again since she spoke so badly of them. She always said her heart was broken after Henri died, and Billie knew they were somehow to blame. Why else had her mother cut all ties?

That night, when she lay in bed in her own little apartment, Billie looked at the framed picture of Elisabeth and her father from their wedding day in Paris.

Her mother was wearing a white shift dress with daisies in her hair, and her father a broad grin. They looked so happy, she thought, so why then did he decide to take his own life?

Chapter 3

Daphné, 1956

Daphné Amyx was eighteen and had two options available to her. Marriage or work. Marriage was possible in the village of Calvaic, but she didn't want a pig farmer with his rough hands and crude tongue. She wanted a man like Jean Gabin, or the American actor, Jimmy Stewart who she saw in the movies at Saint Cere; and she knew that wasn't someone she wasn't going to find in the village.

Not that she had met the man yet, she just knew there wasn't anything for her in the village any more and, as much as she regretted leaving her beloved mother Chantal, she knew it would be better for them both if she earned money in Paris while looking for a husband.

The day she had chosen for her reconnaissance to Paris was going to be beautiful and, as the light rose with the dawn, the garden had never looked as pretty in the growing kaleidoscope from the sunrise. Daphné felt the rising sun on her shoulders as she hung the washing on the makeshift clothesline in their back garden. Her mother's sunflowers were facing east and sweet peas were climbing up the fence, as though greedily trying to get as much of the light as possible.

The morning and evening light was the best, she thought, as the kids danced next to their mothers in the field next to them, their little goat antics never failing to make Daphné giggle.

For a moment, Daphné felt almost nostalgic and then noted the beautifully mended holes in the nightgown she pegged to the line and let go of her sentimentality.

Rural life was hard enough, let alone for a mother and daughter who made a living from the land and making hand-made soap from goat's milk and selling it on the side of the road to the occasional tourist. Lately business had been good with the Americans who passed by. They liked the sweet little labels that Daphné had made and pasted onto the jars. She had even added some pretty linen over the lids and tied them with pink ribbon to really appeal to the customers. But then Daphné, ever the realist, pulled herself from her musing and focused on the day ahead. There was no time to be pondering the light when food needed to be put on the table.

She finished her task and walked back inside the small stone cottage, where her mother sat mending a linen sheet. The cottage was neat as a pin, and everything was polished and folded in perfect order, thanks to Chantal, Daphné's mother.

The bus to Paris would be arriving soon, and Daphné checked her small case of soaps and lotions she and Chantal had made. If she couldn't find a job, then she would sell the stock on the streets of Paris and return next week to try again.

She had a small overnight bag of a change of clothes and a coat belonging to her mother and would stay with the Karpinskis, who had fled Poland and had hidden in their village during the war, finding themselves unable to make their way to London.

The couple now had children and a small jewellery store in Le Marais, which they lived above and where Daphné would stay.

She picked up her case and smoothed her dark hair. 'Mama, I'm going,' she said to the back of her mother who stood at the kitchen sink.

Her mother turned and wiped her hands on her apron. 'Be safe,' she said and Daphné could see the worry in her sad eyes. Losing her husband in the war meant she had little faith in the world to care for her beloved daughter. If Chantal had her way, Daphné would stay at home for ever.

'I will be fine, Maman,' said Daphné sincerely. She was smart, resourceful and brave and a two-day trip to Paris alone didn't worry her like it did her mother.

'You look very pretty,' said her mother, admiring Daphné's figure in the peacock blue dress which Chantal had made from fabric she had saved from before the war. Nipped at the waist, with a full skirt, the shape showed off her tiny waist and the colour complemented her sultry looks.

While Daphné wasn't a beauty, she had an appeal that seemed to make men look twice at her. At seventeen, she knew it was sex appeal but was too shy and far too inexperienced to know its power.

She picked up her case, and kissed her mother on her weather-beaten cheek. Years of being in the garden and tending the animals had created lines on her skin yet it was soft from the goat's milk soap and cream that she made and used.

'I will see you on Thursday,' she said and she smiled brightly as she went to the door. 'Wish me luck.'

'Good luck and give my love to the Karpinskis,' said Chantal, and then Daphné was on her way.

* * *

The bus journey to Paris was long and slow, frequently interrupted by roaming sheep, goats, and even a family of ducks, who insisted on crossing the road in single file.

Everyone on the bus thought it charming, but Daphné just wanted to get to Paris. She knew there was something waiting for her there, but what it was, she wasn't sure.

The only highlight was a women's magazine that a woman had left on her seat after she had departed the bus. Such a luxury wasn't in Daphné's budget and the trip went quickly while she read every article and studied every picture.

When the bus arrived in Paris, it was after lunch and Daphné was tired, grimy and hungry, but she knew she didn't have time to waste. Work was hard to come by in Paris and, as Anna Karpinski had said in her letter to Daphné, only the tenacious survived, but Daphné didn't plan on just surviving, she wanted to thrive in the city.

Of course Anna and her husband Max were tenacious enough to have survived the war in hiding and make a life in Paris, but when Daphné arrived at their tiny shop, and she saw shabby state of their establishment and how rough the neighbourhood was, she wondered if life in Paris was as wonderful as the magazines she read at the village store claimed.

'Daphné,' cried Max, as she opened the door to the store, her eyes adjusting to the darkness.

'Max,' she said warmly and let him embrace her like her father would have.

Anna and Max had moved from house to house for three years during the war and often slept in barns or cellars. They never complained, and always worried for those who were protecting them.

It was Anna who comforted Chantal when the telegram arrived informing them that Daphné's father had died.

It was Max who suggested goats to Chantal, and Anna who taught Chantal how to milk them and make the soap. The oil they needed was hard to come by at the end of the war, so they improvised with lard but it worked, and with some sweet lavender from Chantal's own garden, they had something she could sell on the side of road.

'Anna, Anna,' Max cried up the slim staircase, and Daphné looked around the store.

Dark and dreary, filled with a few cabinets of stock, and a curtain behind to separate the back room from the store, Daphné thought this was no place she would want to buy jewellery, yet she knew Max's work and it was beautiful.

'How is the business?' she asked when Max turned from the stairwell.

'You know, hard, I do what I can with what I have,' he answered vaguely, but Daphné read his face and knew the answer.

Her thoughts were pushed aside when Anna came down the stairs in a rush and held Daphné for a long time, occasionally pulling away to touch her face.

'And Maman?' she asked of Chantal, who was Anna's mother figure as her own mother had never been heard of after the invasion of Poland.

'She is fine, worried about me and you and if the world is going to keep turning,' laughed Daphné.

'Of course, she is a mother,' said Anna and her hands gestured to her children.

Daphné had met them once when they were younger, but now she saw a smaller version of Anna and Max, with the same proud face of their mother and the ingenious twinkle in their eye from their father.

'Peter, Marina, this is Daphné,' said Anna gently to the boy and girl who stepped forward politely to shake Daphné's hand.

Upstairs, Anna had created a makeshift bed on the sagging sofa, but it was warm and clean and much more appealing than the shop.

The children had been sent outside to play, and Anna warmed up some vegetable and barley soup and placed it in front of Daphné with a large chunk of rye bread.

She ate it hungrily, savouring the flavours of the sour bread and the sweet broth.

'How is the business?' she asked as she dipped the bread into the soup.

Anna shrugged. 'It's hard,' she said and Daphné thought she looked older than her thirty years.

As Daphné wiped the remnants of soup up with her last piece of bread, she thought about the store.

'It needs to be lighter,' she said. 'To show of Max's work.'

'But there is no way,' said Anna. 'The only light is from the front windows, and the street is so closed in.'

'Then you must paint it,' said Daphné, thinking of the light that rose over the horizon on the farm.

'Paint it? What colour?' asked Anna, her face bewildered.

Daphné looked around at the utilitarian space. Anna didn't have the time or money to think beyond the practical and everyday survival. 'Why?'

Daphné picked up her bowl and plate and took them to the small tin tub that Anna used as a sink and put them in the water to soak.

'Blush,' she said, 'The colour of make-up powder you see in the magazine.'

She took went to her bag and took out a magazine, flicking to a page and finding an advertisement, showing Anna.

It was a drawing of a woman holding a glass of pink champagne, her face beautifully contoured in shades of pink.

'Pink lightens the skin, it takes away the age lines,' read Daphné and she looked up at Anna and smiled. 'And it's pretty,' she said.

'What sort of pink?' asked Anna suspiciously.

'The sort of pink you see in a woman's face when she's happy, when she's been outside in the sun, but she's not sunburned or hot, she's warm, inside and out,' said Daphné thinking of Chantal. Her mind wandered as she kept speaking. 'The rose in the sky at the end of the day, that looks like old paintings of heaven.'

Anna smiled and touched Daphné's face. 'You mean the afterglow,' she said.

'Is that what it's called?' asked Daphné, surprised there was a name for what she was describing.

'It's also the colour in a woman's face when she falls in

love,' said Anna with a smile and Daphné bit her lip in antici-
pation. She was ready to fall in love, have an adventure, and
to bathe in the afterglow of the world.

But first a job, she thought, as she washed her hands and
combed her hair, and applied a little goat's cream to her face.

'I am off to find work,' she said to Anna and, after picking
up her bag, she headed out the door, waving to Max as she
left the shop.

Paris wasn't so hard to navigate. She and her mother had
been there before, but this was her first time alone.

She paused and thought out the arrondissements in her
head and got her bearings. She needed to cross the river to get
to Montparnasse, where the cafés were. She could become a
waitress, she thought, as she walked with purpose across the
bridge and through Saint-Germain.

Jazz musicians busked on the streets, and tourists wandered
with cameras about their necks. American accents mingled
with the French and Daphné wondered why on earth she
thought she could have stayed in the village. Paris was the
only place for her, she could feel it in her soul, and she started
her job-hunting in earnest.

Chapter 4

Robert

Paris never looked more beautiful than in the autumn, Robert Le Marche decided as he drove under a golden canopy of magnificent beech trees.

Everyone always went on about spring in Paris, but autumn was sublime, with the leaves changing and people looking so chic in their coats and boots.

Robert parked his navy Bugatti on rue de Grenelle and jumped out as two attractive women walked towards him. Just as they passed, he pressed the key to lock the car, making them aware that the machine was his.

The women strolled by in deep conversation, ignoring Robert and his car, much to his chagrin. He had twisted his back getting out of the car gracefully and all for nothing, he thought, cursing the women but not the car that was as low to the ground as a snake on roller skates.

He pressed the security code next to the ornate iron gates and then pushed them open and walked inside, entering the private garden. He ignored the last flush of melon-coloured tea roses that stood proudly in their immaculate beds and an espaliered orange tree ran across the ancient brick wall, bearing the last of the fruit while orange and white poppies waved in the sun.

He could never understand his mother's obsession with the colour orange. She was like Monet, always chasing the light, looking for that 'dernières lueurs'.

He had stopped listening to her ramblings of the search when he was a boy, but Henri had always listened, even encouraging the pursuit, delivering hand-dyed tangerine silk woven with gold thread from Varanasi, amber beads from the Grand Bazaar in Istanbul, even a jar of antique buttons in her favourite shades of apricot and candlelight peach from the Camden Markets.

Henri was always such a sycophant, he thought, as he put the key in the lock of the front door and pushed it open.

The marble foyer and wrought iron staircase met him and he sighed, as he looked upstairs. Why his mother wouldn't get an elevator installed in the place he could never understand. She had the money, but she refused, claiming it was sacrilegious to install such modernity in such an old home.

Robert hadn't argued with his mother because he would never win. He learned that years ago, but now, as he stood in the foyer of the four-storey family home, he felt nothing. He thought he would feel some sort of relief, even some satisfaction that she was gone, but there was only silence in his heart and in the house.

He walked up the stairs slowly, stopping at each level to catch his breath, and silently cursing his addiction to cigarettes.

Finally, he reached the top level and loosened his tie from

his neck. He was once a handsome man, but a lifetime of sunbathing, smoking, drinking and eating rich food had ruined his fine features and had turned him into a doughy version of his former self.

He crossed the room, with its heavy, ornate furniture, and opened the drawer of the Louis XV desk. He pulled out a kidskin file and opened the gold lock with a small key that hung on his key ring.

He rifled through the papers inside and then, not seeing what he wanted, pulled them all out and spread them across the desk.

Birth certificates, the marriage certificate, deeds to the houses and other items that Daphné had deemed important were inside. Everything except the one thing he wanted.

He pulled out his phone, dialled a number and waited.

'Edward Badger please, Robert Le Marche,' he said, as he checked the papers again.

'Edward speaking,' came the crisp English accent.

'Where is the will and the formula?'

'Let me first offer my condolences on the loss of your mother,' said Edward smoothly. 'She was a remarkable woman.'

Robert had never liked him. He tried too hard to be Henri's replacement.

'Remarkable is one word,' said Robert drily. 'I'm at rue de Grenelle, the documents aren't here.'

'The formula is in the bank vault, and the will is in the office, as per your mother's instructions before she passed.'

Robert felt his blood pressure rise. 'She wrote her will three years ago,' he said.

'No, there was a codicil the night before she died,' said Edward.

'A what?'

'A codicil is an amendment to a will,' said Edward.

Patronising prick, thought Robert.

'I know what a fucking codicil is,' he snapped, walking around the top floor, staring unseeingly at the view across Paris. 'When can I see it?'

'We have some details to attend to, and then we will read the will. Madame Le Marche expressed very firmly that it should be after her funeral.'

Robert clutched the back of a gilt-edged chair.

'I need to get things moving,' he said, trying to control his voice.

'Yes, I can understand that,' said Edward and then he paused on the end of the phone. 'We have to wait for Sibylla's response,' he said.

'Sibylla? Henri's child?' asked Robert. He now circled the chair and sat on its overstuffed silk cushion.

'Yes, she's in the will,' said Edward.

'What did Daphné leave her?' Robert ran through the list of chattels and houses. The château now used as a wedding venue, the house he was sitting in, the apartment in London where she died? Perhaps it was some art? Robert could accept some art going to the girl, she deserved that much, and a flush of guilt ran through his body, causing a cold sweat.

'Why do we need to wait for her? If it's an item, we can ship it over, can't we?' Robert's voice betrayed him as his desperation rose.

'That's not going to work,' said Edward. 'Now if you will

excuse me, I have more details to attend to, as I'm sure you do also, for the funeral will most likely be enormous.'

Robert sat in the chair, staring at the wall.

Sibylla Le Marche. He barely thought of Henri's child nowadays. How old was she when he died? Nine or ten? He searched his memory for the girl who had played with Celeste while he and Matilde pointed blame at each other for Camille's death.

She was more like her mother Elisabeth, he remembered, dark haired and quiet, in contrast to Celeste's boisterous beauty.

Just thinking about the past gave him a headache and he decided he needed two things. A strong coffee and blowjob from one of the escorts he used for such purposes.

He dialled a number and waited. 'Anika, it's Robert, can I see you?'

'Darling,' she purred in her German accent, 'I'm in Cannes.' She laughed and he could hear the sound of laughter in the background.

'Why are you in Cannes?'

'I'm with a sheik I met at the festival, who offered me an obscene amount of cash to stay for a while. We've been all over the Mediterranean, and we're just coming back into Cannes now.'

Her voice hushed to a whisper. 'I can pay my apartment off with this trip,' she said.

Robert wasn't sure if he should congratulate her or call Interpol in case she went missing.

'Please be careful,' he pleaded with Anika. She was by far his favourite of the young women he used for pleasure.

'I'm fine,' she said. 'Jesus, you're like my father.' She was laughing as he ended the call.

The thought of Anika's mouth around the sheik's cock made him shudder, but he also felt a searing jealousy, while the thought of the wealth the sheik must have made him livid.

Yes, Robert had money, but he wasn't obscenely liquid like the Middle Eastern sheiks or the Russian oligarchs.

His thoughts went back to his mother's will and he felt a small seed of doubt sprout in his mind. Maybe things weren't going to go to the way he expected after his mother's death, and he wondered why he thought they would since they had never gone to plan while the old bitch was alive.

Leaving the kidskin wallet on the table, he made his way downstairs and through the garden out to the street, where he saw his Bugatti was now sporting a parking fine.

Today was proving to be the worst, he decided, when his phone rang and he saw his daughter's name on the screen. Now it was proving to be even more hellish.

'Celeste,' he barked. 'I can't talk now.'

'Why not?' He could hear the pout in her voice. 'I just want to find out about Grand-Mère's funeral. When is it?'

Robert pulled the ticket off the windscreen and unlocked the car.

'I don't know, I haven't organised it yet.'

'Papa, she died two days ago, what do you mean you haven't organised it?'

'I haven't had time, I have a company to run, not everyone lives your life,' he said as he slid into the seat of the car, cursing his back. He needed one of those driver's pillows he had seen in a catalogue for people with disabilities when he was last visiting his mother.

He made a mental note to get his secretary to order one, as he started the car, the sound of the engine nearly blocking out Celeste's question.

'What did you say?' He wasn't sure he heard correctly.

'Do you want me to organise it?' she asked again, her voice sounding small. 'I thought it might be nice for me to do it.'

Robert paused, the phone still up to his ear, the engine thumping impatiently.

'That would be lovely, Celeste, really, if you think you can handle such a sad affair. I need to be looking at the company and all that it entails, so your help would be so wonderful.'

His charm soothed him, and he felt the anxious grip in his chest loosen.

'Do whatever you need and just send the invoices to Le Marche,' he said. 'Now I must go, darling, about to head to a meeting, message me with any details.'

And he hung up before she could speak.

What a gift, he thought happily, as he pulled out into traffic without looking, knowing he wouldn't be hit by another driver. Who wanted to deal with the insurance on a Bugatti? He laughed as he turned up the radio to a song he didn't know the words to until it annoyed him enough to change it to the jazz station he loved. Soon John Coltrane was playing *Lush Life*, and Robert thought that his life was indeed very lush, and once he had Le Marche sold, then he would be the one sailing through the Greek Islands or the Mediterranean and girls like Anika would never leave him for a sheik again.

Everything was looking up, he thought. He was even feeling generous to Henri's child. Let her have whatever it was Daphné had willed to her, what did he care now. Most likely it was one of her hideous paintings or some jewellery. He was about to get what he deserved and, even though he was fifty-eight years old, he still felt thirty. With this in mind, he dialled another girl he liked.

'Chloe, my place, twenty minutes?' he demanded more than asked and she responded as he thought she might and agreed to see him but for double the price.

But what did he care? He was truly rich now and, as his mother always said, the wealthier you become the more life costs you.

His ex-wife's face came to mind and he felt himself scowl and then stopped. Matilde wasn't worth getting more lines over, he thought, as he glanced at himself in the rear-view mirror. His blond hair had turned silver, which, he'd decided when he turned fifty, was elegant. He could have dyed his hair, like his grandfather had for years, according to Anna. What a pathetic old man, he thought, thinking of Giles Le Marche.

Robert was very proud of himself for growing up without a decent male role model. His father was inept, his brother too. He was his own creation, and now without his mother's domineering influence, he would finally, at the age of fifty-eight become the man he was always knew he was meant to be.

Better late than ever, he said to himself, and pressed the accelerator on the car, making sure he would be able to meet Chloe for his celebratory blowjob.

Chapter 5

Matilde

Matilde adjusted the collar on her black Dior coat, aware that all the eyes of society were on her, and then genuflected at the altar of Sainte-Chapelle.

She had stopped believing in anything when Camille died, but Daphné had believed in God, or so Celeste had said when she planned this spectacle of a funeral.

Daphné's coffin was lying in state, covered in what seemed to be one hundred amber roses, the heady scent mixing with the frankincense that was burning in the brass censers on the altar.

Slipping into a pew further down the back of the church, Matilde looked around at the attendance. A decent enough showing of the right sort of people, she thought, and watched as Paul Le Brun walked up the side of the aisle and slipped into a seat.

News of her daughter's affair with Le Brun had made the gossip pages for a day, until a terrorist threat overtook all other news, and Celeste was spared of too much humiliation. Still, people stared at Paul when he arrived, and she saw their heads joined in covert whispering.

Celeste could do so much better, she thought, as she noted his slightly coloured hair. Matilde was an expert at spotting three things: plastic surgery, hair colouring and sexual attraction.

It had proved to be a very valuable set of skills over the years. She had worked it to her benefit, finding lovers for herself and for her friends, and knowing the exact point in which to topple someone's ego with a well-placed barb about any work they had done to their appearance.

Matilde was known within her circle as a sharp wit; to those outside of it, she was just a bitch.

More faces, known and unknown, walked into the church and soon it was a sea of black with hushed gossip sending waves through the sacred space.

Finally, Celeste and Robert arrived, arm in arm, Robert's face looking concerned and upset, but not so much that he might cause any lines, thought Matilde, with a roll of her eyes.

God, being married to a fop with an unquenchable sexual appetite had been exhausting, and even if Camille hadn't died, she would have left him anyway. She told him then and still stood by her statement. She needed a rest from him, the sex, and his lies.

She saw Celeste glance at her and she raised her head in approval. Celeste had done a wonderful job, with so little time to organise everything. Of course Robert had dumped it on his daughter; he was a lazy son of a bitch, she thought.

Daphné's funeral had only just made the French rule that all funerals needed to have taken place by the sixth day but Matilde knew that people wouldn't miss the chance to see the fall of the last of the Le Marche family.

There were more gossips in this church than friends, thought Matilde, as the priest stood at the altar and the ceremony began, and she stood with the rest of the crowd to say goodbye to Daphné Le Marche, the woman who saved her daughter.

* * *

Matilde was the face of Le Marche when she was nineteen, after Daphné decided that they needed to bring in a model to represent the brand and become more current.

By twenty-one, she was dating Robert. At twenty-two, she was pregnant with Camille.

And at twenty-three, she married him, but only after Robert had been threatened with disownment by Daphné.

Camille had changed Robert's mind about marriage. The moment the child was placed in his arms, he adored her and that was enough for Matilde to forgive him for his transgressions.

There was no father as devoted as him to Camille, and then came Celeste. He would get up to them in the night, which was rare, according to her friends in Paris, and he took them to school. He knew everything that was going on in their lives and their friends and was as much fun as they could wish with a father.

He drove them everywhere. No matter where they wanted to go, he took them, speeding in the latest sports car and bringing back a treat for whoever was at home.

Matilde felt her eyes sting with unshed tears as she remembered, or was it from the incense. She tried to focus on the coffin and the roses, but her mind would not stay with her, and she felt it wander off again and there she was, back as though nothing had changed, and yet everything was about to be shattered.

'Can you take the girls to ballet?' Matilde had asked, knowing he would.

'I'm not going.' Celeste had pouted. 'Camille got new shoes and I didn't.'

Matilde didn't have time for Celeste's sulking.

'Go to ballet, Celeste. You had new shoes last month, and the reason Camille got them was because her feet have grown so much.'

Matilde had looked at her long-legged daughter, who had the best of both of her parents' looks. The blonde beauty of Matilde, and the fine, aquiline Le Marche nose.

She could model one day. Matilde and Daphné had discussed this quite often, while Robert denounced her plans.

'No, Camille will take over Le Marche with me one day,' he had said proudly and Matilde had noticed the shadow cross Celeste's face.

'And then Celeste can join when she's old enough,' added Matilde.

'I don't want to work with Daddy and Camille, I hate them,' Celeste had said, lashing out as she did when she was hurt.

She was so like Robert, Matilde always said to people when they asked about her demeanour, or was it because of Robert.

The priest was now swinging the censer around, the smoke billowing out, lifting up the prayers to heaven, and Matilde felt the tears fall.

The policeman had escorted her to the hospital, with a screaming Celeste, who didn't want to go, and had to be lifted into the back seat of the police car.

Robert was almost unscathed. Camille had died instantly.

It was rare Matilde let herself remember that time, but she was at the mercy of her memory as she listened to the prayers, and remembered the year after Camille had died.

Elisabeth and Henri had brought lovely Sibylla out from Australia to try to be a companion for Celeste, but Celeste had hated her on sight and the trip was a disaster, with Robert and Henri having harsh words before they abruptly left.

What the argument was about, Matilde never knew and she never asked, too caught up in her own pain to care.

Only a year later, Henri had died. The Le Marche family had lost two members in two years. It was the sort of thing that the gossipy society Matilde moved in thrived on.

So Matilde drank, and Robert slept with anything that had a heartbeat, and Celeste was ignored.

Matilde wasn't proud of her mothering. Robert was always the better parent when they were small, but when Camille died, he stopped parenting and Celeste was left with no one.

So she and Robert separated and they sent Celeste away. Out of sight, out of mind, she had thought, but it wasn't Camille she dreamed of; it was Celeste.

And when Celeste broke down about her unhappiness and had tried to kill herself, Daphné had stepped in.

Without Daphné, Matilde might have no living children, and she said a silent prayer for the woman under the roses.

She loved Celeste, she just didn't know how to help her. When she had arrived in Nice last week, her face all tear-stained and so thin, Celeste had wanted to hug her and put her to bed and feed her soup and bread and watch her sleep, but the opportunity for her to be a mother had long gone.

Celeste had resisted hugs, and instead went out on the balcony and stared into the horizon. She refused to speak of her pain, even though Matilde knew it was that arrogant Paul Le Brun, and she glanced at him in the church. Handsome yes, but what good is handsome when you're married to someone else.

Oh, Celeste, don't choose a man like your father, she thought, looking at the back of Celeste's blonde chignon at the front of the church.

So many times Matilde wished she had something wise to say to Celeste, or that Celeste would even listen, but she was scared of her daughter now.

Scared she would lose her like she lost Camille, scared of her temper and her biting tongue, and scared of her restlessness.

Matilde stayed in the past, as the service went on, and when it finished, she was one of the last to exit the church and that's when she saw him.

A man, as handsome as any man she had ever met, in a navy suit, and silk tie, with a crisp white shirt, and a beautiful coat draped over his arm. He had dark, thick hair, cut close to his head, and slightly tanned skin, but it was natural, she could tell. He walked slightly beside her, and they stopped at the entrance of the church, waiting for the crowd to exit.

'I am sorry for your loss,' he said in her ear and she felt a ripple of something in her body—fear or lust, she wasn't sure, but God knows, he was too young for her and too handsome to be good for any woman.

'It is not my loss,' she said firmly, turning to see eyes of lapis blue. 'It is my daughter and ex-husband's loss.'

'But you were sad, *non*? I saw it in your face, you had many memories cover your face during the service.'

Matilde felt herself frown. Where had he been sitting? Why had he been watching her?

'Who are you?' she asked, narrowing her eyes. He was cunning, she thought, cunning was always hard to manage. Daphné was cunning.

'Dominic Bertiull,' he said, extending a hand that Matilde didn't take.

She sniffed as though the name meant nothing to her, and she pushed her way into the crowd and away from the blue-eyed libertine, who still followed her, but Matilde knew everyone who mattered, that was her job in life.

'It must be hard for Robert to have to take over the company when he has not really worked in it for a long time,' said Dominic in a hushed whisper that smacked of false concern.

So the vultures have started to circle, she thought, and she wondered if she should tell Robert that Dominic Bertiull, the corporate raider and slash and burn CEO, was at his mother's funeral.

And then she remembered Camille. Why should she care if Dominic took Le Marche from under Robert's rule? He had lost Camille, now he could lose the company he had always desired to be at the helm of, and only then did Matilde feel that justice would be served.

'I don't know what Robert does and what he will do next.

My only concern is for my daughter, please excuse me,' Matilde said and, with a push, she forced her way through the crowd to Celeste's side, where she took her daughter's hand.

Glancing back to the steps of the church, she saw Dominic Bertiull staring at her and she wasn't sure if she should feel flattered or scared, or a little of both.

Chapter 6

In London, 1983, the cultural landscape was shifting. Nothing was as it seemed and the roles that people were so familiar with were changing before people's eyes.

Boy George was changing music with his gender-bending costumes and make-up, a film about a female welder and dancer was number one and Margaret Thatcher had just been re-elected for a second term as Prime Minister.

It was also the year Elisabeth Herod met Henri Le Marche.

As with the most extraordinary of relationships, their meeting was completely ordinary. Elisabeth worked at the bookstore, Hatchards in Piccadilly, and Henri had asked her opinion on *The Name of the Rose*. She had to admit to him that she hadn't read the book, but she had heard only good things.

She decided that Henri had a look of a poet, taking in his rumpled suit but expensive silk tie and uncombed hair. His French accent was as delicious as a chocolate soufflé and she thought he would be the perfect man to lose her virginity to while she was in London.

He asked what was the last book she read, and she took

him to the poetry corner and pulled out a slim volume and handed it to him.

Henri seemed as interested in her, which was lovely since her dark hair, dark eye combination seemed so uninteresting to English boys at the time. Samantha Fox was on Page Three of the *Sun* and the boys who were living in the hostel had images of her stuck to every bathroom wall.

Just seeing Ms Fox's large breasts made Elisabeth feel uncomfortable, and she always glanced down at her own chest, lacking in everything compared to Samantha's.

Henri turned the book over in his hands and then read aloud in French, 'Louise Lévêque de Vilmorin—*Poèmes*.' And then looked up at her. His blue eyes widened, and his dark hair fell over his face.

She quelled a desire to move it from his forehead so she could see his eyes again.

'You speak French?'

'*Oui*,' she said, aware her Australian accent might ruin the romance of the moment.

'And you read French poetry?' he asked, a smile playing on his face.

'*Oui*,' she said again. Oh yes, she was definitely flirting now.

From the corner of her eye, Elisabeth could see her manager coming towards them and she snatched the book from him and put it back on the shelf.

'Elisabeth, are you helping this gentleman?' asked Bernard, the snivelling manager who reminded her of a court fop.

'She is,' said Henri, in an accent somewhat thicker than he had used with Elisabeth. 'She is so knowledgeable and her taste is sublime, you are very lucky to have such a woman to work for you.'

Bernard almost bowed and then gave a rare, thin-lipped smile to Elisabeth. 'She is a wonderful girl, who knew an Australian could be educated as well as she is. Please let me know if you need anything else.'

Bernard left them, walking backwards, and bumped into a table of discounted travel books. When Elisabeth turned her attention back to Henri, he was holding the book of poems again and he read to her,

'*Fiancée of a million deviations*
what do you hide up your sleeve?
Is it a postcard
from the place where dreams are discarded?
Is it your revenge plan:
a vulture's kiss: stolen and flown?'

Elisabeth felt her heart tighten and her breath squeezed her lungs until she thought she would explode.

'You translated that from French? So quickly?' she asked.

'I know Louise de Vilmorin's work,' he said. 'Did you know she was engaged to Antoine de Saint-Exupéry?'

Elisabeth nodded and she wondered if in fact he would be more than just the thief of her innocence.

'Dinner? Tonight?' he asked, tucking the book under his arm.

'OK,' was all she could reply.

'I will pick you up. Where do you live?' he asked politely.

Elisabeth thought of the grotty hostel and the pictures of Samantha Fox.

'Can I meet you here? I work till late,' she lied.

'Of course,' he answered and he reached down and kissed her on each cheek.

'*Au revoir*, Elisabeth,' he said and then left her alone while he paid for the book at the counter.

It was only after that she realised she didn't know his name and she rushed to the counter to see if he had left a clue with his credit card.

'He paid cash,' said the girl at the till. 'Wasn't half handsome, wasn't he?'

Elisabeth spent the rest of the afternoon as though flying on a flock of wild birds, seeing London below as a fantastic adventure that finally she was beginning to undertake.

* * *

Henri was waiting for her when she left the bookstore at six in the evening. The streetlamps were turning on and the crisp autumn air made everyone look like smokers as they hurried home. Henry was leaning against a post box, wearing the same suit as earlier in the day, but this time with a camel coat draped over his shoulders.

He looked incongruous against the streetscape with a group of punks walking past, their hair pointed upwards and their mouths downturned.

'Hello,' she said as she walked towards him. She was aware of the unfashionable coat she wore compared to his but she had a silk scarf she had found in lost property and had artfully wound it around her neck, just like she had seen Catherine Deneuve do in a television commercial.

He reached out and touched the scarf, 'So chic,' he said with a smile and then leaned down and kissed her on the cheek again.

He smelt of tobacco and soap and something else she couldn't quite name.

'What is that scent?' she whispered in his ear while his face was still close to hers.

'Opoponax,' he said back to her.

She pulled away. 'A pop of what?'

Henri laughed and she thought it was the most beautiful sound in the world.

'Opoponax, it's the sweet cousin of myrrh. It was used by the Ancient Romans as incense and helps people learn others secrets and portends the future like the Sibyls.'

Elisabeth thought her legs would give way and she clutched his arm.

Henri, however, seemed calm as he held her steady.

'You need a drink, *oui*?'

'*Oui*,' she said feebly and allowed him to lead her to the bar at Claridge's.

She didn't know men who wore a scent like Henri and even knew its history. Her father had an old bottle of Eau Savage that Elisabeth's mother had bought duty free on a trip to Singapore, and he wore it only at special events, which was about three times a year.

Henri helped her out of her coat, and she felt ashamed of her wool skirt and plain white blouse so she kept the scarf around her neck.

'What will you drink?' he asked her and Elisabeth shrugged as she slid into the private booth.

'I don't know, what do you think?'

She didn't think she could ask for a pint at Claridge's but she didn't know any other drink other than cask wine.

'Champagne,' he stated and then ordered a bottle of Taittinger for them with a selection of cheeses to share.

Elisabeth realised how hungry she was and placed her hand on her stomach to stop it protesting about the paltry cup of soup that had masqueraded as lunch.

'I don't know your name.' she said suddenly, as though speaking her thoughts aloud.

'Henri Le Marche,' he answered, as he sat back in the booth.

'I'm Elisabeth Herod,' she said and she put out her hand in a formal manner.

Henri laughed and took her hand and gallantly kissed it as Elisabeth laughed.

'Sorry, I think it's the environment, it's very posh, isn't it?' she whispered.

'Shall we go somewhere else?' Henri asked, his handsome face now worried. 'I didn't know where you might like to go, but my mother always says Claridge's is best when you're in London.'

Elisabeth tried to hide her smile as she nodded in agreement but Henri noticed.

'You don't agree?'

'I don't really know,' she said, deciding to be honest. 'I'm from Australia, here on a gap year. The nicest place I've been to so far has been Harrods and even then the staff looked at me like I was going to steal something.'

Henri laughed. 'You will tell me if you're not happy here?'

The waiter arrived with the champagne and made a show of displaying it to Henri, who waved his approval with his hand.

When their glasses were filled, Henri picked up his glass. 'To books,' he said.

She felt herself smiling. 'To books,' she echoed and took a sip of the champagne, savouring the taste.

'Gosh, that's lovely,' she said, as she watched the beads burst up in the glass.

'It is,' said Henri, and he took another sip. 'Beeswax,' he said then paused. 'And blackberries.'

Elisabeth took a sip from her glass. 'And apple,' she added, remembering the cider she had drunk at her brother's twenty-first birthday party.

Henri beamed at her. 'Yes, apple.'

The waiter brought the cheese and they were silent until he left.

'Do you work in the wine area?' she asked, watching how he held his glass by the stem and not the bulb.

'No, I work in the family business,' he said, leaning forward and smearing Brie onto a wafer-thin piece of toast and handing it to her.

Elisabeth took the offering gratefully and popped it into her mouth.

'We make cosmetics,' he said with a shrug. 'My grandfather started it and now my mother runs it.'

'And you will take over one day?' asked Elisabeth, as he handed her more cheese.

'I hope not,' said Henri with a sigh.

'What would you rather do?' Elisabeth sipped her champagne, as he thought.

'I would like to write books,' he said.

She thought her face would crack at the width of her smile.

'Does your mother think you should write books?' she asked.

Henri smiled now. 'My mother doesn't care what I do, as long as I'm happy. It is my brother Robert who will get the company one day.'

'So why are you in London?' she asked, feeling somewhat fortified by the champagne and cheese.

'My mother lives here most of the year, she prefers London for business, so I come and visit her.'

Disappointment rose in Elisabeth that his would be a fleeting visit and she wouldn't see him again.

'But now I know Mademoiselle Elisabeth is in London, I will be here for a while, I think.'

She felt herself smile again and wondered if he could read her mind, or was the opoponax tapping her secrets for Henri's benefit.

'What are Sibyls?' she asked, thinking of his comment about the scent he was wearing, grasping at a casual conversation to try to balance out the sexual tension she was feeling.

'They were prophetesses or Sibyllas from Ancient Greece, who could predict the future. They were very wise and gave sage advice to the priests, but they only spoke in riddles.'

'It's a beautiful word "Sibylla",' said Elisabeth, rolling the word around her mouth like a sweet.

'Yes, if I have a daughter, I would like to call her Sibylla. I think she will be very wise, but that, of course, would come from her mother.'

He looked at her pointedly as he said this and Elisabeth choked on the invisible sweet.

'More champagne,' said Henri, as he lifted the bottle from the silver bucket and refilled her glass and then his.

'Now tell me all about you,' he said. 'And Australia, I've always wanted to go there.'

Elisabeth went through the details quickly. An only child of two working-class parents, she had excelled at school and received a scholarship to a private girls' school. This led to an acceptance at university to study English, which she hoped to be able to teach at high school one day.

'But why high school? Teach at university, become a *professeur des universités*.' He clapped his hands happily at his decision on her behalf.

'You will be the beauty and the brains in your long robe, all the men will desire you and be intimidated by you.'

Elisabeth laughed and blushed. The need to kiss him was disconcerting, or was it the champagne?

'Tell me about you,' she said, desperate to steer the topic from her.

Henri Le Marche was twenty-six years old and the second son of Daphné and Yves Le Marche. What he lacked in ambition he made up for in charm and intelligence.

'You cannot make a living reading,' she said, 'unless you work in a library.'

Henri thought this sounded perfectly reasonable and decided to one day open his own library in Paris when he received his share of the business.

He wanted a simple life. Books, a woman with dark hair and dark eyes who would read him love poems, while she lay naked in their bed, and a child when the time was right.

When he spoke of his last wish, without pressure or

embarrassment, Elisabeth wanted to jump up in the bar and scream, *Pick me, pick me.*

Instead, she felt a quiet calm cloak her and, emboldened by Taittinger and lust, she drained her champagne and stood up. 'Shall we have dinner or go and read naked, in your bed?'

Henri's room was upstairs from the bar, and the walk to the elevator was silent. They were silent as the elevator doors opened, and Henri took her hand and led her into the small space.

He didn't let go of her hand until the doors opened again and he found his room key, then led her down the lush carpeted hallway, past the art that probably cost more than her ticket over to London and towards a door with the number three hundred in gold on the front.

At the door, he turned and held her face in his hands. '*L'amour est la poésie des sens.*'

Then Elisabeth kissed him. Was it the Balzac quote, or the fact that something like this moment happening was so extraordinary to a girl who lived such an ordinary life that she became someone else for a moment? Or was this who she always was?

As they kissed, he managed to open the door and they fell inside the suite, hands pulling at clothes, words in French and English being muttered.

Elisabeth felt as though she needed to feel every part of him inside her. She wanted to touch him, suck him, lick him, kiss him, caress him until she knew every single part of his body and soul.

Naked on the bed, she felt his hands slide up her slim

frame, and gently cup her breast. 'You, Elisabeth, you are my dream.'

'Love is the poetry of the senses.' She repeated the Balzac quote back to him in English, as she pulled him to her.

She never told him she was a virgin. It didn't matter any more. She realised she was only ever meant for Henri.

* * *

Elisabeth spent a week in bed with Henri, learning every part of him and him, her. She was fired from Hatchards at the end of that week and, on the following Monday, she phoned her parents from the hotel.

'Mum, I'm moving to Paris,' she exclaimed.

'Paris? What's in Paris?' her mother asked, confused.

'Henri Le Marche, my future,' said Elisabeth. 'I'm going to write poetry, and become a professor and have a mystical little baby. If it's a girl, we'll call her Sibylla and if it's a boy, we'll call him Antoine.'

'Elisabeth, don't be ridiculous,' her mother cried from the other side of the world.

'There's not a thing you can say to make me change my mind, the heart wants what the heart wants.'

And then she put down the phone and fell back into Henri's waiting arms.

Chapter 7

Edward

After the funeral, Edward took a plane back to London.

Daphné had died in London, but requested to have her funeral in Paris, which was fine, except it took a whole day, and Edward didn't have a whole day to spare, not even for Daphné.

He had avoided Robert and Celeste at the funeral, which was easy since they were surrounded by hangers-on and work associates. He had felt almost sorry for Celeste, having to organise the funeral at such short notice, and, while it wasn't as full of pageantry as Daphné Le Marche would have expected, it was appropriate and the right sort of people had turned up to pay their respects and/or to be seen.

He checked his phone and saw missed calls from the office and from Robert, but no international calls. He opened the world clock. It was midnight in Melbourne, and he wondered if Sibylla Le Marche would still be up. If she were anything like her cousin, then she would most likely still be out, he thought.

Taking a risk, he dialled the number that Elisabeth Le Marche had given him the third time he had spoken to her.

The estranged side of the family was proving to be very difficult, he thought, as he listened to the sound of international connection and then the echoing ringing of Sibylla's phone.

'Hello?' came a muffled voice.

'Sibylla Le Marche?' he asked, needing to be sure.

'It's Billie March, who is this? You do know it's midnight?'

Her accent was jarring after being with the French all day, and he screwed his face up, as though this would help him to listen more clearly.

'This is Edward Badger, I'm your grandmother's lawyer,' he started to say.

'Edward Badger, are you serious?' asked Sibylla.

'Yes, I'm Daphné Le . . .'

'That's quite a name,' she said and he thought she might be laughing.

'What is?' he asked, confused.

'Edward Badger. Teddy Badger. You sound like something from *The Wind in the Willows*. How hilarious.'

Edward was silent. She was mad, he decided. Absolutely, convict raving mad.

'Oh I'm sorry, I've offended you,' she said. 'It's actually quite sweet, isn't it? My name is Sibylla, but I go by Billie. If we got married, I'd be Billie Badger. Teddy and Billie Badger, and their adventures in Toy Town.'

'Have you finished?' asked Edward, ruing Daphné's decision. He had thought it was a good idea, better than working under Robert, but this girl was nuts, and she was rude.

'Yes, I'm sorry. I tend to talk too much when I'm nervous.' Her voice sounded normal now.

'I know my grandmother died, and Mum said she left me

something in the will, but, honestly, I don't want it. I'm fine here. I didn't even know who they all were besides a cousin Mum mentioned and who I have vague memories of, so I don't need any money, I mean we're fine and I work. I have my own little flat, which I'm doing up. It's lovely. I'm going for a whole Nordic feel, very clean lines and bright fabrics.'

Edward listened to her prattle and waited until she realised he wasn't responding.

'So yeah, whatever it is, maybe you can just pop it in the post or whatever . . .' Her voice trailed off.

'It's a bit hard,' he said drily. 'And since you won't be here for the will reading on Friday, I think you should know, she's left you half the company.'

'What?' she yelled and he held the phone away from his ear.

'What about Celeste, or whoever else is in the family?'

'Celeste is the other inheritor,' said Edward, starting to enjoy himself. He had hoped to do this in his office, so he could see the horror on Robert's face when he realised he had lost his bet, but this was almost as good.

'And there is an uncle, Robert Le Marche,' he said, trying not to colour his voice with distaste.

'Oh my God, an uncle? Dad's brother, yes, Mum said he's a prick,' Billie said.

Edward didn't argue with the truth, so he left her statement as it was.

'So you will come?' he asked.

'No. I don't want it, sell it to Celeste or something. She can have the lot.'

'It doesn't work like that, Sibylla,' he said.

'Billie, please, Billie.'

'OK, Billie,' he said, pronouncing her name slowly. 'You will have to come over here and sort out the details, as there are caveats on the will and clauses about selling and so on. I think it's something you will need to discuss with Celeste.'

'Oh for fuck's sake, I'll think about it,' snapped Billie, then there was a pause before she spoke again. 'Sorry, I shouldn't swear, it's just that sometimes I can't seem to find a more appropriate word.'

Edward thought he hadn't been this entertained at work in a long time, and he hoped Billie Le Marche would come to London, just for a while, to shake up Celeste and Robert. With her foul mouth and candour, she was exactly what Le Marche was lacking now Daphné was gone.

Edward's role as the most trusted advisor to Daphné had been accidental, or was it? he wondered now.

He had seen the lack of insight from her lawyers in the London office that represented her. Le Marche might not be their biggest client, but it was certainly their most loyal, and since they were moving their head office to London, Edward saw an opportunity for the firm to step up and create more value for the company.

Except none of the other partners cared to hear his opinion.

'It's an ailing cosmetics brand, run by a French Miss Haversham, what do we care? As soon as she dies, she will leave it to the son, who will sell it off. It's not worth the time. God knows why she's moving the company to London either. I'm sure no one supports that inside the business.'

But Edward could see her reasoning for the move. Closer to the rest of the English-speaking world, and part of the London beauty legend, Le Marche was popular in France, but it was relatively unknown to the rest of the world.

And then he took the biggest risk of his twenty-five years. He flew to Paris on his own ticket and told Daphné that she needed to change legal firms, and explained why. He then said he would be leaving also and he wished her the best. He had always liked the sharp old woman, who spoke to him as though he was more than a junior.

'I don't need a legal firm in London any more,' she said imperiously

'Oh you will, I'm sure, just maybe one that's more respect-ful of what you have achieved and what your international goals are for Le Marche,' he explained.

She shook her grey curls, perfectly set in a chic bob.

'No, I have you, you can be my legal firm, you can come and work for me, and you get some lawyers you like to help you and we can do it together,' she had said with a wave of her crêpe paper-like hand, a huge aquamarine surrounded by diamonds catching the light on her ring finger.

She's mad, he thought, as he pasted a smile onto his face.

'I'm not sure that would work,' he said slowly, trying to make her understand.

'It will work,' she said with a roll of her eyes. 'I know you can do it. I trust you, you just have to trust yourself.'

And so Edward Badger went to work for Daphné Le Marche.

Edward sat in the back of the taxi he had hailed as the driver asked him where he wanted to go.

Edward had two choices, the silence of his riverside apartment, or a ton of work at the office?

No one would begrudge him if he took the afternoon off when the boss had died, would they? Edward thought about his sterile apartment, with its iconic view of the Thames, and made the right decision for him—he went right back to the office. After all, what was waiting for him at home?

The problem with working for Daphné Le Marche was that you didn't get a social life. The woman was working on her deathbed, for God's sake, he thought, as he paid the cabbie and went into the Grosvenor Street address.

Orange roses filled vases in the hallway, and a plethora of flowers with cards attached lined reception.

'Mr Badger, where shall we send these?' asked a pretty receptionist whose name he forgot.

He glanced at the flowers and shrugged. 'Send them to nursing homes in the Greater London area. Someone should enjoy them,' he suggested.

The girl nodded and smiled. 'Good idea, Madame Le Marche would like that.'

Edward thought that Madame Le Marche probably wouldn't care what happened to them, since they were all white. Lilies, chrysanthemums, roses and delphiniums spilled over the desks and he found the smell sickening.

'Take something for yourself,' he offered generously.

The girl blushed. 'Thank you, Mr Badger,' she gushed.

He nearly asked her to call him Edward but then refrained. The last thing he wanted was an office dalliance. The last time that happened, she left him with a set of spreadsheets of their finances and moved to a rival company. He had nearly lost his job, and Daphné had reminded him, no, he thought again, warned him to never mix business with pleasure again, unless it was family.

He strode up the hallway and nodded at those who passed him by, and finally found the silent security of his office.

His capable secretary, Rebecca, barrelled in with her six-month pregnant stomach and barked messages at him, and he listened while watching her bump in its tight jersey top.

'Is that thing moving?' he asked, peering at her.

Rebecca stared down at the bump. 'Yes, they're busy today. It's because I had laksa for lunch and now they're all high on chilli and lemongrass,' she laughed, cupping the twins in their safe house.

Edward laughed but wished for a moment she wasn't going to leave next month to have the babies. How on earth would he replace such a wonderful assistant?

Rebecca was still speaking. 'And Sibylla Le Marche called for you,' she said.

Edward looked up. 'She called here? To the office?' he asked.

'Yes, she said she had trouble getting through to you on the mobile,' said Rebecca, glancing down at the notepad she was holding. 'She said, thanks but no thanks.' Rebecca raised her eyebrows and waited for his instruction.

Edward sighed and leaned back in his chair. This whole arrangement was proving to be more difficult than he had imagined and he wondered if he should have just gone home after all.

He sat thinking. There was no way he was going to leave Daphné's legacy to that useless idiot Robert. He wanted to believe in Daphné's granddaughters, but he had his doubts that the two estranged cousins had anything in common, let alone the ability to turn around a business.

Sometimes Daphné made impossible requests when she was alive, but he did his best to fulfil them. When he made her a promise, he never broke it, which was probably why he wasn't a successful barrister with chambers at Gray's Inn. But there was something about the Le Marche dynasty that was compelling, and Daphné's energy was everywhere, even after her death.

He felt his eyes hurt with unshed tears for his boss and friend and he squeezed them tight to make them disappear.

Don't frown, you'll get lines, he heard her voice say and he smiled to himself as he opened a file. As long as the company was still under the Le Marche name, then it would have his loyalty.

Chapter 8

Giles, Paris, 1956

Giles Le Marche had closed his pharmacy for lunch was and preparing to go home to a cooked meal, thanks to his housekeeper, Bertie.

Giles liked routine, procedure and process, and his owning his own pharmacy in Montreuil, right next to the main Paris bus depot, afforded him a good living with all number of people coming for their travel sickness remedies and medicines they were unable to find in their village.

He adjusted his hat on his dark head of hair—a genetic gift, thanks to his maternal grandfather, but he told his gentlemen customers the bounty on his head was due to the hair tonic he made, and used daily.

Men willingly bought the tonic, just like women bought all manner of balms and lotions for their ageing.

Everyone was looking for something, he thought, as he closed the door and locked it with his brass key and slipped it into the inside pocket of his suit coat and set out on his walk home.

As he passed the bus station, he saw a small group of people gathered, all quibbling over the price of something.

Perhaps it was some delicious figs that a farmer had brought up from Autignac. He had a lovely blue cheese that would go well with the figs and a class of Tempranillo after dinner.

Moving to the back of the crowd, his height gave him a vantage point to see the spectacle below, but instead of a valise of figs, there was a young girl selling what looked to be cakes of soap, wrapped in raffia ribbons. Glass jars of varying sizes were filled with a lotion that the women in the crowd were trying on their hands and arms and murmuring to themselves.

'Very soft.'

'Lovely.'

'How much did you say?'

As the women discussed the product and the price, Giles stepped forward and dipped a finger into the jar that one of the women was holding. He smeared it onto the back of his hand and sniffed it, then gently rubbed it in.

His skin absorbed the smooth emollient and left it feeling fresher and, dare he say it, almost younger.

He picked up a cake of soap and held it to his nose. Lavender, he noted, and picked up another and recognised pungent citrus scents.

'How much?' he asked the girl, who looked up at him with indigo blue eyes, and a shock of dark curled hair.

'The soap? Two francs. The lotion is five francs,' she said, as a woman handed her the money for one of each of the products.

He rubbed the back of his hand again and noticed that his skin was still dewy where he had sampled the cream. There was something different compared to the creams he made in his pharmacy, but he couldn't quite place the core ingredients.

There was lard, which was common, but there was something else.

'What is in it?' he asked her, feeling his stomach rumble. If he had the ingredients, he could experiment in the pharmacy and create his own Le Marche creams.

The girl looked up at him, and he saw her tired smile. It was amused and defeated all at once, and he felt sorry for her for a moment. So many girls like this came into Paris to find work, but the city was becoming overrun with the country mice just like her.

He waited for an answer impatiently. She handed a woman her change and a jar of cream and then leaned over and put her hand on Giles' shoulder and whispered in his ear.

He could feel her mouth next to his skin. Her hair smelt of sunshine but her whisper was redolent with ambition.

'An enchantress never reveals her magic,' she said and stepped back from him. He felt the hairs on his neck rise with a feeling he thought would never visit him again.

'I will buy them all,' he said, without thinking twice.

And later, when surrounded by the cakes of soaps and lotions, he wondered if it was the product he wanted or the girl from the country.

* * *

Daphné Amyx stood opposite him in the small pharmacy, her hands twisting around each other, as though she was resisting the overwhelming urge to touch the rows of perfectly lined up bottles with their pretty labels.

'I can make more,' she said, as she watched the man line up the jars and soap on the marble-topped bench in the dispensary.

'When you're next in town, bring me some,' he said brusquely.

Daphné shook her head. 'No, I mean I can stay here and make more for you. I could work for you. I'd be an excellent assistant.'

He looked up at her, as though seeing her for the first time. She was ten years younger than his own son and yet she had more self-possession and directness than anyone he had met of that age.

He was used to the teens coming into the store, the girls trying to shoplift the peroxide for their hair, the boys wanting the hair cream for their pompadour.

But this girl with the cloud of dark hair and a waist he could have spanned with his outstretched fingers was beguiling him.

'I don't need an assistant,' he snapped.

'I think you could.' She gestured around the space. 'Women like other women to recommend things, it's part of the secret women's business,' she said with that smile that shifted his perspective of the world.

It had been twenty years since he had loved a woman. His existence was carved out of routine and duty, yet this girl turned his mind into a whirling dervish, spinning him back in time before responsibility and duty took over his life.

'An assistant,' he harrumphed. He was fifty years old and being manipulated by a woman. It seemed time didn't change a thing. He liked to sleep with whores, that way there was no misunderstanding about the future.

'Where are you from?' he barked.

'Calvaic,' she answered.

'And your parents?'

'Only my mother is alive now, she works a small property with a few animals and vegetables. If I worked here, I would send her money to help.'

He paused, thinking of Yves, who never asked for anything or ever offered him anything. 'Where would you live in Paris?'

'I have friends in Le Marais I could stay with until I found something more suitable.'

He snorted. 'Le Marais? Jews.' He shook his head as he spoke the last word.

Daphné raised her head proudly. 'Yes Jews, and my friends. My mother and I hid them for a time during the war, and I would do it again for anyone, even you.'

Giles looked up startled at the hardness that crept into her tone. 'Of course,' he said quickly. 'I agree. I am just commenting on them taking my business. There are more and more pharmacies opening and a few of them are run by Jews.' He felt ashamed as he spoke, realising his shame at not doing more during the war, in fact, avoiding it at all costs.

The war had interrupted his routine. He'd sent his son Yves to Switzerland to finish school and stay safe with his chemistry teacher's family from university and, since then, Yves had stayed there, much to Giles' disappointment. A trip back to France once a year for a weekend didn't allow them to connect as a father and son. Instead, they were polite, like cousins once removed, knowing the skin of each other's life but not the bones.

Yves mother, Louise, was the unspoken ghost in their lives, dying when Yves was fourteen years old.

The conversations about Louise and her death hadn't evolved into a respectful mourning from both of them, and then the war started in earnest and Yves was sent away.

Daphné adjusted the belt on her teal dress, which was well made from shabby fabric. She would need clothes, he imagined, and he thought of the pharmacies on the Champs-Élysées where the women wore white shirts with little black bows tied around their necks.

'I can pay you sixty-four francs a week,' he said, waiting for her to argue. Instead, her eyes opened wide and she smiled with such radiance, he thought he might be thrown backward by the force of her happiness.

What had happened, he thought, as she clapped her hands? How had he been so bewitched by her? He had lost his mind, he thought, and was about to rescind his offer when she leaned forward and touched his face with her soft hand. Too soft for a rural girl, he noted, as she leaned into his ear again, whispering conspiratorially.

'Goat's milk,' she said and pulled back, and he saw amusement in her eyes. She smiled again and he inhaled sharply, as everything within him that was dormant woke.

* * *

Daphné went back to Calvaic to get her possessions and see her mother again, on the strict instructions from Giles she was to return in three days' time, ready to work.

She was all he could think about during those three days, with her absence draped around his mind and body.

Daily he told himself off for his desire, nightly he indulged in fantasies far beyond anything he and Louise had experienced during their marriage, or even anything he had done with the occasional whore he found in the back alleys of La Marais.

Then she walked through the door on the third morning. He could hardly concentrate all morning, waiting for her arrival, just before he set off home for Bertilde's leek and Gruyère tart.

'You're here,' he stated, as though she wasn't going to come back to him.

The girl nodded, and he saw her eyes her were red, and she was pale.

'Your farewell to your mother was difficult, I imagine,' he said, somewhat more kindly.

She nodded, and he saw her eyes fill with tears again.

'Have you eaten?' he asked.

She shook her head and he picked up his jacket from the hook next to the dispensary and slipped it on, adding his hat and picking up his keys for lunch.

'Home then,' he said and he walked out of the shop with Daphné following him, locking the door after them.

Bertilde had left him the tart, still warm, covered by a linen tea towel on the dining room table. A small salad but enough for two sat next to it in a glass bowl, with a vinaigrette in a little jug. It was all exactly as it was every Thursday but to Giles it felt unusual and exotic.

Daphné stood in the middle of the room, looking around at his life and he wondered what she saw. The orderly room now looked sterile to his eyes. The darkness from the blinds being half closed felt ignorant and the closed windows suffocating.

He threw up the shades and opened a window, letting the warm air inside.

'Shall we eat?' he said, gesturing to the table.

Daphné sat down opposite him and watched him as he served her and then himself. He gave her more than him, and she looked up and smiled at him.

'You should take the bigger piece,' she said.

'I don't want to put on weight,' he said, touching his flat stomach. He was in excellent shape, from his programme of walking every day and exercising self-discipline in all things.

They ate in silence and Giles watched, as she carefully used her knife and fork. There was something so endearing about her, and he wanted to protect her, teach her, love her.

He stood up and poured himself a glass of wine.

'Wine?' he asked Daphné who shook her head in refusal.

He saw a flush building on her neck, and he wondered if the air from the open window was too warm on her.

'Are you all right?' he asked her.

She paused, as though finding the right words.

'Do you expect me to have sex with you?' she asked, her bluntness outweighing any shame she might feel at the honesty of her question.

'What? No,' he cried and it was true. He had long ago given up having expectations from other people.

'It's just Mother said some men hire young girls so they can have something to toy with at work, and a wife to cook for them at home.'

Giles gestured around the room.

'I have no wife, as you can see. I have a son, who I barely see who lives in Switzerland, and I have no desire for anything from you but the formula for your creams. I think we could make a very good business if we tried.'

Her eyes were downcast and then she looked up at him, her eyes meeting his, and he saw something that he imagined was disappointment in them for a moment, but then he remembered that Louise had said he had always been a fool, except now he was just an old fool.

Chapter 9

Dominic

Dominic Bertiull left Sainte-Chapelle with no more idea of what was next for the Le Marche dynasty than any of the mourners. His strategy to approach the ex-wife hadn't played out as he had hoped. Usually they sang like birds, bitter and twisted with their place outside of the family, ready to spill their opinion on everything wrong with the past and placing curses on the future. But Matilde Le Marche hadn't said a word. Dominic's charms hadn't worked; in fact, he thought, as he sat back in his office, they had quite the opposite effect.

Most women fawned over Dominic, particularly older women. He was deliberate in fashion, preferring expensive suits, silk ties and handmade shoes. He only wore shades of blues and greys, with black saved for casual wear and black tie events.

He knew he was pleasant looking, but good clothes and a slim and muscular frame ensured he went into the next category of class, and money lifted him up one more level again.

He was rich, beautiful, successful and single. Europe was

his oyster and beautiful women his pearls. Born in London to his diplomat French father and a German mother, he was educated in England but went to university in America, much to his father's disappointment. But Dominic wanted to become wealthy by the time he was thirty and money and America seemed to go hand in hand. He came back to Europe and set up an office in Paris, ready to embrace his Gallic blood, and to use his French charm to buy and sell companies for a profit.

He was rich by the time he was thirty, obscenely rich by the time he was thirty-five and, by forty, he was bored.

Matilde Le Marche came into his mind and he typed her name into his computer.

Photos of her came up from her modelling days, and he still saw the beauty in her face, although it was lined from sunbathing.

She was fifty-five years old, he noted. Ten years older than him and he wondered what she would be like in bed.

Dominic had slept with women older than Matilde, and younger than eighteen—he wasn't an ageist. Sex was sex and he liked it because he was good at it.

He typed Celeste's name into the computer and images of her filled the screen. She was attractive, he thought, but not like her mother had been. Celeste had sad eyes that caused her mouth to turn downwards, as though she was disapproving of everything around her.

Maybe she was like Daphné, he thought, amused at the idea. He had heard the stories of the woman's iron fist in a velvet glove.

He flicked through the images and read some more about the company he had been watching for the last year.

There was nothing he didn't know about the company.

Giles Le Marche, a chemist, had started the company in Paris in 1902. He married a French woman called Louise who had died just before the Second World War started.

Daphné married Yves in 1956 and was soon working in the company, turning it from a small family concern into a product that was found in every pharmacy across France.

In 1978, Yves died and Daphné took over the running of the company and soon the products were across most of Europe, but they never made it to the same level of success in America or the United Kingdom where French pharmaceuticals were seen as indulgent or too foreign.

There was a head office in London, and an office in Paris attached to a laboratory. They had excellent skin products and their lipsticks were moderately successful, but the rest of their line was struggling. Cosmetics was competitive and it wasn't enough to have appropriate colours; they needed to have an edge, and Le Marche had lost its edge twenty years ago when Henri had died.

Dominic sat back in his chair and stared at a picture of Daphné and her two sons. They must have been sixteen and nineteen, he imagined. Robert looked like a younger version of his father, and Henri looked like a young Alain Delon.

Dominic peered at the image on the screen. Henri had a casual elegance that Robert didn't, he noted, and he wondered what would have happened if Henri had survived and worked in the company.

He scratched his head, careful to smooth down his dark hair again and clicked through the pages on the computer again. Yes, he knew everything about the company and the basics of the scandals that befell them, with tragic deaths and any number of rumours that followed them through the years, but what he didn't know, and what he needed to know was what were Robert's plans for Le Marche.

The Japanese company was desperate for an established cosmetics company with a European presence they could build on, and Le Marche was perfect if Dominic could get it for the right price.

He had two choices—he could pay what it was worth and have the deal done in a matter of months, or he could try to lower the value of the company, so his client paid less and he was paid more as a bonus.

Dominic thought for a moment and then decided he never liked to pay full price for anything and so he began his war on the House of Le Marche.

* * *

Edward Badger was still at his desk when Dominic Bertiull rang him from Paris.

'I have a client who is interested in purchasing Le Marche,' Dominic said, then paused for effect, 'and the formula.'

Edward cleared his throat, 'Madame Le Marche has only just been buried today, Mr Bertiull. I don't think we're in the position for any such offers at the moment.'

Dominic heard the tiredness in the man's voice and he smiled. This was going to be easy, he decided. The lawyer and right-hand man of Daphné Le Marche was most likely sick of his position. No doubt he was already looking elsewhere for another job. No one in their right mind would work under Robert Le Marche, everyone knew how hopeless he was.

'When do you think you will be ready?' asked Dominic, with just the right amount of respect.

'I will have to speak to the family,' said Edward.

The family? thought Dominic. That's interesting. Perhaps Robert isn't the only concern. Perhaps the granddaughter got a slice of the company also?

That was easy enough to handle, he thought. He'd done his homework on Celeste and saw she was having an affair with a married man and had no real career. She would take the money in a heartbeat.

He clicked on the screen again and saw images from *Paris Match* of a small dark-haired child at the funeral of her father.

Henri's child, he reminded himself, but then dismissed her. Daphné and the mother of the child hadn't spoken since Henri had died and, according to his private investigator, she hadn't been back in the country since the funeral.

There was no chance the woman would make a claim now, was there? He made a mental note to speak to his private investigator to find out her whereabouts, and if she was still in Australia.

'When will the reading of the will be? Perhaps I can speak to Robert directly?' he offered smoothly. 'I know how busy you must be.'

'The reading of the will is actually none of your business, but you're more than welcome to speak to Robert, as that's none of my business,' countered Edward with the same slick tone.

Dominic ignored the barb and kept focused.

'Robert mentioned the formula. He said his mother told him she had discovered something that would change a woman's face, make her look younger, more beautiful. He said it was being trialled around the world.'

'I have no idea what you're talking about,' said Edward. 'I have to go. Goodbye, Mr Bertiull.'

Dominic hung up the phone and sat in thought.

Something odd was going on. Edward Badger was very cagey about the formula, and then said that the decision to sell the company would be made as a family.

He needed to know more, but he didn't want to scare the granddaughters away. His eyes turned to the computer screen, and settled on Matilde. Perhaps he might try seeing what she would reveal away from the Le Marche and Paris gossips. According to his sources, there was no love lost between her and Robert, so no doubt she would be happy to spill the secrets for some revenge and a price; there was no doubt that she would be left nothing by the old woman, and Robert wasn't going to share anything he had with his ex-wife.

Robert really was a repugnant man, thought Dominic, as he left the office and got into his waiting car. When Robert had first approached him with the news that his mother was dying, and would he want to buy the company from him, Dominic wasn't interested, but then he spoke of the formula. A contact at the private bank, Lombard Odier, told him there was a sealed envelope in a vault belonging to Daphné Le Marche with the words written on the front—

To be opened according to the instructions in the Last Will and Testament of Daphné Le Marche

It was a perfect mystery, and if he could get his hands on

the formula, whatever it might be, and strip the company and sell it to the Japanese concern, everyone would be happy. Well, at least him and Robert.

His phone chimed with the reminder that he had a date tonight with a twenty-three-year-old Russian supermodel, who was walking for Chanel and Givenchy. She was utterly perfect to look at, but about as interesting as a clothes hanger.

He sighed, thinking about the evening ahead. He knew how it was going to play out. She would wear a slip dress, her nipples hard through the fabric, making everyone in the restaurant turn. She would order the crab soufflé and barely touch it, while drinking too much wine. They would return to his apartment, where she would allow him to have sex with her, while she did nothing more than lie there. Her belief in her beauty meant she didn't have to contribute, as her looks were enough.

He thought about cancelling and then changed his mind. He had nowhere else to be, and any company, even Masha the model, was better than none at all.

Chapter 10

Anna, 1956

Daphné pushed her way through the curtains that were supposed to keep out the cold winter wind and into the Anna and Max's flat.

Paul and Marina were at the table, eating dinner, while Anna was stirring a pot on the stove.

'Hello, everyone,' said Daphné happily.

Anna merely nodded, as the children talked for over each other telling Anna about their day.

After they had eaten, Anna sent them downstairs to be with their father while he closed up the shop.

'What's wrong, Anna?' asked Daphné, her face worried.

She had changed since working at the pharmacy for three months. Now she looked like a chic Parisian girl, with make-up, and a little white shirt and a peach scarf tied around her neck. She had lost a little weight, and had a confidence about her that Anna had been searching for her whole life.

Anna had only been into the pharmacy once, and had found both it, and Giles, intimidating, but she had seen the way he looked at Daphné when she spoke. The way his eyes followed her when she moved, and Anna knew desire when she saw it; that's why she was so upset now.

'I'm pregnant,' she said, and sat at the table and put her head in her hands.

'Oh,' was all Daphné said.

'Yes, oh,' said Anna. 'I cannot believe this happened. Marina is at school, I can't have another child, I'm forty years old for God's sake.' She shook her head and thumped the table with her hand.

'You could have used a condom,' suggested Daphné.

Anna looked up at her. 'How do you know about these? What is happening with Giles?' she demanded to know.

Daphné burst out laughing. 'Nothing, I sell them, that's all. They are very popular with the country women who don't want any more children.'

Anna sighed. 'I think that horse has already bolted.'

'Does Max know?' Daphné asked.

Anna shook her head, 'No, I am afraid to tell him. Business is slow, babies cost money.' She felt her eyes fill with tears and she was angry with herself for allowing this to happen. Usually, Max pulled out but they had been carried away one lunchtime, with Daphné and the children away, and Anna had thought she was too old.

It seemed her body didn't get the message.

They sat in silence, both thinking of the options, then Daphné stood up. 'Well, we might as well get on with it,' she said.

'What do you mean?' asked Anna.

'I mean, you can't change what's happened and if it's money that's worrying you, then we need to get the business to make more money. I told you to paint the shop, make it look nicer, now we must do it.'

'With what money, Daphné? And how do we know it will make a difference?' Anna felt exasperated at the girl. She may look grown up, but she still thought like a child.

'I know it will work. The jars of Le Marche crème are walking out the door, because of the labels I made for them and had printed. A little bit of pomp with a crown and some fancy writing and now women think they are buying Marie Antoinette's own recipe.'

Daphné was at the kitchen bench making coffee. Her energy was unrelenting but also infectious.

'So you think painted walls will make a difference?' said Anna, with a smile that she reserved for the children.

'I think it's one of the things you could do,' said Daphné, as she turned from the stove. 'I think about these things you know. I'm always thinking of how to make Le Marche better or the shop downstairs. It's fun.'

Anna couldn't help but laugh. What was a weight to her and Max was a game to Daphné.

'So tell me everything then,' said Anna and Daphné brought the coffee to the table and sat, warming her hands around the cup.

'Get a pencil and paper, we're going to make a list.'

* * *

Later that night, while the children were upstairs asleep, Daphné and Anna sat with a shocked Max.

'Another child,' he kept saying, as though he hadn't heard correctly the first, second or third time Anna told him.

'Yes,' said Anna patiently, as he processed the news.

Daphné watched the snow fall outside and sighed then pulled her woollen cardigan around her a little tighter.

'It's cold down here,' said Anna, rubbing Daphné's slim shoulder. 'You can go upstairs if you want?'

'No, we have to finish this conversation,' said Daphné adamantly and she cleared her throat and lifted her head.

'Max, I know the baby is a big issue financially, but Anna and I have written a list of things I think you could do in the shop, to make it as good as the jewellery you sell. Your work is beautiful and needs to be in a beautiful space.'

Anna watched as Daphné cajoled and flattered him. She didn't know this side of Daphné, who had always been like a little sister. This girl knew how to work Max and his ego and again she wondered about Giles.

She believed Daphné when she said nothing had happened between them and that she had never thought of Giles that way, in fact she had been shocked when Anna had mentioned it a few times.

'He's like my father,' said Daphné but Anna knew enough about older men and younger women to know someone was filling some sort of role in the other's life.

'I don't have the money to do even half of what's on that list,' said Max, defeated before they had even started.

'We will find a way,' said Daphné determinedly and Anna saw the same quiet determination that was in her mother Chantal who had hidden them from the Germans all those years before.

'I think she's serious,' said Max, turning to Anna.

'I think she's remarkable,' said Anna and she leaned in

and kissed Daphné on the cheek. 'We live because of you,' she said, feeling tears swelling in her eyes.

But Daphné shook her head in refusal to accept the weight of Anna's comment.

'No, you live because you choose to. Every single decision you have made has led you to this moment—knowing to escape Poland when you did, knowing to trust my mother and the Resistance, knowing to come to Paris and let Max open the store, letting me into your home, and even this baby. What you make in life comes from your ability to trust yourself and your decisions.'

Anna looked at Daphné in awe. 'Thank you.'

Daphné picked up the list that Anna had written, ran her finger down it and read aloud. 'Painting, new display cloths, new window decorations, a sign above the shop, new boxes.' she looked up at Max.

'You need a name. You can't just call yourself Marais Jewels, you need something better.'

'What sort of a name?' he asked.

Daphné chewed at the end of the pencil and then wrote.

'Karpinski,' she said firmly.

'That's my name,' said Max, looking bewildered. 'It's also a Polish Jew name—we're not popular.'

Daphné looked at Max, holding his eye contact. 'You have to honour your heritage, Max. All across the world, jewellers are called by their surname—Cartier, Boucheron, Mellerio dits Meller.'

'How do you know these names?' asked Max, looking at Anna who shrugged.

'I walk at lunchtime,' said Daphné. 'I like to go to all parts of Paris. I have seen these stores on Rue de la Paix. Some of them let me try on the jewels. They are very elegant.'

Anna felt her mouth drop open. 'I would never go to those stores, what on earth possessed you?'

But Daphné just laughed. 'Why wouldn't I go to these stores? They need customers and, one day, I might be able to afford a little gold chain from them. They are no better than me, if they come to me for some paracetamol or laxatives.'

Anna burst out laughing. 'You are too much, Daphné, just too much.'

* * *

The next afternoon, the sound of the bell on the door ringing made Anna and Max look up from their calculations of the list in front of them.

'Hello,' said Daphné proudly, as she stood in the door-way, with Giles Le Marche standing behind her, looking as uncomfortable as anyone Anna had ever seen.

'Max and Anna Karpinski, this is Giles Le Marche,' said Daphné dragging Giles by the hand through the door and into the dark shop.

Max shook his hand and Anna nodded at him, as she glanced at Daphné to see what she was up to.

'How can I help you, Monsier Le Marche? A trinket for your wife perhaps?' asked Max and Anna wanted to elbow him for his lack of subtly.

'No, no,' was all Giles said, waving his hand over the cases.

Daphné placed her handbag on the glass counter, and walked behind it, picking up the list, leaving Giles alone in the middle of the store looking like someone about to face the firing squad.

'Giles has agreed to lend me the money to help you fix up the shop,' she said, waving the list at Anna and Max.

'What? No,' Max cried.

'Why?' asked Anna.

'Because we don't know him,' Max started to say but Anna shook her head and looked at Giles.

'No, I mean, why would you lend us the money?' she asked carefully.

Two men's egos were at stake here and, judging by the puce colour of Max's face, so was their health.

Giles took off his hat and placed it next to Daphné's bag; Anna noticing that Daphné moved it so they were closer together.

'Because Daphné made a compelling argument as to why, and above all she said you were like family to her.'

'What do you get out of it?' Anna asked, narrowing her eyes, as she took in his perfect cuffs and well-laundered suit. Nothing was out of place, except his heart, she thought, as she saw him look to Daphné for support.

She stepped in to catch him. 'Giles thinks that it would be a good investment, and you can pay him back over time, or he can keep his stake in the business, it's entirely up to you.'

Max looked at Anna, who in turn looked at Daphné.

'Can we have a word, Daphné?' asked Anna.

She and Max left the shop and went into the back room.

'One moment,' said Daphné, as she followed them, closing the door.

'What on earth are you thinking?' asked Anna, trying to keep the anger from her voice.

'What? It's a good idea,' said Daphné.

'What will you have to do for this money?' asked Max, who had crossed his arms and was looking at her like he did when Marina was cheeky to him.

'Nothing,' said Daphné, turning red. 'He's not like that.'

'I don't want an investor,' said Max.

Anna turned to him. 'You're not thinking of taking it, are you?'

Max shrugged, 'You have to spend money to make money, anyone knows that, and if Daphné can convince a man like him to lend us money, then we must have something going for us.'

'It's because he's in love with her,' hissed Anna.

'That's ridiculous,' said Daphné, now crossing her arms like Max.

'So you don't think we have anything going for us?' Max asked his wife.

Anna groaned. 'Don't start that, it's not what I am saying,' she said.

'Please don't let your pride stand in the way, Anna. Please see that this is exciting and Max's work is beautiful and should be known,' Daphné pleaded.

'Yes, I promise this will work. I feel it,' said Max.

Anna rolled her eyes at him 'Eggs and promises are soon broken,' said Anna quietly, but Max and Daphné were already back in the shop speaking excitedly to Giles. Anna sat on the chair at Max's workbench, realising she was never going to win against Daphné, she was just glad she was on her side.

Chapter 11

Billie

Billie was feeling empowered when she woke on Saturday morning. She had told the lawyer with the stupid name that she didn't want her share of the company. She wanted nothing from that family. She was still cross with her mother for not telling the whole truth about her father. But would that have changed anything? she wondered. Her life was pretty great as it was. Besides her lack of sex and love, she wouldn't change it for all the skincare empires in Europe.

She showered and headed out in her little car, which she had bought when she first started to work at the laboratory. She had been there for five years and, while it wasn't exciting work, it was steady and secure and she liked that more than anything else.

She stopped at her local café and rushed inside, where the barista knew her order.

'Usual?' he half yelled, trying to be heard over the din of milk being steamed and the clashing of teaspoons on saucers and chatter from the Saturday morning crowd.

'Yes please,' said Billie, as she peered into the glass cabinet of pastries and treats.

Usually, she was a fruit muffin kind of a girl but today, in honour of her father, she chose an almond croissant.

Her ties to France were limited to liking the food and being able to speak a smattering of the language, most of it gone with her father, who was the only one who spoke French to her.

She knew Elisabeth knew more French than she said she did, but she understood why she wouldn't want to speak the language of their love.

'Hey there,' she heard and looked up to see Nick.

'This isn't your café?' she half joked. She knew Nick lived nearby but she had never seen him around the neighbourhood.

'You went on about the coffee here, so I thought I should try it.'

His face was slightly red, and she wondered if he had bicycled to the café, but there was no sign of a helmet either in his hand or on his head.

'You alone?' he asked with a smile.

'I'm about to go and see Mum,' she said, taking the takeaway cup that was offered to her. 'You?'

'I'm meeting someone,' said Nick, his eyes scanning the crowded café.

Billie's heart sunk a little. Of course he would be meeting someone, he had a life outside of the laboratory, she thought.

'Enjoy your weekend,' she said and then, taking her croissant and coffee, she left, as though she hadn't a care in the world.

As she drove to her mother's house, she sipped her coffee and ate her croissant, enjoying the sweetness, ignoring the icing sugar that spilled across her lap. Nick was a work friend, and that was all, she reminded herself. There was no need to get obsessive over a man she barely knew other than being a brilliant chemist. She had seen Nick's résumé and knew he was wasted at a laboratory like theirs, but jobs in science were hard to find at his level in Australia at the moment and even Billie knew not to make any rash decisions when employment was unreliable.

A huge truck was in the driveway, with several men already loading on the larger pieces of furniture while her mother was sitting on the brick fence, a cup in her hand.

'Hey, Mum,' Billie said as she approached.

'You have dusty jeans,' said her mother with a smile.

'I just ate an almond croissant,' Billie said, returning the smile.

'Your father's favourite,' said Elisabeth and she sipped her tea.

'I know,' said Billie, as she shoved her hands into the back pockets of her jeans and watched the work being done by the removal men.

'Where's Gordon?' she asked.

'At the other house, unpacking a carload,' said Elisabeth. Billie nodded. 'So what do we do now?'

Elisabeth shrugged and smiled. 'There isn't anything to be done. We did it all yesterday. The men have a plan and I'm not prepared to deviate from it. They're almost as bossy as you.'

Billie snorted. 'I doubt that. Well, can I take over some more valuables, things you don't want to go in the truck?'

Elisabeth shook her head and pushed herself off the fence, groaning a little. 'I'm too old for this moving business,' she complained.

'I hardly think fifty-three is old, Mum,' said Billie, poking her mother in the back.

The house was slowly emptying and Billie wandered into her bedroom. She had lived in this room from the age of ten until she moved out at twenty-one. There were stickers on the back of the door, her height recorded in pencil on the doorframe and the outline of the prints that had been on the wall for those eleven years.

She had planned revenge and world domination in this room, dreamed of her wedding and winning a million dollars. She had been a pop star and an actress, a world leader and the most popular girl in school.

Except none of it had happened.

She touched the faded blue curtains, remembering the chinks of light that came through them from the streetlamp.

When had she lost all of her courage? She couldn't name the day or the time but the more aware she became of her father's decision, the more it impacted her and, eventually, she just chose the easiest and safest options in life. She chose the career in science, even though she was also good at art, because there was comfort in the guarantee of work.

She chose the sensible car over the pink Beetle that she had yearned for as a child, promising she would one day own the coolest car on earth.

She said no to more dates than she went out on because she didn't want to have to trust and have her heart broken like her mother.

Tears filled her eyes and she wiped them away quickly with the back of her hand.

She had written poems for her father in this room, and

imagined his suicide note. She had never asked to read it and hadn't wanted to until now, but she would never ask her mother to invade her privacy. If Elisabeth had felt she needed to know then she would have told Billie.

'Everything all right, darling?' Elisabeth stood in the doorway.

'Yes, just remembering when I was going to be Kylie Minogue.' Billie laughed and Elisabeth joined in.

'Gosh, you loved make-up back then,' said Elisabeth.

'I know,' said Billie with a roll of her eyes. 'How things have changed.'

'I have something for you,' said Elisabeth.

Billie shook her head. 'Mum, honestly, I don't need anything else from here, you've already given me those towels and the chairs,' she said, as she followed her mother into her bedroom. The room was almost empty, but a cardboard box sat on a chair, marked 'Billie'.

'This is yours,' said Elisabeth, picking up the box and handing it to her.

Billie looked down at it. 'What is it?'

'Take it home, don't open it here. It's just things, stuff, memory bank withdrawals and deposits.'

Billie saw the shadows across her mother's face and she nodded, aware it was more than what Elisabeth had said.

'I'll put it in my car.'

Outside, she placed the box in the boot of the car and ran her hand over the top where her mother had scrawled her name.

Part of her wanted to open it now, but she knew she should honour her mother's request, and she slammed the boot shut and went back inside to help with the rest of the move.

* * *

In the evening, after a shared fish and chip dinner with her mother and stepfather, all of them dirty and tired but moved into the new house, Billie went back to her flat.

The silence, which was welcoming on most nights, seemed heavy tonight, as she carried the box inside and placed it on the sofa.

She stared at it and then went and ran a bath, dosing the water with jasmine and vanilla oils. She also lit a cassis bark candle.

These were her luxuries and, as she undressed and lowered herself into the warm water, she felt her aching muscles unknot and the frown on her face relax.

Was there anything better than a bath? she wondered as she soaked, the steam flushing her face. She lifted a leg and assessed it objectively. It was an OK leg, as far as leg shape went, it got her around, but she remembered Celeste's long legs. Even as a child, Billie was aware of her shortcomings and short legs compared to Celeste and Camille.

Why hadn't she got her father's legs or her mother's breasts? Instead, she was told she had Daphné's figure.

Another reason to hate her for her rounded bottom and small breasts. Her best feature was her waist, which was rarely shown off by her shapeless white lab coat.

Her toe played with the faucet as she tried to relax, but the box with her name on it called from the other room until she could ignore it no more.

Splashing her way out of the bath, she pulled a towel

around her body and dried herself off, then pulled on her soft robe and padded out to the living room, leaving a trail of wet prints behind her.

She stared at the box and then sat next to it; just being in its presence was causing her to feel sick, and she wished she had the courage to have said to her mother she wanted no more memories. That she had enough memories.

But she didn't and now she had Pandora's box on her Ikea sofa.

Taking a deep breath, she opened the box and peered inside.

School reports greeted her and she pulled them out and leafed through the pages.

The same thing was said every year, six different ways of commenting that Billie was clever and quiet, and could do anything she wanted. And she had. Hadn't she? Self-doubt filled her and she put down the reports and picked up a pink cloth-covered book that felt familiar. As she opened it, she saw her handwriting, and closed it again.

She didn't want to remember those times, she thought, and she put the book under the school reports.

There were photos and letters to her mother from camps and when she stayed with her maternal grandparents in the Victorian country. Memories of happier times, she thought as she flicked through them, laughing at some of her spelling and phrasings.

And then she saw it: an A4 yellow envelope at the bottom of the box, addressed to her in her mother's writing.

Billie, this is your father's letter. If you want to read it now, then do so, it might help you come to a decision about your

grand-mère*'s will. If you don't, then I understand and you
can return the letter to me and we will never discuss it again.*

   M

   X

Billie held the envelope in her hands and stared at it, as though
trying to use X-ray vision to see into the contents without
having to move.

Did she want to know? Hadn't she made her decision
about Le Marche?

Courage, Billie, she told herself. When was the last time
she had courage? And without a further thought, she opened
the envelope and pulled out a piece of fragile airmail paper.

Darling Elisabeth,

*Life is so hard for people like you and I, but you have
Sibylla to keep you going. I cannot give her anything any
more. I am going mad. This news from Robert has sent me
over the edge and into the void.*

*I was born from betrayal and it is too heavy a burden to
carry and then I betrayed you. I should not have been born,
but perhaps I was born so Sibylla can carry on my work.
Maman wants me back in Paris to take over, you want to stay
in London, how can I keep you happy? How can I go back to
my mother now knowing what I do? It was nothing you did,
or Sibylla, our little prophetess. Maybe she will take over as
I cannot? Perhaps she is the future? She will be my future.*

I love you so much, darling. I'm sorry.

Henri

Billie's eyes pricked with tears and frustration. What was he thinking? Why did he do it? What had Robert told him? How had he betrayed her mother?

She picked up her phone from the table next to her and dialled her mother.

'I read it,' was her greeting.

'Yes,' said her mother, as though she had known Billie would.

'Why did he do it? What was so bad? You have to tell me.'

Elisabeth paused and then replied, 'I did not know how to reach him, how to catch up with him . . . The land of tears is so mysterious.'

'*The Little Prince*,' said Billie, feeling tired, as her eyes scanned the letter again for a clue.

'What had Uncle Robert told him? What was so bad?'

She could hear her mother sigh softly. 'That's what I don't know. Robert said he hadn't told him anything, but they had a fight in Nice when Camille had died, and your father was dead a year after that. He had cut ties with Daphné and Robert, and it didn't matter what I said or did, he wanted nothing to do with them. Now I look back, the depression was always there from the beginning. The restlessness, the migraines, and then the sleeping. It was only a matter of time before he spiralled out of sanity. I didn't know what to do. He was very good at masking it in some ways, and yet it was patently obvious that day by day he was leaving the world.'

Billie had never heard her mother be so raw and real about her father's death.

Usually, it was platitudes about him being sick and mental

illness is an illness and we don't ask why some people get cancer and so on.

Now it seemed as though Elisabeth was speaking to Billie as an equal. They were two women who loved Henri Le Marche and were trying to understand his final decision.

'How did he betray you?'

'I don't know,' said Elisabeth quietly. 'Maybe by dying, I don't know.'

'Do you think I should go over there and ask Robert?' she asked.

'He won't tell you anything,' said Elisabeth, 'and what does it matter now? I think I just wanted you to see he thought you were his future and saw a role for you at Le Marche.'

'Jesus, Mum, that's a lot of pressure,' she snapped.

'I know,' said her mother. 'It's up to you, but make sure if you say no, or if you have said no, that you're doing it for the right reasons. Perhaps your father saw in you something that you can bring to his future that he could not.'

Billie hung up from the call and stared at the letter again, rereading it several times, then she dialled her phone again and waited for an answer.

Finally, someone picked up the line, and she spoke before they could.

'Edward Badger, please. It's Sibylla Le Marche.'

Chapter 12

Celeste, London

The London offices of Le Marche were so dreary, thought Celeste, as she climbed the stairs to the front entrance.

Why Daphné had opened a London headquarters was beyond her but that wasn't her problem now, it was her father's.

The peach walls made her feel nauseous or was that the wine headache? She needed to lay off the Pinot Noir, she thought, as she passed wilting flowers at the reception desk.

The reception girl went bright red when she saw Celeste, but she ignored her, not wanting to have to pretend to care about an employee she would never see again after today. Most likely the girl had heard about her affair with a married man, but Celeste held her head high. She wasn't the first and she wouldn't be the last to succumb to the admiration of a powerful man.

Celeste glanced around the office. She had spent no time in the business, but the staff obviously knew who she was, she thought, as she was directed to the office of her grandmother's lawyer and advisor. No doubt he would be a crotchety old man, with soup on his tie and a plastic comb in his top suit jacket pocket, she thought, as she pushed open the door.

Her father sat inside, texting on his mobile phone.

He was wearing jeans that were too young for him, and she was sure he had a fake tan. It was surprising that he and Matilde had ever split up, she thought, as she shrugged the trench coat from her shoulders and dropped her bag onto the floor, as though she didn't care it was worth two thousand euros.

'Bonjour, Papa,' she said politely, as he glanced up at her. The affection between them was frosty at best, and on a good day it was polite.

'One moment, I'm finishing an email,' he said and she rolled her eyes. No doubt selling the company as we speak, she thought, tapping her Chanel loafer.

'Where is this lawyer? I want to get this finished, I have to go back to Paris, I hate London,' she complained, bored already.

'I am the lawyer, Edward Badger, and yes, we can start,' she heard and looked up to see a pleasant-looking man, who she guessed was in his late thirties, without what looked to be soup on his blue spotted tie, wearing a navy suit with a red pocket square, standing in the doorway staring at her.

'Can we start? I hate London,' she repeated, feeling herself redden. Perhaps he too knew of the affair. She was about to add a poisoned comment about his tie, when she saw he wasn't alone as he walked into the room.

A dark-haired girl, in jeans and a puffy jacket, walked in behind him, her feet in Converse sneakers, and a backpack on her shoulder.

'*Merde*,' said Celeste, as Robert looked up.

'Celeste, Robert, I'm sure you remember Henry's daughter Sibylla?' Edward said, as he went behind his desk and sat down.

'Billie,' she said, as she placed the backpack down on the floor.

'How are you?' asked Robert charmingly, but Celeste noticed she looked at him as though he were the devil, which, according to Matilde, he was.

'Fine, thank you,' she said politely, before giving Celeste a thin-lipped smile. 'Hi,' was all she offered.

Celeste felt herself nod back, unable to speak from shock.

So far, her grandmother's will was proving to be surprising and they hadn't even started dividing her assets yet.

Edward cleared his throat, and opened up a folder that he had carried in with him. He looked down and then up again at them.

She'd better not get the Paris apartment, thought Celeste, as Edward spoke and then she concentrated on the final wishes of her grandmother.

Edward cleared his throat, took a breath and then spoke.

'"This is the last will and testament of Daphné Hélène Le Marche. I hereby revoke all my formers wills, and appoint my lawyer, Edward Badger to be the executor and trustee of this will."'

Celeste noticed her father's head snap up at the announcement and she wondered if he had other expectations about today's reading. She didn't expect any surprises, although the arrival of her cousin was a fly in the ointment.

Edward was reading again.

"'I give the sum of fifty thousand pounds to each of the Karpinskis' children, who are living at the time of my death.' he said and Celeste saw Robert roll his eyes and snort.

He listed various charities for refugees and mental health to be bequeathed cash and art, and Celeste felt herself softening at her Grand-Mère's generosity. She would get the Paris apartment for sure, she thought, and maybe Billie the London one. That would keep everyone happy. She turned her attention back to Edward.

"'To my former daughters-in-law, Elisabeth Le Marche and Matilde Le Marche, I leave the sum of one hundred thousand pounds,'" he said and Celeste and Billie glanced at each other in surprise.

"What for?' Robert cried and Celeste thought that her mother probably deserved more after being married to him.

"'And to my only surviving son, Robert, I leave the Paris apartment,'" Edward said.

'*Merde*,' Celeste said again and slammed her hand on her lap, as Robert gloated at her.

"'And seven hundred thousand pounds,'" Edward finished.

Celeste stood up and started to yell. 'This is bullshit, what do I get? I don't want to live here, did she leave me the London place? I don't want it.'

But Edward shook his head, 'No, she left the London residence to you and Sibylla,' he said.

'Billie,' Celeste heard her cousin correct him, but she ignored her.

'Great, so now we have to sell it? Utterly ridiculous, don't you think?' She turned to Billie who was silent.

'And the company,' Edward said slowly for effect.

Two Le Marches turned their heads and stared at him.

'Excuse me? Can you explain further?' Celeste asked, as though he was offering directions.

Edward ran his finger over the words as he read them out.

'"After payment of debts, taxes, funeral expenses and testamentary, I give my entire estate and company to Celeste Sophie Le Marche and Sibylla Antonia Le Marche. They must work at Le Marche for a year and one day, and cannot sell it until that time has passed. They cannot pass on shares or dividends in the business, and are hereby given equal shares in the business until one year and one day. Once this has passed, they may sell the business to each other but if both wish to sell, then they must close the company."'

He paused.

'She can't do that,' cried Robert, clutching his phone tightly in his hand.

Celeste didn't know whether to laugh or cry. 'She cannot be serious,' she said, shaking her head.

'I already have a job back in Melbourne,' said Billie and then Celeste started to laugh.

'She is crazy, like truly crazy,' she said. 'Maybe she was demented at the end.'

But Edward held up his hand. 'She was the least crazy person I knew. I haven't finished yet,' he said and Celeste was silenced by the tone and respect in his voice.

'"I have discovered a formula that will cause a revolution in skincare. It is currently being held in a bank vault and it can only be opened by my granddaughters after their first year of working together, and when they have committed to running Le Marche. If they decide they do not wish to run the company, or they sell it, the formula must be burned, unopened by the executor of this will, Edward Badger, in the presence of my granddaughters, Celeste and Sibylla.'"

'This is intolerable. I'm going to contest it. This goes against French law,' said Robert, now shaking his phone at the room.

'You will be wasting your time,' said Edward easily. 'She left it in the family, she left you a large sum of money and a property worth millions, you will be fine. She has both a French and English will. She was very careful about this.'

Celeste watched her father crash and burn and tried to feel sorry for him. No doubt he had already sold the company in his mind, probably had even promised it to a stranger over a cognac and a handshake.

'You did this, you set her up for you own benefit,' cried Robert, shaking a fist at Edward.

'If I did, then where is my share?' asked Edward calming. 'If you remember, I wasn't named as a beneficiary.'

Celeste admired the tone that the man took with her father. Calm but not condescending, something she knew her father didn't respond well to in the best of times.

But her father was a fool, she thought, and the warm feelings for her grandmother intensified.

'A year and a day,' she said aloud, but Robert turned to her.

'This is never going to happen. You're ridiculous. You don't know anything about running a company,' he spat.

He always knew how to press the button that made her furious.

'And you do? I seem to remember Grand-Mère saying

that business was at its worst when you were at the helm for a while.'

'You're a bitch like her,' he muttered.

Celeste didn't know if he meant it for her, her mother or for Daphné, and she noticed Edward flinch at the way he spoke to her. But she didn't care, she had been called worse by him. Her father had a big mouth, and an even bigger temper that was always getting him into trouble.

'We will need to work out the details of the share between you both,' said Edward to Billie and Celeste, as he shuffled papers.

'I don't want it,' said Billie quietly.

Everyone turned to her and waited for her to go on.

'I don't want it,' she repeated.

Celeste glared at her. 'Why not?'

'I have a job,' Billie stated. 'Back in Melbourne.'

'As what? A science teacher?' Celeste sneered at her.

Before Billie could speak, Edward jumped in. 'I can understand this is all quite a shock,' he said calmly. 'Why don't we take a break and think about Daphné's decision and come back tomorrow and discuss the finer details?'

'No,' said Billie and Robert simultaneously. They glared at each other.

'I'm going to see my lawyer,' claimed Robert. 'French law states that she must leave it to her heir.'

Edward nodded. 'And she did, she left it to your issue and Henri's issue, who are Celeste and Sibylla.' He gestured to the women. Now he was being condescending, Celeste thought, and she waited for Robert to explode.

But instead she heard her cousin's voice. 'Billie. Not Sibylla.'

It was Celeste who lost her temper. 'We get it, OK, stop with the correcting, it's so pedantic and annoying.'

Billie lowered her eyes and for a moment Celeste felt bad. This was just as surprising to her as it was to Billie, probably more so, she thought.

'If Billie and I go and talk about this by ourselves, maybe we can resolve something,' she offered, using Billie's pre-ferred name as peace offering.

But Robert was already out of his seat at the door.

'You will be hearing from me,' he said to the room, his face red and his eyes narrowed to slits. He then turned and slammed the door behind him.

Celeste and Billie stared at Edward.

'Well, that went better than I expected,' said Edward with a smile and Celeste found herself starting to laugh. Not just at the ridiculous performance of her father's but also at the absurdity of her grandmother's decision.

'I think we need lunch,' said Edward with a firm nod. 'No good decision can be made on an empty stomach.'

Celeste smiled at him and then looked at Billie and shrugged. 'We might as well eat and talk about our options, *oui*?'

Billie sighed. 'Fine. But I can't stay. I have a life back home.'

'Excellent,' said Edward, pulling on a camel coat that Celeste noted was of extremely good quality.

Obviously her grandmother paid him well, she thought, wondering if he would stay on at Le Marche.

If she and Billie did take it on, there was no way they could make it work without his insider knowledge.

'Where shall we eat, Edward?' she purred.

'The local pub is good,' he said.

Celeste felt herself scowl. A pub? How awful.

Billie seemed fine with it, as she walked out of the office with Edward, her hands stuffed in her coat pockets.

Celeste followed them out, pretending to check her phone as they discussed London and all its highlights, or lowlights, as Celeste thought.

The pub was on the corner and, thankfully, it wasn't as dire as Celeste had thought. It was quaint without being kitsch, and the smells emanating from the kitchen were making her mouth water.

They sat at a booth, Billie on one side and Celeste and Edward on the other.

'Did you want to sit together?' asked Celeste bitchily. Sometimes she just couldn't help herself and she regretted it as soon as she spoke.

Billie and Edward looked at her as though she was stupid, which she was now feeling in bucketloads, and she studied the menu that was placed in her hands.

'So this is all very odd, I'm sure,' Edward started.

Billie shook her head in agreement. 'I thought maybe I would be given a painting or something, but the company? I don't know anything about that,' she said.

'Why don't you?' asked Edward and the women looked at him in surprise.

'What do you mean?' asked Billie.

'You work in scientific research. You understand formulas

and all that it takes to create something out of different ingredients. Your grandfather was a chemist. Maybe you will know what this secret formula is?'

'He was a pharmacist,' corrected Celeste.

'One and the same,' said Edward, with a wave of his hand.

Billie shook her head. 'I don't want to run the company. I don't know anything about cosmetics or marketing or whatever else that needs to happen to make the brand successful.'

Edward ordered wine from the waiter and then turned back to them.

He was actually very smooth, thought Celeste, as she watched him order. He had very good manners, which was certainly something her father needed.

'That's where Celeste brings value,' he said and she felt herself frowning, but not caring about the lines being created on her forehead.

'Me?' she said.

'Yes, you're a well-known person, there are blogs about your style, you're very chic. Sort of like a younger Inès de la Fressange.'

Celeste pulled out her phone and Googled her name and flicked through the results. 'God, I had no idea.'

'I think your relationship with Paul Le Brun has helped your profile,' he said.

Celeste glared at him. 'Are you judging me?' she snapped. She looked in her bag for her painkillers and then washed them down with some water.

Edward shook his head. 'Not at all. It is none of my business who you are in love with, but there is a certain cachet with being the lover of a man like Paul Le Brun.'

Celeste could feel Billie looking at her with interest, but she was more fascinated with Edward's attitude.

'I thought you English were stuck up about those things?'

But Edward merely laughed. 'There have been too many politicians having affairs in our parliament for us to be stuck up about anything. It seems it goes with the political territory.'

The waitress came to take their orders and Celeste decided on the salmon and salad, sharing some baby potatoes with Edward, who had ordered the beef.

Billie looked up at the waitress. 'The garden salad, please,' she said.

The waitress paused. 'With anything else?' she asked, but Billie shook her head.

'Your grandmother would disapprove,' said Edward, with a raised eyebrow and Celeste nodded in agreement.

Billie scowled. 'She's dead, so what does it matter?'

'Maybe you can share some of the potatoes,' suggested Edward kindly.

Celeste was about to snap at Billie when she saw her face. She looked like Camille, with her wide eyes and worried expression. All Camille had ever wanted was for Celeste to be happy, and had even offered her the new ballet shoes on the day she died, but Celeste had responded with a tantrum and Camille had died. Celeste wished she could have that day back again and her eyes fill with unexpected tears. She looked at Billie and locked eyes with her cousin.

'Please eat something, Billie. You cannot think properly on just a salad. Have the salmon, it's good for the brain.'

Billie swallowed and then looked at the waitress. 'I'll have the salmon,' she said in a small voice.

Celeste felt herself smile with approval at her cousin's choice and, tentatively, Billie smiled back. They were strangers related by blood, but now bound by the will of their grandmother, for a year and a day.

Chapter 13

Daphné, 1956

In the weeks that followed Max and Giles' handshake of an agreement, Daphné looked at Giles in a different way. She had never been so close to a successful man and she found the way he spoke about money to Max both intimidating and exciting. He was like the King in *The King and I*, the movie she had seen last week, except without the bare feet and bald head, she thought. He was commanding and even rude sometimes, but this made Daphné more intrigued with him than ever. 'I want to learn everything from you,' she said one day as she watched him take her recipe for their Le Marche crème and better it, distilling it into lovely jars for selling.

'I can teach you whatever you want to know,' said Giles, concentrating on his work, and Daphné felt herself wonder what she meant.

She watched his forearms with his sleeves rolled up, the muscles flexing as he pounded the coconut compound, the sweet smell making her dizzy, or was that Giles?

Anna must be mistaken about him loving her, she often thought, when he had snapped at her for her customer service or her attention to detail, but sometimes she found him staring at her from across the shop and, when she smiled at him in return, she saw him blush.

He was equally endearing and frustrating, and when she told Anna this she answered that Daphné was falling in love with him.

'I'm not,' she had answered, but was less sure this time.

She glanced at the clock and saw it was close to closing for lunch, so she set about tidying up. She took the cash from the till and placed it in the little safe in the storeroom.

She closed the door and locked it and then went and placed the keys in Giles' jacket. She knew the routine as well as him now, she thought proudly.

'Are you going to the Kapinskis for lunch?' he asked, but she shook her head.

'No, it's too far to walk for such a short time, and they are up to their eyes in paint,' laughed Daphné. 'I'll go for a wander and buy something when I'm out.'

Giles frowned. 'The first lesson I have to teach you is to never buy food when you can make something, it's a waste of money.'

'Perhaps,' she said and she smiled at him, 'but I am currently sleeping in the living room with four other people and a baby on the way. I don't have the luxury to make lunch or have lunch made for me.'

She said this without blame or accusation and Giles gave her a rare smile.

'Then you will lunch with me, just like you did on the first day,' he said and stood up. He slipped on his jacket, patted where the keys were in his inside pocket, put on his hat and walked to the door.

Daphné stood in the dispensary, unsure if he was serious or not.

Giles kept the boundaries very well at work, so this was unlike him.

The rumbling in her stomach reminded her she shouldn't say no to a meal and she grabbed her bag and was soon walking down the street to his apartment.

She knew the way, because she had walked it many times before, not that she told him this information.

She walked to his apartment in the hope of seeing the world through his eyes and what he saw every day.

He stopped as the cars passed on the busy streets, putting his hand protectively in front of her. She felt his fingertips touch her stomach and her hunger pain was now replaced by butterflies that danced through her stomach and down beneath her pencil skirt.

Oh God, she thought, as they crossed the street to his apartment building, perhaps it was love after all.

Giles seemed not to have noticed a thing, as he opened the wood and glass door for her and then the grate on the tiny elevator.

She stepped inside and Giles stepped in after her, and she could hardly breathe for his closeness.

They travelled the five floors, Giles watching the arrow move as they went higher, and Daphné wondered if she was going crazy.

Just as she was doubting her sanity, the elevator stopped with a jerk and she fell forward into Giles' body, his arms holding her up, as she stared into his eyes.

Kiss me, she begged him in her mind. *Kiss me now.*

But unhearing, he propped her back onto her feet and opened the grate. He stepped out and let Daphné pass him. They walked in silence to his door, where he fumbled with his keys, and, as he tried to open the door, she saw his hand shake.

She wasn't imagining it, she thought, as she walked into his orderly world.

Giles was pouring himself a glass of wine, and Daphné, who hadn't drunk it before, felt she needed something to calm the butterflies.

'Can I please have one?' she asked and Giles handed her his and then poured another one.

She sat on the edge of the chair, which was all the tight pencil skirt would allow, and sipped the wine. It was dry but nice, reminding her of sunshine and currants.

'The Karpinskis' store is going to look wonderful,' she said, noticing how tightly wound up her voice sounded in the room.

Giles nodded, and sipped his wine, crossing his elegant legs in his armchair.

Daphné sipped more of the wine, and then more again, until she felt warmth flooding through her body, and she shifted in the chair, noticing how everything felt alive and on edge.

Giles was also drinking his wine with rapid pace, and she wondered what was in his head.

'What are you thinking about?' she asked, noticing the blinds on the windows were up this time.

'You,' said Giles with more candour than she expected, and she nearly dropped her wine.

'What about me?' she asked carefully.

'I was wondering how you bring so much light into people's worlds, it's quite a gift you know,' he said and she saw the sadness in his eyes.

'Do I bring light into your world?' she asked, putting the glass on the small mahogany table next to her, ensuring it was on the coaster.

Giles swallowed his wine and then placed his down on the table next to him, missing the coaster, but only Daphné noticed.

'You make me feel alive,' he said.

With more courage than she knew she had, she walked to his chair. She got on her knees in front of him, lifted his hands and kissed them.

He took a sharp breath in and closed his eyes. She raised herself, so she leaned on his legs.

'I love you, Giles,' she whispered.

'I am an old man,' he said, shaking his head.

'And I am a young woman who is in love.' She smiled.

'You can do better than me, someone who you could marry and have children with,' he said, as he touched her face.

'I don't want children, I want you,' she said, and she pulled his legs apart and moved in to be closer to him.

And then he kissed her, pulling her up onto his lap, as his tongue explored her mouth and she felt herself take his hand and place it on her breast. He moaned.

'Make love to me,' she whispered, but Giles kept kissing her.

'Please,' she said again, and pulled away from him. 'I need to feel your hands on me, without clothes, please.' She felt her voice crack from desire and felt his hardness beneath her, knowing he wanted her.

But still he didn't respond. He just kissed her neck, his hand moving from her thighs to her breasts and then back again.

His hands were lovely, she thought, and she kissed him back, and then pulled herself off his lap. If he wouldn't take her, then she would punish him, she decided, and she stood up and straightened her clothes.

'So what's for lunch?' she asked.

Giles looked confused as she walked towards the kitchen and he followed her.

'I don't know,' he said.

She noticed his erection beneath his suit pants, and she leaned in and kissed him, and squeezed it with her fingers, feeling him swell and cry into her mouth.

'What are you doing to me?' he asked, as he pulled at her skirt.

But Daphné pulled away again. She lifted the tea towel from the plate on the bench and saw cold chicken and salad. She poked it with a fork. 'The breast or the leg?' she asked innocently.

Giles' face had changed and she saw him pull off his tie and move towards her. 'Are you playing games with me, Daphné?' he asked, his face unreadable.

Daphné thought she might melt onto the floor in a puddle of longing.

'Yes, I am. You won't take me to bed, so we will have lunch instead,' she said and pulled out a chair to sit.

'Take off your clothes,' he demanded.

Daphné froze. 'Pardon?'

'Take off your clothes, I want to see you,' he said and as

fast as the nerves had rested in her, they were gone. She pulled at the scarf tied around her neck, and undid the buttons on her white blouse, until it was open, showing her lace camisole that her mother had sent her.

Giles swallowed as he stared at her. 'More,' he said.

She slipped the shirt from her shoulders and it fell to the floor. She then unzipped the back of the skirt, and wiggled her body from its casing, and stood in her white camisole and white knickers.

'More,' he said again. He was undoing his shirt now, and she felt her body respond, as she pulled the camisole over her head, showing him her modest bra.

His shirt was open, and she smiled at him.

'More,' she said, with a smile and he returned it, as he shrugged it from his shoulders.

His pants were undone, and he stepped from them, his hardness causing his boxer shorts to balloon. Daphné wanted to touch what was beneath them.

They stood, neither daring to make the next move and then Daphné undid her bra, and let her breasts make the move for her.

Giles was at her side, kissing her. His mouth was on her nipples, his hands down her underwear, probing her wetness, making her moan as he tickled his way inside her.

She was pulling at his shorts, releasing his penis into her hand. She ran her fingers over the tip, as he lifted her onto the table, and opened her legs.

'I need to be inside you,' he said, as his cock touched the entrance of her lips.

She grabbed the base of the shaft and pushed him into her,

biting her lip at the rush of unfamiliar pain and pleasure. She held on to him, as he moved inside her, and then he pushed her onto her back and pulled her body forward as he moved.

'I need to see you,' he said, as she put her hands above her head and arched her back.

'God, you're beautiful,' he gasped, as he held her legs and she wrapped them around his body.

'A condom,' she said, as his movements became faster.

Giles stopped. 'I don't have one,' he said, his face falling.

'I do, in my bag,' she said.

He pulled out and rushed to the other room. On returning, he undid the packet, his hands shaking, and she sat up and helped him guide it onto his hard penis.

'You're very experienced,' he said, awed, as she moved her hand down to check it was correctly fitted.

'Not really,' she said.

She eased him back into her. She needed to feel him again, and she touched her own breasts, as he watched her. His head leaned down and pulled on her nipple until she felt the electricity between her legs and she opened them wider for him.

'God,' she moaned, as he worked her other breast, and then she started to move with him, the table rocking under their weight. Daphné's last thoughts, before they came together, were: Is this what Anna and Max did? Will the table hold up? And how long before we can do it again?

Chapter 14

Dominic

'That certainly complicates things,' said Dominic down the line to an almost hysterical Robert.

As always, Dominic was calm in a crisis. Robert had promised him the company and the formula but now Robert wasn't a factor any more. He wanted Robert off the phone so he could plan his next move.

'I am planning to take this to court,' said Robert imperiously.

Dominic rolled his eyes at the largesse of the statement, but he knew that Robert taking his own daughter and niece to court would be bad for him and for the deal.

'Let's just wait on that,' he said slowly. 'I think it might be more worth your while to see what decision the girls make.'

'They won't want the responsibility. Sibylla is a sullen thing who works in science, she's incredibly unattractive, obviously takes after her mother, and Celeste, well, we all know Celeste.' He laughed at his own joke and Dominic disliked him even more for his disloyalty to his daughter.

'I have to go to a meeting now,' he said. 'Leave it with me.'

Without waiting for Robert's reply, he put down the phone and stared at the screen. Matilde Le Marche stared back at him. According to Robert, her ex-mother-in-law had left her a sizable amount of money in the will, and he wondered if it was to keep the secrets of the family safe.

He picked up the phone again and called his assistant.

'I need to go to Nice straight away,' he said.

He would flatter Matilde until she spilled any information she had on Celeste and Robert and the formula, and then he would make his move.

***

The private plane landed in Nice, and a car waited for Dominic, ready to take him to Matilde's villa.

'We need to stop en route,' Dominic told the driver, adding specific instructions about the stores he wanted to visit.

Judging from the stories and snippets of tales in *Paris Match* and online, Matilde liked to drink, gossip, play tennis, and she was notoriously against plastic surgery and remarrying.

Forty minutes later, Dominic was standing under the cerise bougainvillea at Matilde's door holding a new Technifibre tennis racquet, a bottle of Taittinger and the latest copy of *Paris Match*.

Matilde opened the door, dressed in a striped T-shirt and denim skirt, which made her look younger than her years, and certainly showed off her lithe figure from tennis.

For whatever reason, she didn't seem that surprised to see him at her door, and instead smiled at him in a lazy, cynical way, which he found off-putting—usually all women responded to his charms.

'Hello,' she said, her eyes running from the top of his head down to his leather loafers.

'Madame Le Marche,' he said, with his most charming smile.

'Is dead, as you know.' She kept her arm on the door, creating a barricade between him and her home.

'Then what should I call you?' he asked.

'Matilde is fine,' she said. Her blonde beauty was still intact, more so because of the haughty look on her face.

'Matilde,' he said, starting again.

'Yes?' She arched one eyebrow at him.

He felt himself stutter. 'I've . . . I've come to talk to you,' he said.

'Oh? I thought you were here to play tennis,' she said. She moved her arm from the door, and walked inside, leaving him no choice but to follow her.

'This is for you,' he said, feeling stupid as he offered her the gifts.

'Thank you,' she said, but took nothing that he offered, and walked into the kitchen.

The villa was filled with cushions and Moorish bits and pieces, offset by some significant art, probably picked up after her divorce, thought Dominic, but it was all surprisingly modest.

Stone fruit sat in a bowl in the kitchen, an iPad was on the table, and a cat walked through the space, waving its tail at Dominic imperiously.

'Don't mind Tarot, he's a prick of a cat, but he does kill the rats,' said Matilde, as she took the champagne and magazine from his hands, leaving him holding the tennis racquet.

This wasn't going the way he had planned. She was more self-assured than he had imagined, and she certainly wasn't impressed by his presence. In fact, she acted like she had been expecting him.

'You don't seem surprised to see me,' he said, as the cat circled his legs. He resisted the urge to kick it away.

'I'm not surprised by anything any more,' she said. 'Drink?' She held up the bottle.

Dominic nodded. Champagne at two in the afternoon wasn't something he usually indulged in but he had the feeling all bets were off with Matilde Le Marche.

She opened the champagne expertly and then took two fine glasses from the cupboard and poured the liquid gold into them.

After handing him one, she lifted her own glass.

'Here's to you and your nefarious undertakings,' she said and she took a sip.

Dominic didn't know if he should laugh or be insulted.

He decided on the latter, taking a drink before he spoke. He needed the courage in the face of such disdain.

'Why do you think my visiting you is corrupt?'

'Because you're clearly here for two reasons,' said Matilde.

'Oh really?' He walked to the balcony, and looked outside, hearing the waves crashing on the rocks. A little like his plan, he thought.

He assumed Matilde would be grateful for a man like Dominic to show her some attention, and to drink and flirt with him, but he was wrong, and he was not used to the feeling.

'You're here to flirt with me, get me a little drunk until I hand over the Le Marche secrets, making your movements on the company brutal and easy.'

Dominic sat on the cane lounge, and she sat on the matching chair opposite him.

He drank a little more and then looked at her, now nursing her drink bemusedly with her legs crossed. She had very good legs, he noticed; he'd always been a leg man.

'What if there was a third reason?' he asked, his eyes running up her body to her face.

Did he see a flicker of interest? A quiet blush on her décolletage?

'Do tell.' She raised an eyebrow in amusement.

'What if I were here to seduce you?'

'Then you better hurry up because I have tennis in an hour,' she said, a smile playing at her lips.

Dominic hadn't seen such rudeness since he had bedded the Russian supermodel a few days ago.

He drained his glass and stood up, feeling himself become more aroused with every moment.

He walked to her, took the glass from her hand and lifted her hand to his mouth.

'Shall we?' he asked.

Matilde laughed and snatched her hand away. 'You would have sex with an old woman to try to get information for your scheme? You mustn't have any morals at all.'

'You're not that old,' he said, in his best seduction voice.

'Oh stop it, you're ridiculous,' said Matilde, shooing him away with her hand, as though he were a pestering child.

'Ask me what you want and, if I choose to answer, I will,' she stated.

'And what do you want?' he asked, sitting down on the lounge again, disappointed that he wasn't going to take her to bed. She really was quite intriguing, he decided.

'You can come to tennis with me,' she said, 'and then stay for dinner.'

'I can't play tennis in this,' he said, gesturing to his suit.

'You can buy something,' she said.

'I have a dinner meeting,' he said. The woman was insane, he decided.

'Cancel it.' She smiled.

'Why do you want me to stay and yet you won't let me make love to you?'

Matilde's eyes met his and she held his stare, as the soft breeze brought with it the scent of salt and something more mysterious to his senses.

Matilde looked out at the ocean. 'Not everything is about sex,' she said.

'I disagree, everything is about sex, even this moment. We are hitting the ball between us like we are in a game, and whoever wins the point gets the prize.'

'And what is the prize?' she asked, turning her face back to him.

Dominic thought for a moment. *What is the prize?* he asked himself. He had money, he had power, he had lovers lining up to share his bed. But he knew was tired of the game, and Matilde seemed to see it in him.

'I want to know how I can get your daughter to sell me her share of the company,' he said.

Matilde smiled and stood up. 'I will betray my ex-husband,

I have no loyalty to him, but I will not betray my daughter or my mother-in-law, they don't deserve that.'

'But you're not close to her, nor were you close to Daphné,' he argued. 'Why did she leave you so much money?'

'I think I deserve it for being married to her son.'

Matilde walked inside the house, and he followed, watching as she opened her refrigerator and poured herself more champagne, but not offering him any.

'And the formula? What do you know about that?'

Matilde shook her head. 'Nothing and, if I did, the answer would still be nothing. My daughter deserves more than you tearing her down. Her father has been doing it to her her whole life, and the men she chooses to be with. Don't you dare even think about ruining her life and this opportunity. If Daphné believed in my only surviving daughter enough to leave her the company, then I will do everything in my power to ensure she and the company are safe.'

Dominic drew breath, realising he had been holding it the entire time she was speaking.

'You love Celeste very much,' he said, leaning against the counter.

'I do. I don't deserve to have her in my life, I don't know how to have her in my life, every time I see her I am reminded how I nearly lost her, and yet she returns. One day I hope I can be the mother she deserves.'

As she spoke, her face was troubled, clouded in something he couldn't describe. It was more than pain, he thought, it was as though she hurtled back into the past, and was facing the internal war all over again.

Dominic pushed himself from the counter and walked to her, and kissed her on the head.

'You're a good mother,' he said.

'No, I'm not,' said Matilde, 'but it's too late now.'

Dominic took the glass from her hand and placed it on the bench, and then tilted her face towards him.

'It's never too late,' he said and then he bent down and kissed her.

Her mouth was surprised, but soon he felt her respond to him, and her arms wrapped around his neck, until she pulled away.

'Don't try to seduce me to learn secrets, because I won't tell,' she said, her face close to his, but her eyes steely in her resolve.

'I'm not. I don't care if you don't tell me anything,' he said, his voice catching as he spoke. 'I just needed to kiss you.'

And then her mouth was on his again, and she was desperately pulling at his suit pants.

He pulled her skirt up to her waist, and pulled down her underwear, then lifted her onto the tiled bench. He felt her grasp his hardness, and guide him inside her, as her legs wrapped around his waist.

It was fast, and she matched his passion as he felt her start to quiver, and then moan. The sound of her unashamed pleasure turned him on even more, and, just as he thought he would explode, she went first and then he joined her, and they cried out in the kitchen.

'Jesus,' he said, his head on her shoulder, as he tried to regain his breath.

He pulled away and she was off the bench, adjusting her clothes.

'You should go now,' she said, as though nothing had happened.

'Don't you want me to play tennis?' he asked, feeling as though he was being dismissed.

'No thank you,' she said. She walked to the door and opened it for him to leave.

He was being dismissed. He couldn't believe it. He had just fucked her, and she should be grateful, he thought, as he walked to the door.

'Is that it?' he asked, unsure of the feelings welling in him.

She shrugged and smiled a little. 'You came for conversation and you ended up getting sex, some men would be happy with that,' she said.

'Fuck you,' he said half jokingly, as he walked through the door.

'You just did,' she laughed after him and she closed the door with a bang.

Dominic Bertiull wasn't used to being played, nor was he used to not getting what he wanted. He was also unfamiliar with being used and dismissed. It made for an uncomfortable change, he thought, as he leaned back on the comfort of the leather seats of the car, and he wondered when he could see Matilde Le Marche again and what his excuse would be.

Chapter 15

Billie

Billie let Celeste open the door to the London apartment. It seemed only right, since she was the elder cousin, and she already knew the place, but she mostly let Celeste have her way because she was afraid of her.

Celeste had flirted with Edward throughout the lunch, largely ignoring Billie, unless it was to make an acerbic remark about Billie's lack of sophistication.

Billie had ignored her, reminded by her mother's words that Celeste had known great loss, but, as Billie watched her take the keys from her large handbag, and fit them in the door, she wondered why Celeste's loss was greater than hers?

Celeste opened the door and screwed up her perfect nose.

'God, it smells terrible,' she said in her lilting transatlantic accent.

Billie had thought she would have more of a French accent but Celeste had told her that was impossible when she spoke three languages and had been educated in Switzerland.

Billie had wanted to ask her about the reactions of positive ions when mixed with sodium hydroxide but she held her tongue.

Celeste was an odd combination of confidence with an air of anxiety about her when she wasn't speaking, as though she needed to keep talking to remind herself she was still in the room.

Celeste flicked on the light switch and Billie's eyes adjusted to the low, soft light, as she dropped her backpack with a large thump onto the floor.

'Grand-mère preferred pink light bulbs. She said they softened the lines on her face,' said Celeste. 'That's why everything looks so foggy.'

But Billie wasn't looking at the light globes. She was entranced by the room and its interior. Linen lined walls, and elaborate sconces surrounded the delicate furniture covered in silk, and silver-framed photos of Celeste, Camille and Billie were on every available surface.

Billie as a baby, toddler, with her father, with her mother, with her cousins, and then the timeline stopped when her father died.

Her mother had obviously sent them, thought Billie.

'Isn't it awful?' said Celeste, sprawling on a love seat.

'No,' said Billie, as she picked up a beautiful nautilus shell and turned it over in her hands.

'You like this sort of thing?' scoffed Celeste. 'Of course you would, you're Australian.'

Billie put down the shell. 'What do you mean?'

Celeste shrugged and closed her eyes. 'I wish I were back in Paris.'

'Then go,' said Billie, as she walked out of the room.

Celeste was awful, she thought, as she opened the door to what was the main bedroom. It was lined in pale orange silk, with a huge fireplace at the end of the room, facing the bed.

'I bags this room,' she called out to Celeste, knowing it was childish but not caring.

'Take what you like, I'm going to stay at the Conrad,' she called back.

Billie made a face at the wall. How on earth was this ever going to work, she thought, as she moved through the rest of the apartment.

Another two bedrooms, a small kitchen, two bathrooms, and what she presumed was her grandmother's study. A book-lined room with a desk she could imagine Marie Antoinette sitting at to write her daily correspondence.

If Billie had to choose a place to live, this was it, she thought, as she pulled at the desk drawer, only to find it locked.

'I'm going,' said Celeste, standing in the doorway, looking around at the books. 'God, it's all so old,' she said, making a face of disgust. She walked to the door, her shoes making an echo on the parquetry floor.

'Tomorrow we will sort this all out,' she said to Billie as she stepped into the hallway.

'Sort out what?' asked Billie.

'How we can make this all work.' Celeste gestured to the apartment.

'You could just stay here,' said Billie. 'It would be cheaper.'

Celeste shook her head. 'No, we cannot live together and work together.'

Billie felt her mouth drop open. 'You don't actually think I'm going to work at Le Marche, do you?'

Celeste smiled at her and then pressed the elevator button.

'Grand-Mère always got what she wanted, there is no point fighting it,' and the elevator doors opened, and Celeste stepped inside and disappeared without another word or even a wave.

Billie shut the door behind her and leaned against the heavy wood.

'Grand-Mère can jam it,' she said aloud, as she walked back to the locked desk drawer.

She was here to find out what her uncle had told her father before he died, then she would take her share of the estate, give it to her mother, and go back to her life in Melbourne.

She rattled on the drawer again, and then searched for a key.

After turning up nothing, she rang Edward Badger, not thinking it was after nine in the evening.

'Billie?' he asked.

'How did you know?' she asked, surprised.

'My secretary put your name into my phone with your details, much easier, don't you think?'

Billie shook her head at his old-fashioned words.

'Is there a set of keys that I don't have? There is a desk in the apartment that is locked.'

'I don't know, I would have to go through the particulars tomorrow,' he said.

Disappointed, Billie sat at the desk. 'Celeste has gone to a hotel,' she said.

'Yes, that's Celeste's style,' he said with a small laugh.

'It's really quiet,' she said.

There was a pause.

'Did my grandmother die here?'

'Yes,' said Edward without any hesitation. 'It was her favourite place.'

'Why not Paris? All Celeste does is extol the virtues of Paris above any other major city in the world.'

'I don't know,' Edward said. 'Your grandmother was very private.'

'Were you close to her?' Billie asked.

'As close as you can be to a woman who scares the living daylights out of you when she demands you come to her office.' He laughed again, and Billie thought he was quite honest and she decided she liked that about him.

'I will look for the keys tomorrow for you,' he said.

Billie smiled at the phone. 'Thank you,' she said and then went to drag in her backpack to the bedroom where she presumed her grandmother had passed, but she was too tired to care about anything but sleep.

* * *

Billie woke at seven in the morning, as the sun rose, and realised she had forgotten to close the curtains.

The light caused the orange silk to give off an amber glow and Billie thought how lovely it would be to have a fire in the room when it was winter.

She stretched and pulled the linen sheets up around her ears, enjoying their heavy softness.

The sound of someone knocking at the door made her jump. She climbed out of the large bed and pulled on an old cardigan to cover her tank top and some sweatpants.

She padded to the door, and peered through the peephole.

'Edward, gosh, hi,' she said, as she opened the door.

He was in a suit, looking extremely polished and awake, and she wrapped the cardigan tighter around herself, feeling frumpy in his presence.

He held up his hand. 'I have the keys, they were in the safe deposit box with the jewellery.'

'You've already been to the bank? It's seven in the morning,' she exclaimed.

'Money never sleeps for the wealthy,' he said, as he handed her the keys. 'There is twenty-four-hour access to the safety deposit boxes.'

'Should I require access to the family tiara at two in the morning,' she said, as she held the set of keys in her hand.

'Exactly,' laughed Edward and he turned around and went to the elevator.

God, he looked good in a suit, she thought, wondering why she hadn't noticed it earlier. No wonder Celeste had been flirting with him so madly through lunch.

'Why are you leaving?' she asked, wondering if there was anything in the kitchen to offer him.

'I have to go to work,' he said.

Billie nodded, the weight of the keys heavy.

He went to speak and then stopped as the elevator doors opened. He pressed the button to go down.

'I will see you later,' he said in a professional tone, and then, like Celeste, he disappeared without another word.

Billie went to the desk and started to try the various keys until she found one that fit and turned easily in the lock.

She pulled open the drawer, feeling a sense of trepidation and disloyalty. She knew nothing about her grandmother and now she was rifling through her locked desk drawer.

Inside were leather-bound notebooks, with different years stamped in gold on the front of each one.

She picked up one marked '1970' and opened it, only to find it was written in French.

'*Merde*,' she said, as she sat on the chair and started to read.

Her French was rusty to speak, and even more so to read, and, for a moment, she thought about asking Celeste, but Celeste seemed bored by everything Billie said or did, and she had the feeling these journals would have the same impact.

She needed to translate them herself, so she could get into the head of her grandmother, and then she might find out what happened to her father.

Billie went to her backpack, and pulled on warmer clothes and shoes, and then went downstairs to find a coffee shop.

Fifteen minutes later, she was back at Daphné's desk, with a coffee, a croissant from a cute café that was almost like one back home, and a new notepad and pen from the newsagent.

She found the earliest date on a journal, back in 1962, and she opened to the first page.

'*Trouver la couleur du matin.*'

Billie rubbed her sleep-filled eyes and took a large gulp of coffee.

This wasn't going to be easy, she thought, as she started to write down the translation.

'Finding the colour of morning,' she said aloud and then shook her head. What on earth did she mean? Was this the research for the formula? Billie was comfortable with research, and she opened another journal and started to read the difficult handwriting, and then sighed. She had the feeling this whole exercise wasn't going to be easy, and she didn't just mean the translation.

Chapter 16

Yves Le Marche arrived at the apartment exactly at midday when he knew his father would be home for lunch. He adjusted his tie, and instinctively brushed the lapels of his blue wool suit, and only then did he knock on the door. His father had never given him a key, since he told his son that Switzerland was obviously his home.

It wasn't a gibe, just a statement of fact, and Yves hadn't argued the matter. It was true that Switzerland was more of a home to him than Paris, but if he was truthful with himself, he never felt at home anywhere.

Yves had felt restless for his entire twenty-nine years yet he lived the life of a hermit. He felt as though he was always looking for something, but he hadn't quite discovered what the prize was on offer.

Yves was slim and with a forgettable face. He was neither handsome nor ugly, he was just ordinary, or, as his father reminded him, he looked like his mother. Light brown hair, with brown eyes, his best features were his long eyelashes, which he had decided weren't an admirable trait on a man.

The door to the apartment opened and a girl answered, the light behind her shining like an aura. Her face was flushed, and the buttons on her blouse were done up the wrong way.

'Yes?' she asked.

'I'm here to see my father,' he said, taking in the open blinds behind her. His father lived in half-light at home; why were they open now ?

'Yves?' she cried happily, as she pulled at his coat and dragged him inside.

'Giles, Yves is here,' she called, and his father walked from the kitchen, impeccably dressed as always. No button undone, or even a hair out of place.

Maybe this girl was the new housekeeper, and didn't have fine motor skills down pat yet, he told himself, as his father stepped towards him, his face stern as always. Yves felt himself shrink back in his presence.

'Yves, you should have called,' he said, but putting out his hand in welcome.

'I thought I would surprise you,' he answered.

'Surprises are for children,' said Giles.

The girl stood to the side, and Giles turned to her.

'You can leave now, the shop will need to be open soon for Christmas gift buying,' he said, and Yves saw her mouth drop open.

So she was the shopgirl his father had spoken of in his letters, Yves thought, and his eyes ran over her shapely figure. He wondered what on earth she thought she would get from having an affair with his taciturn father.

'Of course,' she said.

Yves saw the glisten of tears in her eyes, and he felt sorry for her.

'I didn't get your name,' he said in kind voice to try to offset his father's tone.

'Daphné Amyx,' she said in almost a whisper.

'Yves Le Marche,' he said and he took her slim hand in his.

The touch of her made his skin tingle and, when she looked at him with such gratitude in her eyes for his kindness, he thought he wanted to protect her forever from his father.

She let go of his hand and took a coat from the rack by the door and did it up, this time not missing any buttons, and then left without another word.

'She's a bit young isn't she, Father?' he said, aware of the recrimination in voice, or was it jealousy? He immediately regretted his question.

Giles walked towards him, so his face was almost touching Yves. 'She's none of your business,' he said and Yves nodded, wishing he had stayed in Zurich with his surrogate family.

The men stood facing each other, and Yves half wanted to leave and take the next train to Switzerland but then he wouldn't see Daphné again.

'How is the law?' asked Giles, as he stepped into the kitchen that Yves had spent his early years in, being told off by his father for poor table manners, while his mother fussed to the point of anxiety making sure everything was perfect for Giles.

'It's fine, busy,' said Yves. The law wasn't a passion but it was a job and he was busy enough in the patents office in Zurich to use it as an excuse to not visit Paris more often.

'You should be married,' said his father. 'You're nearly thirty.'

Yves said nothing about his father's hypocrisy or his ideas for his life, instead he sat at the table, and lifted the cloth that the housekeeper had covered the lunch with.

A quiche, he thought, with a sigh. It seemed nothing changed in some respects of his father's daily life.

They were like strangers sharing a table, as Giles carefully portioned the meal for them. They ate mostly in silence, with an occasional comment on the weather and the state of business at Christmas, which Giles said was going very well.

'I have a new line of products, made with goat's milk,' he said. 'They are walking off the shelves.'

Yves was surprised at the appearance of his father's entrepreneurial side. The man hadn't created anything in his life, besides him, and now he had his own line of product. Wonders will never cease, he thought.

'And Daphné? She works in the shop, you said?'

'She is a shopgirl, nothing more,' said Giles sternly, so Yves said nothing in return.

'I have to go back to work. You are staying here?'

It was a question, not an invitation, and Yves shook his head. 'No, I won't get in your way. I'll stay at a hotel. I won't be here for long,' he said.

He had planned to stay till New Year, but his father's welcome had ensured he would stay till Christmas Day and then head back to Zurich.

'Good,' said Giles to his only child. 'I keep very long hours and like to rest when I come home.'

Yves piled the dishes in the sink and poured water on

them, but his father was already by the front door, hat and coat in hand.

'You can walk me to the store,' he said and Yves nodded at his demand.

'What will we do for Christmas ?' asked Yves, as they rode down in the squashed space of the elevator.

'What we always do,' said Giles, staring ahead.

Christmas Eve drinks alone, early to bed, the passing of one present each in the morning and then a hot lunch of duck and vegetables, cooked before by the housekeeper, and warmed up on the day, and then a cold dinner with leftovers.

Yves wondered if he could think of an excuse to return to Zurich early, as they walked towards his father's business.

The store was open, and Daphné was repositioning things in the window when they arrived. She glanced up at them, and he saw her face turn red.

Giles turned and shook his son's hand. 'I will see you tomorrow for lunch?' he asked.

Yves nodded. There was no arguing with his father. He never had, not since his mother had died.

Daphné watched them as they shook hands, and then Giles walked to the pharmacy area.

Yves stepped into the store, and looked at the boxes in pastel colours she was arranging in the window.

'They're very pretty,' he said, picking one up and turning it over in his hands.

'They're creams for the body and face,' she said shyly. 'You might like to give one to your wife or lady friend for Christmas.'

It was Yves' turn to blush. He didn't have either and, with

his terrible luck with women, he doubted he ever would. Women seemed to pass him by in life. He was pleasant looking but he didn't have the confidence of some men his age, or the money of others. A junior lawyer in a patents office in Zurich wasn't exactly honey to the bees, and his nights were spent in his room at the professor's house, reading and listening to contrapuntal music.

But mostly his loneliness stemmed from being afraid of a relationship. He had seen the one between his father and mother, and that was enough to make a man a bachelor for ever.

He glanced at Daphné. Her dark hair and ink-blue eyes against her pale skin were so arresting, and he reached out and touched her arm.

'Be careful with my father, he can be . . .' He paused, trying to find the right word, but in the end there was only one word he could think of to describe him. 'Cruel,' he said.

She went to speak, her mouth slightly parted, and he wondered why she would allow it to kiss his father, the man who had sent his own wife and his mother to an early grave.

'Daphné,' he heard his father call, and she walked away from him towards his father.

Chapter 17

Celeste

Celeste knocked on the door twice, then again, as per the agreement, and a fumbling with the chain made her anxious. Once, she found the clandestine nature of her affair with Paul exhilarating, especially when they were fucking in his office, but now it caused her to look up and down the hallway like a stray cat, and, when the door opened an inch, she pushed her way inside.

'The stars have aligned,' said Paul, wearing a robe. 'Excellent luck that we're both here at the same time.'

The robe made Celeste angry, as though he was just waiting for sex, and, to make her point, she sat on the sofa.

'If you left your wife, we wouldn't have to wait for the stars or anything else to line up,' she snapped. 'Instead, you denied everything, and then did that sickening spread in *Hello!* magazine with your family.'

Paul sat on the chair opposite her and crossed his legs, giving her an eyeful of testicles. She felt sick. What was she doing here?

'Let's talk. You know it's going to take time to work everything out,' he said with a smile, as though she was a child.

'There isn't any more time. I'm here to break up with you,' she announced, as surprised as he was.

'What? Why?' He frowned.

'I have a company to run,' she said, knowing she sounded childish and self-important, but it made sense to her in that moment.

Daphné's belief in her meant more than she realised, but Paul threw his head back and laughed as though she had just told a wonderful joke.

'You're not serious, are you?'

'Deadly,' she said, staring at him.

Why hadn't she noticed earlier how much he looked like her father?

His jowls were thickening, and his nose florid from daily lunches with wine, and the robe was pulling around his stomach.

'Your father wants to sell the company. He told me so at the funeral,' he said.

'My father wasn't left one share in the company,' she answered, enjoying knowing something that he didn't. 'I was left the company.'

'You?'

His incredulity made up for his rudeness and she decided to leave Billie out of the picture. Eventually, Billie would sell and Celeste would make something of Le Marche and herself.

She stood up. 'Yes, me. Goodbye, Paul,' she said. She walked to the door, but Paul, for all his extra weight, got there before her and put his hands on her slim shoulders.

'You're not leaving me, I love you,' he said and, for a

moment, she nearly believed him, but then she saw him glance at himself in the glass of the picture hanging by the door.

'No, you don't, Paul, you only love yourself,' she said and she opened the door.

'Celeste,' he said, pulling on her arm. 'Come inside, let's make love, let's talk,' he pleaded, his hand pinching her skin.

'Let me go, or I will scream,' she said in a quiet voice.

Paul reluctantly dropped his hand and Celeste walked away, not turning, even when he was hissing her name.

She didn't turn around once.

Paul was history. She was about to make her own future, and that meant not being second to some dowdy wife.

She was going to run Le Marche, but to do that, she needed an excellent advisor. That wasn't Billie, with her sanctimonious airs about her education and her cheap clothes.

The girl looked as though she shopped in a charity shop, she thought, as she walked through the foyer and into the street.

She walked until she found another hotel, not as nice as the Conrad but she couldn't be near Paul. She shuddered to think of him in that robe.

What had she been thinking when she was pining after him?

She needed someone younger, more stylish, more in the know, someone who would be grateful to be with her.

She went up to her room, kicked off her shoes, lay on the bed and closed her eyes.

Edward, she thought. He fitted the bill perfectly, and she opened her eyes and stared at the ceiling.

Yes, he would be just fine, and once she had used him for her benefit, she could let him go. Lawyers always found jobs, and he seemed to be quite good at his, at least her grandmother had thought so.

In the morning, she dressed carefully, trying to look sexy without being overt. Black cigarette pants, a cream silk shirt and black heels. A simple gold bracelet, and her hair in a messy ponytail with only a touch of lip gloss and mascara. Edward didn't look like he appreciated a woman who drew too much attention to herself and, for a brief moment, she wondered if he had a wife, or a girlfriend.

Not that it mattered, he wasn't going to be here forever, he was useful to her, and that was all.

The office was quiet when she arrived, and the girl at reception told her Mr Badger was in a meeting.

Celeste wasn't pleased. 'Did you tell him it's me?' she snapped at the girl.

'Yes, I did,' she answered, looking as though she might cry.

Celeste glared at her, and went and sat on the sofa in the foyer. She leafed through an old copy of British *Vogue* and then put it down, and checked the dates on the other magazines.

She stacked them and then carried them to the girl at the reception desk.

'Can you throw these out?' she said, dropping them in front of her with a large thump.

'Excuse me?' Her scared eyes looked up at Celeste.

'These are all out of date by at least nine months. If we want to be seen as relevant, then we must have more relevant publications.'

The girl looked at the pile of glossies on her desk. 'These are the magazines that we advertised in,' she said in a small voice.

'So get the new ones that we advertise in,' said Celeste impatiently.

The girl swallowed, and her face was puce. 'I can't.'

'Why not?' Celeste was losing what little patience she had left.

'We haven't advertised for over a year,' she said.

Celeste was silent, and then her eyes roamed around the office. The paint was dull, the furniture out of date, the carpet was old and the boxes of product that lined the glass display cabinet were dusty and faded.

Le Marche was so tired, it was nearly dead.

'I need an office,' she said to the girl. 'Actually a desk will do, with a computer and a phone line.'

The girl nodded, seemingly pleased to be given a task by the intimidating granddaughter of the founder of Le Marche, who she had never met.

'Your grandmother's office is free,' said the girl, 'Otherwise I could get you a desk somewhere else.'

'My grandmother's office is perfect,' said Celeste. 'Show me the way.'

The girl led Celeste down the hallway, and Celeste noticed she was wearing very nice shoes, and her clothes were subtle.

'Would you like to be my assistant?' Celeste asked, as they reached a closed door.

'Excuse me?' the girl spluttered.

'I need an assistant, and you look like you know your way around here,' said Celeste, as they stood in the hallway.

The girl nodded. 'I would like to move up in the company, but I didn't know if there was going to be a chance, since Madame Le Marche died. Everyone says your father will sell it.'

Celeste smiled at her. 'My father wasn't left the company, I was,' she said, once again leaving out Billie.

'Gosh, wow,' said the girl.

'So, you will help me?'

'Yes please, that would be wonderful,' the girl said. 'I do have a degree in business administration, but I could only get entry-level jobs.'

'Excellent,' said Celeste. 'What's your name?'

'Gemma,' she said, 'Gemma Taylor.'

'Celeste Le Marche,' she said with a smile. Gemma seemed very capable, and exactly what she needed.

'Thank you, Ms Le Marche,' Gemma stammered.

'Celeste, please,' she said, as Gemma opened the door to her grandmother's office.

It was exactly like her home in London: all silks and Louis XV furniture with the faint smell of a perfume and old age.

'*Cette est horrible*,' exclaimed Celeste.

'It is sort of old-fashioned,' agreed Gemma. 'Your grandmother didn't come in very much.'

'I can see why,' said Celeste, as she walked to the desk. She ran a finger along its surface, and then spun the chair before sitting down.

'Where is the computer ?' she asked.

'Your grandmother didn't use one,' Celeste heard and she looked up to see Edward standing in the doorway.

'Good morning, I'm here to start work,' said Celeste with

her most seductive smile, then she turned to Gemma. 'Get me a computer right away.'

'You're here early,' he said.

He looked good in a suit, she thought. He seemed less stressed than yesterday, more powerful. His hair was a little grey at the temple, and probably needed a decent cut at a salon, not at a barber's, but he had potential.

'I have much to do,' she said.

'Oh?' Edward looked surprised.

'I'm not as stupid as you think I am,' she snapped.

'I don't think you're stupid, I think you're just what we need,' he said sincerely. 'I'm just happy that you want to make this work. It has so much potential.'

Her eyes met his, and captured her attention. They were blue. She wasn't used to being complimented about something other than her looks, and combined with such sincerity, she thought she might fall apart at the desk in front of him.

This wasn't what she wanted to be like in his company. She wanted to be cool and sexy, and now she was acting like a needy teenager.

'Is Billie in yet?' she asked, desperate to change the subject.

'Not yet. I dropped something off to her at the apartment and she said she had something important to do.'

'What did you drop off to her?' asked Celeste, feeling an uneasy jealousy. Yesterday at lunch, Billie and Edward seemed to talk so easily about all manner of subjects while Celeste was left floundering, cursing her cousin for her education and Edward for not seeing how much she was flirting with him. She had resorted to the worst version of herself, trying

Kate Forster

to make Billie feel inferior so she could feel better. Even now she felt ashamed thinking of her behaviour.

'Just a set of keys for things around the apartment,' said Edward with a smile.

Celeste nodded, and ran her hands over the empty desk.

'What did my grandmother actually do when she was here?' she asked, looking up at him.

Nerves rattled inside her as though she was on an old roller coaster, and she wondered if she could actually do this job, or any job for that matter.

Edward sat down opposite her at the desk. 'What do you like to do?' he asked gently.

Celeste wondered if she should say what she thought he might want to hear, but then she didn't want to start out setting herself up to fail.

'I like imagery, interiors, art, design, things like that,' she said, aware of how scant her interests sounded. She could have mentioned wine, Marvin Gaye and shopping, but she edited those out.

Edward smiled. 'It's as good a place to start as any.'

Celeste leaned back in her grandmother's chair. 'How bad are things here ?'

'You mean the financial part?' he asked.

'I mean in all parts,' she said.

Edward stood up and paused. 'Perhaps we will wait until Billie is in, she is your business partner now.'

Celeste felt herself scowl, but she knew he was right. Even if Billie didn't care about the business, she still had to include her for the sake of the inheritance.

'When will she be in?' asked Celeste with an eye roll.

'When she's ready,' said Edward in a firm but polite tone, and Celeste wondered if it was Billie and not her who had caught his eye and she hated herself, and her cousin, for the fifth time that morning.

Chapter 18

Edward

Edward sat the end of the boardroom table and shuffled some papers, as Billie and Celeste sat on either side, like warring divorce parties.

Both seemed wary and defensive of each other, their faces careful to mask any emotion other than disdain.

Women like Celeste scared him, with her haughty beauty and slightly too thin face. He preferred the sultry yet accessible looks of Sibylla, who seemed like she might be fun to have on a table at a trivia night, the sort of girl he could take to his mother up in Sheffield.

As one of six boys, Edward was the last one to be married, so naturally his family assumed he was gay. His mum had even put a rainbow sticker of support on the old Mini Minor, despite his protestations that he liked girls very much, they just didn't seem to like him in return.

In the end he found it easier not to argue, since they kept telling him he was in a supportive environment, and once he accepted it, everyone would be a lot happier.

Edward was also the only one to attend university. He

had lucked out at school, and found that remembering things came easily, and he didn't have nerves in a test. All he had to do was repeat what he had learned and everyone was happy.

A scholarship to the London School of Economics decided his future, and soon Eddie Badger of Broomhall Road became Edward Badger of London.

He wondered what Celeste would make of his childhood back in Sheffield, sharing a room with two brothers, and a dad who drank and sang to his mother on a Friday night, and the endless worry of money for his parents. Women like Celeste had no idea about true struggle, he thought, a rare stab of envy in his heart causing him to frown.

'I am not going to pretend that things are going well here,' Edward said tersely. He was never one to fluff about with the truth. He liked to point out the problem and then work on the solutions, part of why Daphné loved him so much. It was a shame his candour at work wasn't translated to his love life.

'The sales are down across all products. In the last focus group that was done by the previous marketing manager, the participants said the creams are seen as out of date. Old-fashioned.'

'Where is the marketing manager now ?' asked Celeste.

'Your grandmother fired her.'

'Why?'

'Because she didn't like being told she was out of date.'

Celeste shook her head and looked down at her blank notepad.

'What do you think ?' asked Billie to Edward.

He tapped his pen on the table and then stuck to his motto

of telling the truth. 'I think they are out of date and old-fashioned.'

'But there is nothing wrong with history,' said Celeste. 'Fashion houses have traded on it for years.'

'But I think it's different with skincare. The old names and branding does makes it seem like the product is actually old,' Billie added.

'Oh, thank you Miss Marketing, don't you have some atoms to split ?'

'I'm a chemist, not a physicist,' said Billie with a roll of her eyes.

Edward watched the exchange like a tennis match and then cleared his throat. 'Actually, I think both of you are right,' he said.

Celeste snorted. 'That's a cowardly response. Pick a side.'

'Why do I have to?' he asked pleasantly and they stared at each other, refusing to break eye contact first.

'So we're doing this?' asked Billie, leaning forward with her hands on the smooth wood of the table.

'Doing what?' asked Celeste and both she and Edward turned.

'You and I are going to run Le Marche for a year?'

'Of course,' said Celeste. 'What did you think we were doing?'

Edward saw the bewilderment on Billie's face and he felt sorry for her. Celeste had the pushy energy of her grandmother, which could be both a blessing and curse at times.

'I assumed you had both talked about it,' said Edward.

'We haven't yet, not properly,' admitted Celeste.

'I only arrived two days ago. I'm barely getting my head around London, let alone running a company.'

'So are you going to do it?' asked Celeste impatiently.

'I don't know,' said Billie.

'Oh for God's sake,' said Celeste, standing up and walking to the window.

Edward looked at his papers for a while, thinking about Daphné. It meant so much to her to leave the business to Billie and Celeste yet he didn't want to pressure Billie. She had a life back in Australia, whereas Celeste saw it as an opportunity to get a life.

There couldn't be more different women in the world than Celeste and Billie, he thought.

Then Celeste turned to Billie.

'You owe me this,' she said, her arms crossed and her face frowning.

'Excuse me?' Billie looked at Edward, who seemed as shocked as her.

'I had to cope with this family alone. My grandmother, my father and mother, the legacy. It's exhausting being a Le Marche. I want someone to share it with.'

Edward snapped his head towards Billie, who was now standing.

'The last thing I want is to be a Le Marche, trust me. Why do you think my mother took me so far away? She hates your family.'

Edward cleared his throat, but Celeste was now yelling about Billie and her not understanding, and Billie was now yelling and crying.

Edward slammed his hand on the table. 'I cannot listen to

family dramas, I'm not paid nearly enough,' he said forcefully.

He looked at Billie, her quite lovely face tear-stained with mascara.

'It meant more to your grandmother than you know for her to leave you Le Marche. She followed your life from afar. She was extremely proud when she learned you would be attending university. She had hoped for law, like her husband, but she said you must take after her, with a nose for concotions and laboratories.'

Billie stared at him for what felt like an age and then she spoke. 'My father died when I was young. He killed himself.'

Edward nodded. He knew the facts.

Then Billie looked back to Celeste. 'And it was your father that made him do it. So, if either of you can explain to me why I would want to stay here and work in the place that is a daily reminder of the woman who shunned my mother and myself for the past twenty odd years, I'd like to know.'

Edward was speechless at her outburst, desperately trying to find the right words, but coming up empty.

'Grand-Mère didn't shun you or Elisabeth,' said Celeste from over by the window.

'How do you know ?' said Billie.

Celeste walked towards the table and sat down wearily in her chair. 'Because I've seen the letters that your mother returned. The gifts, the photos, so many of me, which I apologise for,' she said, with a rueful smile.

Edward watched as Billie slowly sat in her chair and stared at Celeste wide eyed. 'She wrote to me? For how long?'

'Until you were eighteen. She said you could reach out to her as an adult after that.'

Billie sat in silence, as she took in the information.

'Perhaps we should take a break,' Edward said to them both.

Celeste stood up. 'I'll be in my office,' she said hautily and stormed away.

'Her office?' Billie asked after she had slammed the door with some force.

'It was Madame Le Marche's,' said Edward. 'She got in first.' He shrugged, embarrassed.

'I don't care about that. Can we get out of here?' she asked.

'Of course, do you want to get a coffee somewhere?'

'No, I need to walk,' she said, pulling on her puffy jacket.

'Then we will walk,' said Edward cheerfully.

They walked through the streets, Edward in his overcoat and Billie in her jacket, looking as odd as any pair on the street, he thought, as he glanced at them in the reflection of a shop window.

Billie's dark mood was matched only by the dark clouds gathering overhead.

'It's going to rain,' said Edward, feeling like a typical Englishman.

They were walking along the river, sidestepping tourists and buskers, but Billie didn't look at the sights, she stared ahead, her hands shoved deep into the pockets of her jacket.

Then finally she stopped, which was just as well, Edward thought, as his shoe was rubbing on his left heel.

She leaned on the fencing along the river, so he joined her.

'My mother never told me Daphné wrote to me,' she said and then she turned to face him. 'So why would she tell me that you rang her after my grandmother died?'

Edward shook his head. 'I don't know, you would have to ask her.'

Billie turned back to her view of the grey water. 'Do you know what my uncle said to my father before he died?'

'I don't,' he said truthfully.

'If you did know, would you tell me ?' asked Billie.

The rain started to fall in slow drops. They were heavy and cold.

'Come on,' he said, pulling at her hand.

'No,' she said, standing still. 'Would you tell me if you knew?'

'If I had promised your grandmother, then no, I wouldn't,' he said, feeling the rain falling harder now, and dripping down his neck.

Billie didn't seemed perturbed at this. Instead, she asked, 'And if you did know?'

'I would tell you,' he said. They stood still, as people scattered around them like tenpins.

She really was quite beautiful, he thought. Her dark hair and blue eyes were so unusual, and the way her lips parted slightly to show her white teeth.

'I don't trust anyone in my family any more,' she said, and he saw tears forming in her eyes.

'You can trust me,' he said and then felt foolish. Never trust a man who says 'trust me'.

'You're almost like family,' she said. 'Besides, I don't know what to do. Do I give up my life and try this, where I think my own uncle wants me dead, and my cousin loathes me? Or do I go back to my life that is actually quite boring, and face my mother who lied to me for years?'

Edward smiled. 'I can't tell you what decision to make.'

'You could advise me. Isn't that what lawyers do?'

The rain was coming down in sheets, the wind driving it into his face, and he laughed.

'Do what feels right,' he said.

'That's a stupid answer,' she said and then she started to laugh. 'We're in the rain,' she said.

'I know,' he said with a shrug.

'Thank you for walking and being in the rain with me,' she said and she smiled. 'I bet my grandmother liked you a lot.'

He nodded, feeling his throat tighten. He hadn't acknowledged his grief about Daphné to anyone. She was only his boss, but he knew they both meant more to each other than that. He was her most trusted person, and he vowed that he would do anything to protect her granddaughters.

'Do you miss her?' she asked.

He nodded again, afraid to speak.

Billie took his hand and led him under a nearby awning over a café.

'I'll stay,' she said.

His face flushed. 'You will?' He felt like hugging her, but knew it was unprofessional and that Daphné would have told him off, so instead he put out his hand for her to shake.

'Congratulations, Miss Le Marche. Welcome to the family business.'

Billie made a face that he couldn't quite read but it didn't matter.

Billie Le Marche was staying, and Daphné was one step closer to her dream of having the next generation of Le Marche women at the helm.

Chapter 19

Giles' dismissal of Daphné in front of Yves wasn't mentioned, but she knew he was aware she was upset with him. However, her feelings were second to the business needs, and the Le Marche stock was sold out by the time the shop closed on Christmas Eve.

Then she had taken the brave step of speaking to Giles before he left for the night. He had given her four days off to go back to Calvaic to see her mother but she couldn't go, not without him knowing.

Giles was locking up the drugs in the back, when she stood in the doorway watching him. He was so handsome, she thought, and she felt the familiar ache between her legs that happened whenever she stared at him for any length of time.

'I'm pregnant,' she said.

Giles looked up at her and frowned. 'How?'

Daphné felt her voice falter, all the bravery having gone into the one statement. 'I don't know but I am,' she said, hearing the defensiveness in her voice.

'We will have to take care of it,' he said in his firm manner, and Daphné unclenched her fists, grateful for his sensible manner.

'We could marry when I come back from seeing Maman,' she suggested. She had dreams of wearing a cream wool suit with a simple strand of pearls borrowed from the Karpinskis, and lunch at Le Grand Véfour.

Giles looked at her askance. 'We cannot get married, what will people say?'

Daphné felt as though the world was falling away from beneath her. 'What people?'

'My customers, my son, your mother, the Karpinskis,' he listed.

'I don't think they would care, as long as you love me and I'm happy.' Her hands were in tight balls by her sides again.

'I'm too old to be a father,' he stated.

'You're not,' she implored.

'I don't want a child,' he said. 'I have one, that was enough.'

'One that you barely know,' she snapped.

She had seen the way Yves looked at his father with a mix of dislike and fear.

Giles had never mentioned what happened to his wife, but Daphné had the feeling Yves blamed his father.

Two days ago, he had warned her about him, and she had dismissed him, but now, his forewarning seemed justified.

'Don't tell me about my son, you're a child,' he scoffed.

She felt her anger rise. 'Then I'm a child with your child.'

Giles glared at her. 'I never wanted this,' he said, his voice rising.

'You wanted me,' she cried.

'You seduced me.' His hands were shaking as he spoke,

and part of her wanted to go to him and hold them but another part knew she could never forgive him.

'You did this to trap me,' he hissed and she saw his face contort with anger.

'I didn't, I love you.'

But he wasn't listening. His back was to her, as he tidied up the counter, and locked the cabinets.

What were her options now? Find a woman in a room somewhere in Le Marais who could take care of it, but risk infection and death like Anna had told her about, or head home to Calvaic and burden her mother with another mouth to feed and no money coming in?

She wanted the baby. She had seen Anna's youngest, Julia, grow over the past year, and even though they all still shared a house and it was crowded and noisy, Daphné had loved the child as though she were her own. Her chubby little face beamed at everyone, and she could charm strangers in the street with a wave of her pudgy fist.

They stared at each other, each waiting for the other to relent, until Daphné realised she would lose. She had nothing and he had everything, and at that moment she hated him.

She picked up her coat and bag, and looked at him. 'I'm going,' she said in a dull voice.

'I will see you in four days,' he said, turning away from her.

She took a package from her handbag and left it on the counter.

She had saved her money, going without lunch for a month to buy him a pair of kidskin gloves, lined in the finest cashmere, from Hermès.

Just walking into the store on Rue du Faubourg Saint-

Honoré made her feel special. Now she felt exhausted and the tears burned her eyes as she walked through the store. She wouldn't be back, she couldn't come back and face him after his words.

He made her feel like a cheap whore and yet there had been times when she thought he had loved her. When they lay in his bed, and he couldn't stop exploring her body until she was shaking with delight. When he gave her the extra pastry with coffee on their break, or when he told her that they would make double his profit thanks to her creams.

As she pushed open the door to the street, she saw Yves about to turn into the store.

'*Joyeux Noël*, Daphné,' he said and she tried to focus on him, her eyes blinded with tears.

'Yves,' she gulped.

He held her arms. 'What's happened? Is it my father?' he demanded to know, but she just shook her head.

'I have to go, I won't be back,' she sobbed.

'Did he fire you? Why?' Yves was leading her away from the store.

'I'm leaving,' was all she could say.

'Why?' Yves face was so kind and concerned, she broke down, and she felt his arms around her, holding her close.

'I'm pregnant,' she said, his coat muffling her words, but she knew he had heard by the sound of the sharp breath he took.

He held her while she cried, until she slowly regained composure. The air was freezing, and she shook in her less than adequate coat.

'And my father doesn't want it or to marry you?' asked Yves, his voice sounding resigned.

She nodded.

'So what will you do?'

Daphné watched everyone returning home for their Christmas Eve, and she thought about going home to the Karpinskis but she couldn't face Anna's disappointment in her, when she had been the only person to question Giles' intention with Daphné.

'I don't know,' said Daphné. 'Probably go home to my mother in Calvaic.'

Yves shook his head and then reached into his pocket and took out his wallet. He peeled off some franc notes and handed them to her.

'Take this,' he said.

But Daphné shook her head. 'I don't want money. I want a life. I thought I could have that with Giles.'

'You don't want that with my father,' said Yves, his brow furrowed as he spoke. 'He's a cruel man. He wants what he wants and then discards the mess of consequences.'

A cold rain began to fall, and Daphné looked up at the sky.

'My mother will be so ashamed,' she said, and she closed her eyes.

'Let me speak to him,' said Yves quickly and, before Daphné could protest, he was inside the store.

She waited by the wall, afraid to even see what was happening between the father and the son, but hope swelled in her, and she instinctively placed her hand on her belly.

'Maybe,' she said aloud, when she felt a hand on her arm.

'Let's go,' he said, and he pulled her along the street.

'Where are we going?' she asked, as she tried to look back to see if Giles was following them. 'What happened?'

Yves turned to her on the street. The rain had soaked her jacket, and she shivered.

'Do you want to be married? Do you want to have your child raised in a proper home?'

Daphné nodded, hopeful that perhaps he had talked sense into his father.

'Then we will go to Calvaic and marry tomorrow,' he stated, as though this was always an option.

'What?' Daphné screamed, not seeing the people who turned and glanced at her.

'My father is a man of extreme anger, and the worst thing you could do is to be married to him.' Yves was breathless as he spoke, but his conviction was strong.

Daphné felt as though her world was turning upside down, and she grabbed his arm.

'I cannot marry you,' she said, shaking her head. The rain was hurting her eyes but she couldn't close them, because she didn't know what would happen next.

'Why not?' asked Yves.

'Because I don't know you.'

He must be insane, she thought, as the wind blew up, pushing her towards him.

'We can know each other over time, plenty of marriages start like that.'

'But you live in Switzerland,' she said, trying to find reason.

'And you can live with me. I lead a respectable life. You will want for nothing.'

'But I like to work, I like what I do,' she said, feeling as though she was clutching at straws.

'You can work if you wish, you can do anything you want, just marry me,' he said, his voice urgent, and his face serious.

'Why?' she asked for the final time.

'Because I want you,' was all he said.

Daphné ran through her options in her head. Switzerland would be far enough away from Giles to make him see he had made a mistake, and then he would ask for her back.

Yves would understand when they were reunited. Perhaps this was his plan all along?

'We can't get married on Christmas Day,' she said.

'We can. A judge will marry us. I can ask as soon as we get to your mother's house.'

Daphné tried to imagine him in her mother's cottage and failed.

'She is very poor, most of my money goes to her,' she said, blinking away the rain.

'And we will keep helping her,' said Yves solemnly.

And in that moment Daphné knew he was not his father. Not once did Giles ever enquire after her mother, or offer to help her with money to send home. He acted as though she was entirely independent of anyone and completely dependent on him.

'But I don't love you,' she said, finally, having exhausted all her other excuses.

'Love has nothing to do with this,' said Yves and, for a moment, he looked like Giles again and her heart warned her to think again.

But what options did she have?

'Then I will marry you,' she said in a low voice, and she

felt Yves' mouth on hers in a stiff-lipped kiss, his lips cold on her warm mouth.

They were married on Christmas morning at the police station. The judge was a friend of his chemistry teacher guardian, Dr Aberle, from Switzerland. Daphné's mother gave her her own wedding ring to use for the ceremony and, when they returned home to her mother's house, she had made a roast chicken for lunch. They had no gifts to give, but Yves made her mother laugh and he carved the chicken correctly. They lay next to each other that night in Daphné's mother's bed, the linen sheet soft and comforting; strangers now married.

Chapter 20

Celeste

'We need a new product,' said Celeste, lining up the products on the desk, as Billie walked into her office.

She looked up at her cousin. 'Why are you so wet?'

'I got caught in the rain.'

Celeste looked out of the window. 'London loves to rain,' she said and went back to the products. 'It's one of the few things it does very well.'

'I'm staying,' said Billie.

Celeste looked up at her again. 'Of course you are,' she said.

'You thought I would stay?'

She sat in the chair and looked at her dripping family member. 'I didn't think you had a choice.'

'We all have choices,' said Billie.

'Not really,' Celeste laughed. 'We think we do, but really, we have to do what is best.'

Billie was silent.

'We need a new product, something special,' she said, thinking aloud. The products were boring, and dated. The packaging was old-fashioned, and probably the ingredients were as well.

'Don't you want to wait for the formula? Then we can turn that into the next product?'

Celeste shook her head. 'I don't think we have that much time. I get the feeling things aren't very good as far as sales are concerned. What do you think of this?' she asked, unscrewing a jar of their least popular cream.

Billie scooped it out with her fingers and smeared it on the back of her hand, rubbing it in slowly, feeling the texture.

'It's quite greasy,' she said, looking up at Celeste.

'*Oui*, it would leave a shine under make-up,' Celeste said, and she picked up the box, and read the ingredients out loud.

Billie nodded. 'Yes, that's all standard stuff. It's got a lot of lanolin in it, that's what's causing the grease slick that's left over.'

Celeste made a face at the cream, and went through the others, finally coming to the last jar of their best-selling line, Le Marche Moderne.

'And this?' she asked, handing it to Billie.

Billie opened it and sniffed it. 'It smells nice,' she said, and went through the same motions, rubbing the cream onto her other hand.

'Less lanolin in this one,' she said.

Celeste leaned back in the chair, and put her hands behind her head. 'There are so many products, it feels like Grand-Mère just put out anything without thinking about it in regards to the others already for sale. I think some of them are the same with a different name.'

Billie laughed a little and Celeste felt herself smiling in return.

'You need to make a new product,' she said.

'What? I don't know how to make a product,' said Billie.

'Then find someone who does,' Celeste said, moving the boxes into little stacks on her desk.

'These ones have to go, we can't sell them. They are probably costing us money instead of making it,' she said firmly. 'These one are OK, but need improvement, and these few are safe, for now,' she added, gesturing to one of the ordered columns.

'Gosh, you really know your stuff, don't you?' said Billie and Celeste felt her head snap up at her words. Was she being rude about her lack of job experience?

But Billie's face was without anything but admiration.

'I just like products,' said Celeste shyly. 'I love pharmacies and make-up counters.'

Billie was quiet for a moment. 'What about a lipstick?' she asked.

'We don't do make-up,' said Celeste, shaking her head.

'Why not? We could. What if we did a nourishing lipstick that had some tint to it? We could sell it as a skincare and a make-up product.'

Celeste tied her hair up and secured it with a rubber band from the desk drawer. 'I like that idea. Can you make it?'

'I can't, but I know someone who can,' said Billie slowly.

'Then bring them here. Tell Edward, he can work it all out,' she said, with a wave of her hand.

Billie stood up and smiled. 'I'll get back to you,' she said, but Celeste was already quickly writing on a notepad.

After Billie left, Celeste gave a huge sigh of relief. For a moment she had thought Billie was going to walk away and she would lose this whole opportunity, but thankfully Edward had saved the day again. She really should thank him properly, she thought, as she looked at the boxes stacked into three piles on the desk.

The three stages of Le Marche's history, she thought, as she picked one up. The beginning, the middle, and the end, but there was no way she was going to let this be the end.

She thought about the women she knew who still used Le Marche. They were all older, like her mother, and even older again.

Le Marche needed something that she would use, she thought, and then she had an idea. She started to write in her notebook. Three pages later, she took it down to Gemma at reception. She was looking bored.

'Gemma,' Celeste said.

The girl jumped at her name being used. 'Yes?' she asked.

'You will have to come and work near me. There is a desk for an assistant outside my office, and it would be easier if you came there,' she said.

Gemma nodded. Celeste waited and gestured at her.

'Now? You want me to come now?' Gemma asked, her face flushing.

'Yes, I said I needed an assistant and I chose you, so hurry up, we have a lot of work to do,' she said and started to turn back to her desk.

'But who will answer the phone?'

Celeste shrugged. 'I don't know, get one of those temperamental people.'

Gemma stared at her and then she nodded. 'A temp, you want me to bring in a temp?'

'Yes,' said Celeste impatiently. Maybe this girl wasn't so bright.

'Give me half an hour,' said Gemma, in an efficient tone, which inspired some confidence back in Celeste about her decision to promote Gemma.

Celeste went back to her office and stood in the middle of the room, assessing the changes she needed to make in order for it to be acceptable to her taste.

She wrote more notes, and even drew a new floorplan, and then she heard a knock at the door and Gemma walked in.

'You ready to start working?' she asked, and then she saw that Gemma's face looked very close to tears.

'What is wrong?'

'Mr Badger said I can't work for you as your assistant and he said you can't have a temp,' Gemma said, looking down at the floor.

'Mr Badger? Who is this? Your imaginary friend?'

'I'm Mr Badger,' Celeste heard and she looked up to see Edward in the doorway. 'Surely you know my name?'

'I don't pay attention to names, but that's a silly name,' she said.

'I'm quite aware of that fact,' he said and he turned to Gemma. 'Thank you, Gemma, that will be all.'

Gemma rushed from the office and Celeste glared at him.

'You can't treat me like that,' she said, crossing her arms. 'And don't be rude to my assistant.'

Edward looked furious; a little vein in his neck was throbbing and his brow was creased.

'I'm not treating you like anything, I'm just stating that we can't afford another staff member, and now Billie wants to bring in some new flash chemist to make a lipstick. I know you don't know anything about the business, but surely you understand how dire things are?' She could hear him trying to control his voice, and she wondered if he yelled at his girlfriend or wife.

Celeste walked to him and put a cool hand on his brow. 'Don't frown,' she said. 'You'll get wrinkles."

His eyes caught hers and he blinked a few times, as though trying to focus.

'You sound like your grandmother,' he said, in a low voice.

'Is that such a bad thing?' she asked, feeling her insides turn dramatically. This wasn't right, she thought. She wasn't supposed to feel anything real for Edward, she had planned to use him for his knowledge about the company.

She saw the flecks of yellow in his green eyes, the way his eyelashes curled at the ends, the perfect shape of his nose, and the tiny cut on his chin from shaving. Her hand ran down his face, and she put her finger on the mark.

'You need to be more careful,' she heard herself whisper.

He swallowed and then blinked, breaking the spell.

'You must run things by the accounts department and myself before you spend money,' he said, his demeanour softening a little but he had stepped away from her.

'I know how to save money,' she said and she walked to the desk and picked up a jar of cream.

'We need to stop making this,' she said, holding it out for him.

'This?' He took it from her.

'It's not selling, it's old-fashioned. No one will mind, anyone who uses this is probably close to death anyway.'

Edward put the jar down on the desk.

'We could lose these two also,' she said, pushing the others towards him. 'What we save on these, we can put into new products, and Gemma,' she said, raising a shaped eyebrow.

Edward sighed. 'Anything else?' he asked, crossing his arms.

'And new furniture for this room,' she said, looking around. 'It's hideous.'

He laughed. 'While you're at it, why don't you redo the whole office?' he said.

'Oh I plan to,' she returned.

He peered at her. 'You're not serious, are you? Did you hear anything I just said?'

For a moment she wondered what he would be like in bed. Would he be strong and controlling, or demand she do all the work like Paul?

She preferred something in between but so far hadn't lucked out with the lover who met her needs. Matilde said it was because she had father issues. Celeste just thought it was because she liked wealthy men, and it was a known fact that wealthy men were terrible at sex.

'Do you have a wife?' she asked.

Edward frowned again and she refrained from touching him.

'Excuse me?'

'A wife? A girlfriend? A boyfriend?'

Edward shook his head. 'No to all of them,' he said, his face bewildered.

She checked her gold wristwatch, and then picked up her handbag. 'I'm starving. Let's get lunch,' she said, and she walked to the door, where a nervous Gemma was sitting outside on a gilt chair.

'We're out for lunch,' Celeste said to the girl. 'Please organise all the furniture from my office to be gone by tomorrow.'

Gemma went red, her mouth opening wide. 'Where will I send it?' she asked.

'I don't know,' laughed Celeste. 'I don't care. Do what you want with it.'

She turned to Edward. 'Now I want to hear all about you and your life. You certainly know enough about mine,' and she realised as a bewildered Edward went to get his coat that her head wasn't hurting today, and she really did want to know about him, and that she wasn't sure which revelation was more surprising.

Chapter 21

Daphné's cries filled his ears, and Yves rushed out of the house and into the garden. Standing under the lilac tree, he looked up at the window of their little house, where Daphné was labouring under the eye of a midwife.

For eight months they had lived in Switzerland, and with every day that her belly grew, she became more and more depressed and nothing Yves said or did could move her spirits.

And now his father was causing her more pain.

Yves had never told Daphné what had happened in the shop that day before they left for Calvaic, but Giles' words were the permanent soundtrack to every day for the past eight months.

Condemning Daphné and her child to a life with his father was too much for any person, he had thought, and while his proposal was noble, it wasn't entirely selfless.

He yearned for Daphné the same way he had the first time he saw her and yet they were still strangers physically. She had her bed, and he had his, and never the twain shall meet, he thought every time he went to sleep.

He had told Daphné it was best that she not contact Giles,

and she had agreed, but then she had agreed to everything Yves had suggested, including the small house and the names for the baby.

Robert for a boy, after his professor, and Louise for a girl, after his mother.

There was a final cry from the open window upstairs and Yves clutched at a branch of the tree, causing a shower of lilac petals to fall onto his unknowing head.

Then the cry of a baby echoed out and Yves ran back into the house and up the stairs. He opened the door a little, and closed his eyes.

'All is well, my dear?' he asked in a calm voice.

'Come in,' he heard Daphné say, and he stepped into the room.

Daphné lay on the bed, her head covered in perspiration and pride, with a red-faced babe in her arms.

'Come and meet Robert,' she said and he tiptoed to the side of the bed, and looked down at the child.

His face was angry, and his fist clenched, and when Yves went to touch his head, the baby roared as though he knew who Yves was, and Yves felt nothing but pity for him.

'Isn't he beautiful?' asked Daphné, her face shining with joy.

Yves just smiled and kissed her on the top of her head. 'You already look like the perfect mother,' was all he said in return.

'I'm going to be the best mother there is,' she determined, and Yves nodded, as the baby closed his eyes and nuzzled at her breast.

But he wasn't sure if she was speaking to him, the baby or Giles, far away in Paris.

* * *

For the next three months, Daphné was true to her word, and Robert wanted for nothing. He didn't even have to cry to be fed, or changed. She was so intent on making her baby happy that Yves wondered if she even remembered he was in the house with them.

Then Daphné announced she would be taking the baby to Calvaic to see her mother.

'You won't go and see my father, will you?' he warned.

Daphné shook her head. 'No,' she said emphatically, 'I have no desire to see him again.'

She reached up and touched Yves' face. 'How lucky I am to have you and not him,' she said, but her words sounded hollow to his ears, and the light in her eyes that once danced was now dulled, framed by black circles.

'I can come with you,' he said.

'No, I want to spent some time with Maman. You will be bored and it's very cramped,' she reasoned.

Yves couldn't argue with that and yet something didn't sit right inside his heart and head.

'If you see Giles,' as he now called him, 'and he learns about us, and sees you've had the baby, he will punish you.'

But Daphné waved away his concern with her hand. 'I promise you, I will not see him.'

There was nothing Yves could do, but to let her go.

***

Two days had passed since she took the train to Paris with Robert in his pram, and he had easily settled into his bachelor existence again. He thought he would enjoy his time alone, but he missed the sounds of Daphné chatting, and the smell of casseroles cooking, or his morning coffee waiting for him on the table with a little pastry alongside.

He liked to come home and see the washing snapping on the line, and seeing Daphné in the garden, Robert on a blanket under a tree.

Now the house felt empty when he came home at the end of the day, and when he went to their room, he lay on her bed and inhaled the scent of her perfume on the pillow.

The thought of her lying next to him made his insides turn upside down, and he felt himself harden at the thought of her unlacing her nightgown for him.

Would any woman ever do that for him? Marrying Daphné was the bravest thing he had ever done and he did it to spite his father, and she had said yes to avoid a life of poverty and shame, but it wasn't a foundation for happiness.

The sound of the telephone ringing pulled him from his self-recrimination and he rushed downstairs.

'Hello?'

'Yves?' He heard Daphné's voice and he breathed out with relief.

She had agreed she would use the phone at the police station in Calvaic, since her mother didn't have one and wasn't likely to ever have one installed.

'How is Calvaic?' he asked, sitting at the table, noticing the snapdragons in a blue enamel jug on the table were wilting.

'Yves, something terrible has happened.' Her voice was dull, and he felt himself sit up straight, readying for the news. She wasn't coming back, he thought. She decided a life without him was more preferable to one with him. His father had wooed her back to spite him.

'What has happened?' His voice sounded tired, even to his own ears.

'I'm in Paris,' she said and she paused, but he said nothing. Of course she would go back to him, why did he believe her when she promised she wouldn't?

She would always choose his father over him.

'I saw Giles,' she said, 'and showed him Robert. And then I told him we were married.'

Yves closed his eyes, and sighed. 'And what happened?'

He waited for the resolution, which he was sure wasn't going to go his way.

'He told me I was a whore, and I forced you to marry me and because you're weak you did it, and then he told me I betrayed him.'

'And?'

'And then I left to see the Karpinskis and was going to see Maman the next day but in the morning a solicitor delivered a letter to Anna and Max from Giles that said they had thirty days to pay him back the money he lent them or he was going to bankrupt them.'

Daphné was crying now, and then he heard Robert crying in the background, and a voice soothing the baby.

'Where are you now?' he asked.

'At the Karpinskis', I can't leave them now, it's terrible,' she sobbed. 'I should never have taken him to them. They don't have that money, the shop is just making a profit now.'

'I'm coming to you now,' he said. 'I'll be on the next train.'

I should be there by tomorrow. Don't do anything till then and stay away from my father.'

Yves arrived at the Karpinskis' shop the following morning, when the upstairs house was chaotic with babies crying, and children ready to go to school.

He hadn't met Anna and Max before, but Daphné spoke of them so highly, he was more ashamed than ever to be his father's son.

However Max behaved as though Yves had no relation to Giles, and warmly shook his hand.

Yves looked around the crowded upstairs space. 'You all live here?' he asked, astounded.

'We were going to move with the money we have saved, but since the letter that doesn't look likely,' Max said lightly, but the worried lines on his forehead told Yves otherwise.

Anna glanced at them and he was met with a stony face, as she bustled two children out of the door with a kiss on their heads and a reminder to come home straight after school and no dawdling.

The memory of his mother telling him the same thing as a child pierced his heart, and he looked at a sleeping Robert in a wicker washing basket on the sofa.

'I knew he wasn't to be trusted,' Anna exploded, as the sound of children's feet on the stairs faded away.

Yves glances at Daphné, who was looking ashamed, and he felt more for her than he ever had. It was one thing to suffer for your choices but another to bring an innocent family into the situation.

'He hates Jews, you can see in his eyes,' Anna stated and Yves didn't argue. His father was anti-Semitic, but he always served them at the shop, as he said, 'Their money is as good as anyone else's.'

What Yves couldn't understand was why his father had invested in the business in the first place. Giles was careful with money, and a whimsical investment in a jewellery store didn't seem like something he would do lightly.

Daphné was chewing on a fingernail, and staring at her feet. She looked so young and vulnerable, and his heart lurched.

All this time he thought his father had just used Daphné as a sexual release, but now he realised he actually loved her and was completely unable to bypass his own pride and expectations to give himself happiness.

Yves sat at the kitchen table, as Anna made coffee for them all.

'We need something to leverage off,' he said, thinking like a lawyer instead of a son and husband.

Daphné looked at him. 'What? He hates me, so it won't be that.'

'We need to have something to take back from him, something that will hurt him enough to make him reconsider.'

All three pairs of eyes stared at Daphné.

'I know nothing about anything, he didn't even let me count the till at the end of the day,' she cried.

'You must have brought something to the business, or have seen something,' Yves coaxed and then Anna leaned forward.

'The creams,' she said. 'Daphné brought him the recipe for the creams and lotions and soaps.'

'Is that true?' Yves asked.

Daphné nodded. 'But they're just goat's milk and some

other things, anyone could make them. I don't own the idea for that. It was Anna who taught me.'

But Anna was shaking her head and a small smile crept onto her worried face.

'You added the oils and the herbs. You went out and looked at the other stores and what they did. You made the logo and encouraged him to make special packaging for them. You created that whole line, Daphné. You're good at it, and the women trusted you. I know those creams have made the difference to his store. You could see it in his nature. He's an arrogant man but more so now.'

At Anna's impassioned speech, he saw Daphné eyes fill with tears and she nodded.

'I did always like that part of my job,' she said in a soft voice.

'Then we will get it back for you,' he said and then he looked at Anna. 'Don't worry about the store, I know exactly what I'm going to do.'

He felt Daphné's eyes on him. 'What's wrong?' he asked.

'Nothing's wrong. I've just never seen you like this,' she said.

Yves felt his face redden under her gaze. He wondered if he should be more powerful, more often. Maybe then Daphné would unbutton her nightgown for him, and give him a child of his own, and not of his father's.

The thought of it thrilled him, and he leapt from his chair.

'I'm going to make this all go away for you,' he said and, on impulse, he leaned down and kissed Daphné on the mouth.

And, from the sofa, Robert roared his disapproval.

Chapter 22

Celeste

Gemma put her head around the corner of the door, where Celeste was sitting at a wooden desk, on a plastic chair, with no other furniture in the room.

'Your next meeting is in the boardroom. I'm going to head off now, it's after six, if that's OK?' she said nervously.

'That's fine,' sighed Celeste, as she glanced up at Gemma. 'How am I supposed to get any work done with these stupid meetings. 'Who am I seeing? And why?'

'Accounting with Billie and Mr Badger,' Gemma answered.

Celeste started to laugh at the sound of the names.

'Billie and Mr Badger,' she giggled to herself, as she picked up her notebook, and walked to the boardroom. Yesterday's lunch with Edward had been nicer than she had imagined. He was funny, and smart and he spoke so well of her grandmother she wished she had known her better.

She pushed open the glass doors to the boardroom, where Edward, Billie and two men with large files sat at the table.

'Bonjour,' she said to them all as she joined them at the table.

She had woken that morning in her hotel room, and was straight out of bed. She wasn't used to having somewhere to go in the morning, especially somewhere that wanted her. She had a real job for the first time in her life, and it was exciting, even if it was still her first week.

'We have to go through some paperwork to look at your allowance from your grandmother, and the salary you will receive,' said Edward, taking the papers from in front of him and pushing them towards Celeste. He was acting very professionally, as though they hadn't drunk wine at dinner three nights before on a whim, and she hadn't heard about his family thinking he was gay, and where she had divulged that she could barely remember her sister.

While it wasn't a fair trade on secrets, she did feel she knew him a little better.

She glanced down and then looked at Billie. 'Are you doing this too?'

Billie shook her head. 'I never got an allowance,' she said. Celeste frowned. 'That's not very fair.'

'There is a provision put aside for Billie that Daphné put money into every year, which she can access now,' Edward said.

Celeste thought for a moment. 'You said this allowance was from my grandmother?'

Edward nodded.

'But I never got anything from her, only from Papa,' she said.

Edward frowned. 'No, the money was from your grandmother, given to your father until you were eighteen, then it was to be directed to you.'

Celeste felt her stomach drop back to when she was eighteen. She was living between the eating disorder clinic and her grandmother's apartment in Paris, and not speaking to her parents. She couldn't quite understand what Edward was saying.

'I got two thousand euro a month from him, and nothing from Grand-Mère.'

Edward looked at his papers, and then he looked at the printouts on the desk in front of the men from accounting while Billie was looking down at her hands.

'No, you were given five thousand euros a month from the day you were born, and it was put into your father's account. Here are the records.'

He pushed them to Celeste who took a cursory glance at them. She didn't have to look to know what experience had told her. For the past thirty years, her father had been stealing from her.

She looked at Edward and held his gaze. He looked embarrassed for her, but she didn't want his shame or his sympathy. Her father was a selfish, greedy man, and she was ashamed of their shared blood.

'I want you to sue him,' she said to Edward. She felt Billie's eyes on her and shrugged her shoulders. 'My father is a shit,' she said.

Billie nodded. 'I gathered as much,' she said in agreement.

'Suing him will be expensive and very public. Do you think you want to drag the brand through the papers when you're trying to create a new image?' asked Edward.

She looked at Billie who threw her hands up. 'I don't care about that, if you want to do it, then do it.'

'I want to do it,' she said and she saw Edward sigh.

'Do you think that's wise? What sort of a message is that sending out about Le Marche?' he asked.

Celeste pushed back her chair and stood up. 'That Le Marche women are not to be underestimated.'

And with that she walked out of the boardroom and back to her office, where she told Gemma not to disturb her, as she had phone calls to make.

It was only then, sitting on the plastic chair in her near empty office, that she let the tears fall.

Why did her father hate her so much? Perhaps he wished it were her who died and not Camille? Her whole life she had been a disappointment to him, so much so that he felt he had to take money from her as though she were paying him to be her father. The need to be with her mother didn't come often and, when it did, she knew it wasn't to be trusted, but right now, she thought of her mother's hands on her hair, telling her everything would be all right, like she used to do before Camille died.

A knock at the door interrupted her thoughts.

'I said I was to be left alone, Gemma,' she called out, but the door opened and there was Edward.

'Hello,' he said in such a kind voice that she burst into tears again.

'Don't,' she said holding up her hand, 'I don't even know why I'm crying. It's not as though I don't know my father is a bastard.'

'But it still hurts,' he said.

She nodded through her tears, and looked up at him. 'I think he wishes I had died instead of my sister,' she said. 'I was always the more difficult one.'

'Perhaps you should go home for the rest of the day,' he suggested, which made Celeste sob harder.

'I don't have a home, I'm living in a hotel.'

'Come and live with me in the apartment,' Celeste heard and she looked up to see Billie in the doorway.

'Oh God, why don't you bring Gemma in as well,' she shouted, and, seconds later, Gemma was next to Billie.

'Did you need me?' Gemma asked.

Celeste didn't know whether to laugh or cry at the sight of the three of them.

'Come home,' said Billie and she walked forward and took Celeste's hands. 'It's lonely living alone, it would be so nice if we could get past our parents and create something between us,' she said with a smile.

Celeste nodded through her tears. 'That would be nice,' she said and she looked up at Edward. 'I meant what I said, I want you to sue him for the money he took from me, and then I want you to give it to the charities that Grand-Mère mentioned in her will.'

Edward nodded. 'I will set the wheels in motion.'

Celeste looked at Gemma. 'If you tell anyone you saw me crying, you will lose your job, do you understand?'

'I would never,' said Gemma, her eyes widening at the threat and Celeste believed her.

Celeste took a large pair of sunglasses from her handbag and put them on.

'Let's go,' she said, and the cousins left the office for their grandmother's house.

* * *

That evening, Billie and Celeste ordered pizza and they ate it with a glass of wine from the stock in Daphné's cupboards.

'Why is my father such a bastard?' asked Celeste as she poured Billie more wine.

They were sitting on the sofas, which were more comfortable than they looked, and the pinky lamplight made everything look softer and somewhat more bearable.

'I can't answer that,' said Billie with a shrug. 'I just know he said something to my father before he died, something that caused him to kill himself.'

'Does your mother know?' asked Celeste, as she picked salami off the pizza and ate it slowly.

'No.'

Celeste wiped her hands and leaned back in the chair. 'I never thought I would see you again,' she said.

'I don't really remember you,' answered Billie truthfully. 'Now I've spent time with you, I see flashes of memories, like photographs really, but nothing substantial.'

'Perhaps if our parents weren't so angry, we might have been friends,' Celeste thought aloud.

'Do you remember anything about Camille?' asked Celeste. Her only memories were so used they were tattered like a book that had been read too many times.

Billie thought for a moment. 'I remember she was nice to me, and that she helped me when my ice cream ran down my arm.'

Celeste smiled. 'She was sweet like that.' She paused. 'And what do you remember about me?'

Billie laughed. 'I remember you yelling at your dad for something.'

Celeste laughed loudly. 'Well, nothing much has changed there.'

Billie smiled. 'And what about me? What do you remember?'

Celeste met her eyes and she held them as she spoke. 'I remember I was so jealous of you.'

'Me? What for?' Billie cried.

'For everything you had that I didn't.'

Billie laughed. 'And what was that?'

'Love,' Celeste said slowly. 'Your parents loved you so much, and Camille and I used to wonder what it was like to have that sort of love from your parents. The way Uncle Henri let you ride on his shoulders, and how you were allowed to sit on your mother's lap during dinner. They would both read you a story, and greet you in the morning as though you had been away for days. I cannot imagine being loved like that. Your parents are what I hope to be if I ever have children one day, you were so incredibly lucky.'

Billie looked down at her hands, and then up at Celeste. 'But then the luck ran out,' she answered.

And Celeste knew exactly who was to blame for it and she hated him even more.

Chapter 23

Billie

The light in London made Billie feel like she was living in a Turner painting with the dark, sullen skies, but she was missing the Melbourne light, warmth and coffee, and the simplicity of her life, and she missed Nick. She didn't realise how much time they spent together at work, and how often she would have coffee or lunch with him, or even a quick drink at the pub after work on a Friday. He was her best friend and she missed him. But most of all she missed her mother, yet she couldn't bring herself to call her when she was still so confused and upset about her mother's decision to keep Daphné's letters from her.

Perhaps there was an explanation for what happened to her father?

Perhaps Daphné knew and Elisabeth didn't want to listen?

Perhaps Daphné just missed her granddaughter?

Billie was avoiding her mother's calls and emails; instead she had sent her a text message saying she was very busy and would get back to her soon, but that was now three weeks ago.

She and Celeste had settled into some sort of a routine,

where they left together every morning, taking a taxi to work, even though Billie told her they could ride bicycles, or take the bus. Celeste was always perfectly attired, in her signature slim cigarette pants and some sort of fabulous top with labels that Billie wasn't familiar with, and with a quilted Chanel bag with a chain handle that was heavier than it looked.

Billie was in jeans and a sensible sweater, with her puffy coat, and her hair in a ponytail. The only thing that was shared between them was Daphné's extensive perfume collection.

There were two silver trays filled with bottles of rare and unusual fragrances, all bottled in the same brown slender glass with their names handwritten on the labels.

Billie was enjoying the tuberose and Celeste was obsessed with the lemon and black tea blend that was half full.

'Do you think the formula is a perfume?' asked Billie, as they opened the vials and gently let the scent drift to them.

'I have no idea,' Celeste had said. 'It could be an anti-ageing cream, or a perfect primer. What we need is someone to refresh everything and help us create new products, but I don't know anyone in that world and by the time we start a recruiting process and we interview, it could be months before we find someone, and we need them soon.'

Billie thought of Nick. 'I might know someone,' she offered.

'Call them, see if they will come and work here,' Celeste almost yelled.

Billie waited until that evening, until she knew Nick would arrive early at the laboratory in Melbourne.

'Nick? It's Billie, Billie March.' She still wasn't used to

her proper surname, and the last thing she wanted to do was throw too much information at Nick.

'So you finally called me? I thought it was something I said,' he laughed.

'What do you mean?' Billie was trying to remember when they last spoke, and she realised it was in the café in Melbourne.

'Did I promise to call you?' she asked, worrying.

'No, but I thought you might at least explain where my best scientist had gone,' he admonished. 'One day you're at work, the next I get wind that you've upped and left for London, and no one knows anything more. Everyone was saying you'd fallen in love and followed the bloke there.'

Billie laughed. 'Not even close,' she said and explained the situation.

'Jeez, that's intense,' Nick had said. 'But you have a full lab, and staff?'

'Yes, we have two labs, one here and smaller one in France. There is no real leader, and they just churn out the same stuff. Celeste and I think we need a refresh and new products.'

'Celeste, as in the cream with the sperm whale head?' he laughed and Billie remembered their conversation back in Melbourne.

'I don't think she would appreciate that,' she giggled, thinking of Celeste's lack of humour about herself.

God, she had missed his stupid sense of humour.

Billie ran through the offer that she and Edward had worked out and Nick was silent.

The salary was double what he was getting in Melbourne, and he had a generous relocation allowance, but a move to

London would mean he would leave behind his friends and family, and maybe a girlfriend.

'I don't know if you have others to think about,' she said.

'No, I don't,' he said quickly and she felt her heart skip a beat. Her crush on Nick hadn't waned, she realised, and she crossed her fingers as he decided.

'If you need more time—' she started to say but Nick interrupted her.

'No, no.' He paused.

Billie closed her eyes and sent a little prayer up to her grandmother.

'I'll do it,' he laughed, and Billie gave a little scream and started to laugh with him.

'Oh my God, that's so exciting,' she said, jumping up and down in the apartment, as Celeste opened the door and stared at her and then closed it and walked down to her bedroom.

'When will you come?' she asked, sitting down again and trying to be professional.

'I'll give them two weeks notice here and then come over and get an understanding of your set-up, and look for an apartment.'

'I can't wait,' said Billie, 'I've missed you.'

The words spilled out of her mouth before she realised, and she gulped.

Nick said nothing in return and Billie felt her cheeks redden. God, she was so stupid, she thought, and she put on her best Celeste tone.

'I will have my assistant send you all the details, Nick, thank you so much. I look forward to you joining the company.'

She figured she could get Gemma to send the details, and pretend to be her assistant.

'That's great, Billie, looking forward to it, thanks for the opportunity,' he said.

Billie put down the phone and lay on the sofa. She covered her face with a pillow and then yelled into it and kicked her feet up and down in frustration.

When she stopped, she removed the pillow and saw Celeste sitting on the armchair, her legs crossed in her elegant black pants, a red-soled shoe hanging from her foot.

'Have you finished?' Celeste asked drily.

Billie sighed. 'I just made an idiot of myself,' she said.

Celeste shrugged. 'You'll survive,' she said. 'Get dressed, we have to go out.'

Billie sat up. 'Out? Where?'

'We have a networking event,' said Celeste. 'I told you about it the other day, it's the European Businesswoman Awards, Grand-Mère is receiving a lifetime achievement award.'

'But she's dead,' said Billie, trying not to laugh, but Celeste didn't seem to see the funny side.

'She was offered it before her death. Papa was supposed to represent her, but instead, it will be us.'

'Can't you go?' sighed Billie. 'I don't have anything to wear.'

'You can borrow something of mine,' said Celeste.

'If you have two of the same and sew them together, then maybe it would fit,' Billie suggested.

Celeste stood up. 'Come and we will get you something suitable.'

Billie followed her up the hallway and then into the room Celeste was sleeping in.

'I told you, nothing of yours will fit me,' said Billie, but Celeste didn't say anything; instead she opened a large armoire and gestured at the dresses inside.

'These will fit you,' she said and she pulled out a sleeveless Indian pink beaded top and matching slim skirt.

'Wow,' said Billie, as she reached out and gently touched the beads.

'Or this,' said Celeste, putting the pink outfit on her bed and taking out a black knee-length cocktail dress, made of jersey, draped so it hung beautifully on the hanger.

'This is perfect,' said Celeste, thrusting it at her.

'Whose clothes are these?' asked Billie.

Celeste closed the cupboard. 'They're Grand-Mère's, she saved everything. Do you have black heels?'

Billie nodded, thankful that she had brought a pair with her in case she had to attend a memorial service.

Billie went to her room, changed into the dress, and slipped on her heels. The dress fell perfectly around her frame, showing off her décolletage and her long neck.

She went to Celeste's room. She was wearing a long red dress with a plunging neckline and Billie felt silly in her grandmother's hand-me-downs next to Celeste's chic presence.

'You look good,' said Celeste, her eyes running Billie up and down.

'I feel stupid,' said Billie. 'Like I'm playing dress-ups.'

Celeste shrugged. 'You're wearing a vintage, silk jersey YSL dress that would probably fetch a few thousand online, it's not dress-ups, or whatever you call it.'

'This is Yves Saint Laurent?' Billie felt very differently about the dress, and hoped she wouldn't spill anything down the front.

'You need some make-up and then we can leave,' said Celeste, as she applied red lipstick to her mouth without using a mirror.

'I don't really wear make-up,' said Billie.

'You do tonight,' said Celeste and, ten minutes later, Billie was wearing a dark smoky eyeshadow and a pale lip gloss. Celeste had suggested she pull her hair down from the ponytail and let it fall around her face, and Billie did as she instructed and then looked in the mirror. She looked like a sultry version of herself, as though the vixen had been released.

Of course, only Celeste could entice her inner vixen out, thought Billie, as she adjusted the sleeve of her dress.

'Let's go,' said Celeste and, in a moment, they were in a taxi, heading across London.

Celeste had refused to let Billie wear her puffy jacket over her dress, so she rubbed her arms in the cold air when they alighted from the car.

'We're at Claridge's,' Billie said, as she looked up at the awning of the hotel.

'*Oui*,' said Celeste, as she ignored the doorman and walked to the door.

Billie stared up at the hotel and heard her mother's voice from far away.

'You were made in a suite at Claridge's on our first wedding anniversary. We were drunk on love and Taittinger. Your father read me the poems of E. E. Cummings, and we dined on chocolate and strawberries.'

Once upon a time, Billie had made faces at this story, repulsed by the idea of her parents being intimate with each other. Then, over the years, she had rolled her eyes at her mother's lush memory, but now, as she stood outside the entrance to the grand hotel, wearing an Yves Saint Laurent dress of her grandmother's, her glamourous French cousin calling her name from inside the doorway, Billie understood the intoxication her mother must have felt when she met her father.

The Le Marches were so bewitching that not even she, the girl who had tried so hard to be unlike her dreamy father and her romantic mother, could resist the spell, and here she was, back to exactly where she had started in life.

Chapter 24

Daphné, Paris, February 1958

The judge shuffled some papers and cleared his throat and then looked over the bench at Yves and Daphné, who in turn, felt her stomach lurch with nerves.

In a chair near her sat Giles, his legs crossed and hands clasped in his lap. She could see a glimpse of skin between his socks and the hem of his trousers and, for some reason, it made her sad.

Once they had lain in each other's arms and she knew every inch of his skin, but now the inch of exposed flesh seemed unfamiliar.

The judge started to speak, narrating the sequence of events that brought them to this moment.

Daphné half listened, as she glanced behind her, and saw Max sitting proudly in the gallery, his hands in his lap, wearing his only suit, which Daphné had seen Anna mend the day before.

Robert was at home with Anna and Julia, happily spoiled by the older children, giving Daphné space to concentrate on the moment ahead, yet her mind wandered.

She tried to focus on the words swirling around her.

Trademark. Debt. Contracts. Logo. Formula.

And then Yves took her hand and squeezed it firmly.

She felt Giles look at the action, and part of her wanted to pull her hand away to show him she still cared, but Yves was clutching on to it, and then the judge stood up and everyone else stood up in return.

'What happened?' asked Daphné. 'Is he coming back?'

'No,' said Yves, a broad smile on his face. 'We won. Giles has to stop using the Le Marche name and your recipe and he has to honour the agreement he had with the Karpinskis.'

Daphné looked around for Giles, but he was already gone.

The victory felt hollow, even when Yves slapped Max on the back, and suggested they all go out for dinner, even the children.

Everything Daphné had wanted and had hoped might resolve, ending in her and Giles reuniting, was over with the judgment.

She had lost her lover, her father-in-law and her child's father.

Daphné and Yves had checked into a small hotel in Le Marais, near Anna and Max, and, later that night, after a loud dinner with children and wine, she lay in her single bed, listening to the sound of Robert snuffling in the basket on the floor.

Yves had saved her, but now it was time she saved herself. She owned the Le Marche cream now, and if she sold enough jars, she might be able to pay off the Karpinskis' debt to Giles sooner, freeing them all from the tie to him.

The problem was the cream didn't have a very long shelf life, and needed to be used within thirty days. If she wanted to sell more, she would have to have it in more stores, and it would need to travel.

'Yves,' she whispered in the dark.

'Yes,' came the reply. His voice sounded hopeful and worried, and Daphné closed her eyes.

They had been married for nearly a year and they still hadn't shared a bed. She had expected that Yves would just come to bed one night and take her, as was his right, but he didn't and she didn't ask. She could still remember every touch of Giles, and the memory burned in her heart and between her legs.

But Yves had rescued her from a life of poverty, and Giles hadn't cared. It was Yves who grabbed her hand in the court room today. It was Yves who saved the Karpinskis from his father, who had given her back her recipe for the creams.

Self-recrimination swept over her for even wishing Giles would change his mind, and her breasts ached, not with milk but needing to be touched.

'Can I lie with you?' she asked shyly.

There was silence and she wondered if he had gone to sleep, and then she heard him turn over to face her.

'Yes,' she heard in the darkness.

She moved to his bed, and lay next to him, their bodies close in the thin bed.

Tentatively, she moved her hand to his back, and pressed herself against him. She felt his hardness against her stomach and she arched her neck, so her mouth was on his.

His mouth parted in surprise, and she realised he had no idea what to do with her advances or body.

'Have you been with a woman before?' she asked.

His silence was her answer. She sat up in bed, undid the buttons on her nightgown and then pulled it over her head, while she felt his eyes on her silhouette.

She lay down again, and took his hand and placed it on her breast, as their mouths collided again. This time his tongue joined hers and she slid her hands down his body, undoing his pyjama top until his chest was bare, and their skin touched.

He was on top of her now, her legs around him, and she pulled at his pyjama bottoms impatiently.

They didn't speak, but they seemed to understand each other. His hands knew what to do and, when she grasped him in her hand, she felt him shiver with pleasure.

Slowly, she eased him inside her, and she held him close. 'Be still,' was all she said. And he was.

Then she felt him start to move and she met his rhythm in the small bed, their mouths searching for each other. It felt like he couldn't get enough of her, kissing her mouth, gently moving her hair from her face, his hand touching her breast as though it were a priceless item.

His tenderness made her want to cry, and she understood he loved her. This was what Anna called '*faire l'amour*', not just sex. She thought Giles had loved her, but nothing had felt like this with him, and even Yves' inexperience couldn't mask his passion.

His body shifted and she pulled him closer as she felt the orgasm rise within her and, as she came, he joined her.

Yves lay beside her, their bodies breathless.

'I love you Daphné,' he said, his hand on her stomach. 'I know you love my father, but maybe one day, you might love me, but if not, then this is enough.'

Daphné was silent in the darkness. She thought that she loved Giles and he loved her but perhaps she didn't know what it was, and maybe Yves was the one to teach her?

She put her hand on his, and buried her head into his shoulder.

'I could love you,' she whispered into his shoulder, and she felt him kiss her head.

'Then that is enough,' he said and, at that moment, she thought it was enough.

***

Their private train compartment was silent on the trip back to back to Zurich. Daphné watched the lazy farm animals staring at the train impassively as they passed, while Robert was asleep in her arms.

She wished he would settle for Yves like he did for her. Robert was such a demanding baby, and she wondered if she and Yves had made another baby last night.

Maybe it would be a girl, she thought, and she looked over at Yves, who was asleep, his head lolling against the side of the train.

Robert whimpered in her arms, and she slowly rose, placing him into his basket, and tucking a warm blanket around him.

She steadied herself against the rocking of the train by holding on to the luggage rack, and then moved to Yves' lap, which she half fell onto.

'Hello,' she said when he opened his eyes, surprised.

'Hello,' he said, a small smile on his face.

'I enjoyed last night,' she said and she saw him blush.

'Yes, I also,' he said and she felt his hands on her waist.

She leaned down and kissed him on the mouth, a slow, sexy, languorous kiss that made her feel like she was melting.

She felt him harden against her leg, and she moved slightly, causing him to moan.

'Daphné,' was all he said, as she lifted up her skirts and released him from his pants.

'Yves,' she answered, as she looked into his eyes. 'I do love you. I have loved you since the night you arrived at your father's apartment.'

She remembered the shame of the dismissal from Giles, and Yves' gentle sympathy, which felt like a salve to the burn on her heart.

'Say it,' said Yves, as he pulled her down onto him.

'I love you,' she whispered.

'Say it again,' he said, his breath becoming ragged.

She did, and then he climaxed, saying her name so loudly, she thought the entire train would hear.

***

There was a telegram waiting for them at their house when they arrived home. Yves ripped it open, and read it quickly, his eyes darting over the paper

'What is it?' asked Daphné. They hadn't even walked inside yet.

'Father,' was all he said, and he handed her the note.

She read with the same speed as Yves, as there were few words, leaving no questions for either of them.

Wish to advise that Giles Le Marche was found deceased in his home by his housekeeper. Cause of death appears to be suicide by poison. No statement or notes were left by the deceased. Please advise of funeral arrangements.

Robert cried for her breast, as the cold air from the mountains nipped her cheeks, and Yves carried the bags inside.

'Come on in out of the cold,' he said.

She stepped over the threshold, as Yves dropped the bags and took Robert from her arms.

'Shhh,' he soothed the child and, to her surprise, the baby stopped his fretting.

'Sit down and feed Robert, and I will make you coffee,' he said.

She sat in the armchair by the fire.

'Giles is dead', was all she heard in her head, as she went through the automatic motions of feeding Robert.

Yves brought her coffee, and lit the gas fire, while chatting about the week ahead. She was silent until she could bear it no longer.

'But your father, what about him? He died, he died because of us and what we did,' she cried. 'We are guilty of his death.'

But Yves shook his head. 'The only death anyone is guilty of is my father, who killed my mother,' said Yves in a matter-of-fact tone.

Daphné felt her mouth drop open at his statement, but Yves said nothing more.

'Giles killed your mother?' she asked. She thought she

might have fainted if not for the tugging of Robert on her nipple.

'Yes,' said Yves, looking at her. 'And if you had stayed then you would have ended up the same way.'

'But why wasn't he charged by the police?'

'He said it was suicide, used one of her diary entries as a note, claimed she stole the drugs from the shop.'

'How do you know she didn't?' Daphné didn't want to think how he knew but she needed to know.

'Because I saw him inject her when she was passed out drunk. My mother was an alcoholic, but he drove her to drink. Always critising her, demeaning her, belittling her. It wore her away until there was nothing left. And then I saw him in her room, the tourniquet on her arm.'

Daphné felt bile rise in her throat at his words.

'My father didn't send me away because of the war, he sent me away because I saw, and I didn't return because I had seen what he did.'

Robert detached himself and snuffled into her breast. She had given birth to the child of a murderer and she wondered if in fact she should have listened to his words telling her to be rid of the baby, but then she wouldn't have Yves, and her creams and a future that seemed safer somehow, now Giles was dead.

She started to weep.

'Don't cry for him, Daphné, he doesn't deserve your tears,' Yves said.

But she shook her head. 'No, I'm crying for you and for Robert, having such a horrible man as father.'

'I'm fine,' said Yves with a smile, 'and Robert won't know

any different. He will grow up believing he is my firstborn, and he will never, ever find out the truth.'

And Daphné almost believed him, but her mother's words rang in her ears: the truth and moon eventually always come out.

Chapter 25

Celeste

The champagne was making Celeste light-headed, and she drank some water to try to sober herself before the speech. The red dress was probably too much for such a staid event as this, she thought, looking around at businesswomen with straightened, smooth hair and simple black dresses. Her plunged gown, showing off her slender bust and beautiful skin was a dress for a man, not a room full of powerful women.

Celeste was used to feeling like she didn't fit in around women, but she felt she was being judged by everyone, or was she judging herself?

Billie was chatting happily to a woman who owned a chocolate company, and who looked like she tried too many of the samples, Celeste thought and then told herself off. That was something her father would say, and God knows she didn't ever want to be like him.

Excusing herself from the table, she went to the bathroom to check her lipstick and take a moment away from the room.

This wasn't so hard, she told herself. Billie had said she had to do the speech as she was French and sexy, and they would love that more than an Australian speaking about the woman she couldn't remember.

Edward had written the speech for her that afternoon, and Gemma had printed it out onto paper in a large font, so it would be easy to read. It was all done for her, except she felt sick with nerves.

The bright lights of the bathroom were hurting her eyes, and she stepped back into the lobby and looked around for an escape route, when she heard a voice.

'Is it so boring in there you have to come out here looking for something fun?'

Celeste turned and looked at the most handsome man she had ever seen.

'It's not boring, it's that I have to make a speech and I haven't ever given a speech, and I may throw up, or run away, I haven't decided yet.'

The man smiled at her, his eyes surrounded by laughter lines and the slight tan making him look a little like Cary Grant, but more handsome, she decided.

He looked smart in a charcoal suit, with a periwinkle blue shirt to match his eyes, and a silvery tie.

'Curl your toes,' he said, looking down at her feet in gold strappy sandals.

'Pardon?'

'If you curl your toes then the tension goes into your feet and not into your stomach,' he said.

'Is this true?'

'I promise you, it is true. I do it and I give speeches all the time,' he said.

Celeste smiled, her nerves forgotten for a moment. She

knew his suit had to be Jil Sander or Tom Ford, and he wasn't wearing a wedding ring, and his eyes had danced over her exposed décolletage. Yes, he was interested and so was she, she decided.

'Perhaps you can come and watch me and give me some pointers,' she flirted and, to her delight, he laughed, throwing his head back so she could see his lovely neck.

'I am your public-speaking coach now, am I?'

'A position just became available,' she said.

'Then I would love to take you up on your offer,' he said, and Celeste suddenly didn't care what the women in the room thought about her any more. What mattered was the admiration of this man, any man, she thought, and she took his arm.

'Walk me in?' she purred.

'Of course,' he said, and just as they opened the door to the room, her name was called, while a frantic-looking Billie was waving at her to get onstage.

Celeste allowed the man to walk her to the podium, where she held his hand and stepped up to the microphone. It was only when she looked down that she realised she had left the speech on the table.

She took a deep breath and curled up her toes, and then looked around the room, finding Billie in the sea of faces.

'My name is Celeste Le Marche and I am the granddaughter of Daphné Le Marche who many of you may know passed away a few weeks ago.'

She paused, trying to think what Edward had written in the speech, but she had only glanced at it, and now she regretted lying to him that she would read it in the taxi. Her mind went blank, and she closed her eyes for a moment and then she spoke.

'My grand-mère was ahead of her time in every way. She was a founder and creator of the Le Marche brand. The recipe we still use is based on the original one she brought to Paris with her from her village of Calvaic. She convinced my great-grandfather to make her creams and then married the boss's son. She worked when many women didn't, and dedicated her life to creating creams that worked, and creams that were a part of every woman's day.'

She saw Billie staring at her, and curled her toes up once more.

'My cousin, Sibylla and I have been left this legacy by our grandmother. Not just the company, but also the expectation that we will bring her brand of fearlessness and her avant-garde ideas to the company. Sibylla and I both hope we can do this, and we want to do this. Not just for our grandmother, but for every woman who is told no by a bank manager because of her gender, or whose father told her she was useless to him because she was a girl, or whose lover told her that her job was just to look pretty and be quiet.'

Celeste slowly uncurled her toes, and she grasped the edge of the stand.

'The Le Marche woman is extraordinary, and we want to remind the world that she matters. Thank you for reminding my grandmother she mattered, and for allowing me to stand and speak to you tonight. It is an honour to be here and an honour to be a Le Marche.'

She stepped back from the microphone and heard the loud

applause, and she smiled, took the award from the presenter, posed for photographs and then went back to the table.

'You're amazing,' said Billie, her face shining with tears, and she pulled her into a hug.

Celeste was stiff in her acceptance of her affection, and she looked around the room, over Billie's shoulder and then saw the handsome man leaning against a wall, slowly clapping and nodding in approval at her.

'Here, you take this home,' said Celeste, shoving the glass award at Billie.

'Where are you going?' asked Billie, frowning.

'I have a date,' said Celeste, and she picked up her small clutch purse, and swayed over to her admirer.

'I will have to resign, you have no need for me,' he said with a smile.

'I curled my toes and I was fine,' she said, as she took his arm. 'Shall we get a drink?'

'I couldn't think of anything else I'd rather do,' he said.

'Oh I can,' she whispered, as they walked into the bar of the hotel.

If he heard her he didn't say anything, and they settled in a booth.

'Champagne?' he asked.

'No,' she said, and she glanced at the drinks menu. 'A glass of Château Cos d'Estournel.'

She looked to him to see his response. At one hundred and ten pounds a glass, it was a test to see if he flinched. Paul was always so stingy with wine, not allowing her to order anything over twenty-five euros.

He didn't blink, as she ordered two glasses of the wine,

and then he sat back in his chair. The sounds of conversation and glasses tinkling made her happy, and she looked at him, waiting.

'Celeste Le Marche,' he said with a smile.

'*Oui*.' She smiled and then she leaned forward. 'And your name is?'

'Dominic,' he answered, 'Dominic Bertiull.'

Chapter 26

Daphné, Zurich, March 1958

It was as though Giles' death hadn't happened. Yves didn't even return to Paris to make arrangements for a funeral. Instead, Giles was cremated and his ashes left on the shelf of the funeral home to be forgotten about until one day during a clean-up, or a change of owner, they were discarded with other long forgotten or disowned urns.

But for Daphné it was different. She spent her time consumed in guilt when Yves wasn't home, and then masking her emotions when he returned. She felt sick to the stomach, not able to keep a crust of bread down, and was too tired to look after a very fractious Robert.

'You must go to the doctor,' urged Yves. 'You're not well.'

But Daphné ignored him, convinced instead that this was her punishment from Giles, and that he was haunting them from the beyond.

Spring was peaking its nose from behind the carpet of snow, with forest violets becoming visible when Daphné walked Robert in his pram. The wheels crushed their hearts, sending their scent into the crisp air.

She picked a small posy and took them back to the house, placing them in a small jam jar on the windowsill.

Yves was home for lunch, and he lifted them to his nose.

'The tears of Cybele and Attis,' he stated.

'What?' Daphné was only half listening, as Robert was starting to cry.

'In Greek mythology, the goddess Cybele loved a mortal named Attis, though he didn't love her, but she didn't mind, because she was a goddess. Eventually though, she hounded him until he castrated himself, and then impaled himself on the branch of a tree. So the myth claims that where his blood fell on the ground, the violets grew.'

'That's so sad,' said Daphné, ignoring Robert's cries for a moment.

'For her or for him?' asked Yves and Daphné realised she couldn't quite find an answer.

Was she Cybele, who pursued Giles until she sent him to his own death, by his own hand?

Yves put down the violets, and kissed her cheek.

'You need to start to think about your creams. You could do one with a violet scent.'

Daphné looked at the small flowers in the jar, the scent of them sweet and slightly sickly now she knew the mythology of them.

'Perhaps I do need a task,' she said.

'Don't lose the light inside of you, Daphné. I know how much you loved work. If it makes you happy and will stop you from being sick with guilt, then start tomorrow.'

She felt tears spring to her eyes, as she took his hand.

'Why are you understanding? How can you be so true, and me so unworthy?'

'Stop,' he said and he kissed her mouth. 'I don't want to hear any more of that. My father made his choice and paid for it with his life. I made mine and every day I arrive home so thrilled you are inside it, and my heart.'

His growing confidence was soothing to Daphné. She liked it when he was firm, but he was never cruel. It was as though every time they lay in each other's arms, he grew stronger and more certain about life.

Yet Daphné couldn't lose the feeling she was being judged by Giles, that he was watching them, planning their downfall.

Perhaps Yves was right. She should do something with her time, and the creams did sell well in France.

'The problem with the creams is they have a short shelf life,' she said, picking up Robert, and kissing his fat cheeks. 'I need to find something to put in them to make them last longer so I can send them back to France and even beyond. Imagine if I could sell them in London?'

Yves kissed her shoulder. 'Let's speak to Doctor Aberle and see what he thinks. He might know of some element we can add.'

Daphné looked up at him and smiled. She liked him using the word 'we'. It was so loving, and inclusive. Giles was only ever about what he would do, as though Daphné had brought nothing to the recipe or the success of the creams.

The next day, she had Dr Aberle and his wife Greta to the house for lunch, where Robert sat on Greta's knee, charming her with his boisterous demands for clapping games and sweet pastry tidbits, and Daphné showed Dr Aberle the creams.

He opened the jar, smeared a little on his hand and then sniffed it and looked at the jar's contents.

'This is nearly off,' he said and Daphné nodded.

'You need something called propylene glycol,' he said. 'If you mix it with the cream, particularly with botantical extracts, it will extend shelf life.'

'Where do I get some?' asked Daphné, feeling a surge of excitement. She could imagine neat rows of her Le Marche creams sitting in pharmacies across France.

The older man looked at her. 'It needs to be gently agitated into the cream, and then any fragrance added,' he said and Daphné nodded, listening.

'Where is your laboratory?' he asked.

The reality of her situation struck her, and her shoulders dropped. 'I don't have one,' she said. 'I was going to make it here.'

How silly was she? Of course she couldn't make it at home. She wanted to produce more product than Giles had produced at the shop, and she thought she could do it in her kitchen?

Dr Aberle must have seen the defeat on her face and he reached over and patted her hand.

'You need a laboratory, my dear, but don't despair, you can use a commercial science facility who will make your product to order, until you have enough to set up your own one day.'

Daphné smiled at him and laughed. 'I doubt I'll ever need to do that, but thank you for your faith in me.'

'It is Yves' faith in you that I trust. He is a very clever man, but not so good at being with people, yet you help him. His father was very kind to introduce you both and encourage you to be with Yves. His father must have been a wise man like his son, may he rest in peace.'

Daphné felt her skin prickle at his words, and she glanced through the window at Yves, who was outside with Greta and Robert, looking at the erlicheer that was waving in the breeze.

What tales had Yves spun to Dr Aberle and Greta about her and their son Robert? Did it matter? All that mattered now was that they were a family, but she couldn't shake the feeling that perhaps Yves had embellished too much. And for what reason?

'Did Yves say anything else to you about us meeting?' she asked gently. 'It's just he's so reserved in his emotions and a wife likes to know sometimes that she matters.'

Dr Aberle threw back his head and laughed. 'Of course, a wife can never know enough that she matters.'

Daphné laughed also, not because it was particularly funny but because she wanted the old man to tell her more.

'He said to me that he met you and fell in love the minute you shook hands at his father's shop, and that you were swept away by him. Having no real experience with men, he was very careful not to scare you but you soon wanted him the way a wife should.' The man looked at Robert, now in Yves' arms.

'Anything else?' she said lightly.

'Nothing else, besides his father being very sad at you leaving, but giving you his blessing. Such a shame his heart gave out when it did. He would have liked to have seen you and Yves so happy with Robert and another one on the way.'

'Another one?' Daphné shook her head.

'Of course, dear, Greta was first to notice, and then Yves said you were ill to me, so I put two and two together.'

Daphné sat back in her chair and was still, listening to her body, and realised it was true. She was pregnant. She hadn't been sick with Robert, but this must be it, and her monthly was late, and her breasts swollen. Pregnancy disguised by grief and guilt.

She looked at the doctor. 'Do you think that a baby, while it's growing, takes on the emotions of its mother?'

'I am not a biologist, I am a chemist, but it would be hard not to assume that the mother's countenance must have some impact on the child.'

Daphné was silent and then the man patted her hand again.

'If this is true, then your baby will be the happiest child in the world, since its mother is surrounded by so much love and joy.'

The sound of Robert's cries entered the room, along with a gust of wind, causing her to shiver.

'Did someone walk over your grave?' asked Dr Aberle, laughing and Daphné said nothing as she took Robert from Yves and buried her face in his hair.

'I am so sorry I made him your father, and not Yves,' she whispered, as she took him up for his nap.

She could hear Yves laughing with Doctor Aberle downstairs and she closed her eyes for a moment, listening to the jolliness and the sound of coffee cups being placed on the table.

Yves had created a fantasy about them, where they were the opposites of each other. Did he wish he were more like the man in the story he told people? The confident, skilled man who wooed a scared little country girl into marrying him?

Part of her felt offended at his fairy tale. He became the hero and she was subjected to being the passive bystander in their life, where in fact, they were as mutually brave as each other when they married as strangers on Christmas Day in Calvaic.

That night in bed, Yves moved towards her but she turned over.

'What's wrong?' he asked, his hand resting on her back.

'Why did you tell the doctor all those lies about us?'

'What lies?'

'You said I was naïve and your father introduced us and that he was very happy for us.'

Yves lay back on the bed, removing his hand from her back. 'Would you have preferred me to have told the truth?'

Daphné lay on her side, staring into the darkness.

'I didn't like that you made me so pathetic,' she said softly.

'I saw you as you were, and pathetic wasn't it.'

'Then what did you see?' she asked, feeling tears of shame rising. 'A whore? A fool?'

'No,' came Yves' quiet voice in the dark. 'I saw a woman who deserved more than she thought she did.'

The tears fell and Daphné rolled onto her back, and felt for his hand and clasped it tightly.

'I'm pregnant,' she whispered.

Yves squeezed her hand back in return.

'Thank you,' he said, and they slept hand in hand, just like they did on their wedding night.

Chapter 27

Robert

Robert was having a late breakfast, and had just finished toast with apricot jam and a coffee, served by his new housekeeper, Mary, who came from the Phillipines, and had very large breasts. She was the mother of three children, who were being minded by her elderly mother, so she could send money home, and he had no doubts she was an illegal immigrant.

Robert was reading *Le Monde*, when Mary told him there was a boy who needed to speak to him at the front gate, and it was urgent.

He had gone to the front and had seen a scared-looking teenager with acne and a satchel bag crossed over his body.

'What do you want?' he called.

'Are you Robert Le Marche?'

'Yes, why?'

Then the boy reached into his bag, and Robert thought for a moment he was going to be shot. Instead, the kid pulled out a white envelope and handed it to him.

'What the fuck is this?' he yelled, taking it and starting to rip it open.

The kid turned and jumped on a bicycle that was leaning against a tree and rode away, not waiting to answer Robert's question.

He glanced over the papers, and then started again, trying to understand the claim, then he went inside and picked up his phone, his hand as shaking so much it took him three times to get the number right.

It went through to voicemail.

'You're suing your own father? For the loss of your allowance? You lazy, money-grabbing bitch,' he yelled and then he hung up and dialled another number.

This time it was answered.

'Good morning, Mr Le Marche,' came Edward's voice.

'You put her up to this, didn't you?' he yelled.

'I do wish you'd stop blaming me for everything that doesn't go your way, it's really quite boring,' said Edward.

'I owe her nothing,' said Robert.

'No, according to our figures, you owe her six hundred and sixty thousand euros or roughly forty hundred and eighty thousand pounds. Either currency will be fine.'

'What does she need the money for? She has the company.' Robert was pacing about the apartment, surrounded by his mother's life. It should have been Celeste here, not him and he hated his mother for her decision.

'It's the principle,' said Edward.

'She has no principles, it will be spent on her stupid lifestyle.'

'No, she has asked it be donated to the charities that your mother chose in her will, so you can donate to them directly, and send us a receipt, or you can send me the money and I will divide accordingly.'

'I owe her nothing,' Robert yelled so hard his throat hurt. 'Do you think that her schooling was free? She went to the best boarding school in Europe.'

'That was your choice to send her there, she should not be made to pay for something she had no decision in.'

'And those hospitals after she tried to kill herself, who paid for all of those?'

Edward was silent and Robert laughed.

'You didn't know about that, did you? Oh yes, she is quite the drama queen. Stopped eating at boarding school because the other students were mean to her or some rubbish, and then she tried to overdose in Paris. My mother pandered to her and of course Celeste manipulated her like she is doing to you now. You're a fool.'

'Pay the money by the close of business today, or I am going to the media with this,' said Edward and Robert heard the line go dead.

Then he made his final phone call.

'Paul Le Brun, it's Robert Le Marche,' he said and then he waited.

'Robert, what a surprise,' said Paul.

'I need a favour,' said Robert.

'Before you go any further, I think you should know that Celeste and I have finished our friendship. She became far too needy and was very threatening,' said Paul.

Robert rolled his eyes at the phone. 'I'm not surprised, my daughter is very unstable.'

'Yes,' answered Paul, 'but if I can help you, I will.'

Robert thought for a moment and then continued. 'I am very concerned about the state of the product of Le Marche since my mother died last month. As you know my daughter and her cousin were left the company, which was a huge shock, particularly to the staff, who were expecting me to take over.'

'Yes, I'm sure,' said Paul sympathetically.

'A few of them have contacted me and stated that the laboratories in London aren't making the product according to the proper safety guideline, something about them being told to save money, and they are concerned that the product being shipped into France is contaminated with a fungus, which if applied to broken skin could cause infection, or even death.'

Paul was silent so Robert went on.

'I am not sure what to do about it. I don't want to upset the company or my daughter, but I need to make sure that people aren't harmed by silly decisions in order to try to save money.'

'Hasn't this happened before at Le Marche? When you were in the company?'

Dammit, thought Robert. That had been twenty-five years ago; he wondered how Paul knew about it. Thankfully Daphné had managed to stop the creams from actually going into stores, but a few media outlets had picked up on it and they had watched a drop in sales that took years to recoup.

'It was in my mother's time, I worked in another area,' he lied.

'I am the minister for trade, so yes, it is important that I know if contaminated items are entering our country. I can't personally deal with it but I can get the right people to start looking into it. In the meantime, we will put a hold on the import of the creams until everything is cleared.'

'Thank you,' said Robert with a smile. 'I would hate the

Le Marche name to be destroyed by something like this. My mother worked too long and hard to see it ruined by two silly girls who are out of their depth.'

He put down the phone and smiled to himself.

Celeste, Sibylla and Edward could all go and die, as far as he was concerned at this moment.

He called for Mary to come into the living room.

'Yes, sir?' she asked.

'Take off your dress and come and suck my cock,' he ordered.

Mary stared at him, as though she couldn't understand what he was saying, but he saw a flicker of disgust in her eyes that turned him on.

'Do it or I'll have you deported,' he said. 'I know you're not legal.'

Mary started to cry, which bored him.

'Oh be quiet, I hate crying,' he said and he waved his hand at her. 'Go away, I was only joking.'

Mary scuttled from the room, and Robert sat on the sofa and thought. He had money, he had a wonderful home, but it wasn't quite enough. Nothing was ever enough for him, and he wondered what else he could do to hurt Celeste. He had one thing he could use but it was so dynamite that he knew he had to save it for the right time. He didn't want to waste all of that wonderful shock that would rock her world.

He called out to Mary again, asking for a coffee, but she didn't answer. His throat already hurt from yelling at Edward, and so he got up and went to look for her.

There was no sign of her until he found a note, written on his mother's stationery, stuck to the fridge.

Go suck your own dick. I quit.

The note made Robert laugh for the rest of the day, and then he rang the immigration department to report an illegal person from the Phillipines, who lived over in Corbeil-Essonnes, and gave them all the details he had on her, including her bank account, where he had paid her wages.

Chapter 28

Daphné heaved herself off the kitchen chair, as the sounds of Robert came down the stairs.

'I'll go,' said Yves, taking his soapy hands from the sink and drying them on a towel.

'You cooked dinner and did the dishes,' she said, 'I can't have you do everything, people will think I'm a terrible wife.'

'No, people will think you're days away from having a baby,' said Yves before kissing her head.

Daphné sat down again and smiled at him gratefully. 'Thank you,' she sighed.

Yves took the stairs two at a time, buoyed by the scent of Christmas in the house, and the sense of purpose. Life seemed almost too glorious to believe.

Daphné had just sent off the first shipment of creams to Paris, all with a shiny new label on the front, the new preservative in the lotion to keep the cream viable for longer, and bearing the new violet, rose and lemon scent.

But the pièces de résistance were the elegant, bevelled, glass jars with the brass lids copied from one that Anna had found in a Paris flea market, and had sent to Daphné as a sample.

A glass factory in Zurich had made them for a fraction of the cost that a French company had quoted, adding sophistication to the simple creams.

Yves had gone to Paris with her and Robert to sell the creams, and he had put the Paris apartment on the market, hoping for a quick sale.

All the furniture had been sold or sent to the junkyard, and all that was left was an empty shell where Daphné had lost her innocence and found a life.

There was a peace in Yves' world that he hadn't known before. When he had lived in solitude, too afraid to truly exist, he had thought that was peace but now he knew he had been mistaken. Peace only comes when you are satisfied with your life, or choices, or that exact moment that you are experiencing.

He opened the door to Robert's room, where the child was standing in his crib, his red face roaring in anger.

'Hello,' said Yves gently, and lifted the boy up into his arms, and slowly rubbed his back.

Usually Robert would only let Daphné soothe him, as though he knew his parentage, and this was Giles' last way of exercising some control over his son, but now, Robert leaned his hot, tear-stained cheek against Yves' shoulder and sighed heavily with the weight of his sadness.

'It's all fine,' whispered Yves. 'Soon you will have a brother or a sister, and you will play together and love each other very much, just as your mother and I love each other.'

His mind tripped backwards to his own parents, and their stifled existence, bordered by expectations and disappointment. How did Daphné ever fall in love with his father? He had never understood it, and it still seemed like a mystery. But what was being 'in love'? He knew Daphné loved him, but he didn't think she was in love with him. Perhaps that was for innocents like himself?

Every move she made, every word, every new part of herself that she revealed to him was like a new treasure. Slowly, he was collecting them, each foible was a jewel, each quirk a charm bracelet, every smile a brooch to be worn with pride.

Robert snuffled into his chest, and he felt the child's breathing slow and his chubby body became heavier in his arms. He kissed the boy, smelling the scent of his skin and rocking him back and forth in the quiet of the darkened room.

This was peace, he thought and he could not think of anywhere he would rather be right now, than with this child in his arms.

* * *

Daphné gave birth to Henri Yves Le Marche on New Year's Eve. It was an easier birth than Robert's, with the midwife in attendance for the last part, although later Daphné had said she could have done it all by herself.

Yves didn't disagree. Daphné was proving to be an expert at whatever she took her mind and hand to. She was the most naturally gifted person Yves had ever met.

'Do you wonder what you might have been if you had had a proper education?' he asked her once, as she poured over a book of fragrances, while breastfeeding Henri, and peeling an apple for Robert.

She had looked up at him and smiled. 'But I am everything

I ever wanted to be, so how would more school have changed that?'

Yves' work was busy, and he had been promoted. He knew that having a pretty wife and two boys went a long way to boosting his career, and Daphné was always ready to entertain, or come with him to boring law dinners, leaving the children with Greta, or one of the older women from down the road.

He knew Daphné was playing a role when she went to these events, never mentioning her growing business of Le Marche creams that were now being stocked in Zurich as well as Paris.

Soon she would be making as much money as he made, and he found he didn't mind at all. He didn't particularly love his job, and Daphné loved hers so much that he wondered if in fact they should swap roles.

Daphné laughed when he casually mentioned it to her one morning.

'Imagine what people would say if you were the house-wife?' she laughed.

Yves just laughed with her, but the more he thought about it, the more he imagined the life he would lead with the boys. He loved Henri and Robert equally, which surprised him, not that he would have admitted it to anyone.

Robert had settled down, Henri was a dream baby, and he thought about all the things he and the boys could do together as they grew older. All the things he and his father never did. Build tree houses—not that he knew how, but he could learn, he told himself—or read them the classic stories of his childhood that got him through the painful silence of living with his parents.

He pushed Daphné to venture further with her creams than Paris and Zurich.

'I can't leave Henri while he's still feeding,' Daphné said and then he had an idea.

'I could go and sell it for you,' he said.

'You?' She started to laugh again. 'Buying face creams from a man?'

Yves shrugged. 'Why not? Women buy clothes from men.'

Daphné thought for a moment. 'How would you do it?'

'I could travel to different places and ask them to stock it for a period of time. If nothing sells then we will take it back at our cost; if they sell it then they become a preferred distributor.'

'And where will you go?' Daphné asked, her face intrigued and bemused.

'All over France for a start, and then—' he thought for a moment '—the world.'

'Your faith in the cream is very touching,' Daphné said.

'It's not the faith in the cream, it's my faith in you,' he answered. 'I think I can sell the cream and the woman as a package deal. The Parisian who moved to Switzerland to harness science for her product—it's a good angle.'

'You should be in advertising, not law,' she said, but she thought about it for a few weeks, and then, at the start of summer, she decided that she would try Yves' idea to sell more products.

Yves resigned from his job, taking a large amount of holiday pay and bonuses, and soon he was off to Geneva, Berne and St Moritz with the samples.

As the orders came in, Daphné doubled the laboratory's

output, but as Yves travelled for a week at a time around Switzerland, Daphné missed him more and more.

'I wish you could come home faster,' she said to him one night as she lay in his arms after making love.

'The trains take such a long time,' said Yves. 'Perhaps I should take an aeroplane between cities.'

'But they're so expensive,' Daphné said.

'But so quick,' countered Yves.

So it was decided that he could do twice as many places using a plane in a week, compared to a train, which meant he could be home longer at a time.

Yves had never flown before, but the first time he knew he was hooked. The ordered seats, and elegant travellers. He could even drink wine with his compartmentalised meal while up in the air, it was all so modern and exciting. His life with Daphné never seemed to stop giving him new and exciting experiences.

The schedule was proving to be a bonus, with their orders growing, and his time at home being more blissful than ever.

Daphné relished his time back, and developed new ideas for the brand, and even designed an advertisement like she had seen in a women's magazine.

'We can do this for next quarter,' said Yves, looking over the orders in the green ledger, and flicking ahead to the calendar in his diary.

'You're so organised,' Daphné said, kissing his cheek.

Yves blushed at her praise. He was still not used to compliments, but Daphné's were the ones that meant the most to him.

'I'm going to Bordeaux tomorrow, and then to see what I can do in Monte Carlo, so we will organise the advertisment when I'm back,' he said, writing a note down in his elegant hand.

'Monte Carlo?' Daphné exclaimed.

Yves shrugged. 'There are many older women trying to look younger in Monte Carlo, it seems the perfect place to sell Le Marche creams.'

That night Daphné was more passionate than she had ever been, leaving the light on so he could see her naked pleasure.

'You look so beautiful,' he said to her, admiring the blush in her cheeks, and the glow of her skin.

'That's because I'm in love,' she said, as she leaned down and kissed him, her breasts tempting him with their gentle touch on his chest.

'Don't ever leave me,' he whispered, as he pulled her to him, and moved to be on top of her.

'Never,' she said, their eyes meeting and, in that moment, he believed her.

* * *

The plane to Bordeaux arrived on time, and he rang to tell Daphné he was safely on the ground. She didn't answer and he assumed she was out with the boys.

I will call her from Monte Carlo, he thought as he set out to meet his scheduled appointments.

The plane for Monte Carlo wasn't full that afternoon, and he sat back in his seat, grateful for the empty space beside him. He had a good many orders in Bordeaux and was expecting Monte Carlo to be even better.

The whirring of the engine started and he saw the stewardesses strap themselves into their seats.

The plane started down the runway and he closed his eyes, ready for a nap between countries, when he felt the wheels shake beneath them, and the stewardesses looked at each other nervously, and then the plane veered off the runway.

The last thing Yves saw was the look between them, and then nothing. He only felt the heat, as the plane burst into flames.

Part Two

Summer

Chapter 29

Billie and Nick sat opposite Celeste in Nick's office.

'I told them there is no bacteria,' said Billie, her face red with frustration.

'I know, but they're insisting we have the last shipment recalled, just to be sure,' said Celeste, as Edward walked into the office.

'Paul Le Brun ordered the recall,' he said, looking pointedly at Celeste.

'That bastard, and I bet I know who put him up to it,' she said and she stormed out of the office.

Edward raised his eyes at Billie who shrugged. Robert's attacks weren't a surprise but all she could think about was the reputation of the company and her name, now that she was supposedly in charge of the laboratory.

'There is no bacteria in this lab, in fact Nick has made the process even more stringent since he started.' She smiled at Nick who looked pleased but embarrassed.

'Just doing my job,' he said, a red flush appearing on his neck.

'Then make sure you keep doing it, and keep it bacteria free,' snapped Edward and he turned on his heel and shut the door rather too firmly behind him.

'What's got into him?' asked Nick.

'He's a bit worried, I think,' said Billie, but the truth was she had no idea why he was acting so weird, and it always seemed to be around Nick.

Nick had settled in to his job easily and, within a week, he had the laboratory running seamlessly, and had tightened up production and all the staff were in love with him.

Billie noticed his eccentricities seemed less pronounced in London, or perhaps she was so pleased to see someone from home that they didn't matter any more.

Going to work was a pleasure, and even Celeste seemed to like him, although she regularly asked Billie why didn't she just take him to bed.

But Billie didn't want to ruin her crush by making it a reality. She preferred to dream about them living happily ever after and putting Daphné's secret formula together and improving it, then changing the world of skincare for ever.

However, Nick didn't seem to see her any differently than the girl that he used to work with back in Melbourne. They ate lunch together most days, and talked constantly about Le Marche and London, and went on the search for a perfect cup of coffee.

They were friends, and that was it, she decided. She would never act on her feelings and she didn't want to ruin their friendship.

But, sometimes she caught him looking at her in meetings, even when she wasn't speaking, and sometimes he seemed to seek her out just to chat, or with some small question about work that she knew he knew the answer to, but then nothing happened.

Billie constantly felt like he was going to the edge of the diving board, looking down, and then turning around and climbing down.

'Maybe he's gay,' said Billie to Celeste when she went to see her after the meeting.

'He's not gay,' Celeste answered, as she tapped viciously on her phone screen.

'How do you know?'

'I just do, he's not gay,' she said, not looking up from her task.

'He's thirty-five and never mentions a past girlfriend.'

'Edward is thirty-eight and doesn't mention one either, do you assume he's gay?' Celeste said, still not looking up from her messaging.

'Oh, I thought he was gay.' Billie laughed.

'He's not, he has a little crush on you, I think,' Celeste said and then put her phone down.

'Me?' Billie sat on the only other seat in the office, which was now half painted in an ecru, with navy edging on the walls.

Celeste had a large glass desk and an office chair, and a see-through plastic Louis-style armchair.

Billie was afraid to ask if this was it for the office decoration, or if Celeste planned to add any more pieces to the room as Celeste's confidence in her style was intimidating, especially since a photo of Billie from the awards night had landed her on a fashion website as a vintage style leader.

Billie knew nothing about fashion, nor did she have much idea about men either, she thought.

She had been about to question Celeste about Edward when the phone rang and Celeste answered it, then started screaming rapid French into the receiver.

Billie stood up to leave, but Celeste gestured wildly at her to sit down again.

Billie could only assume it was Robert, as she tried to catch some of the words she knew, but it was too fast and too angry for her to understand.

Celeste's office door opened, and Nick and Edward stood staring at her and then at Billie and Celeste then gestured for them to come in. Nick closed the door and lowered his head, as though he were at a funeral, which he may have been, thought Billie, as Celeste yelled bloody murder down the line.

Then she slammed down the phone and put her hands on the desk and looked up at Nick, Edward and Billie.

'We cannot let my father win, do you understand me?'

Her chest was heaving, her face was flushed, her hair tousled, and, in her black high-necked dress with her red lipstick, she looked formidable, Billie thought. She turned to Nick and saw the way he was staring at Celeste, and she realised that not only was he straight but he was absolutely enthralled with Celeste in that moment.

Her stomach dropped and she stared at her cousin again, just to ensure she was right. Celeste was now talking and Billie tried to concentrate on her words.

Nick had come away from the wall and was standing next to Billie.

'You said that he was deliberately attacking the business and that you would sue him,' Nick said.

'You speak French?' asked Celeste, looking slightly impressed.

'Yeah,' said Nick, with an embarrassed shrug. 'I wasn't trying to listen in, but you were quite loud.'

Celeste laughed, and Billie noticed how beautiful she was when she wasn't being self-conscious.

French? Nick spoke French? Billie wanted to shake him for not telling her but then, why should he have to tell her everything about himself? Their friendship was superficial at best, she thought, and she wondered why she was so stupid to have a crush on him.

Edward was standing next to the window with a scowl on his face, but Billie couldn't tell if it was about Robert or Nick.

'I can sue him all I like but that won't change the fact that he's a bastard,' she said as she sat down.

The room was silent, and then Celeste looked up at Billie.

'We need more than one lip gloss; we need something exceptional and ways to improve these products.'

She placed pushed forward the three best-selling jars of cream from their line.

The three stared at the jars, and then Nick moved them apart and stared at them.

'What are you thinking?' asked Billie, watching him. She knew this look on his face, the way his eyes squinted and he scratched his head, causing his hair to stick up, but not realising it was stuck up in the air.

Billie suppressed a need to smooth it down and waited for him to air his thoughts.

He picked up the first jar, read the label, and then did the same with the others and then looked at Celeste.

'You know your grandmother was quite brilliant, even if she didn't realise it,' he said.

'How so?' asked Billie.

'These creams already contain three different ingredients, three simple things that separate them and yet they're all perfect for different skin needs.'

Celeste shook her head and threw up her hands. 'I don't really think that's so brilliant, it's just her creams.'

'If you got your marketing figures, you would find the younger women buy this one,' he said, pushing aside a jar.

'The middle-aged women would buy this one,' he said, gesturing to another. 'And the older women, those who remember when Daphné was still a part of the brand, would buy this one,' he said, holding the original cream.

Celeste was nodding. 'That's true, I've already seen the breakdowns from marketing. So what's your point?'

But Billie stood up, excited. 'We already have the products, we just have to improve them, and then we can market it as three phases of ageing with Le Marche.'

Celeste was thinking, and she moved the jars around, as though she was a street hustler moving cups for a bet, and then she looked up.

'The stages of age with Le Marche,' she said aloud and she tapped the desk with a fingernail.

'Three women, three creams,' she said and then she clapped her hands. 'Each stage has the cream as the pièce de résistance and we create a suite of products to accompany it, for what women need for each new stage.'

'Exactly,' said Nick, looking pleased.

Celeste grabbed his arm. 'You're brilliant, you should be in marketing,' she cried.

'No thank you,' laughed Nick, 'I prefer the lab.'

'This will cost a fortune,' said Edward from the side of the room.

His words brought them down to reality, as Billie tried not to focus on Celeste's hand still on Nick's arm.

'He's right,' said Nick.

'What about if you and I go through the costs with the savings from the discontinued lines and we try to see what we can come up with?' she asked Edward.

'We can try but it's an enormous investment,' he said, less aggressively, and he paced the room, his arms crossed. 'It's a bloody good idea, Celeste, and it would be a fantastic opportunity to relaunch you and Billie as the new Le Marche brains.'

He looked up at Billie and then at Celeste. 'Your grandmother would be proud of you,' he said and he walked to the door. 'I'll get the figures and we can meet tomorrow, OK?'

Celeste nodded and smiled and, when Edward left, she walked over to Nick and kissed him on the cheek. 'You're a saviour,' she said, as Nick turned red.

'I have to go to a meeting,' lied Billie and she rushed from the office and went into the bathroom, and locked herself in a stall.

She was so stupid for bringing Nick here, of course he would fall for Celeste. Why would he have meatloaf when he could have filet mignon?

And Celeste's silly idea that Edward liked her just made

things more awkward at work, she thought, and she had such a desperate need to talk to her mother that she burst into tears.

Why was she in this city? To prove something to herself, her mother, her father, her cousin, her uncle or her dead grandmother?

And she left the bathroom, got her handbag and her jacket and went home to call her mother.

Chapter 30

Dominic Bertiull was proving to be fascinating company. He was knowledgeable about business, he paid her compliments on more than her looks, but what intrigued her the most was that he hadn't yet tried to take her to bed.

They had been on four dates to dinner, where he didn't balk at her ordering the vintage Krug champagne, or when she sent back her soufflé twice, and they stayed for an extra hour because of her request.

They could talk for hours, but he didn't make a single pass at her, and it was driving her mad. Usually men would try to seduce her from the minute they laid eyes on her but Dominic wanted to know about her, and the more questions he asked the more she told him. He was wise, thoughtful and very inquisitive.

'Tell me about your mother,' he asked, as he sipped his espresso.

Celeste thought for a moment. The usual snappy one-liner about having a model mother who couldn't mother didn't feel right. Matilde had been trying more since she had found out how awful Robert had been, and while Celeste appreciated the concern, it did feel unfamiliar and uncomfortable.

'My mother is a divorcée who lives in Nice and plays tennis a lot,' said Celeste, smoothing out the napkin on her lap.

She had dressed for sex tonight, in a chiffon cocktail dress that was cut so it showed off her svelte shape and highlighted her long legs.

'Are you close?'

'No.'

'And your father?'

'Is a prick,' said Celeste with a smile.

'OK,' laughed Dominic. 'Why?'

'Because he's angry I got the company. He wanted to sell it off and buy prostitutes and yachts with the money, and now he can't because I'm going to save it.'

Dominic was silent. 'Perhaps he thinks your company isn't worth saving,' he said finally.

Celeste felt her loyalty to Daphné rise, and she folded the napkin and placed it on the table.

'The company is worth saving, we're already in motion to make exciting changes.'

'Oh yes? Such as? Tell me your grand plans.'

His bemusement annoyed her and she picked up her clutch purse.

'I'm ready to leave,' she said and she pushed back her chair and stood up.

'Oh don't be silly, I was teasing, I'm sure you have wonderful ideas,' he said not moving, but Celeste felt a chill down her spine, and instead she just nodded.

'Goodnight, Dominic, thank you for the dinner,' she said

and she turned and walked out of the restaurant. She stood on the kerb, and hailed a taxi.

'I can take you home,' she heard him say, but she didn't turn around.

'No thank you, I have plans for tomorrow, and I have to be up early,' she said, as a car pulled up to her.

'Celeste, please, I didn't mean to insult you,' he said.

Then she turned and looked at him, their eyes meeting.

'I don't know what you meant but I know I don't like to be made to feel like I'm ridiculous and stupid. If I wanted to feel that way, I would have dinner with my father.'

She opened the door to the taxi, and sat back in the seat, while Dominic stood outside on the kerb, his face expressionless.

'Mayfair,' she said to the driver, and the car pulled into the traffic.

* * *

It was Saturday morning, and Celeste woke with a bad headache. She thought about cancelling her meeting with Edward at the office, but instead dragged herself out of bed, being careful to not wake Billie.

She pulled on her jeans and loafers, and an oversized cashmere sweater. She then tied up her hair with a scarf, and didn't bother with make-up. The light in the bathroom was hurting her eyes, and she pulled on her sunglasses and left.

The sound of the traffic hurt her head, as she hailed a taxi, and headed to the office.

Edward was already in the boardroom, dressed in jeans and a hoodie, looking like his naughty twin brother, surrounded by stacks of paper, and two laptops open, and a stack of freshly sharpened pencils.

'Good morning,' said Edward, as Celeste tried to summon some enthusiasm.

She took off her sunglasses and squinted in the light.

'A little hung-over?' he joked, but she said nothing.

Of course he would assume she was hung-over, like Dominic thought she was a silly fool playing businesswoman, and her father thought she was a bon vivant, not that he could cast any aspersions.

A roll of nausea came over her, and she swallowed to still her stomach.

She knew what was coming, and she knew she had to leave soon.

'Can we hurry up?' she snapped.

'OK,' said Edward, looking upset.

Celeste was about to apologise, when she stood up, and tried to rush to the bathroom, but dizziness stopped her and she felt the vomit rise, then she threw up over the stacks of paper and then collapsed to the floor.

'Celeste, Jesus,' said Edward, who was on his knees by her side. 'I'll call an ambulance,' he said.

Celeste shook her head. 'Migraine,' she whispered, and shut her eyes tightly.

'You need medication,' he said.

'In my bag.'

She heard him rifling through her handbag, and then he was back with a glass of water, and two tablets in his hand. He helped to put them in her mouth, and she swallowed them, and then lay back down.

'Let's get you home,' he said, but Celeste shook her head.

'Let me stay here until the tablets work,' she said.

She could hear Edward cleaning up her mess, and she tried to find the energy to say sorry but failed.

The tablets were strong, and she hadn't eaten yet, and she felt them coursing through her system, yet her head still felt like it was being slammed by a hammer.

'Come on, I'm getting you home now,' she heard Edward say after a while, as he helped her to her feet.

They were in the elevator, and the motion was making her feel sick again, and she covered her hand with her mouth.

'Here you are,' he said, holding her around the waist and he produced a waste-paper basket for her to be sick into.

She wanted to laugh at his ingenuity but instead she retched, grateful they were only on the fourth floor.

They walked through the foyer, and then Edward settled her in a seat downstairs, as she heard a whistle outside.

'Come on,' he said and Celeste somehow managed to walk down the stairs, even though her legs felt disconnected from her body.

She fell into the seat in the cab, and the last thing she remembered was Edward saying her name and then nothing else but silence.

When she woke, she was in what she assumed was Edward's bed. The room was darkened, but she could make out the shape of the furniture. She was still fully clothed, with a mohair rug over her legs, and there was an empty bucket by the bed, and glass of water, which she sipped slowly.

Her migraine medication was powerful, especially with a

stomach filled with alcohol from the night before and nothing else.

She wanted to feel embarrassed but she didn't have the strength. Instead, she sat on the edge of the bed and saw that Edward had only undressed her feet, with her loafers lined up next to the bed. There was something about this deliberate attention to detail that made her smile. She walked to the door and opened it, the light hurting her eyes for a moment. She closed them, and then opened them slowly, allowing them to get used to the shock, and then she looked around the space.

A warehouse by the river, she noted, and she smiled at his orderly taste. Two matching armchairs, and designer sofa. Lamps from a generic store, but nothing tasteless, and no art or photographs to be seen on the tables.

The only real life in the room was a floor-to-ceiling bookshelf, filled to overflowing with books of every size and colour.

'Hello there,' she heard and Edward walked from behind the bookshelf, wiping his hands on a tea towel.

'Hi,' she said, and she shook her head. 'I am so, so sorry.'

'For what?' he asked, his face surprised.

'For vomiting on your work, and for obviously passing out, and for you having to bring me here.'

Edward just smiled. 'That's what friends are for, aren't they?'

Celeste blinked a few times, as she tried to understand what he had said. 'Are we friends?'

'I like to think so, even though we work together. It is friendly, isn't it? I mean, it is for me,' he said with a shrug.

Celeste felt herself smile.

'You've been asleep for the past six hours,' he said. 'Are you hungry?

She thought for a moment and then nodded. 'I am.'

'Then sit down. I've made Amatriciana pasta and I have a lovely bottle of cheap and cheerful plonk from Spain that will match it perfectly.'

Celeste sat on the sofa, and sank into the cushions. Edward thought he was her friend, which would mean he was her first ever male friend.

But, more than that, it felt quite nice to be looked after for once in her life, and there to be nothing given in return except company.

Chapter 31

Daphné, Paris, 1971

Yves' death hardened Daphné, as though cutting off the supply to her love.

She went through the motions of parenting, but, whenever possible, she let others look after her sons.

It was too painful to see Robert looking for Yves, or the way Henri was turning into his father's doppelgänger.

So Daphné worked, and the more she worked, the more the business grew, and eventually, she was what others would consider to be a successful businesswoman.

So she did what all the other successful men did and sent her children to boarding school in Allemagne.

Henri was twelve and Robert was fourteen, and neither of them wanted to go. Robert was stoic, showing nothing of his emotions to her, but Henri was inconsolable.

'Look after your brother,' was all she said when she said goodbye to them at the gate, after they were all settled into their rooms.

Robert turned and walked inside, but Henri had watched her get into her car and drive away, her tears hidden until she was out of sight.

They had been there for a month, with a weekly phone call permitted and letters written home every Saturday. They seemed fine, if not distant, she thought, and part of her missed them but part of her was happy to not have them in her way.

Being a parent was so difficult and she constantly felt torn. She needed Yves, and missed him every single day since his death, but the real reason she sent the boys to boarding school was because she liked to work, and she felt guilty for not enjoying parenting more.

Robert had always been a difficult child and, as he became older, he became nasty in his lashing out, particularly to Henri.

Daphné was at a loss as what to do with him. She had tried stern nannies, kind nannies, and a therapist who specialised in angry children, who said Robert needed a father figure.

But Daphné refused to remarry. She was married to her work now, and Robert would have to find his own father figure. Men chased her: golddiggers, diplomats, and other successful businessmen, but Daphné stayed alone. She arrived at parties alone, and left alone. There would be no more lovers for her in her lifetime.

The answer seemed to lie in a strict boarding school for boys in the Alps, with skiing lessons and a focus on routine.

Of course Henri would have to go also, but Daphné hoped that Robert would keep an eye out for his brother. Both of her boys were like their fathers, not that she ever told Robert who Giles was. Some things were best left hidden, she told herself, whenever she wondered why Robert was so different.

She tried to remember if she had treated him differently, but she couldn't say. All she knew was that it was easier to love Henri than it was Robert. He was easier in every way, as though he knew he was born into drama, and his role was to stay in the wings. But Robert? He was always at the centre of every fight, every altercation with a child at the local school, he had even been suspended for three days for putting drawing pins on the teacher's chair. Robert was difficult, and Daphné didn't have the time or energy he needed.

Now with a small office in Paris, and her laboratory in Geneva, Daphné was torn between the cities. She missed Paris, but Geneva was Yves' emotional home.

Paris reminded her of Giles, and guilt seemed to stand on every street corner, accusing her of ruining the lives of the two men she loved.

And she did love Giles for a time. Or was it more obsession?

When she looked at the photos that Yves had taken of her before he died, she looked like a different person. Happy, content and in love.

She wondered if she had ever looked like that when she was with Giles.

An invitation from Anna to visit in Paris and see their new store and apartment was enough of an excuse to leave Geneva.

Arriving in Paris, she went to her small but comfortable hotel near Rue de la Paix, so she could walk to the Karpinskis' new store. They had grown to be one of the finest new jewellers in Europe, worn by Princess Grace and Princess Margaret. The wealthy Europeans flocked to wear Max's elegant, yet modern designs, but Daphné refused to wear jewellery other than her wedding ring.

A note from Anna was at reception, inviting her to dinner at their apartment. Part of Daphné wanted to rest, but she wanted to see Anna desperately. Her own mother had died the year after Yves, and while it wasn't unexpected, the double loss had shattered Daphné's strength.

Later that evening, Daphné arrived at the apartment on Boulevard de Courcelles and the door was answered by Chantal, her mother's namesake and Anna's youngest child. At sixteen, she was already a beauty, with skin like a peach.

'You won't need any of this,' said Daphné, lifting the bag of sample creams she had brought for Anna.

'No, but I will,' said Anna appearing in the doorway and smiling at Daphné.

She was dressed in a chic purple shirtdress, with a beautiful brooch of a peacock attached to the front, and Daphné felt positively dowdy in her plain black dress.

'You don't need this either,' said Daphné admiringly. 'You look amazing.'

She had stopped caring about clothes after Yves died. Getting dressed was enough of a chore, without having to make choices. She chose black and plain and, while she thought this would be easier, it was suddenly proving depressing next to Anna in her splendour.

As she walked around their new apartment, Daphné marvelled at the elegance of Anna's choices in furnishings and art.

'Wealth suits you,' said Daphné, as Anna made them a drink with a silver swizzle stick in the gold-dipped glasses.

'It seems I was always meant to be rich, I just didn't realise it until we made money,' Anna laughed, gesturing for Daphné to sit on the silk sofa.

'The shop must be doing very well,' murmured Daphné.

'The store is very popular,' said Anna.

Daphné couldn't help notice the small correction. A shop is not a store, she thought, as she handed Anna the bag of samples.

Anna placed it by her side but didn't look at the products.

'How are the boys?'

'In boarding school,' said Daphné.

'Oh?' Anna raised her eyebrows.

'They've only just started; we will see how it goes.'

'Do you think that's a wise choice for Henri?'

Daphné felt herself bristle at Anna's question. She had seen Anna a few times over the past ten years, and suddenly Anna was an expert on Henri's temperament?

'Henri needs to be more stoic,' snapped Daphné.

Anna looked down at her drink, and slowly swirled the ice with her silver stick. 'If they were my boys, I wouldn't have them together unless I had to.'

Daphné felt a shiver at her words. 'What do you mean?'

Anna paused.

'Tell me,' Daphné demanded.

Anna stood up and walked to the door and shut it quietly.

'When we came to see you in Gstaad last year, Chantal saw some things that upset her. She spoke to me about it, and I was going to say something to you and perhaps suggest that Max speak to Robert, but you left for the emergency at the laboratory, and it was too late.'

'What did she see?' Daphné tried to remain calm but her insides were churning.

Anna looked Daphné in the eye. 'She said that Robert would hurt Henri.'

'Oh that's normal boys playing,' laughed Daphné. 'You never had that because Marina and Peter are older.'

But Anna shook her head. 'No, it wasn't like that. She said that Henri would shake when Robert came near him. That Robert would suffocate Henri until he couldn't breathe.'

Daphné swallowed bile that had risen into her mouth. 'He's just a little rough, I'll have a word to him,' she said.

'No, I don't think that's it,' said Anna and she leaned forward. 'Does Robert know about Giles?'

'No, and I will never tell him. He doesn't need to know,' snapped Daphné.

'Do you think that perhaps he knows there is something different between him and Henri?'

'How can he know? There is not difference, they even look similar.'

Anna held her stare. 'I meant the way he is treated.'

Daphné slammed her drink down on the glass-topped table, and stood up. 'I'm not listening to this,' she said.

'You must.' Anna was by her side, holding her arm. 'If I can't tell you, nobody can.'

'Tell me what? That I favour one son over another? That Robert hurts Henri deliberately, to get to me?'

'Yes,' Anna said.

Daphné wrenched her arm away. 'You are not my mother,' she hissed.

'I'm trying to be your friend,' said Anna, and Daphné saw tears in her eyes.

'I don't know what you're trying to do, but whatever it is, it's hurtful to my sons and me as a parent.' Daphné picked up her handbag and walked to the door.

'Don't leave it like this, I want to help,' said Anna, but Daphné was already out of the door and walking down the stairs.

She could hear Anna calling her name, but she was out on the street. Walking to her hotel, her mind filled with Anna's words, and flashes of times when Robert had made Henri cry. But that was normal, she told herself, as she went up to her room and sat on the bed.

She wished for Yves to come and tell her he would talk to Robert. She wished she could wind back time and tell Anna she was sorry. She wished Yves was Robert's father and not Giles.

She lay on the bed and closed her eyes, as tears found their way out and ran down her cheeks.

She would call Anna in the morning and apologise, and then she would call the boarding school and make sure the boys were safe.

But until then, she would cry. As she rolled over and stared at the empty side of the bed, the phone rang and she sighed. Anna had got in first, she thought, as she picked it up.

'Anna?' she said.

'No, is this Madame Le Marche?'

'*Oui,*' she answered.

'I am the school nurse at Allemagne, your son has had an accident and has broken his arm.'

Daphné felt herself gasp. 'Henri?' she cried.

'No,' said the nurse. 'It's Robert.'

'Robert?'

'Yes, apparently he fell down the stairs, only his brother saw it.'

Daphné shook her head. Anna must have been wrong, she told herself.

'I will return at once,' she said.

'He has a cast on and will be fine. Perhaps call him tomorrow and then come for a visit?' said the nurse. It was more of an instruction than a suggestion and Daphné acquiesced.

'There is one thing that the headmaster wants to discuss with you upon your return though,' the nurse said.

'Oh?' Daphné's stomach dropped even further.

'Robert says that Henri pushed him, but Henri denies it. Is that something that seems out of character for either of them?'

Daphné closed her eyes as she thought. 'Robert can be dramatic, and is very competitive with his brother. I am sure he fell when they were playing, and Robert wants someone to blame.'

'I will let the headmaster know,' said the nurse, sounding relieved. 'Don't worry Madame Le Marche, we will take excellent care of your son.'

Daphné carefully replaced the receiver and sat with her hands in her lap.

Anna must have been wrong, she thought. If Henri pushed Robert, then they were just brothers jostling and playing and nothing more. She went to bed feeling satisfied that Anna was overreacting, and brothers were just brothers.

Chapter 32

Nick

Nick rode his bicycle home to his little flat near the office of Le Marche, weaving through the traffic, thinking about the night ahead. He was facing another night of takeaway curry and watching reruns of *Myth Busters* and then tomorrow, on a Saturday, he had planned the exciting task of doing his washing at the laundromat.

He thought coming to London would make him braver and pull him out of his comfort zone. Instead, he was living exactly as he had in Melbourne. Still pining after Billie, who was far too young and beautiful for him, except now he worked for her. And she was his best friend, actually his only friend in London.

Perhaps he should leave and go back to Melbourne, he thought, as he arrived at his flat and walked his bike up three flights of stairs.

Inside the flat, he hung his bike up on the rack he had attached to the wall, and turned on the lights.

Everything looked so drab and depressing, he thought. He really must get some more homewares—maybe Billie could help him with that? That might be a nice outing to take together? He thought about texting her with an invitation to go to Ikea tomorrow, but then he had heard she went home early, so he left it.

He'd ring her tomorrow, he thought.

He washed a few mugs with half-drunk cups of tea in them, turned on the television and then ordered a chicken tikka for home delivery. Feeling adventurous, he added some naan bread to the order. He sat on the sofa and stared at the television screen.

He hated Fridays. It would be two days until he saw Billie again. Sometimes they did things together at the weekend. They went to a movie once, and another time they went to see the Changing of the Guard at Buckingham Palace, but mostly their socialising was confined to lunch hours.

Billie was different to Celeste, who was showy and confident in herself and her role in the business, but yet Nick saw what Billie brought to the company. She was more than just a scientist, she was a strategist and had business skills, even if she didn't see them.

The knock at the door stirred him from musing about Billie. He answered it, and paid for his dinner, then took it straight to the sofa, and ate it out of the container, using the plastic fork that was wrapped up in a cheap napkin.

He flicked the channels on the television, taking a chance and spurning *Myth Busters* for a documentary about penguins.

As he watched the penguins search for the smoothest stone to woo a mate with, he thought about what he could bring to Billie. Smooth stones weren't the answer, but smooth waters perhaps. Stability and calmness?

There had been no indication of anything from Billie aside from friendship, and yet he couldn't stop thinking about her. He thought about her in Melbourne and now he thought about her in London.

Was it just chemical attraction or was it love?

He would go and see her tomorrow, he decided, and once and for all find out if he was manipulating the data or if it was the real thing.

Love hadn't hit Nick before. A few quick relationships, where the women soon tired of his eccentricities and he soon tired of their games. That's why he liked Billie. She was straightforward and uncomplicated and she laughed with him at his oddities, not at him.

Filled with a desire to see her, he picked up his phone.

Was it too late to call? What was his excuse?

No, he would leave it to the morning, he decided, and went to bed to dream about offering Billie stones shaped like letters.

It was only when he woke that he realised what they had spelled out in his dream.

Light.

Was she his light? Was he her light? What the hell did it mean?

There was only one way to find out. He picked up the phone and dialled her number.

'Hey,' she answered, less than warmly.

'What are you doing?' he asked, feeling like a teenager calling his crush for the first time.

'Reading my grandmother's journals, or at least trying to,' she answered.

'How's that going?'

'I'm unsure. They're in French. Right now I can't work out if she's saying we should put a roof on our face or a window on our head.'

This was his opportunity, he thought.

'I'll come and help you,' he said. 'I can bring coffees and we can research together. You know I love to research things.'

Billie was silent on the other end of the phone. 'OK, but Celeste isn't here, in case you're wondering. She's working with Edward and is probably going out later with the guy she's seeing.'

'I wasn't coming for Celeste,' said Nick, wondering what she meant.

'Oh? You seem to be quite smitten with her,' said Billie.

Nick was confused. 'Do I? I just think she's fairly remarkable, that doesn't mean I am desperately in love with her.'

There was a pause. 'Yes, she is remarkable, considering what a dickhead her father is.'

'So can I come over?' he asked, his fingers crossed.

'Sure,' said Billie, and Nick did a small fist pump in the air, which was entirely unlike him and slightly embarrassing, but it felt so right that he did it again just to celebrate his success.

Chapter 33

Dominic

The air was cool, and the wine crisp and, from his yacht, Dominic could see the lights of Nice and his mind strayed to Matilde.

His mind strayed to Matilde more often than it should, especially since he was seeing her daughter, not that anything had happened between them. Celeste was prickly and wary, which was understandable with her pig of a father, but on the odd occasion he saw a glimpse of her mother in her. The way she looked vulnerable when she spoke about anything remotely emotional, and when she spoke of her sister. She had only mentioned her once, but the pain on her face had hurt Dominic's chest and he had wanted to hold her for a long time.

Yet he couldn't bring himself to touch her. Not when he couldn't banish Matilde from his thoughts.

When he returned to Paris, he had sent her a case of Krug and a can of tennis balls, and his phone number.

She had sent him a text.

Don't you need your balls?

He had laughed and had texted her back.

They're all yours.

He waited for her reply, feeling like a schoolboy.

Lucky me.

And that was as far as their communication had gone.

Then he met Celeste, or, if he was honest, he had sought her out with the intention of finding out everything he could about her plans for Le Marche, including the secret formula, and then make the deal, but he just couldn't do it.

She was fragile, and she worried him. There was a distant look on her face at times that he couldn't break through and he knew it wasn't his place. He wanted to call Matilde and tell her to come and make sure her daughter was safe, but how could he?

Music pumped through the speakers on the yacht, and Dominic watched as two girls, hired for the occasion and wearing tiny bikinis, danced seductively on the deck, as his guest, a Chinese billionaire and political advisor, cheered and drank his champagne from a wine glass.

He stared at the coastal lights, trying to work out which one might be Matilde's and wondered if she was awake.

The girls were making out with the billionaire now, and Dominic nodded at one of them to take him downstairs to the cabin. He was close to making another fortune on a deal if the man committed to investing in Dominic's proposal.

A few well-timed photos of the man and the girls would be all the signature he needed and he drained his wine and signalled for the deckhand to come to him.

'Get me the speedboat,' he ordered. 'And take me into shore.'

The deckhand rushed to Dominic's bidding and soon he was speeding across the water and into dock in the harbour.

'Shall I wait?' asked the deckhand.

Dominic alighted and checked his watch. 'No, it's late. I'll call in the morning. Tell Mr Zhào that I had urgent business to attend to, but that I will contact him as soon as possible.'

The deckhand nodded and expertly backed the boat from the dock and soon Dominic was standing alone on the dock.

It was eleven at night, and he could hear a few people laughing from boats nearby.

He walked out to the road, got his bearings, and then started to walk up the hill to the houses that looked over the cliff.

This was madness, he told himself, but he couldn't stop walking. Cars passed him, taxis slowed as they neared him, but he waved them on. He needed to make this pilgrimage, to be sure of his intended destination. He could turn around any time. He had his phone on him, and his credit cards. He could leave, but yet he could not stop walking until he arrived at her door.

The lights were on, and he could hear music. He listened carefully, trying to make out the tune. He knew the melody, and he hummed along, but couldn't place the singer.

A thought came that horrified him. What if she had company?

He was about to turn away, and take a few moments to think about what to do, when the door opened and there she was.

'What a surprise,' she said, not looking surprised at all.

'Matilde,' he said, feeling his mouth become dry. 'How are you?'

'Tired,' she said and she opened the door wider and gestured for him to come inside.

'How did you know someone was at the door?'

'Tarot told me,' she said.

'The cat?' He looked around.

'No, the cards,' she said and he saw a spread of richly coloured cards on the table with an empty wine glass next to them.

The song kept playing as Matilde walked around the room turning off the lights, and locking the front door.

'Bed?' she asked, but it was more of a statement.

He nodded, as she took his hand in hers. At the touch of her hand, he felt himself come to life, and he pulled her to him and kissed her.

Her arms snaked around his neck, and he thought he would never be able to get enough of her heady scent and soft mouth.

His hands pulled at her summer dress, but she stepped back and looked at him.

'Let's take this to bed. I'm too old for this standing up business.'

Dominic laughed, and he followed her down a hallway lined with art, and then into her bedroom.

The bedside lamps were on, and he could see the doors were opened to the small balcony, the sound of the waves crashing beneath them.

The bedcovers were cream, and the walls were unadorned. Not a single piece of art. All that decorated the room were plants. Large ferns and small pots of unusual plants he couldn't name.

The breeze was slowing outside, and he felt the mists of midnight coming through the doors.

He turned to look for Matilde, but she wasn't there.

'Matilde?' he called.

'In the bathroom, one minute,' he heard from behind a closed door across the hall, and he walked to the balcony and looked out. He wondered which yacht was his, and he found he didn't really care. This was always his destination.

'Dominic?'

He turned to see Matilde in the doorway, wearing a simple white nightgown.

'Are you coming to bed? There is a spare toothbrush on the basin in the bathroom.'

Dominic smiled and shook his head as he went to the bathroom and cleaned his teeth and then went back to her room, where she sat in bed, wearing glasses and flicking through her phone.

He felt stupid as he sat on the side of the bed and took off his shoes and clothes, but he left on his underwear, not wanting to assume, and got in under the covers and turned on his side.

'You look very sexy with glasses on,' he said.

Matilde peered over the top of them at him. 'Do you have mother issues? Is that why you're here?'

Dominic's laugh filled the room. 'No, I love my mother very much, but I have no Oedipal issues to deal with. I just find you absolutely fascinating. I can't stop thinking about you. I think you're my drug.'

Matilde took off her glasses and placed them with her phone by the bed, and rolled over to face him.

'It's been a long time since anyone said anything like that to me,' she said and he saw the same vulnerability in her face as he saw in Celeste's sometimes.

He leaned forward and kissed her gently on the mouth. Her minty breath made him smile, as he felt her body respond.

God he wanted her so badly he ached. His hands cupped her bottom as he pulled her close so she could feel him.

She took a sharp breath in and, with a surge of power, he was on his back and she was on top of him.

She sat up, her legs astride, and she smiled, then lifted her nightgown above her head.

She sat shamelessly, allowing him to see the creped skin of her chest, the sagging of her breasts and the softness of her belly.

His hands touched every part of her until she was moaning, and she tugged at his last item of clothing.

'Take these off,' she snapped.

Dominic laughed again, and did as she said and then pulled her to him so he was on top of her.

Holding the back of her head, he smiled as she opened her legs for him, and he eased inside her, rocking his hips back and forth, loving the way she closed her eyes with pleasure.

He felt her hands on his back, and he lifted onto his toes and forearms. 'Look at my cock inside you,' he whispered, as she opened her eyes and looked down at their bodies.

'God,' she moaned.

'I love to watch my cock slip inside you, Matilde,' he whispered in her ear. 'I think about fucking you all the time.'

He felt her breathing change, and her legs were wrapped around him now.

'Dominic,' she said and he felt her come around him and then he joined her.

He collapsed to the side of her when he finished.

'Jesus Christ, that was incredible,' he said and he opened his eyes and saw her staring at him.

'To be honest, I thought you would have lasted longer,' she said and he saw a glint in her eye.

'If you weren't so fucking sexy, then I would have,' he said, and it was her turn to laugh.

'I bet you say that to all the women over fifty you sleep with.'

That look was back, and he reached up and touched her lovely face.

'I've never been with a woman over fifty,' he said and they held each other in their gaze.

The sound of a bell came into the room, and then a thump on the bed broke the spell.

'Tarot will be very put out by you taking his side of the bed,' Matilde said.

'He better get used to it,' he said, surprising himself. This was the only place he wanted to be in the world right now.

Matilde went to the bathroom and then slipped back into bed, her nightgown back on.

'You won't be needing that,' he said, pulling at the lace.

'I can't sleep naked, never have.' She shrugged, as she settled down on her pillows.

Dominic played with her hair, twisting it around his fingers. 'Did the Tarot cards really tell you there was someone at the door?'

Matilde laughed. 'They did say I had a stranger coming

from across the sea, but I also saw you on the security camera, bobbing your head in time to the music.'

'What was that song? I knew it, but can't remember who sang it.'

Matilde frowned, and then smiled. '"You're All I Need to Get By",' she said.

'That's it,' said Dominic and he hummed a little, and Matilde joined in for a few bars.

'Who sang that?'

Matilde smiled and sighed. 'The only man who never let me down, the one and only Marvin Gaye. A man I loved introduced him to me and, whenever the nights are too long, Marvin helps me through.'

'But now you have me,' said Dominic, hating himself for sounding so needy.

'For now,' said Matilde and she turned over and clicked off the light.

He lay next to her, hearing her soft breathing as she drifted into sleep, and he wondered why she thought he wasn't a long-term investment.

It was then that Dominic Bertiull realised that he was in love for the first time in his life. He loved this mystery of a woman, and yet he hardly knew her.

He stared into the darkness, feeling the cool air in the room, and listening to the waves crash outside, comforted by Matilde's quiet breathing. A list of the things he needed to do ran through his mind.

He had to tell Celeste about his feelings for her mother. He had to tell Matilde he knew Celeste. He needed to tell Robert the deal was off. There was no amount of money that could buy the way Matilde made him feel.

He would tell Celeste first, and explain that he had fallen in love with her mother, and then he would tell Robert that the deal was off, and then he would come and take Matilde back to Paris with him. It was all so easy, he decided, and he rolled over and closed his eyes, feeling more content than he had ever been before.

Chapter 34

Billie

The apartment was empty when Billie woke, then she remembered that Celeste was working with Edward at the office.

She thought about ringing Nick and seeing what he was doing but then she remembered the way he had looked at Celeste and him not telling her he spoke French and not seeing how much she liked him, and she resolved to never talk to him again about anything other than work.

After yesterday's tears in the bathroom, she had gone back to the apartment to call her mother, but couldn't bring herself to ask why she had kept the family from her for so long.

She had enough to deal with, without having more secrets and confessions revealed.

A rare glimpse of sun was shining through the window in the study and, taking a cup of tea, she went and sat at Daphné's desk, and took out the journals. There were twenty in all and every one of them in French, with bits of dried flowers in between many of the pages.

Maybe the formula was for a perfume, she thought, but perfume was hardly going to revolutionise the cosmetic industry.

She leafed through them, picking up the odd word and sentence, enjoying the solitude.

The more time she spent with Celeste, the more she liked her. She was blunt and easily annoyed, but she was also smart about the business, and intuitive. But sometimes she saw a passing look on Celeste's face that she couldn't name. It happened when she was unsure of herself, or if she thought she had made a mistake.

She wondered what Celeste's life would have been like if she had been told she had the capability to be anything in her life, like Billie had been told.

Her phone rang and she picked it up, as she opened a new journal.

'Hello.'

'Morning.' The sound of Nick's voice came over the line and she made a face at the phone.

'Hey,' she said curtly.

'What are you doing?' he asked.

'Reading my grandmother's journals, or at least trying to,' she said, peering at a word.

'How's that going?'

'I'm unsure. They're in French. Right now I can't work out if she's saying we should put a roof on our face or a window on our head.'

As soon as she said it, she regretted it, as she knew what Nick would do.

'I'll come and help you,' he said. 'I can bring coffees and we can research together, you know I love to research things.'

Billie was silent. She didn't want to see him, but she needed help and she could do with a coffee.

'OK, but Celeste isn't here, in case you're wondering. She's working with Edward and is probably going out later with the guy she's seeing.'

'I wasn't coming for Celeste,' said Nick.

'Oh? You seem to be quite smitten with her,' said Billie, wishing she could shut up. She knew she was behaving like a child.

'Do I? I just think she's fairly remarkable, that doesn't mean I am desperately in love with her.'

His grownup words made Billie feel petty and small and she softened. 'Yes, she is remarkable, considering what a dickhead her father is.'

'So can I come over?' he asked.

'Sure,' said Billie, surrendering to her crush. She gave him the address.

When Nick arrived, she was wearing her soft sweatpants and a T-shirt, and one of the cashmere cardigans that were in Daphné's closet.

Since she didn't quite believe Nick's words about Celeste, she didn't feel she had to make herself any different to what she would normally wear on a Saturday. With her hair piled up in a topknot, she opened the door and took the coffee he held out to her.

'Come in,' she said.

Nick stepped inside, and looked around the room. 'Gosh, this is a bit nice,' he said.

'Yes, it's gorgeous,' said Billie, seeing the room through his eyes. The quiet elegance never failed to calm her, and she loved knowing her grandmother had chosen everything in the room. It felt like a way to get to know her in absentia.

'Come through,' she said, leading him to the study, where she had neatly lined the journals up on the desk, and had placed a pad and pencil on each side of it, with a chair for Nick.

'You're very organised,' he said with a laugh.

'What do you mean?' she asked.

'It's like an exam,' he said. 'I feel like I should have studied.'

Billie sat on the chair and sipped her coffee and she felt Nick look at her closely.

'It's not a criticism, it's a compliment.'

'It feels like veiled insult.' She looked him in the eye.

She felt a new boldness inside her, as she spoke her mind. Perhaps knowing he had a crush on Celeste, even though he claimed he didn't, was giving her the fuel to be honest.

'This isn't a test, I just wanted to be organised for your arrival. If that comes across as controlling, then I apologise. Please feel free to go. I don't expect you to give up your Saturday for me.'

Nick reached out and took her hand. 'Billie, I want to be here. I can think of nothing better than spending a Saturday with you.'

She said nothing and instead looked at the plastic top of her coffee cup.

'And I love the way you're organised. That's why I love to work with you. I'm just nervous I won't do you and your grandmother justice.'

His hand stayed on hers and Billie looked up at him, hating the tears in her eyes.

She wanted to punch herself for being so stupid. She didn't have a crush on Nick. She was in love with him.

And in her new-found boldness, she did what she always did at the start of a relationship, she ruined it.

'I think you should resign and go back to Australia.'

'What?' Nick was looking at her incredulously.

'I don't think we can work together any more,' she said, trying to summon the imperious tone that people said Daphné had when she spoke to staff.

'What have I done? Is my work not good enough? Why are you saying this?'

Nick looked so hurt that Billie felt like crying, but there was no way she would reveal herself to him, or anyone else. She dealt in science, not emotion.

'I just think this isn't working,' she said, knowing she sounded ridiculous.

'You do?' he asked softly. 'Billie, what is going on?'

His eyes were so kind and confused, she burst into tears.

'You're in love with Celeste, and I can't stand it, so you have to go away from me. Far away.'

'Oh, Billie,' was all she heard, and then she felt him take the cup from her hands, and pull her to him and kiss her gently and then pull away.

'Not everything has to be difficult, Billie. Sometimes the experiment just works, you know?'

'Am I an experiment?' she asked.

'No, Billie, I love you,' he said. 'I'm using that term because I know nothing about love except I know that I've loved you from the first time you told me I had my helmet on in the lab back home.'

'I have loved you from when I saw you had one leg of your trousers tucked into your sock,' she said, and then she kissed him in return.

'When you asked me to come here, I couldn't believe it, and then I saw you with Edward, and I saw the way he looks at you, and I thought perhaps I was deluded.'

Billie laughed and cried simultaneously, and held his handsome face in her hands. 'No, we're just two dorks who are pretty hopeless at reading other people, especially each other.'

Nick kissed her again. 'I'm not very good with people, but I feel amazing when I'm with you. That's why I was looking at Celeste with such awe yesterday. You two are so similar,' he said. He kissed her gently and then pulled away. 'But it's you I want.'

Billie stood and held his hand. 'Come to bed with me,' she said, wondering who she had become but liking herself more and more.

Nick's jaw dropped and he blinked a few times. 'Really?'

'Unless you don't want to,' said Billie, as coquettishly as she dared.

Nick's kiss told her what he wanted, and they somehow managed to walk to her bedroom, while simultaneously stripping each other's clothing off and kissing.

Billie ran her hands over Nick's chest, and kissed it, as they stood naked by the bed.

'You're so lovely,' she said, as she took him in her hands and felt his moan.

'It's been a while,' he said.

She looked up at him and smiled. 'Me too.'

'I haven't had many . . .' His words trailed off.

'Me neither,' she said, biting her lip to stop from laughing.

'I think we're meant to be together,' said Nick, as they fell onto the unmade bed.

'I don't think anyone else could handle us,' said Billie.

She felt his hands caress her body and then he slipped further down the bed, so she could only see the top of his head, but she could feel his mouth on her, his tongue rattling over and over, until she was clutching the linen sheets and arching her back with pleasure.

And then he was inside her, pinning her arms on the bed, and she thought she would die with desire.

'You seem fairly confident for a man who claims to not have had many lovers,' she whispered, then kissed his throat.

'You make me confident,' he said, as they rolled over, Billie on top of him.

Her dark hair had fallen from the topknot and hung around their faces like a curtain.

'I love you,' she said, looking into his eyes.

'I love you too,' he said and she knew it was true.

She moved slowly, enjoying the feel of him inside her, and then she pushed herself up, her hands on his chest, still moving but needing to see all of him.

The air in the room felt magical, with the soft sunlight making the room glow pink and coral. Nick watched her, lust and adoration on his handsome face, and Billie thought she had never felt more sexy or beautiful in her life.

When it was over, and they lay on the bed, naked, and touching each other, Nick moved her hair from her face and touched her cheek.

'I don't think I have ever seen you look more beautiful than you do now. You're glowing.'

Billie smiled and kissed him. 'That's because I'm in love.'

'Stay that way,' he whispered and then he kissed her and they began all over again.

Chapter 35

Matilde, Paris, 1985

It was late when Henri arrived at the apartment.

'Robert isn't here,' Matilde said when she opened the door. 'And I have no idea where he is. He's probably in some whore's bed.'

Henri didn't look surprised or ashamed at his brother's behaviour, instead he just stepped forward and hugged Matilde.

'I'm sorry Robert is such a prick,' he said.

Matilde pulled away and gestured for him to come inside.

'Shhh, Camille is asleep,' she said, as they moved into the spacious living room. It was opulent to the point of ostentatious but none of the heavy drapes and gilded furniture was Matilde's choice. It was Robert's money and he chose where and how they lived.

'Where is Elisabeth?' she asked, as she poured herself more wine, and found a glass for Henri and handed it to him.

She had tried to like Elisabeth, but she was a strange girl, and terribly nervous. She often told Robert that it was like being around a rabbit when they socialised together.

Henri's announcement he was marrying an Australian girl was seen as a betrayal by Robert, and with disinterest by his mother. Daphné was travelling most months, growing Le Marche and losing contact with her sons. She had only seen Camille a few times, much to Matilde's disappointment.

She had hoped for a doting grandmother to her daughter, but Robert had laughed at her complaints.

'She wasn't a doting mother, so why would she be a doting grandmother,' he had said bitterly.

But Matilde knew she loved her sons, and she loved Camille, she just wasn't very good at showing them.

She often wondered what had happened to make her mother-in-law so distant from those she loved, as though she was afraid of losing them.

Once, when Matilde suggested that Daphné take up an offer of a night at the opera with a widower she knew, Daphné had scoffed.

'I am bad luck to men,' she said.

Matilde wondered if this was why she remained at arm's length from her own sons.

Henri sat on the sofa, and adjusted the overstuffed velvet cushion, eventually giving up and putting it on the floor.

'Elisabeth is going back to Melbourne,' he said and then took a sip of wine.

Matilde put down her glass on the table. 'For how long?' she asked.

'Don't frown, you'll get lines,' he said, mimicking his mother, but Matilde ignored the joke.

'What's happened?'

Henri shrugged and then she noticed the dark circles under his eyes, and the state of his rumpled shirt, which was normally perfectly pressed.

He drained his wine, and then stood up. He walked to the window, opened it and sat on the sill and looked down.

'Henri?' Matilde jumped up and then walked slowly towards him.

He turned to her and took a joint out of his shirt pocket and lit it. He took a long drag and then held it to her. She shook her head and waited. He smoked for a while and then he turned to her, his back to the sky.

'I cannot give her what she needs,' he said, somewhat hopelessly and Matilde wanted to drag him away from the window.

'What does she need?' she asked carefully.

She felt like any fast movement would send him reeling in every sense.

'A baby, of course,' he said as his eyes became more bloodshot. 'She wants a baby and a little house, and sunshine and friends and family.'

'She can have all of that,' said Matilde.

'We have tried for two years, and nothing,' he said, putting his hands up, and knocking ash onto the carpet, but Matilde didn't move.

'Go to the doctor and get checked. There are many reasons why it might not have happened yet,' she said.

'See that's why you're so sensible,' said Henri.

He walked away from the window to the collection of records on the sideboard and pulled one out. He put it on, the scratching of the needle sounding like it was heralding the start of something Matilde couldn't name.

Music filled the room, and Matilde rushed to the door to protect Camille from the sound.

When she turned around Henri was dancing by himself with his eyes closed.

'You're stoned,' she admonished him, as Henri took her by the hand and spun her around. He then took her into his arms, as he hummed the tune in her ear.

'I love Marvin Gaye,' he said.

'I know you do, you gave me the album for my birthday,' she laughed, as he twirled her again, and then held her close.

They moved wordlessly, until Matilde felt the energy change between them. 'When will Elisabeth be back?' she asked, trying to bring him back into the room and out of his head.

Henri had always worried her. His moods were unpredictable and most of his despair seemed to be directed at himself, unlike his brother, who blamed anyone within a finger-pointing radius.

Even now he assumed that it was his fault that Elisabeth couldn't get pregnant, and she rubbed his back gently.

'You need to be kinder to yourself. Go to the doctor with Elisabeth, get a check-up, get the results and then make a plan. They can do amazing things now. That little baby Amandine was born a few years ago from a test-tube implant.'

But Henri wasn't listening. The music changed and the beat filled the room. He smiled at her.

'You're so clever,' he said. 'You always know the right answer for everything and everyone.'

Matilde was used to hearing her beauty praised but not her intelligence, and she felt herself blush.

'I'm just pragmatic,' she said, brushing away his compliment.

'And charismatic, and dramatic, and dynamic and ecstatic,' he said and twirled her with each word, until Matilde was laughing and wondering if she had inhaled enough second-hand smoke from the joint to feel as high as she did.

Henri had the sort of power that could make or break a party, and when he was good, like he was now, he was intoxicating. He was everything her husband wasn't, and she missed having fun with someone. She missed being twirled and told she was smart and clever, and then she did the unimaginable.

She kissed him.

Henri was still for a second and then he joined in her touch and soon they were on the carpet, Marvin crooning to them, as they pulled at their clothes.

It wasn't the best sex, but it wasn't the worst, she told herself later, but it was the touch she needed more than the climax. Henri called out Elisabeth's name when he climaxed, but she didn't say anything. She didn't think this was the start or finish of a great love affair. It was just two lonely people reaching out for a moment.

Afterwards, Henri sat on the carpet and cried. 'I am so sorry,' he said.

'What for?' She smiled. 'It happened and we will never mention it again. It was just two friends who found comfort in each other.'

'What should I do?' He looked up at her with tear-stained cheeks.

Her heart broke for him, and for Elisabeth. It wouldn't have been easy to be married to such turbulence.

'Go and find your wife,' she said. 'Make a little home, let her be with her friends, and work together to find a way to become a family.'

Henri nodded, like Camille did when she was being very sweet, and she leaned over and kissed his cheek.

'Go and find her,' she said, and Henri was up and at the doorway.

'Thank you for being my friend, Matilde,' he said and she smiled at him.

'But what about you?' he asked. 'My brother isn't a kind man.'

She shook her head slowly. 'I chose him and I married him. My vows are forever in the eyes of God.'

'What if there is no God?' he said. 'What if you're unhappy for a lifetime because of an imaginary friend's opinion?'

Matilde laughed. 'Then I will have to find out myself,' she said.

Henri gave her a broad smile, filled with affection.

He was so handsome, she thought, and she said a little prayer for God to look after him.

'Goodnight, Matilde.'

'Take care, Henri,' she said, and he closed the door.

Matilde pulled on her clothes and sat on the floor, listening to Marvin sing 'Trouble Man', and she wondered when she would see Henri again.

She moved to sit on the edge of the windowsill and she remembered her grandmother using the phrase '*l'appel du vide*'.

The call of the void.

She knew that Henri knew this call. She saw it on his face

when he sat on the windowsill. She knew he heard it in his poems, and in the silence between the notes that Marvin sang. She just hoped he would one day have a child whose laughter would drown out *l'appel du vide*.

Chapter 36

Edward

Edward was used to spending his nights alone, so having Celeste on his sofa, eating pasta, should have been jarring to his routine but she was surprisingly good company.

They talked, and sipped the wine, which Celeste said she thought was quite good for something so low cost, and he nearly believed her.

Then he made them cups of tea, which Celeste had turned her nose up at, but drank anyway, but black. She laughed as Edward's shortbread biscuit broke off as he was dipping it into his tea and he had to fish it out with a teaspoon.

And then he did the dishes, insisting Celeste not move from her sofa, and when he came back to the sofa, he found her asleep, her blonde hair falling over her face.

He sighed and looked at her. The wine and the medication were clearly not a wise idea, he thought, and he somehow managed, thanks to his regular gym routine to stave off the loneliness, to carry her to his bed.

He laid her as gently as he could on the bed, but she opened one eye.

'The wine,' she murmured.

'I know, I'll sleep on the sofa,' he said.

But she shook her head. 'No, sleep here.'

'No, I can't,' he said.

But Celeste waved a hand at him, as though she were swatting his words away.

'You can, don't be silly. I know you're in love with Billie, so I am safe.'

'What? No,' he said far too quickly.

'Yes, but you should know, she is in love with someone else, so you should try to look somewhere else,' she slurred and rolled onto her side.

She took his hand and pulled him to her. 'Come on, lie down and we can snore together, for evermore,' she said.

Edward lay next to her, the words spinning in his head.

Billie loved someone else.

He knew Celeste didn't mean her words to be cruel. They were clumsy and straightforward, like her, but he was grateful to know all the same.

He wasn't in love with Billie, but he could have been. He thought about his family's beliefs regarding his sexuality and his lack of confidence around women and he wondered why he couldn't bring to his personal life the focus and dedication he brought to his job.

But then he thought about Le Marche. He had been there for fifteen years and, while the money was fine, he could have done more with his career.

He could hear Celeste singing to herself. 'What are you singing?'

'A lullaby my mother used to sing to me,' she said, and she started to sing again.

'Go to sleep,' he said.

'You go to sleep,' she said, and continued her song.

Edward sighed in frustration. He was trying to have a crisis and Celeste was singing in his bed.

'Can you be quiet? I'm thinking,' he said crossly.

'About what?' Celeste leaned up on her elbow and stared at him.

'Work,' he said.

'Boring,' she said and collapsed on the pillow again.

They lay in silence.

'Do you think I'm beautiful?' she asked.

'You know you're beautiful,' he answered impatiently.

He didn't have the patience to deal with her insecurities after she had told him about Billie.

He rolled over and looked at her profile.

'Would you have sex with me?'

'What?' he screeched and nearly jumped off the bed.

'That's not an invitation, it's a question,' she said, sitting up and looking at him. 'I have been seeing a man and he is very attractive and we get along well. Well, I thought we did, but he hasn't touched me. He recoils from my advances, but I know he's straight. I don't understand. What is wrong with me?'

'Maybe he wants to be friends,' he said.

'I didn't think men and women could be friends, until I met you,' she said.

He could feel her sadness and confusion in the room, and

he reached out and took her hand. 'Celeste, there is nothing wrong with you.'

'I just want to be loved,' she said, her voice small in the semi-darkness.

'We all do.'

'Would you have sex me if you were him?'

'Constantly,' he said with a smile.

She laughed. 'That sounds very optimistic.'

Edward thought about what it would be like to be loved completely by someone and he squeezed her hand.

'Don't assume he isn't interested in you, Celeste, he might just be taking it slow.'

'I don't like slow,' she said.

'I've noticed.'

He let go of her hand and reached down and pulled the coverlet over them.

'Get some sleep,' he said and he closed his eyes.

Then he felt her hand in his and he smiled.

'Goodnight, Miss Le Marche.'

'Goodnight, Mister Badger.'

* * *

They woke late, but it was easy between them.

Edward made them coffee, and toast with boiled eggs, and he drew a face on hers, which made her laugh.

'My mum always did this when I was kid,' he said, enjoying her amusement at the sight.

'My mum used to draw me a face on a champagne bottle,' she said.

'Really?'

'No.' She looked up at him and laughed.

'I'll take you home when you're ready,' he said and, for a moment, he saw a shadow cross her face.

'Don't you want to go home?'

'Not really, I like being here,' she said with her usual candour.

He smiled and touched her shoulder. 'I like you being here also, we would be good room-mates.'

She nodded, and gathered her things.

They drove across London, to the apartment.

'I'll see you up,' he said, parking in the street outside.

'You don't have to,' she laughed.

'I do. You've been ill,' he said and he jumped out and opened her door for her.

Celeste hugged him when she got out of the car. 'You're amazing,' she said. 'The girl who falls for you will be very lucky.'

They walked up the stairs and into the elevator and rode in comfortable silence.

Edward had never been this content in the company of a woman besides Daphné, but she was more of a mentor than a friend. He saw much of Daphné in Celeste but also something that was entirely unique to her.

Daphné had never lacked confidence in life, but Celeste was more vulnerable than she let on, he thought, as they got to her door.

She pulled out her keys. 'Want to come in?' she asked, as she opened the door, and there, wrapped in a sheet stood Billie, with Nick in a pair of jeans and nothing else, holding pizza box.

'Hi,' said Billie, her face bright red.

'Pizza?' asked Nick, holding out the box to them, his face reddened also.

'No thank you,' Edward said abruptly, and turned to Celeste. 'Please get some sleep, and call me if you get sick again.'

'You're sick? What happened?' Billie tried to rush forward, but became tangled in the sheet, so she merely semi-swayed on the spot.

'Just a migraine, it's nothing,' said Celeste quickly. 'Thank you,' she said to Edward, but he needed to leave. Seeing Billie with Nick made him realise how lonely he was. He realised it wasn't even Billie that he wanted, it was the idea of her. He chose Billie to be his crush because she was suitable and she was like him in many ways but of course he should have seen she was with Nick. They were probably together before she came to London.

'See you tomorrow,' he said to the three. He turned to the elevator to press the button to go back to his uninspired life, when the doors opened and there stood Dominic Bertiull.

'Dominic,' said Celeste with as much surprise as he was feeling.

'What are you doing here?'

'I need to talk to you,' he said to Celeste, pushing past Edward.

This single act of rudeness caused him to break.

'Celeste, what the hell are you doing with him?'

'We've gone out a few times,' she said, and he saw her look down. So this was the man that would't sleep with her but wanted to talk business.

'You do know he's trying to take over the company with your father,' Edward said.

'What?' Billie and Celeste cried out in unison.

'Let me explain,' started Dominic, but Celeste was holding up her hand, and Edward saw tears in her eyes.

'You were using me for my father's benefit?'

'Yes, well, sort of, but it's not like that now,' Dominic said, looking exasperated.

'I think you should leave,' said Celeste.

'I can't leave.'

'Why?'

'Because I'm in love and I need to talk to you about it,' he said, tripping over his words.

Where was the smooth confident man that Edward had dealt with? This bumbling version of Dominic Bertuill wasn't anyone he had spoken to, or watched slash and burn companies over the years.

Celeste groaned, rubbing her temple. 'I have a headache, I can't deal with any declarations of love from you. We have had a few dinners. I don't know how you can be in love with me when we haven't even kissed.'

Edward moved forward as the colour drained from Celeste's face. She had a slight sheen of perspiration on her forehead, and he put his hand on her shoulder.

But Dominic didn't notice Edward's protective hand on her, instead he was shaking his head. 'No, no, it's not you.'

Celeste looked at Edward as though Dominic was crazy and he was beginning to wonder himself, when he stepped forward and took Celeste's hands.

'I need to come and tell you the truth about everything,

but the first thing you need to know is . . .' He paused and swallowed loudly, and then he looked around at them and then back to Celeste. 'I'm in love with your mother.'

And at those words, Celeste fainted into Edward's arms.

Chapter 37

Celeste

'Darling, I had no idea.' Matilde's voice came down the line, but Celeste was too tired to know if she was telling the truth about Dominic.

'It doesn't matter, Maman, I just thought you should know he was seeing me before you. I'm not sure he isn't still working with Papa.'

'Did you sleep with him?' Celeste could hear the strain in her mother's voice at the question.

'No.'

'Good,' Matilde said, but Celeste didn't know if that was because Matilde just didn't want to have to compete with her daughter.

'I have to go, be careful with him,' she said. She hung up and looked at Edward, who was sitting on the other side of her desk.

'She says she didn't know.'

Edward raised his eyebrows, but Celeste just shrugged.

'If my mother wants to be with him, then good luck to her, I just have to make sure we're protected.'

She sat back in her chair and rubbed her head tiredly. The headaches were getting worse, like they had when she was back at Allemagne.

'You should go home,' Edward said, his face worried, but he looked as tired as she did, she thought.

'Home? I don't have a home,' she said. 'Nick has been at our place every night this week. I'm thinking I should charge him room and board.' Then she sighed. 'I'm sorry, I know how you feel about Billie.'

Edward shook his head. 'I don't feel that way about her. She was an object of desire based on supposed similarities, but she and Nick are the perfect combination of beauty and the geek. I think I just wanted something that was close to Daphné after she died.'

Celeste peered at him. 'Were you in love with my grandmother?'

Edward laughed. 'No, but if she were fifty years younger and I didn't work for her, then yes, I think I would have fallen in love with her.'

'Why?' Celeste felt her left temple throbbing, but she wanted to know the side of Daphné that Edward knew and loved so much.

'She was . . .' He paused, trying to find the right words. 'Formidable. Like you when you're on the phone to your father.'

Celeste heard herself laugh loudly. 'Some men find that intimidating.'

'Some men, but not me. You haven't met my mum yet.'

Celeste pondered on his words later. *You haven't met my mum yet.* Did that mean he intended for them to meet? Did

Edward feel something for her? She didn't feel any frisson between them. They were friends and nothing more, but he was her only friend right now, since Billie was so enamoured with Nick.

Loneliness was something that Celeste was used to. She remembered the nights in the dormitory at Allemagne and the sounds of whispers around her, and no one talking to her.

She was known as the angry girl whose sister had died.

Wasn't that enough of a reason to be angry? When she looked back at the five years of constant bullying at Allemagne, she still wondered why the school was so lacking in empathy or kindness.

At times it felt as though she was being punished for Camille's death, not just by her parents for sending her to the school, but also by the school itself.

Remembering caused her head to hurt, and she tried to concentrate on the notes that Nick had left her for the new products, but she couldn't see the words clearly.

Rummaging through her handbag, she found the tablets, and the order of service from Daphné funeral.

Why had she been carrying it around with her, she wondered, and she took it out and smoothed the bent edges of the booklet.

A publicity photo of Daphné from her seventy-fifth birthday was used on the front, and she traced her grandmother with her finger.

She was so beautiful, thought Celeste, noting her perfect make-up and pearl studs in her ears. Her hair was set, and her lipstick was red. She was never afraid of wearing red lipstick, even as she aged.

'It brightens the face,' she remembered her mother saying to her.

More women should wear red lipstick, she thought, and then she picked up her phone and dialled, tapping her nails on the glass desk.

'Hey,' she heard Billie's voice.

'Red lipstick.'

'Is this code for something?'

'No,' Celeste said, standing up and walking to the window and staring out at the grey skies. She needed to see Paris and its particular light. The homesickness was so painful, she closed her eyes and leaned her head against the glass, the coolness relieving her headache for a moment.

'Grand-Mère always wore red lipstick. She had them in all different shades of red. It was her thing, but people were always commenting on her skin, they didn't notice her lipstick.'

'So you want us to create a red lipstick? We had already decided on doing a lipstick.'

'No, I want us to do a whole series of red lipsticks. The best colours for everyone's skin colour. Name them after wines or types of wines, something like that,' she said, thinking of her grandmother's wine collection.

'That's great, I'm going to talk to Nick and the team now,' said Billie excitedly.

'And then next year we can do a perfume collection, based on the ones in her room.'

'She was reading a book on fragrances; it's still on her bedside table,' said Billie.

'Great, I'll look at it tonight.'

'This is all so great, Celeste, you're a powerhouse of ideas,' Billie enthused, but Celeste felt too awful to accept the compliment.

'We still have a lot of work to do,' she said abruptly, as a sharp pain stabbed her behind her eye and she hung up the phone without saying anything more.

Everything seemed overwhelming. Dominic, Matilde, the business, her father, the new products. She sat in her chair, closed her eyes and felt her head thumping.

Maybe she should take some more pain relief, she thought, trying to remember when she last had the medication and then she reached into her bag and found the tablets. She washed them down with a cold cup of coffee and closed her eyes again.

Maybe she would just sit still for a while, she thought. If anything important happened, Gemma would let her know, and she felt herself drift into sleep.

'Celeste, Celeste?' She heard her name being called, and she tried to open her eyes.

There was a hand on her shoulder. 'Celeste,' the voice said. Gemma, she thought. She really should open her eyes, but they didn't seem to be connected to her body.

Then there was silence, and feet running, and then Edward's voice.

The sounds drifted in and out, as though she was turning her to head to a speaker and away again, and she tried to lift her hand to her face but nothing happened, except the pain in her was excruciating.

Edward was telling Gemma to call an ambulance, and she could feel his hand on her arm. 'Celeste, wake up, Celeste,' he was saying repeatedly.

She wanted to snap at him and say that if she could wake up she would, but she was helpless.

Then the pain came back again, and she wondered if there was a knife being put into her brain by an unknown party in the room and, with that, she passed out completely.

When she woke, she could hear the sound of strangers talking by her side.

Was she lying down? She couldn't be sure.

Was that Billie talking? She was saying something about medication, but someone else said it wasn't the medication.

Why didn't they just ask her? she wondered. She could tell them about the headaches, and the tiredness, even the heat in her face and tingling in her hands.

Why didn't anyone ask her?

And then she heard her mother talking in French and crying, saying she had to call Robert.

She didn't want to see her father. She tried to raise her hand, but then she heard Edward speak.

'I don't think Robert will do anything but cause her more stress at this time. Let's wait.'

And she felt herself relax at his words. Edward understood her, she thought, and she fell back into the darkness again.

Chapter 38

Robert, Paris, 1997

From the balcony of the apartment, Robert could hear Matilde's sobbing. It was a raw sound, like an animal in pain, he thought, and he was envious of her ability to weep like she did. He wished he could let the pain out like Matilde, but then he would need to drink two bottles of wine in one night.

'Robert,' he heard and turned to see Henri in the doorway. 'Celeste is calling for you.'

Robert lit a cigarette, not noticing the one already burning in the glass ashtray.

'You go, I can't right now,' he said. He took a long drag and blew the smoke out into the night air. It drifted across the light of Paris.

'Robert, she's asking for you,' Henri insisted.

'If she's asking for her father you should go,' Robert sneered.

Henri turned and walked back inside, where Robert could see him whisper to Elisabeth.

Dowdy, timid Elisabeth, he thought. No wonder Henri slept with Matilde. He hated them both so much. Why hadn't

Celeste been the one to die and he could have had Camille, and Henri and Matilde could be together?

Tears hurt his eyes, but he brushed them away, as he saw Matilde swaying towards him. He felt sick at the sight of her face.

She pushed open the door to the balcony and stood, leaning against the door for support.

'Your daughter is calling you,' she hissed.

'I told Henri to go,' he answered, looking out at the lights.

Everyone was in their happy little homes and he was mourning the loss of his beloved Camille, with his drunken wife, and disloyal brother. Life was cruel.

'Stop this, she adores you,' said Matilde. 'You're the only father she knows.'

'Perhaps we should tell Elisabeth and then she can have the other child she wants so much.'

Matilde's face dropped. 'Don't you dare,' she said.

They stood facing each other and then Robert put out his cigarette. 'Tell them to leave, they're not helping,' he said.

'They're helping Celeste,' Matilde answered.

He leaned on the edge of the balcony and put his head in his hands. He wished he could cry, but maybe Matilde was right, maybe he did have a stone heart.

It had been three months since Camille's death, and Henri and Elisabeth came to Paris as often as possible to help with Celeste and to ostensibly ease his and Matilde's pain, but the only thing that could help with that would be to wind back the clock and change everything so Camille could stay.

His mother hadn't helped much, caught up in her work and her inability to speak about feelings.

'I want to send Celeste to boarding school,' he said.

'What?' Matilde suddenly seemed to sober up.

'She needs to be away from us and from the misery. She needs to be with friends who can help her be a child.'

'No,' cried Matilde, reaching out and grasping his arm.

'Yes, and when she is away we can separate,' he said.

'I don't want to separate,' Matilde said, shaking her head wildly, her lank and dirty hair hanging over face.

'Why? You don't love me,' said Robert.

'I never lied to you, neither did Henri. I told you about what happened, I told you I would leave then, but you wanted me to stay. You promised to raise Celeste as your own, but now you want to send our daughter away? This is punishment, isn't it?'

Robert didn't answer her.

'You're a fucking bastard,' she hissed.

'You're a whore who fucked my brother.'

'And you killed your own child,' Matilde screamed, and immediately Robert lashed out and slapped her face.

Matilde fell inside and Robert lit another cigarette.

He had known about Celeste's true father from the minute Matilde told him she was pregnant. He knew it wasn't his, since they hadn't had sex in over a year. But Matilde refused an abortion, and he refused a divorce, so they made the best of it. For a time, Robert had even believed it didn't matter. He knew Henri and Matilde didn't love each other, and he knew Henri felt terrible about betraying Elisabeth, but now he was without Camille, he felt cheated. Henri had always taken what was his, he thought.

His mother's love, and now she had given him the title of

CEO in Le Marche. Robert deserved that role, but Daphné had said he wasn't responsible enough.

Taking on his brother's secret child wasn't mature enough?

He hated everyone, but most of all he hated himself. If he hadn't been showing off to Camille how fast the car went. If he had remembered that the seat belt on that side wasn't as secure. If he had let Celeste come, then she would have been in Camille's place, and it would be Henri weeping instead of him.

Henri came out to the balcony. 'Maman wants you to go and see her,' he said.

'I'll see her tomorrow,' said Robert.

'No, she wants you to go now,' said Henri. 'Matilde was just on the phone to her.'

Robert swore under his breath. Matilde always ran to Daphné when Robert didn't do what she asked, or when he slept with another woman, or when he didn't come home.

Robert knew he didn't have a choice. He relied on Daphné for his lifestyle, and she used this against him, any chance she could.

Half an hour later, Robert was sitting in her apartment, on a Louis XV chair, opposite his mother.

'Why are you threatening Matilde and Henri?'

'Elisabeth should know, and so should Celeste,' he said, crossing his legs.

'Why?' asked Daphné.

'She should know who her real father is. It would change everything for her.'

His mother swallowed for a moment, and narrowed her

eyes. She was dressed in her customary black, with a large abstract brooch attached at the collar. Her hair was perfectly set, the dark sheen glossy in the pale light. His mother wasn't a beautiful woman, but she was chic, and, at this moment, she was more intimidating than she had ever been.

'Do not hurt a child to alleviate your own pain. You are the only father Celeste has known, and I believe and so does Matilde, that you have done a wonderful job in loving her.'

Robert felt his throat constrict with the pain inside his heart and he looked down at his hands.

'You need to know something about your own father,' she said, her voice hard.

He looked up at her words.

'Before I married your father, I was in love with your grandfather.'

Robert felt his stomach give way and he fell back onto the chair.

'Your grandfather was a difficult man, and when I learned I was pregnant, he told me to get rid of you. I didn't want to, but I also didn't want to be a single mother. It was impossible then.'

He said nothing, as she spoke, so she continued.

'Yves married me. He was the kindest man I have ever known, and he loved you like his own, if not more. He didn't know Henri like he knew you, and you loved him so much.'

Robert tried to remember him, but he couldn't recall much of anything from his childhood besides tormenting Henri as much as he could.

'You had sex with Papa's father?'

'I was in love with him, and he broke my heart,' corrected Daphné, but Robert wasn't listening.

'Why are you telling me this?' He stood and started to pace the room. 'You're trying to hurt me, aren't you?'

'No, Robert, I'm not,' said Daphné with a sigh, which only made him angrier.

'You are, you've always hated me,' he spat at her.

'I don't hate you,' she cried. 'I'm trying to tell you that you can't be so cruel to Celeste. She is your child because you have raised her, just as you're Yves' child because he was there from before you were born.'

Robert shook his head. 'You had an affair with Papa's father,' he said to himself.

'No, I was in love with him and he told me he didn't want me with a baby.'

'And then what happened?'

Daphné paused, and Robert saw a flash of pain cross her face.

'We moved to Geneva and you were born.'

'What happened to my father? Did he ever meet me?' He was leaning on the chair, trying to steady himself from his shaking knees.

She looked up at him. 'No, he never did. He died not long after you were born.'

'From what?'

Daphné was silent.

'I can look it up in the records, he is a blood relative. You might as well tell me.'

'He killed himself,' she said. 'A drug overdose.'

Robert stared at her unblinkingly.

'It wasn't because of me, he was a very unhappy man. Yves said he and his wife's marriage was very difficult.'

'Is that what you tell yourself?' asked Robert, unable to rid his voice of his hatred of her.

'I don't tell myself anything but the truth,' said Daphné, her face hardening.

'So you slept with Papa's father, then ran away with his son, and then you two stole his formulas for the creams, went to court, and then he died of a broken heart and a broken business?'

'How do you know about the court case?'

'Max told me years ago,' he said. 'But it never made sense until now.'

'You should have asked me about it. It's not like you think,' said Daphné.

He was pleased to see her stoic face was breaking and there were tears in her eyes.

'It is exactly like I think. You and Henri are exactly the same.' He walked to the door.

Daphné looked at him and straightened her shoulders, lifting her chin so her eyes met his from across the room.

'If you ever tell Elisabeth or Celeste who her father is, then I will disinherit you. I will ensure this is stipulated in my will also. You have no skills, no real education in anything except debauchery and you have no money. This is your only warning. Do you understand me?'

'She should know,' he said, his hand on the door handle.

'No, she loves you and you, I think, love her. Be a father to the child you have left. And stop hurting people because you're in pain.'

'I always knew I was different. I thought it was me, I thought I didn't fit in, but now I see it was you. You treated me like you hated me. You always have.'

He turned the handle and left his mother behind him.

She was right, he thought. He had no skills, and now Henri was going to be CEO. What on earth would he do without his mother's success? But what price did his father pay for her benefit?

He wondered who he could make pay for her sins.

Chapter 39

Billie

Matilde was as beautiful as Celeste but more so, and even more intimidating, so Billie didn't spend much time at the hospital with Celeste.

Their first meeting was tense, and strained, with Matilde staring at Billie as though she was the one who had caused her illness.

Billie knew there was nothing she could do for Celeste now. The doctors had to take over, and Billie needed to be at Le Marche.

Nick and the team were in the lab, finding possibilities for new formulas for the creams and lipsticks and Billie remembered the colours that Celeste had promised them.

She pressed the intercom for Gemma to come into the office.

'Yes?' Gemma appeared, looking worried.

'I need twelve shades of red for the new lipstick line, a selection of colour for every skin type.' Billie said to the girl.

Gemma's mouth opened and shut.

'What? It can't be so hard can it?' she asked. 'Just give us some ideas for the lab.'

'Choosing colours for a make-up brands can take months, according to what I've read,' Gemma ventured.

Billie sighed. She really had no idea about this world, she thought.

'How can it take months? I see articles like this online. The best reds for pale skin. The best red for dark skin. Surely there is a formula? Why can't we take all that research and just get the best colours according to skin type on the research that's already been done? Isn't there a YouTube video or something?'

Gemma clapped her hands and sat down opposite Billie.

'There are lots of YouTube stars who do these beauty blogs and some of them are very influential, which one do you want me to ask?'

Billie laughed and shook her head. 'Right now I am wearing ChapStick and Nivea, do you think I know anything about that world?'

'But I do,' said Gemma slowly.

'Yes you do and, in absence of Celeste, you're marketing manager until she's back on her feet.'

'Really?' Gemma's eyes widened. 'But I don't want to do it under these circumstances.'

Billie shrugged. 'We don't have a choice, we have to get on with it.'

Gemma nodded and Billie handed her a pad and pencil.

'We need twelve lipsticks, twelve names, and twelve beauty vloggers with different skin types to discuss the brands. We need to launch the new creams with new faces, and a campaign that isn't going to ruin us financially.'

Gemma furiously wrote notes as Billie spoke.

'Speak to Edward about budgets, but I know there isn't much. We're going to have to be creative with our few pennies.'

Gemma looked up at her. 'I'm good at stretching pennies, I work here.'

Billie laughed. "If you make this work, you will get a raise, I promise, but we need it to work. A rising tide lifts all boats and all that.'

'I don't know about tides, I never did like the ocean, but I know how to talk beauty,' Gemma said and she walked to the door as Edward entered.

'Gemma is our new marketing manager while Celeste is ill,' Billie said to him.

Edward nodded, as though distracted, and closed the door behind him and sat down.

'It's meningitis,' he said. She thought she hadn't ever seen anyone look more tired than Edward at that moment.

'Christ. I should go down there,' she said.

'She's having high doses of antibiotics, and her mum is there. And, to be honest, we need you here.'

Billie nodded, but she wished she could do more.

'You look exhausted,' she said. 'Why don't you get some sleep and come back. I know you were at the hospital all night.'

'No, I can't sleep, I'm too worried,' he said, clasping and unclasping his hands.

'OK, so where are we at with everything?' she asked, trying to sound professional.

Edward raised his eyebrows at her. 'Where do you want me to start?'

'From the beginning. List the problems from beginning to end and tell me which ones are under control and which ones aren't.'

She ripped off Celeste's notes and picked up a pen and waited for Edward to speak.

'Robert still hasn't paid the money back from Celeste's allowance but she's lost confidence in chasing him.'

Billie wrote down the name, *Robert*.

'The shipping is still being held up in Europe, and no amount of calls to Paul Le Brun from myself or Celeste have made any difference.'

Billie wrote down Robert's name again.

'What else?'

'We need capital to make these new products happen, and we need a solid marketing campaign, with no marketing manager or team.'

'Gemma is all over that.'

'Can she do it?'

Billie shrugged. She didn't have time to assess CVs and ruminate on potential. 'I don't know but I don't have time to find out.'

Edward sat in thought and then looked Billie straight in the eye. 'And I don't think we can go on if Celeste doesn't survive.'

Billie looked down at her list of names and wrote in careful script. The name of her cousin seemed so certain when written down.

'I know,' she said quietly.

They sat in silence, when a knock at the door broke their individual prayers.

'Billie, there's someone to see you,' Gemma said, her face looking confused, as Billie looked up.

In the doorway stood Elisabeth, her face pale but filled with love.

'Mum,' Billie cried, and she jumped up and ran to her mother, forgetting about her professional game face.

Hugging her mother made everything fade away, and she felt herself start to cry deep, racking sobs that hurt her chest and she was grateful when she saw Edward slip from the room.

'Darling, what's happened?'

'It's Celeste. Isn't that why you're here?'

Elisabeth shook her head. 'No, I'm here because you don't answer my calls and I was worried.'

Billie looked down at the ground, noticing her mum's silver sequined sneakers.

'You're wearing silver shoes,' she said incredulously.

Elisabeth looked at them. 'Yes, aren't they lovely? I bought them in Singapore on the way over here.'

Billie couldn't believe her academic mother was wearing such outrageous shoes.

'They're very silver,' said Billie, forgetting her tears for a moment.

'They make me happy,' said Elisabeth. 'And judging from

your reaction at seeing me, I think I should have bought you a pair also.'

Billie was silent.

'Why haven't you called me?' asked Elisabeth but she looked more worried than angry.

Billie went to Celeste's desk and sat down, exhausted, and it was only ten in the morning.

'Why didn't you let Grand-Mère contact me?'

It was Elisabeth's turn to be silent now. Then she said, 'I wanted to punish her.'

'What for?' Billie demanded to know.

Elisabeth was startled at her question. 'You seem different, what's changed?' she asked.

'Everything,' said Billie. 'Now tell me why you kept the Le Marches from me?'

'I knew they'd get you in the end,' sighed Elisabeth.

'They're my family,' said Billie, hearing her voice rise, but she was unable to lower it. She never spoke to her mother like this. It had always been them against the world, particularly the Le Marche family. That was their shared passion and now Billie had been disloyal.

'They're dangerous,' cried Elisabeth.

'You told me to come.'

Their voices were louder now but Billie didn't care.

'I thought you would get some money to set you up and perhaps Daphné might have left some evidence as to what Robert said to Henri, not that she would take you away from me and give you the moon.'

Elisabeth was crying as she spoke but Billie shook her head.

'Whatever imaginary battle you're fighting is only in your mind,' she said quietly, as she looked at the list of names on the pad in front of her.

Robert

Robert

Celeste

She looked up at her mother. 'My battles are real and right now, they're life and death. You can help me and support me, or you can keep imagining that the Le Marches are out to get you, not that there are many of us left.'

The thought of Celeste dying felt like a punch in the stomach, and she tried to take a deep breath, but instead she gulped for air until she finally found her voice.

'Celeste has meningitis,' she said. 'She's in intensive care, Matilde is with her.'

Elisabeth nodded and stood up. 'Then we should go.'

'To the hospital?'

'Of course to the hospital,' said Elisabeth.

'I can't. I have so many things to do here. Robert has made all sorts of trouble for us. He's a fucking nightmare.'

'Then tell me where she is and I will go and see her,' Elisabeth said.

'Really? Matilde is there,' Billie warned, although she wasn't sure why.

'Matilde was never the problem,' said Elisabeth.

Billie wrote down the name of the hospital and walked her mother to the elevator.

'Call me when you've finished,' said Elisabeth. 'I can take us to dinner.'

Billie paused, trying to think of the right words.

'I have a boyfriend,' she said, wishing she had waited to formulate a better sentence.

Elisabeth merely smiled indulgently. 'Then bring him for dinner also.'

'Will you stay at the apartment with me?' asked Billie.

'No, I have a room booked somewhere already,' Elisabeth said, as the door to the elevator opened and she stepped in.

Billie didn't have to ask where she had booked her room. Elisabeth hadn't been in London since before Henri died, but her heart was still in a bed in Claridge's, waiting for her lover to return with champagne and poetry, and promises of five hundred bells to ring to celebrate their love.

Chapter 40

Elisabeth

Matilde was sitting beside Celeste's bed when Elisabeth arrived. Her head was lowered as though she was praying.

Elisabeth placed her handbag onto the spare chair and Matilde looked up at the sound, seemingly unsurprised to see her; instead she just nodded, as if they were neighbours who passed each other in the street each day.

'I'm sorry I interrupted your prayers,' said Elisabeth, standing at the foot of the bed.

'I wasn't praying, I was telling God what a bastard he is,' Matilde said, taking Celeste's hand.

Elisabeth may not have seen Celeste since she was child, but she couldn't easily forget her remarkable beauty.

Even with her hair lank, spilling out on the white pillow, she looked serene and just like her mother, but the Le Marche bone structure was evident. The same cheekbones as Billie, as Daphné, as Henri.

'How is she?' she asked, sitting on the chair, not moving her handbag. She couldn't imagine seeing Billie like this and her heart split in two for Matilde. Two daughters, one gone, one just hanging on to life.

'She's having antibiotics,' said Matilde, gesturing to the IV that hung above Celeste like the Sword of Damocles. 'All we can do is wait.'

And so the women waited.

It was as though the past had been pushed back by the present, and Celeste was a hand on the clock.

When dinnertime came, Elisabeth managed to convince Matilde to come with her to dinner with Billie.

'We won't be long, you need to eat,' said Elisabeth firmly.

'I can't eat,' Matilde argued.

'You have to,' said Elisabeth. 'You'll be no good for Celeste if you're wasting away.'

They walked to an Italian restaurant near the hospital, which Billie had recommended, where Billie and Nick waited for them.

'This is Nick,' said Billie. 'This is my mum Elisabeth and my aunt Matilde.'

Nick smiled at the women and took Matilde's hand. 'I'm so sorry about your daughter, but they are doing all the right things at the hospital, from what Billie told me.'

'I should hope so,' snapped Matilde.

Elisabeth glanced at Billie, who looked upset, but Nick didn't seem to notice anything rude in her reply.

They sat, the tension as the unwelcome guest, and the waiter handed them menus.

'I don't want anything,' said Matilde, closing hers. But when the waiter came, Elisabeth ordered her a bowl of fresh pesto pasta, which was soon in front of Matilde.

'You need basil,' she said to Matilde.

'Why?'

'The Greeks say that basil restores a family,' she answered, digging into her carbonara.

'We should have all got the pesto then,' said Billie darkly, and Elisabeth laughed a little, enjoying the creamy dish.

Matilde took a small piece of penne and nibbled at it, and then another, and soon the bowl was empty, the remaining sauce wiped up with some soft bread.

Elisabeth chatted to Nick, while Matilde kept glancing at her phone which lay on the table.

'They will call if anything changes,' said Elisabeth gently.

'Nothing will change for a few days,' said Nick. 'The antibiotics take between five and ten days to work, if they work.'

Elisabeth saw Billie's hand jab him in the leg and he shook his head. 'Sorry, that was a terrible thing to say. This is why I work in a lab, and not in a hospital. Of course the medicine will work.'

But Matilde shook her head. 'We don't know if it will. There is no point pretending that she will be OK. We know nothing. We are nothing. Camille, Henri, Daphné, now Celeste. This family is cursed.'

Elisabeth stared at her bowl. Was it cursed? She couldn't lie and say she hadn't thought about this before. So many poems and stories had been written about curses on families. Had she married into one?

'What utter bullshit,' Elisabeth heard from across the table, and she saw Billie's face was furious.

'The only curse this family suffers from is poor decision-making.'

'Billie,' Elisabeth hissed.

'Don't Billie me,' her daughter said. 'If Daphné hadn't slept with Giles, then she wouldn't have had Robert and then Robert wouldn't have been such a prick.'

She looked at Matilde. 'Sorry, I know you had daughters with him but he is truly awful.'

Matilde nodded, her eyes wide with what Elisabeth presumed was shock.

'And if Robert had put Camille on the right side of the car, with the seat belt that worked, then she wouldn't be dead.'

Billie paused, and Elisabeth held her breath.

'And if Dad had gone and got real help, instead of writing a poem about it, then he might have survived to see me here now.

'And, as for Celeste, she has the worst taste in men I've ever seen. First that politician prick, and then the finance guy who was playing you and her.' Billie looked at Matilde. 'If everyone just could become a bit more sensible about their decisions then this family might not need so much pesto.'

She slumped back in her chair and the table was silent.

'What did you say about Giles? And Robert?' asked Matilde slowly.

Elisabeth looked at her and back to Billie.

'It's in Daphné's diaries, in the flat. I have been reading about it. I mean, Nick reads it and translates it for me, but yes, Robert's father is Giles.'

Matilde was shaking her head and looking more dazed.

'This can't be right,' said Elisabeth.

'I want to read them,' said Matilde, her face pale.

'I can bring them to the hospital,' said Billie, and Elisabeth saw tears in her eyes. 'I'm so sorry, I didn't know, I thought it was common knowledge, and why Robert was so mean. I thought everyone knew.'

Matilde shook her head.

'We can go and get them now,' offered Billie.

Matilde stood up, her chair making a scraping sound on the tiles of the restaurant.

'*Oui*,' she said and she swung her bag onto her shoulder and walked to the door.

'Christ, Mum,' Billie whispered, 'did you know this?'

'How would I know?' she answered. 'This family has more secrets than an MI5 Christmas party.'

Nick had hailed a taxi, and Matilde and Billie hopped in.

Elisabeth watched the car drive away, then turned to Nick, who seemed lost without Billie by his side.

'You do understand that this family is exhausting and all-consuming,' she said to him.

He nodded. 'Yes, I'm beginning to see that,' he said slowly.

'And if you decide to be with Billie, you will be drawn into the web of Le Marche.'

Nick shrugged, and shoved his hands into the pockets of his pants. 'I'm already done for,' he said. 'I love her. We fit together in every way. She is remarkable, and I think she might be just like her mother.'

Elisabeth felt her eyes sting with tears. 'I always thought she was so like Henri. He was creative and passionate, and had wonderful ideas, but couldn't fulfil them. Billie used to be so creative, and then, as she became older and learned more about her father, the more she pushed that side of her down until it's gone. She became safe and I worried. I had protected her so much, she had forgotten how to be brave.'

Nick frowned. 'But she was brave in even coming here. And then standing up to Robert and even Celeste at times, she's pretty amazing. And she's taken me on, and I'm just a dork with little to no social skills.'

'You're OK.' She smiled and slipped her arm through his. 'You can walk me back to Claridge's, and I can interrogate you about everything that a future mother-in-law may need to know.'

To his credit, Nick didn't balk at either suggestion, and they walked slowly to the hotel, as she learned everything she could about the man who loved her only daughter and what had been happening in her daughter's world without her.

Chapter 41

Robert, Paris, 1998

A cold wind blew across La Villette cemetery, as the sound of dirt hitting the top of the coffin was interspersed with the sound of Elisabeth weeping, but Robert stared unseeingly down into this brother's grave.

Words spun around in his head until they re-formed into something he could make sense of, something he could live with.

He had wanted to hurt Henri for as long as he could remember, but he didn't think that Henri would have the final word and crush himself more than Robert had ever done.

Matilde stood next to him, her hands clasped, and he wondered if she was praying. She used to be so religious, but since Camille, she seemed to have lost her faith in everything. She was cynical and bitter, both emotions draining her beauty.

He never had any faith in anything bigger than himself, least of all now, however he wondered if Henri was now in limbo. But hadn't Henri always been in limbo?

The priest handed Robert a small silver trowel, and a bucket, filled with dirt, and he took his turn at covering Henri.

His mother turned and walked towards the car, not waiting to see her son be covered by soil for all eternity, and he understood her pain.

Slowly each of the mourners left Henri's graveside, until it was just he and Matilde left standing side by side.

'Come on,' she said, pulling at his sleeve.

'No, you go. I want to make sure he's OK,' Robert said not looking at her.

Matilde turned and left him alone, as a man drove a small yellow earthmover onto the grass and began to push the large pile of dirt into the grave.

When it was done, the man climbed down, took a shovel and smoothed over the grave. He then began piling the flowers that were alongside the plot onto the freshly turned earth.

Robert thought he might help, but then thought better of it. When the man had finished, he nodded respectfully at Robert and crossed himself at the grave and then drove away in the machine.

It was done, Robert thought. Henri was gone from his life. And yet he felt nothing.

'Silly fool,' he said to the grave. 'You utter idiot.'

The scent from the lilies rose and their thick perfume stuck in his throat.

He wished he could take it all back. The beatings, the bullying at school, the cruel words and the lies.

What did you say to him? He heard Elisabeth's accusations over and over in his mind, but he denied saying anything to Henri.

But what if he told her about that night? For the past week he had run over the last time he had seen Henri.

They had been drunk, and Robert had told Henri he was sending Celeste to Allemagne.

'But you can't!' Henri had said, pushing his wine glass forward, so claret spilled onto the white tablecloth of the restaurant.

Matilde pushed her chair back from the table.

'I'm going back to Elisabeth and the girls,' she said.

Henri watched her go.

'Matilde doesn't want to send her there,' Henri said.

'Matilde doesn't make the decision for our child, I do,' Robert had answered. He watched the way the colour drained from Henri's face when he mentioned Allemagne and he enjoyed it. Tormenting Henri was once a sport, but since the birth of Celeste, it was harsher and then when Camille died, it became necessary for him to survive, and Henri became the vessel for his pain.

Henri had swallowed more wine, and then took a deep breath.

'Do not sent Celeste to that school, I implore you.'

'It was a perfectly fine school; she will enjoy it like I did.'

'It was hell,' said Henri.

Robert brushed invisible crumbs away from the cloth, and folded his napkin into a neat rectangle.

'Celeste is stronger than you were, she's not as emotionally weak,' Robert said with a small smile.

'I wasn't weak, you and your friends were bastards,' Henri hissed and Robert felt his stress lessen at the sight of Henri's distress.

'Come on, that was just a bit of school fun,' Robert said. 'Why do you take everything so seriously?'

The waiter came to the table and filled their glasses, and the men were silent for a moment.

'I'm begging you, do not send Celeste to that school, Robert. I know I haven't raised her and I have never interfered with your parenting but this is the one thing I cannot watch happen.'

Robert twisted the glass around on the table, as though he were winding a clock.

'What's it worth to you?' he asked.

'Pardon?'

'For Celeste to not go to Allemagne, what will you give me?'

Henri had looked confused. 'What do you want?'

'CEO,' Robert said.

Henri sat back in his chair, his shoulders slumped. 'You want CEO of Le Marche? You hate the company. Why?'

'Because you have that role, and I want whatever you have.' Robert smiled as he spoke.

'OK,' said Henri with a shrug, and Robert couldn't believe Henri would capitulate so easily.

It wasn't the outcome he had expected. He wanted Henri to fight more, so then Robert could be cruel and release the pain inside.

'You're so like your father, he was a weak man,' Robert had said with a sneer.

'Our father?'

'No, *your* father. You know about that, surely Maman told you?'

Henri's face told him he didn't know and he sighed with satisfaction, disguised as boredom.

'Maman had an affair when she went to Paris with me as a baby. You're Giles Le Marche's child. I'm Yves' son. You're my grandfather's child.'

'What?' Henri's cry caused diners to turn their heads, but Robert ignored their stares: he was having too much fun.

'Yes, you're Giles' child. He killed himself after Maman refused to be with him. Of course Yves let her stay, but the damage was done. That's why she loved you more than me, because you were her lover's bastard.'

'That's ridiculous, I'm going to call Maman,' said Henri, his eyes glazed from wine and disbelief.

'She'll deny it, but Anna told me, and Maman confirmed it. She didn't tell you because she didn't want you to know you were the son of a man who killed himself.'

Henri was silent as Robert spoke.

'Did you know that in Louis XVth's time, it was against the law to kill yourself and, if you did, your body would be dragged through the streets to show people what ingratitude looked like, and then your estate was taken from your heirs and given to the monarchy?'

'You're lying,' said Henri, his face pale.

'No, you know it's true, you know you're not stable, that you've always felt different. You must have inherited it from Giles.'

Henri's face was blank, and Robert wondered for a moment if he had gone too far, and then he imagined Henri inside Matilde, and his anger swelled again.

'I think Maman is ashamed of what she did, especially when Papa was so instrumental to her business. I mean he really made it happen, didn't he?'

Henri pushed back his chair and stumbled towards the door of the restaurant. He turned to Robert.

'I'm going to find out about this from Maman.'

Robert picked up his wine. 'If you do, I will tell Celeste who her father is, and then I will tell Elisabeth and Sibylla what you did to my wife and you will lose it all.'

He raised his glass to Henri and then took a sip, and that was the last time he saw him.

Then the call came from Elisabeth that he had jumped from the bridge at Parc des Buttes-Chaumont and had left a letter that mentioned him.

He denied any knowledge of Henri's claims. He knew Elisabeth didn't believe him, but it was his word against Henri's and he always won.

And now he was buried with his secrets, and Robert's secrets also and he walked away, still surprised that he felt nothing for his brother in life and especially in death.

Chapter 42

Edward

Edward ran along the path near the Thames, his feet aching but his mind still overflowing. Usually he ran to clear his thoughts but now it felt he picked up more troubles along his path.

The list of problems was growing longer and his mind ran through them again.

Celeste was in an induced coma.

Billie was in love with Nick.

Dominic Bertuill had pursued Celeste and God only knew what she had told him before he revealed he loved her mother.

Robert was too silent for Edward to feel comfortable. He knew he was up to something.

Their products were being held from importation, and they were running out of money to make the new line that their future depended on.

He stopped running and bent over, his hands on his knees, trying to catch his breath, and, for the first time in thirty-eight years, Edward thought about giving up and going home.

Finally, catching his breath, he looked out at the London

skyline. He missed Daphné. She would know what to say to him in a time like this, but with her wise words came her secrets and sometimes they felt too heavy to carry and hide, especially now Celeste was in the hospital.

If only he had taken her to hospital instead of trying to impress her with his cooking, he thought for the thousandth time.

Instead, he had tried to be gallant, and kind, and let her sleep in his bed, and he hadn't touched her, even though when she rolled over and he saw the glimpse of skin on her hip where her T-shirt had rolled up, he had never wanted to touch anything more. She was his friend, he reminded himself.

When he thought about Celeste, she reminded him of Daphné. She had the same spirit as her grandmother, but seeing Daphné lose her health over the years, and the last time he had seen her, so small and birdlike in her bed, he knew he couldn't bear to see Celeste so vulnerable.

He needed to do something to help, but he felt helpless. All he knew about was contracts and fine print. What Celeste and Le Marche needed now was boldness and power and then he had a thought. An idea so audacious, it would either save them all or ruin them, and he closed his eyes for a moment, and silently asked Daphné, wherever she was now, if he was completely barmy or brilliant and if there really was a difference.

Two days later, he sat opposite Dominic Bertuill in the bar at Claridge's, both nursing a whiskey.

'How is Celeste?'

'The same.'

'Is Matilde with her?'

Edward nodded, taking in the dark circles under Dominic's eyes, and the way he ran his hand nervously through his hair.

'She won't return my calls,' he said.

'She has much on her mind,' said Edward.

'I know, I want to help,' Dominic said.

'That's why I asked you to meet me,' Edward said, placing his glass on the table.

Dominic did the same and the men stared at each other as though about to draw swords, each waiting for the other's first move.

'First, I have to say that your behaviour with Celeste was unacceptable.'

It was Dominic's turn to nod. 'I know it was, but I didn't tell Robert anything. I did it to find out more about the company and the legacy that Daphné left, but then I met Matilde, and then Celeste. I liked them both, but fell in love with one.'

'Robert Le Marche is a toad and when you do business with toads, people assume you're just like them.'

Dominic didn't look offended at Edward's words; instead he laughed. 'Except I was kissed and have been transformed.'

But Edward wasn't moved, nor convinced.

'Money means a lot to you, how can I assume that you're telling the truth? Matilde is fifteen years older than you. She can't give you children. She doesn't live in Paris or London, she likes to do puzzles and play tennis. Your lives are so disparate it is impossible to believe that you want a future with her.'

'Why?' Dominic's voice rose above the elegant clatter of conversation and glasses clinking in the bar. 'Sometimes the heart wants what the eye cannot see. What is meant for you in life.'

'Antoine de Saint-Exupéry?' asked Edward.

'Who?' asked Dominic.

Edward shook his head. 'Doesn't matter.'

'I love her, and she won't see me, if you have a way of helping me show her how I want her, I will do it. I don't even need to be told the plans.'

His earnest face made Edward smile a little, and he reached for his drink.

'Even if it costs you a large amount of money.'

Dominic shrugged. 'Money can be found anywhere. On the street, in an old jacket pocket, but love cannot. You must make your choice when you find it, but so few make the right one.'

Edward looked down at the fine whiskey in his glass and thought of Billie.

A crush wasn't love, he reminded himself, and he looked up at Dominic.

'I want you to invest in Le Marche. Buy some bonds and pay off some debt. You will receive interest on these bonds should the company succeed. Of course Celeste and Billie will have control and they own their grandmother's legacy entirely. If they choose to use the recipe or formula in the company, then it will still be owned by them.'

Dominic stared at Edward. 'Is there a clause in the will that allows this?'

'Daphné stipulated not sales, but she didn't mention investments.'

'What's the return on my bonds?' asked Dominic.

'One per cent.'

Dominic laughed loudly. 'That's a terrible return.'

Edward raised an eyebrow. 'So is being alone.'

'Oh I didn't say I wasn't going to do it, I'm just stating it's a terrible return on my money.'

Edward nodded. 'Yes, it is, but that's what you get for being a toad.'

To his credit Dominic laughed again and put his hand over the table to Edward.

'Send me the papers tomorrow morning and I will have the requested amount in your account by the afternoon.'

'You don't know how much I'm going to ask for yet,' said Edward, giving Dominic a wry smile.

'It doesn't matter, just tell Matilde will you?'

Edward nodded. 'I will.'

Dominic stood up, drained his whiskey, and put the glass down.

'You can get the bill,' he said and, without another word, he turned and left the bar.

Edward nursed his drink and thought about how he would tell Celeste and Billie that he had just taken Dominic on as an investor.

The sudden need to see Celeste was overwhelming. He threw a handful of notes on the table, and left his drink unfinished.

Celeste would understand what he had done, he thought, as he hailed a taxi and told the driver the address. She would know exactly what he was doing and she would respect it, perhaps even admire him for making such a bold and unusual decision.

She would make it right with Billie, and they could save Le Marche, bring it back to how it once was, and then the sky would be the limit.

The taxi arrived at the hospital. He paid and alighted, a cold air hitting him and causing him to shiver.

The closer he came to the ward, the more he worried. Perhaps Matilde would tell him to go, or Billie would be there. He wouldn't tell her in front of Billie. This wasn't the time.

He pressed the buzzer and announced himself to the nurse, who let him in through the automatic doors.

The silence was pierced by the occasional ringing of a machine or hushed voices, and the nurse came from around the station and took him to a curtained area.

'She's not awake, although we have lowered her medication. Her mother has just left, so you can sit next to her. We think she can hear us, but she's not responding yet. She's still on antibiotics, but she isn't as unwell as yesterday, which is a huge step forward.'

She moved the curtain and Edward saw Celeste in the bed. Her hair spread out, so smooth, as though someone had just brushed it across the pillow.

He stepped forward and sat next to the bed, and took her hand.

'Hello, it's Edward,' he said feeling silly, as though he was talking to himself.

Her hand was soft and warm in his and he thought about the night they slept holding hands, and his heart hurt, and he could hardly breathe with the pain.

'You need to get better, Celeste, nothing is the same without you,' he said, trying to be light but then failing. 'I'm not the same without you,' he whispered.

He thought about going into work and not having the whirlwind of Celeste barging into his office, or their lunches and laughter. The way she teased him, and the way she looked when she was concentrating.

'I've done something you will either think is brilliant or will get me fired,' he whispered. 'I wish you would wake so I could tell you.'

He put his head down on the bed, and kissed her hand.

'You're my best friend Celeste, and I miss you,' he said and he felt his eyes prick with tears.

And then he cried. He cried for the loss of Daphné, and he cried for Celeste and he cried because talking to Dominic was the first brave thing he had ever done in his life, and he did it for the Le Marche women, not for himself.

'Edward?'

He heard her voice and looked up. Her face was confused and pale and he let go of her hand and quickly wiped his tears away.

'Celeste, let me get the nurse,' he said, but she took his hand.

'No,' she whispered. 'Just be with me for a while.'

'As long as you want, Celeste,' he said, and his thumb stroked her hand, and she drifted back to sleep, with a small smile on her lovely face.

When Celeste woke again a short time later, she was distressed and calling for her mother, so Edward called the nurse, who took over the space.

'Let me get her mother, and let me tend to her,' said the efficient nurse.

Edward moved to the other side of the bed, and took Celeste's hand again.

'I'll come back,' he said, but Celeste didn't seem to hear

him this time and, as a doctor arrived, Edward edged from the room.

The hospital was quiet, with most visitors leaving, and only a few people in the foyer, looking tired.

'Edward,' he heard and he turned to see his former, very pregnant assistant, Amanda, waddling towards him.

'What's happened?' he asked.

'Nothing yet but it's going to, my waters broke.' She smiled gleefully.

'Where's Tony?' he asked, looking for her husband.

'Parking the car. It's OK, nothing else has started yet.' She looked down at the ground as though making sure nothing had fallen out. 'How's work? You missing me?'

'You have no idea,' he said, shaking his head.

'Why are you here?' she asked.

Edward thought about telling her the truth, but it felt too unreal to him yet. 'A friend is in hospital, just thought I'd pop in and say hi,' he said casually.

Before Amanda could ask for more details, her husband rushed inside.

'Is it OK?' he almost yelled.

'Yes, we're fine.' She laughed then she reached out and touched Edward's arm.

'Come and see me when I've had them, you can see your friend and the little people I've grown.'

Edward leaned down and kissed her on the cheek. 'I can't think of anything better,' he said. 'Good luck.'

Amanda and Tony walked to the elevator, and he watched them laugh with excitement, as they chatted.

He wanted that, he realised. He wanted children and a

partner, and a life. He had given everything to the Le Marche family and for what?

Perhaps it was time he moved on and got his own family to take care of, but he wondered if he had anything more to give. Had the Le Marches taken everything from him? And would any of them ever give him something in return?

He thought of Celeste, as he always did. She was always on his mind through the day and night. More than just concerns for her health, he wanted to talk to her about work, have a long lunch and gossip about staff, eat pasta in his flat, and watch trashy TV, lie next to her and hold her hand.

Goddamn it, he thought, and he pushed open the hospital door too hard, so it almost came back and hit him in the face.

He was in love with the woman. What an awful, stupid mess. First Billie and now Celeste. Was he that much of a loser he fell in love with any woman that he interacted with?

But it felt different with Celeste. She was the entire world to him now. The idea that he might lose her when she was ill was too much to bear and, while his visits were wrapped in concern, he felt better when he was with her, seeing she was safe.

No, this would not do at all. A woman like Celeste was a firefly. She wouldn't even look twice at him with his sad little life. She would marry a scion of business, a man like Dominic or Paul Le Brun, not a man named Eddie Badger from Broomhill Road.

The only thing he could do was leave before he lost everything, but he wondered if in fact he already had.

Part 3

Autumn/Winter

Chapter 43

Matilde

The light was different in London. There were often clouds in the sky, causing the city to look like it was bruised from seeing too much sadness. The bleakness fell over Matilde's mind and she missed the Nice sun, Tarot the cat and, most of all, Dominic.

But how could she trust him now? She should have known better than to let him into her house and into her bed. She should have known better to have slept with a man whose primary skill in life was to hypnotise and then disassemble entire companies. He was a charmer and she was lonely, it was a recipe for someone being hurt and, of course, she reasoned, it would be her.

Scammers like Dominic would do anything to get what they wanted but she wondered, why on earth he would want to sleep with a fifty-five-year-old woman when he could have anyone. It wasn't as though she divulged any secrets that would change the future of Le Marche.

Matilde sat in the study of Daphné's apartment, the pile of diaries in front of her.

Why hadn't these been read before? she wondered, but then she realised Robert simply wasn't interested in his mother's life, and there was no one else left to care.

But Matilde had been moved by Daphné's passion and heartache over the years. Losing Yves had been daunting, but losing Henri had broken her. She spoke kindly of Matilde, and Elisabeth, which was more than Matilde had done in public, and she wished she had been kinder to the woman. She had saved Celeste, and she had treated her as though she was the reason Robert was such a bastard.

Her phone rang and her heart skipped a beat when she saw the number of the hospital on the screen.

'Hello?' she asked, clutching the side of the desk.

'Celeste is awake and asking for you,' said a nurse and, before she could say anything else, Matilde was out of the apartment and in a taxi to the hospital.

The hospital was almost too quiet when Matilde arrived, but when she walked into Celeste's room, she was sitting up in bed, but looking pale and anxious.

'Darling,' Matilde cried, but Celeste shook her hand at her.

'I have something called Mollaret's syndrome,' she said.

'What's that?' Matilde sat on the chair next to Celeste, for fear her legs would give way.

'It's something the doctor said causes headaches and the neck pain and even the depression. It comes and goes, but this time it stayed, that's why I collapsed. They said I could have died this time.'

Matilde closed her eyes and took a deep breath, trying to not let her mind go to the place where Camille resided.

'I have to stay here for another week, and if I improve I can go home,' Celeste said, looking uncertain at the idea.

'You can come home with me,' said Matilde firmly.

'I can't fly, Maman,' said Celeste, leaning back on the pillows.

'Then I will stay here and look after you at Daphné's.'

Celeste looked away from her mother, staring at the white wall.

'They said that what I have is hereditary. Did you or Papa ever have these headaches? Or the depression?'

Matilde looked down and swallowed. She knew she needed to be brave, braver than she had ever been and she took a deep breath, as though she was about to swim the length of a pool without stopping.

'Yes, your father did,' she said.

It all made sense now, she thought. Henri's headaches, his mood swings, his weeks in bed. He was told he was merely weak, but he was sick. She desperately wished Daphné were here to understand what happened to Henri was an illness, not a weakness.

'I've never seen Papa sick,' said Celeste.

'No.' Matilde stopped and felt her eyes fill with tears. 'Your biological father is Henri.'

She said it. It was out. She was as raw and vulnerable as she had ever been. She had lost one daughter and now she might lose another.

Celeste frowned, as though she couldn't understand what her mother had said. 'You had sex with Uncle Henri?'

'Yes.'

'Were you in love with him?'

'No.'

'Did Henri know about me?'

'Yes.'

'Did he love me?'

The look on Celeste's face broke her heart. She looked like she did the day Robert sent her to Allemagne—confused, hopeful for a reprieve, but, most of all, she looked lost.

'Yes,' said Matilde, as she locked eyes with her daughter.

A tear fell down Celeste's cheek and she put her hand out for her mother.

'You don't hate me for not telling you the truth?'

'Why didn't you?' asked Celeste.

'Because Elisabeth and Billie don't know,' Matilde explained.

'But you could have told me,' Celeste said, but not taking her hand from her mother's.

'I could have, but I wasn't brave enough.'

The women sat in silence, as a nurse walked in and checked the drip and Celeste's vitals and left again wordlessly.

'Did Papa love me?' Celeste finally spoke.

Matilde thought for a moment. 'He did, he does, he's just a very angry man.'

Matilde wondered if she should tell Celeste about Giles, but then left it alone. This secret was enough for one evening, she decided.

Celeste closed her eyes. 'I'm tired,' she said.

Matilde leaned forward and kissed her daughter's forehead. 'I'll be back in the morning,' she said.

'Goodnight, Maman,' Celeste whispered.

'*Bon Dodo, mon amie,*' whispered Matilde in return, and turned off the light above Celeste's head.

This was her chance to be the mother she should have been when Camille died. She had nearly lost Celeste to pride and then to illness and she wasn't going to let anyone stand in the way of her relationship with her daughter. Not Robert, not Dominic, not even herself.

* * *

Over the next week, Matilde dedicated herself to Celeste's recovery, taking in lavender oil to rub on her temples, massaging her hands and brushing her hair, and, slowly, she peeled back the layers of memories to tell Celeste about her one night with Henri.

'Of course there was no doubt I wouldn't be keeping you, and Robert didn't want to be divorced, so we made the best of it. I thought he could get past it, and perhaps he could have, until Camille died. The anger was so intense, he lashed out at anyone, including you.'

Celeste listened and didn't say much, but Matilde noticed when Billie or Elisabeth came to see her, she became closed, and almost sullen.

If they noticed, they didn't ask Matilde about it, and she didn't pry. She knew Celeste needed time to recuperate and process everything that had happened.

The only person Celeste seemed happy to see was Edward, who arrived every evening at six o'clock, always bearing a small gift of some sweets, or a posy, or a magazine, even a copy of the Babar the Elephant stories.

'I haven't seen these in years,' she said, showing Matilde,

who smiled in return but inside she thought about Robert reading to Celeste when she was a child, and her heart ached for the past.

Perhaps she should speak to Robert, and tell him that Celeste knew about Henri, she thought, but then she wondered what the outcome would be. Robert knew Celeste was ill and hadn't even called to see how she was. Paul Le Brun had sent a huge bunch of roses that had to go home with Matilde as they couldn't be kept in the ICU, and a handful of her Parisian socialite friends had called, but no one else had come to see her and Matilde realised that Celeste didn't really have anyone else in the world.

The week dragged, and Matilde was tired of the daily trips to the hospital, the endless waiting for test results, and the conversations with Celeste that seemed to start in the middle of a sentence and drift into nothing. Matilde didn't know her daughter at all, and she wondered why. She knew it was her self-involvement, but why did she distance herself when she loved her so fiercely?

She thought about Daphné every day, reading and rereading the diaries.

Daphné had closed herself off after each death in her life, and, eventually, her shell was so hard, nothing could penetrate it any more.

Had she done that?

Matilde left Celeste with Edward, and walked through the streets of London.

Christmas was coming, she noticed. Red and green filled the windows, and shiny bright decorations started to bud on the streets. She hadn't spent a Christmas with her daughter for years. Was that her choice or Celeste's?

Usually Celeste was somewhere in the sun, with a lover or her so-called friends.

This year they would be together, perhaps Elisabeth and Billie would want to eat with them. Her mind started to turn with ideas for the dinner. Would they celebrate the French way or the Australian way? Matilde didn't even know what an Australian Christmas was like, and she made a mental note to ask Elisabeth.

As she walked through the crowded streets, her mind whirred with ideas for meals for Celeste and Christmas presents. How long had it been since she had been so busy? Days of tennis and nights of cocktails were not real tasks she began to understand. They were merely place fillers for a woman without any real purpose.

'Matilde.' She heard her name called and she looked up as she passed Claridge's, and saw Dominic standing out the front in a heavy overcoat that looked like it cost the earth.

For a moment she wanted to run to him and tell him everything that had happened, but instead she held her ground and stared at him and then kept walking.

Of course she knew this wouldn't stop a man like Dominic and she heard his footsteps running to catch up with her.

'Matilde,' he said again and grasped her arm and spun her around. 'I've called you so many times.'

'And I've been in the hospital with my daughter, who nearly died, so I'm sorry that you felt neglected, but she takes precedence. Perhaps you know her? Celeste Le Marche?'

Dominic's handsome face flushed red. 'Yes I know Celeste. That's why I've called you—I wanted to know what I can do to help.'

'Nothing,' said Matilde, and she threw his hand off her arm.

'Please, Matilde, I love you. I have to be able to help you.'

'The best thing you can do is leave my family alone. You and Robert will make a fine pair, I'm sure.'

'I'm not working with Robert, I'm now working with Edward. I've just made a huge investment in Le Marche. I want to do everything possible to make it a success for you all.'

Matilde tried to take in his words. 'You've invested in Le Marche? Why?'

'For you, for Celeste, to beat Robert, I don't know, because I've never invest in anything, I only tear things apart, but I want to create something now. I want to impress you.'

Matilde sighed and reached up and touched his face with her cold hand, but he didn't flinch. 'Money has never impressed me.'

'I know, that's why I adore you.'

They stood in silence, the street moving past them like a river, but they were anchored in each other.

'I was wrong to betray you and Celeste, but I never even kissed her. The more she spoke, the more I saw how fragile she is. Her father is a bastard. I couldn't hurt her, and then you, you . . .' His words trailed off. 'I can't stop thinking about you. Your house, Tarot the cat, that night.'

'You should be with a woman your own age, marry, have children, create a dynasty.'

Dominic laughed. 'What for? So they can fight like the Le Marches? No thank you. I just want something simple. I want us.'

Matilde felt her eyes fill with tears and she looked down at her boots, trying to control the sobs that threatened to explode from her heart. 'I can't,' she said.

'Why not?' Dominic's face fell.

'Because I have to be with Celeste. I abandoned her once and I won't do it again. I have to be there for her now. I will care for her when she leaves hospital for as long as it takes, so I can't give you any answers or promises. You aren't part of my future right now, she is.'

Dominic nodded, and she saw in his eyes he understood. 'I will wait,' he said with a smile.

'You're not a patient man, I don't think you have ever waited in your life.'

'I'm learning how.'

'It might be a long time,' she said quietly. 'Or it might never happen.'

'I just have to have faith,' he said.

Matilde shook her head and then kissed each of his cheeks. 'Faith is for the foolish,' she said.

'Then I am your fool, Matilde, now and always.'

Matilde turned and walked away from him, knowing his eyes stayed on her until she was swept up into the river of people.

Chapter 44

Billie

Nick opened the door and Billie smiled at him shyly.

'Are you sure? Are you sure you want to live with a former bachelor? I have a tendency to leave the toilet seat up, and eat food over the sink.'

Billie laughed and threw herself into his arms. 'It won't be for ever, just until Celeste gets well and Matilde goes back to Nice.'

'But what if I don't want you to go?' asked Nick, holding her tight.

'Then I'll stay,' said Billie, as she leaned up and kissed him. Their touch was electric and soon they were in his bed, her clothes strewn across the floor with his.

'How will we get anything done?' he asked her afterwards. 'We always end up in bed together.'

'Then we will have to work from here,' said Billie kissing his shoulder.

Celeste was home from hospital, with Matilde and Elisabeth fussing over her, and while Billie was sorry Celeste was so weak, she was grateful to be able to spend time with Nick again outside of work.

But Celeste worried her, not just because of her illness, but also because she wouldn't look Billie in the eye. She longed to ask if she had upset her in any way but she knew it wasn't the right time. She just hoped Celeste would come to her with what troubled her when she was ready.

But Billie had her own troubles. The business needed Celeste and, while Gemma was doing a great job at naming lipsticks and working with the development team from the lab, there needed to be a strategy in place and Billie had no idea where to start.

'I wish I knew more about everything,' she said to Nick as she stared at the ceiling.

'That's a big ask. Is there something in particular you would like to know more about?'

His rolled to his side and ran his hands over her body, and she felt herself instantly respond to him.

'Wait,' she said, reluctantly removing his hand. 'I need to know more about marketing and advertising. It's all very well to make good products, but we need to be able to sell them.'

'It seems quite simple from my understanding. Get an advertising agency to help.'

Billie sighed. 'I don't think we can afford it.'

'Then get one that wants the work, a young group who are hungry for a chance.'

She thought for a moment, and then grabbed her phone from the side of the bed and rang Gemma.

'Gem, we need an ad agency, know of anyone?'

Gemma was silent, then she said, 'Sure, there are the big ones, but they're very expensive.'

'No, it has to be a smaller one, which doesn't cost the earth. One that is exciting and knows lots about social media and all that stuff you're working on.'

'There is someone I know. I mean—' Gemma's voice was nervous '—they're some people I went to university with. They're great but they're small. I know they would love to have a look at this.'

'OK, get them in,' said Billie, trying to sound professional as Nick disappeared under the bedclothes.

'For full disclosure, I should say, I've been having a thing with one of the owners, so if you're not comfortable, I can find someone else.'

Billie felt her legs open to receive Nick's tongue and she jumped.

'When has that ever stopped anyone at Le Marche. It seems everyone is in everyone else's bed, why stop now.'

Gemma laughed, as Billie felt her free hand clutch the sheets.

'OK, get it happening. I've got to go into a meeting.'

She hung up the phone and she felt Nick's head pop up from under the bedclothes. 'A meeting?' he asked, his face amused.

'Yes, now get back to work,' said Billie giggling.

'Yes, boss,' said Nick and he disappeared again.

* * *

The next day, Billie and Edward sat in the boardroom with Gemma and a young woman and man.

'This is Claire and Will, they're from the Clue Agency.'

Billie took in Claire's edgy clothes and vibrant red hair, and Will's fashionable suit, and thought they were everything she wasn't and she wondered why on earth she thought she could have taken over marketing.

'Hi, I'm Billie and this is Edward. Celeste would be here but she's away today,' she said, as though nothing was wrong.

Claire and William nodded and then William cleared his throat, and handed her a folder with their company brand embossed on the front.

'This is a sample of work we have done that we think might be interesting and relevant to Le Marche.'

As Billie took the folder from him, she noticed his hands were shaking and she smiled at him.

'Just for the record, I'm as nervous as you are,' she said and was rewarded with a smile.

'This is a huge opportunity for us, and we want to prove to you we can do it,' he said, and Billie saw the relief on his face.

'We have experience in below and above the line campaigns and have a sector of our business dedicated to social media marketing with digital strategists and planners, including relationships with the some of the most influential bloggers, vloggers and Twitter users.'

Billie shook her head. 'I have no idea what any of that means but I'm assuming it's good, right?' She looked to Gemma, who nodded eagerly.

'They really do know everyone,' she chimed in and Billie saw William's face turn red.

Billie leafed through the folder, seeing a few ads she

recognised but many she didn't, and eventually she closed it and handed it to Edward.

'So what do you know about us and what do you think we need?' she asked.

Claire leaned forward. 'Le Marche is stale and needs a facelift, as it were.'

Billie smiled.

'Your new products that Gem told us about will help this, but the information needs to be shared and people need to get excited again.'

She nodded in agreement.

'I believe that Le Marche has an opportunity to trade off its history and its reputation with women. It was started by a woman and is still in women's hands. The fact that you're family makes it even better.'

'How so?' Billie asked, trying to understand.

'You, Celeste, your grandmother, your mother, and your aunt, Matilde, who was the famous model, you're all great beauties, you should all be the faces of Le Marche.'

Before Billie could protest about her looks, Claire had reached down and pulled out from under the table large pieces of card.

She stood up and walked to the presentation board, and propped them up in a row.

Each one was a photo of the Le Marche women in black and white. A beautiful photo of Celeste crossing a Paris street, her hair blowing back, and a trench coat swinging out behind her. She wasn't looking at the camera, but her power and style shone through.

A photo of Elisabeth from the dust jacket for a book of

poetry she had written years ago, her were arms crossed, but she was laughing, her fine features highlighted by the contrast in black and white.

And Matilde. Matilde was so beautiful it took Billie's breath away.

Her original modelling photo from when she started at Le Marche, in a field of wildflowers and a look of peace on her sublime face.

Billie was almost afraid to see what image they had used to portray her and she looked up through squinted eyes to see an image from the night of the dinner at Claridge's. It was a closer shot of her face, the night lights behind her, giving the impression she was attending a red carpet affair, not a dinner for business. Her smoky eye was wanton, and her tousled hair as though she had just spent the afternoon in bed with Nick, but it was her face that surprised her.

She looked like Celeste. She had never seen the resemblance before, and she smiled at seeing the similar jaw structure of her father and her cousin, and the seductive expression she thought only Celeste owned.

'Where did you get that?' she asked, peering at herself.

'It was on one of the photo agency sites, we just cropped in and reframed it,' said Claire.

Billie sat back in her seat and looked at the Le Marche women.

'So you want to use us as your models?'

'Not just models, but the brand ambassadors. Your history and the Le Marche struggles, and the fact that the women come out on top in this company are very appealing to the female market right now.'

Billie was silent, so Claire continued.

'Your grandmother is constantly referred to as marrying into Le Marche and taking over the skincare business, but I believe, and I might be wrong, that she is the Le Marche family. I don't think she just took over, I think she started this business, and the patriarchy of the business world prefers that than a woman who created something with her own mind and body.'

Claire's face was passionate as she spoke, and William jumped up to join her.

'Not that we want to get all suffragette on you, I mean we are selling face creams and lipsticks but yes, I think more emphasis should be placed on the female power in this brand.'

Billie looked at Edward, who raised his eyebrows at her as if in agreement. She knew how much Edward loved her grandmother, and she paused, thinking before she spoke.

'I think Celeste and Matilde are perfect, but I doubt my mother would be keen, and I'm not a model, I'm a scientist.'

'All the better,' said Claire excitedly. 'Beauty and brains, it's a formula for success.'

'Let me talk to Celeste. Can I keep these?' She gestured to the images.

'Of course,' said William, as he and Claire sat down again.

Billie picked up her pen and tapped the side of her face.

'You know we don't have a huge budget?'

'We know, that's why using you all as the subjects will lower the costs considerably.'

'And we don't have a lot of time, we need to be ready to launch in eight weeks.'

Claire and William glanced at each other. 'We can work with that.'

'I'll come back to you tomorrow,' said Billie.

Gemma walked them out and then was back in the boardroom, and Billie and Edward went through the images.

'They were very pleasant,' said Edward. 'I thought they might be a bit too cool for us.'

'No, they're not like that,' said Gemma, looking pleased with how the presentation had gone.

'William seems very nice. How long have you two had a thing?' asked Billie, looking up from the image of Celeste.

Gemma blushed scarlet, and then scratched her head and shrugged. 'It's not William I'm seeing,' she said, 'it's Claire.'

Billie felt her eyes widen. 'Wow, I had no idea. Well, she seems very smart and passionate, and she's lucky to have you.'

'What's this?' asked Edward, looking up from his phone.

'Nothing,' said Billie, 'just girl talk.'

And Billie could hear Gemma giggle all the way back to her office.

Chapter 45

Celeste

The ministrations of Matilde were annoying Celeste and, although she tried to be patient, it was inevitable that she would snap at her mother.

'Stop fussing, Maman,' Celeste said from her grandmother's bed.

Matilde had insisted she take the bigger room and Celeste had been too tired to argue, but after two weeks in bed, with an occasional walk to the living room and bathroom, she was decidedly frustrated.

The only thing that staved away the boredom was reading her grandmother's diaries and seeing Edward. Billie was too busy to come as often as she would have liked, but she found she didn't have the energy to worry about work. An agency had been hired, and at some point they were going to take photos of Celeste when she was better.

Asking Matilde to model again wasn't as easy as she had thought with Matilde saying she was too old, too fat, too wrinkled, too much sun, too much everything, but eventually she caved when Celeste suggested they take the photos in

Nice and Celeste would come and stay with her there once she got the all-clear to fly.

'They want to take the images in our natural habitats,' Billie said. 'Me in the lab, Matilde on the tennis court, Mum at her desk.'

But Billie hadn't suggested where Celeste's natural habitat was. The hospital bed? In a married man's bed? In her grandmother's office?

Later, when the sun had gone down, and thankfully Elisabeth and Matilde had gone out to see a show in the West End, Celeste settled on the sofa, wearing her favourite blue spotted pyjamas, and opened her grandmother's diary.

She saw so much of Daphné in herself. The ability to disconnect from emotion, the skill to mistake lust as love, the propensity to self-blame at other's bad choices.

The sound of the door startled her, and she opened it to see Edward.

'Hello,' she said, pleased to see him. 'Come in, I'm just reading my grandmother bitching about Robert, for something new.'

Edward walked in and sat on the armchair, and looked around. 'Is Matilde here?'

'No, thankfully,' said Celeste and then she felt disloyal. Matilde's care for her was faultless, with wonderful soups and casseroles, home-made bread and delicious fruit from the Harrods food hall, flown in from Spain or South America or wherever was offering oranges at this time of the year.

'She needs a night off,' added Celeste quickly.

'I'm sure you do also,' said Edward with a smile.

She laughed a little. 'It's true, adult children and parents have to tread carefully when living together.'

'Yes, I'm aware of that as I head home tomorrow for Christmas with my family. My mother insists I stay at home with her and Dad, even though my room is now her sewing room. I often wake up in a single bed with a pin or three in my bottom.'

Celeste started to laugh and then felt lost at the thought of him being away.

'How long will you go for?' she heard herself ask casually, but inside her heart was beating quickly.

What was happening?

Edward crossed his legs and she saw a glimpse of the skin between his socks and his pants, and felt herself blush.

She was turning into a character from an eighteenth-century romance novel, she thought, and tried to push the image from her mind. She had always been forward with men. One-night stands were nothing to her, and nakedness felt as natural as breathing, but that one inch of skin had made her dizzy. Perhaps it was the left-over infection in her brain?

Yes, she was now brain damaged, she thought, as she noticed the way the light caught Edward's eyes, as he talked about going home.

'I'll be gone for a week or so,' he said, and she noticed he didn't look at her when he said it.

She swallowed, trying to think of what to say. Sexually loaded statements were easy for her, but this wasn't what she needed to say. She felt her hands twist in her lap, and then she looked up at him.

'I'll miss you,' was all she could summon.

Edward smiled a little. 'I have been thinking,' he said slowly.

Her heart leapt, although she had no idea what he was about to say. 'Yes?'

'I think, that when the year is up in the agreement, after everything is settled . . .' He paused, as though trying to find the words.

'Tell me,' she encouraged.

'I think I will resign.'

Celeste felt as though the world had tilted and she was hanging off the edge, about to fly off into space.

'What do you mean? Why?' Her voice spoke the right words, but she couldn't see for the panic rising in her.

'I think it's time I moved on. Le Marche is in fresh hands now, and you girls are doing so well. Now with Dominic's money we are safe against Robert, there's no real reason for me to stay, other than safety. I think it's time I got on with my life. I've given so much to Le Marche, it's time I found what I want.'

'And what is that?' Celeste tried to not show any emotion. She was used to it with Robert, not rising to his barbs and comments about her life.

'I want to find someone to marry, have a family, open a little practice for myself. I can't have that at Le Marche. It's all or nothing.'

Celeste wanted to scream at him, *Yes you can. You can have that. You can marry me, and we'll have gorgeous little Badger babies and live happily ever after*, but she didn't. Instead, she lifted her head and nodded.

'It's probably best then,' she said.

Edward smiled, as though pleased with what had just happened.

'Should we order some Indian? I'd love a chicken tikka.'

But Celeste stood and shook her head, which felt as though it was too heavy for her neck.

'I'm not feeling well,' she said. 'I'm going back to bed. See yourself out.'

She rushed up the hallway and into her room, and climbed under the covers. A small fire was lit in the grate, thanks to Matilde, and the room was toasty and perfect, except her heart was breaking.

'Celeste?' The door opened and Edward stood in the doorway. 'Should I call Matilde?'

His voice sounded uncertain, but Celeste waved her hand at him.

'No, I'm fine, just tired. Bye,' she said into her pillow. The tears were coming now and if Edward didn't leave then he would see a full-blown sob fest. She bit the linen sheets to stop the cries from being heard.

Of course Edward would leave her, she thought. They all did.

'I haven't been in here since the night Daphné signed the will,' she heard him say and she squeezed her eyes shut.

Edward was her North Star this whole time, she realised, just like he had been to Daphné, but she wasn't enough for him to stay, unlike her grandmother, and rage replaced the tears. She sat upright in bed.

'Why am I not enough?' she screamed at him.

'What? Who said you're not enough?' Edward looked shocked and, if truth be told, a little scared.

'Why am I not enough for you to stay? Why did you stay for my grandmother but not me? What's wrong with me?'

'Nothing,' Edward stammered, 'I just think I need a change.'

'A change from what?' she yelled. She was kneeling on the bed now. 'A change from what?'

'I just need it,' Edward said, walking into the room.

'Is this because of me?' she asked.

Edward was silent and she stood on the bed.

'You think I'm foolish, incompetent, like my father, don't you? You don't want to work with me, do you? All those lies you told me out there about how we will be fine, you're running away from me, aren't you?'

'It's not like that, Celeste, please don't do this.' His face was pinched, and she felt the awful words coming faster and she couldn't stop them.

'You're a bastard,' she screamed.

'Why are you doing this? Please come down from the bed,' he pleaded, as he moved to the side and put his hand out for her to take it.

'No,' she yelled.

'You'll fall,' he said, trying to take her hand.

'I already have,' she said and then she collapsed on the bed, sobs racking her thin frame.

She felt his hand on her head, gently stroking her hair.

'It's OK, what's going on, tell me,' she heard him say. And, for the first time in her thirty years, Celeste took a deep breath and said what she was feeling.

She rolled onto her back and stared at the ceiling.

'I'm in love with you, and this isn't your issue, it's mine, but the idea of not seeing you again, even for a week over Christmas was painful, but you leaving—and I understand you want to start a new life without us crazy Le Marche women—makes me wish I had died.'

Edward sighed, and lay down next to her and took her hand. 'That's very dramatic,' he said, and squeezed her hand.

'Don't invalidate my feelings,' she said, remembering her therapist saying that's what Robert did to her.

'I'm not,' Edward said, and he rolled onto his side to look at her.

She couldn't face him, not after she had behaved so badly, and she closed her eyes to avoid his.

And then she felt the softest brush of lips on hers, and then another on her cheek, and on her nose, and her eyes flipped open.

There he was. Her Edward, inches from her face.

'I was leaving because I love you,' he whispered.

'You don't leave when you love someone, you silly man,' she said, feeling more tears coming, but from a new well within her.

'I don't know what I'm doing,' he said, and she saw the fear and love on his face.

'Neither do I, but I'd rather not know with you,' she said, and then he kissed her.

She felt as though this was the kiss the poets her aunt Elisabeth talked to her about described, when she came to read to her, when she told her about the words that she and Henri had fallen in love over. Edward was tentative at first, but, as she pulled him to her, she felt her body merge with his, their legs entwined and hands wandering.

'We can't,' he said, as she slid a hand down the front of his pants.

'You want to,' she said, confused.

'I do, but you've been very unwell, and I think this would be too much.'

Celeste didn't know if she should laugh or cry, so instead she did both, his arms wrapped around her. No man had ever said no to sex with her because they were concerned about her health. No man had ever looked at her the way Edward did, or made her laugh or think or even made her want them like she wanted him right now.

She sat up in the bed, and slowly undid her pyjama top.

'What are you doing?' Edward sounded panicked and she started to laugh.

'I'm undressing,' she said.

She got to the last button and then shimmied the top from her shoulders, so her breasts were exposed.

'Jesus Celeste, you've been sick,' he said, but she could see the lust in his face.

She lay back, and wriggled out of the pants, and threw them on the floor, and rolled onto her side, unashamed of her state.

'What the hell am I supposed to do now?' he asked. 'I'm trying to be a gentleman and you're looking like work of art.'

Celeste smiled and waited. 'You can sleep next to me fully clothed, or naked. Whatever happens, happens, and if it's too much for either of us, I will say stop. OK?'

Edward sighed, and got out of bed.

'What are you doing?' she cried. Was he leaving? Had she been too forward?

But Edward was kicking off his shoes, and undoing his pants, and she squealed and jumped under the covers.

'Do you think I could say no to that?' she heard him ask,

as she covered her head with the quilt and then she felt the bed lower as he slipped in beside her.

Her hands reached for him, and he took hers and she moved to him. Their bodies touched, and they held each other for a long time. At some point, Celeste realised they had fallen asleep, naked, still holding each other, and she kissed his mouth softly.

'Mmmmm,' she heard him say.

'Sorry, go back to sleep,' she whispered.

'Not a fucking chance, Miss Le Marche,' he growled.

Their passion met instantly and whatever Edward was lacking in confidence in life, he wasn't lacking it in bed. Celeste had never been explored like he did, she had never had so much attention, while he ensured she came at every possible moment that he was touching her.

And then he was inside her, and she thought she could die of happiness from the feeling of the way they fitted together. The pieces of the puzzle were finally in place.

When they finished, and lay in each other's arms, Edward stroked her back, while she kissed his chest.

'Would you consider marrying me, Celeste?'

She didn't move a muscle, as though afraid of scaring him away. 'Is that a proposal?'

'Would you like it to be?'

They lay, carefully guarded in the dark, the fire almost burned out across the room.

'If it is, then yes, I would marry you, but on one condition,' she said.

His hand stopped stroking her skin and he paused. 'What's that?'

'I am not changing my name.'

Edward laughed. 'I don't blame you – perhaps I should change mine to Le Marche.'

Celeste looked up at the outline of his face in the darkness. 'No, I like you as a badger,' she said, and she reached up and stroked his hair, where she knew the temples were greying a little.

'I love you, Mr Badger,' she said.

'And I love you, Miss Le Marche.'

Chapter 46

Robert

The Limoges china made a very fine sound when it shattered, but it wasn't quite the crash Robert had hoped for, so he picked up the silver coffee pot and threw it across the room. It hit a very sweet, early Bouguereau painting, and fell down, spilling its black contents onto the apricot silk carpet, giving him a little more release and satisfaction.

All the business media outlets were discussing the news that Dominic Bertiull had invested in Le Marche. The press release was out, including the information that Matilde would be the face of a new product, and Paul Le Brun was quoted as saying how excited he was for the French cosmetic and skincare industry.

There was a photo of his mother staring at him from the front page of *Les Écho*, and a smaller one of Celeste and Billie at a dinner, smiling, with Celeste wearing a dress that showed off too much décolletage.

A whore like her mother, he thought.

He scanned the article, as it rhapsodised about his mother and her granddaughters, and stated he was a retired business-man.

Retired my arse, he thought, as his eyes went back to Celeste and Billie, and then he smiled. He knew what he had to do.

With Dominic's money backing the business, there was no way he could compete, but if he broke up the little happy family again, then the only choice would be to put him back at the helm and, this time, he would have Bertiull working for him.

It was perfect, he thought, and he phoned London to set his plan in action.

Robert arrived in London the next day, with a valise of new clothes from Lacoste and Givenchy. He was trying a new look of sportswear mixed with business that he had seen on some of the rock stars in *Oops!* magazine. Teamed with his Tods loafers, he was feeling younger, more relevant and as though he was about to take over the world.

Eschewing a coat for fashion's sake, he was freezing when he arrived at Le Marche. He ignored the receptionist asking him to wait for Edward and instead made his own way to the boardroom. He sat at the head of the table—his rightful place, he told himself.

Edward soon joined him, and Robert didn't offer to shake his hand, and nor did Edward.

'Where are the girls?' he asked.

'Billie is coming. Celeste is unwell still, I'm sure you've heard.'

Robert shrugged. 'Yes, a migraine, wasn't it?'

'No, meningitis,' said Edward with a frown, emphasising the word, but Robert ignored him.

Celeste had always been a drama queen, he thought, trying to take the spotlight from Camille's death.

'We need to make this fast. I'm leaving for a holiday this afternoon,' said Edward, as though Robert was a pestering child. Robert wanted to punch him, but he knew what was coming was about to level him.

Billie pushed open the door and stared at him.

'I would prefer if Celeste was here,' said Robert. Somehow not having Celeste here dulled the fireworks that were waiting to be lit in the room.

'She's unwell, if you hadn't heard,' said Billie, sitting at the other end of the table, facing him.

It was a bold move on her behalf, he thought, and he smiled at her. He had to admire her gumption.

'How's business?' he asked.

'Great actually,' she answered, not flustered, checking her phone as though she had more important places to be than here with him.

Rude little bitch, he thought. Just like Celeste.

'What do you want?' she asked finally, leaning back in her chair and staring at him. 'You said it was urgent.'

She had entirely too much self-confidence for his liking, and he paused for effect.

'I thought you should know about Celeste, if you didn't already.'

He knew by the confusion on her face she had no idea what he was talking about.

'It's important, now that Mother has gone, that the truth comes out in these situations.'

He glanced at Edward, who was sitting so still it was as though he was steeling himself for the unknown.

'I don't think you should speak of your daughter without her being her to defend herself,' Edward stated firmly.

'That's just the thing,' said Robert with a laugh, 'she's not my daughter.'

'What?' Billie leaned forward now, her hands spread on the smooth wood of the table.

'She's Henri's daughter. He and Matilde had an affair behind Elisabeth's and my back. I'm sure Celeste knows, didn't she tell you she was your half-sister?'

Billie stood up. 'I don't believe you.'

'You don't want to believe me,' he answered. 'You've built up this impression of the tortured, pained poet father. Let me tell you something. He was a lying, cheating, waste of space, drug-addicted, alcoholic dilletante, who manipulated everyone around him, including your naïve mother.'

'You will stop at nothing to ruin us. How could you do this? What did you tell my father before he died? I know you told him something. Is this the lie you told him that made him jump?'

She was screaming at him, and Edward hurried from his chair to her side.

'I simply told him a version of the truth as I knew it then,' said Robert shrugging, as though it was no big deal.

'And what was that?' Edward asked.

'That he is the son of my grandfather,' Robert offered, with a cruel smile at Billie. 'I suppose that made sense as to why he was so useless. His father killed himself, and so did he.

Perhaps it runs in the family? Be careful, you know Celeste has tried before also?'

Edward's head snapped up at this and Robert saw his jaw stiffen in anger.

'The women in the Le Marche family can't seem to keep their legs closed, can they? Are you a whore like your grandmother, Billie? She slept with my grandfather and then my father, did she sleep with you also, Edward?'

It looked as though Edward was about to make a move across the table to Robert, but Billie got there first, screaming something at him that he couldn't quite understand, as she scratched her nails across his face.

'That's a lie,' she repeated. 'You're lying about my father.'

But Robert laughed meanly. 'He then killed himself because he thought he was just like his father, having an affair and a child, then hurting people he loved.'

Billie lashed out at him again, but Edward grabbed her around the waist as Robert stepped away from his niece.

'That's not true,' she cried. 'I've read Daphné's journals. You're Giles' son, you're the son of that cruel bastard, that's why it's so easy for you, isn't it? You told my father a lie, and he died because of it, how can you live with yourself?'

'Very easily,' said Robert, wiping blood from his cheek with his hand, and then he walked to the door.

'This company is mine and you are wasting your time. You and Celeste are the product of the most useless man in the world. I am the rightful owner of this business. My true father created the products, and my bitch of a mother ripped him off just like you're doing to me.'

Billie was crying, as Edward held her, and Robert smiled at them.

'Ask Matilde the truth, she will tell you about Celeste. Those two are evil, and eventually you had to find out. I'm just glad it was me who got to tell you.'

And he turned and walked from the room towards the elevator.

'How can you do this to her?' he heard Edward's voice behind him.

'She deserves to know the truth,' he said, turning to him.

'Not Billie, that's one thing, but Celeste. She loves you. You're the only father she has known and you're constantly punishing her for Henri's mistake.'

Robert was still for a moment. Memories of Celeste and Camille on his lap, or swimming in the pool with him, and tucking them into bed at night, whirled through his mind.

'But I'm not her father,' he said as he pressed the elevator button.

The doors opened. He stepped inside and looked at Edward in the eye as the doors began to close. 'I'm no one's father any more.'

He went back to the hotel, and up to his suite, and dialled a whore named Simone, who said she would be over in thirty minutes.

He needed to taste her. He imagined that's what success would taste like, and he felt himself aroused at what had just happened back in the boardroom.

Billie would leave the company now. Celeste was too sick to work, and Dominic Bertiull would ask him to come and take over. It really was a perfect solution. There was no way they would action the clause in the will that he remain silent or he would lose everything Daphné had left him. There would be too much confusion and hate to worry about that.

He waited for Simone, and he laughed to himself at Billie's shocked face.

It was a shame she had scratched him, but he could always sue her, and he decided that after his visit with the whore, he would do exactly that.

Some days were diamonds, he thought, and this was one of them. A big fat carat of a day.

Chapter 47

Billie

'Is it true?' Billie asked Edward, as she sat with her head between her legs in the boardroom.

'You need to talk to Celeste and Matilde,' said Edward slowly.

'You know, don't you?' Billie put her head up and stared at him.

'I can't say, you need to talk to them. Come on, I'll take you there,' he said, and he called for Gemma to bring Billie's things to him.

He bundled her into a taxi and, as she slumped in the back seat, he gave the driver directions.

She should call Nick, she thought, but then again, did he really want to hear more of her family drama?

By the time the taxi had weaved through the busy traffic to the flat, Billie felt sick. She had woken up feeling sick today, and had told Nick she didn't feel right. She must have known bad news was coming, she thought, as Edward opened the door and she stepped out onto the street.

'I don't want to see them,' she said, losing her nerve.

'You have to,' said Edward gently, and, taking her arm, he led her inside and up to the flat.

When he knocked on the door, Billie thought she might throw up, and when it opened, and she saw Celeste smiling at them, and leaning forward to kiss Edward, she wanted to scream at her, but she found she couldn't use her voice.

'Come in. What's going on? What did Robert want?' she asked, as she gestured for them to sit down.

Before Billie could try to summon the use of her vocal cords, Matilde walked from the kitchen, wiping her hands on a tea towel.

'I'm making coffee, Billie, Edward? Can I get you some?'

The thought of coffee made Billie want to retch, but she swallowed it down.

'Sit down, Matilde,' said Edward, and Matilde did so, still carrying the tea towel, her face concerned.

'Robert came to see us today,' Edward said, but Billie stared at the floor.

'And?' Celeste asked in a small voice.

Billie looked up. 'He said you're my half-sister.'

The only confirmation she needed was the gasp from Matilde and Billie looked at her.

'Why didn't you tell me? Am I a dirty little secret kept all the way in Melbourne? The one you don't bother to contact or tell anything to?'

Matilde's face was ashen.

'It was one night, it meant nothing to Henri or me. Things weren't good in either of our marriages and we found comfort for a moment. It was only once. Celeste came from that, but I didn't want to parent alone and Elisabeth couldn't get pregnant at the time. Henri didn't want to tell her and hurt her. The only reason Robert knew was because we hadn't had any intimacy for so long, it would have been impossible to pretend she was his.'

'Then why didn't you tell me?' She looked at Camille.

Camille looked less guilty than her mother, but Billie still hated her for keeping such a secret from her.

'I didn't find out until I was in hospital, after they gave me the diagnosis. I was too sick to deal with it. Maman said it was like Uncle Henri had—the depression, the migraines, the general unwellness. That's why he died, she thought. He must have had it also because it's hereditary and he must have struggled so much.'

'No,' Billie screamed. 'He died because of all the lies that everyone told him.'

'No, he died because he was sick, Sibylla.'

Billie heard her mother's voice and she turned to see her in the doorway.

'Did you know about Celeste?'

Elisabeth shrugged. 'I had my suspicions, but it didn't matter.'

'Of course it mattered,' Billie sobbed.

Elisabeth was on the floor, sitting at Billie's knees and holding her hands.

'It didn't matter because I had you, and Celeste was all Matilde had left. I didn't want to take her away from her mother. Our girls made us strong. I am glad your father is Celeste's papa and not Robert. I'm glad you two are friends now. I'm glad you're here and the truth is out. It's exhausting having to lie all the time.'

Billie looked up and saw Celeste crying, Matilde crying, and even Edward was wiping away a tear.

'I don't know what to do, I feel so betrayed.'

'I would have told you eventually,' said Celeste, weeping. 'I'm not good with secrets, especially mixed with champagne.'

Billie looked at her aunt. 'You said it was only once?'

'Once,' Matilde said. 'He put Marvin Gaye on the stereo and it just sort of happened.'

'He loved Marvin Gaye,' the women all said at once, as though to themselves.

And they sat in silence, each in their own thoughts, and then Edward spoke.

'Don't let this information tear you apart when you've just come back together. That's what Robert wants, Billie. He wants you to leave and Celeste to collapse and him to take over because of Dominic's investment.'

Billie swallowed. 'Screw all of you, every last Le Marche. You were right to keep me away from them, Mum. They're toxic and filled with lies and hate.'

She picked up her bag and walked to the door. 'I'm going home,' she said and she looked pointedly at Elisabeth. 'And you're the worst of all of them.'

'Billie,' her mother cried, but she had already closed the door.

* * *

For two weeks Billie sat on the sofa in the apartment and cried.

She cried for the loss of her mother and family. She cried for the loss of her job, but most of all she cried for her father. How differently things could have been if he had been well. Perhaps Robert wouldn't be so awful, and she and Celeste could have been friends first, and she might have known Daphné and where she came from. Perhaps she might have been braver, and more like Celeste and Daphné. Perhaps she might have been her true self?

Nick went to work and came home, but Billie never asked him about it and he didn't say a word about Celeste or Edward, until one day Billie looked up from her tomato soup he had heated for her, with a toasted cheese sandwich on the side, and put down her spoon loudly, as though making a point with the cutlery.

'Has anyone mentioned me at work?'

Nick kept eating his soup while he answered. 'Everyone.'

'Who's everyone?' She knew she sounded petulant but couldn't help herself.

'Everyone in the lab, Minnie in reception, Marcel in the French lab, Gemma . . .' His voice trailed off.

Billie picked up her spoon again. 'Is that all?'

Nick looked at her. 'Every day Celeste asks me how you are, if she can call you or if she can come and see you. Every day Edward asks after you, says he misses your sensible management of Celeste's crazy ideas, and Matilde calls me, and your mother calls me twice, sometimes three times a day.'

Billie was silent as she thought. 'I'm sorry I'm causing so much drama.'

Nick shook his head. 'I don't mind. I know you need space. You'll know what to do when the time is right. Sometimes things just solve themselves.'

'Thank you for not pressuring me,' she said softly.

He smiled at her and went back to his dinner.

Later, Billie had a dream about her father. These were rare and this one felt different.

Henri was on the side of a bridge. He smiled at her and she waved back to him.

'Papa?' she called out to him.

'It is easy to be angry, but braver to forgive.' He smiled at her happily as he spoke. 'True happiness comes from the joy of deeds well done, and the zest of creating things new.'

'Do you mean work?' she asked, confused.

But he only smiled and stood on the edge of the bridge.

'Don't do it,' she cried.

'But I was only ever flying,' he said, and with that he took off into the sky, heading upwards to the stars.

When she woke the next morning, Billie felt calm for the first time in weeks. It felt as though a storm had passed, and she got up and into the shower.

Nick had already gone to work, and she took her time as she showered and then dried her hair.

'Deeds well done and creating things new,' she repeated as she dressed. It was as thought Henri had given her permission to let go of the past and create things new again.

She pulled on the black pants from Zara that Celeste had talked her into, and slipped on the silver sneakers her mother had bought her. A black cashmere sweater finished the ensemble. She looked like a Melbourne girl, in their uniform of black, but she was in London, with the love of her life, and she was going to make the most of it, but first she had to go to work.

Minnie was first to greet her, as she arrived at the office, and then Gemma.

'Nick said you've been sick,' said Gemma sincerely.

'I'm fine now,' said Billie. 'Is Celeste in?'

'She's in a meeting with Edward,' said Gemma, 'but I'm sure you can go in.'

Billie steeled herself, and slowly opened the door to Celeste's office.

'Oh sorry,' she said quickly and shut the door again.

Gemma laughed. 'I should have mentioned they might be snogging, but I didn't really know how to say it.'

The door opened and a red-faced Celeste grabbed Billie's arm and pulled her inside.

'I was going to tell you but you aren't talking to me,' she hissed.

Billie stifled a smile and looked at Edward. 'And you, were you going to tell me?'

Edward shook his head, 'No, I wasn't. I imagined Celeste would do it if you ever spoke to us again.'

'Do you understand why I was angry?'

Celeste nodded. 'But you understand I was sick and could barely process it myself let alone tell you.'

She was silent. Then she said, 'You're right, I'm being selfish.'

'No, you're hurt, and it's awful, and to be betrayed by your parents isn't a good thing to feel.'

Billie looked at Celeste and smiled. 'Friends?'

'Always,' said Celeste, as she pulled Billie into a hug.

'So you're back to work?' asked Edward from the window where he stood. 'We have a lot to do.'

'Shut up,' said Billie and Celeste simultaneously.

Work could wait for a minute, right now they needed to be family.

Chapter 48

Celeste

Celeste sat in the passenger seat of Edward's car, and clicked the seat belt into place.

The first snow was falling, and Billie and Nick were still in the street marvelling over it when she and Edward left for his trip back home.

'You don't have to come,' he said, but he hadn't protested too much when she invited herself and her mother along.

'I want to come,' said Celeste. She turned to the back seat, 'Don't we, Maman?'

Matilde smiled happily. 'Of course we do. It's exciting to meet future family.'

Edward started to laugh, as he drove the Jaguar through the streets and out to the motorway.

'Are you sure you want your mother tagging along?' Matilde asked, her hand on Celeste's shoulder.

'Of course, it's Christmas, we should all be together, and besides, if they hate me, you and I can run away together,' said Celeste.

'They won't hate you,' said Matilde and Edward in unison.

'Why are you doing Christmas now?' asked Matilde from the back seat.

'We always do it earlier so Mum and Dad can go to Mallorca,' said Edward. 'They've gone there for the last three years, and they take my youngest brother, Sam, with them.'

'So what happens to the rest of the family?' asked Celeste.

'They spend it with their girlfriends or friends,' said Edward cheerfully.

'And what do you do?' she asked him.

Edward was silent for a moment. 'Oh, you know, just catch up on some work or the like.'

So he spent Christmas alone, she thought, and her heart broke a little for him.

'Aren't you upset at your parents?'

'Why would I be?' He laughed. 'They're adults, so am I. I know they love me.'

Celeste watched the streets disappear and soon they were passing snow-covered fields and pretty cottages.

'I think we should have a cottage,' she said aloud.

'Here or in France?' asked Edward.

'Both,' she answered.

Edward hadn't asked her to come explicitly, but she knew he wanted her to meet his family, and she wanted to meet them. There were sides to him she didn't know yet, and since he knew everything about her family, she figured it was only fair.

But soon the countryside became a blur and the gentle movement of the car sent her to sleep. When she woke, they were at the front of a small brick terrace, with a red foil wreath on the front door.

'We're here,' she heard Edward whisper. Matilde was already out of the car, embracing a round lady with bleached hair.

'That's Mum,' said Edward, as the woman tapped on the glass.

'Come on then, hop out you two. Father Christmas isn't delivering through the sunroof.'

As she opened the door, and was met with a hug and enveloped in a perfume that was so strong, Celeste thought she might sneeze.

'I'm Shirley,' Edward's mum said.

'I'm Celeste,' she answered, thinking she was about to be broken from the women's strength.

'You don't talk like a Frenchie,' said Shirley, as she hustled them inside the house.

Edward reached down and took Celeste's hand and she clung to it gratefully, as they walked into the narrow hallway. The house smelled like roasted meat and sweat, Celeste decided, and she tried to imagine Edward growing up in this tiny house. Worn carpet covered the floors, with a plastic runner that went the length of the hallway, and made a crushing sound as they walked on it.

Family photos lined the walls in a variety of frames, but Celeste noticed the faces were all smiling—at the seaside, at school sports days, blowing out candles on home-made birthday cakes—and she wondered how many photo opportunities of her growing up her mother had missed.

'Here we all are,' said Shirley happily, and Celeste walked into a small living room, where a sea of faces stared at her. Shirley reeled off the names of the brothers, and a man with grey hair, who nodded at her, and went back to watching the television.

Shirley and Matilde went into the kitchen, chatting as though they were old school friends. Celeste swallowed nervously, as she turned to Edward.

'Bringing you here was a mistake,' he whispered. 'They're too much en masse.'

'No, it's fine,' she said brightly, hoping it would be.

'I'll get the things from the car,' he said, and she stood in the room, feeling too French, too well dressed, too everything for the Badger men in front of her.

'Are you Edward's boss?' asked one of the older brothers with reddish hair.

'Um, sort of, I mean, not really,' she said, realising how bad it sounded.

'He's done well, hasn't he,' snickered one and a few started to laugh along with them, and then Celeste felt her temper rise.

'Isn't he a wally woofter?' asked one and more laughter ensued.

Celeste felt the words burst from her mouth, yet couldn't stop them. 'Actually, Edward is more the boss than anyone at Le Marche. He is the reason the company survived, and was the greatest asset to my family and the business, and I'm lucky that he wants to be with me. He's an exceptional man and you should be very proud to be related to him. And yes, we are getting married, and we will work together, and I know that with him by my side, we can achieve anything. So why don't you stop putting him down and enjoy his success. It doesn't make things better for you to put him down all the time.'

She raised her head, and stared down at them, then she felt Edward's hand on her shoulder.

'Everything OK?' he asked, looking confused at the stares directed at Celeste.

'It's just great,' she said and she turned and wrapped her arms around him and kissed him so passionately he dropped the suitcases to the floor.

'I love you,' she said, and he blinked a few times, as though trying to understand what had just gone on.

Whatever Celeste did worked, and she noticed a new level of respect occurring when Edward spoke at dinner, while Matilde and Shirley just got drunk on the champagne they had brought with them.

After dinner, which was so much food Celeste thought she would burst, Shirley insisted on present swapping.

'I'm afraid we didn't bring anything,' said Celeste, feeling embarrassed.

But Shirley shook away her shame and put Michael Bublé on the stereo, and started to sway to 'White Christmas'. 'It's not about the presents, it's about the presence,' she said, laughing at her own joke.

'You're the present,' Celeste heard and turned to see Edward's father in his armchair, his Christmas cracker hat still on his head.

'What do you mean, Dad?' asked Edward.

'All these years, we never met any of Edward's friends. Shirl and I thought he was ashamed of us, but now he brings home the fancy girl he loves and her sexy mum, to be with my Shirl. That's a present enough for us.'

Celeste smiled at him and, judging by the open mouths

from his family, she wondered if that was the most he had ever said in a room to them all.

'I'm not ashamed of you, Dad,' said Edward, reaching out and putting his hand on his dad's knee, 'I've just never been in love before.'

Shirley started to jump up and down and then ran from the room.

'What's bitten her on the bum?' asked one of the sons.

But soon she was back, and she handed Celeste a large white box.

'This is for you, duck,' she said.

Celeste glanced at Edward, who shook his head in wonder. She lifted the lid and was met with layers of tissue.

She carefully lifted them, and then saw the netting, and delicate embroidery, and she picked up the piece of fabric.

'It's my veil, and my mother's and grandmother's, and great-grandmother's. Made by nuns in France.'

Celeste looked at the superb handiwork, and the sheer elegance of the piece. She tried to imagine it on Shirley's blonde shock of hair, and failed.

'You never let my Sharon wear that!' said a larger brother wearing a 'So the f*** what?' T-shirt.

'Yes, and where is Sharon today? Edward is the second son to get married, and his bride deserves something special and from our side.'

'Hope he doesn't get the red hair,' said a brother, holding an orange-haired boy in a headlock.

'Fuck off, Matt,' he said and Celeste started to laugh.

'Your mum told me you're getting married,' said Shirley and Matilde smiled happily, as she sat on the arm of a chair.

'*Mère, pourquoi ne pouvez-vous garder un secret?*' Celeste admonished her mother, who had been sworn to secrecy.

'*Noël est un rien de temps des secrets. Je ai eu assez secrets pendant un certain temps*,' Matilde answered nonchalantly.

'*Oui*,' said Shirley in agreement.

'You speak French?' asked Celeste, surprised.

'No, but I agree with your mother, mothers are always right, isn't that so, boys?'

'*Oui*,' they all answered.

Celeste started to laugh, until she was crying with laughter. 'I love this family,' she said to Edward and she kissed him.

'You say that now. They wear a little thin.'

'Oi,' said Shirley and she flicked his ear lobe, 'you're not too old for me to do that, my boy.'

She leaned down and kissed Celeste on the cheek. 'Welcome to the Badgers, Mrs Soon-to-be-Badger.'

Celeste glanced at Edward, who shook his head a tiny bit and she smiled up at her future mother-in-law.

'I can't wait to be a Badger.'

Matilde sat swaying on her arm of the chair. 'And I'll be a Badger's mother,' she said and, with that, she promptly fell off the arm and onto the floor.

Chapter 49

Dominic

Dominic sat at his desk and opened his email, and there was an alert under the name Matilde Le Marche that he had set up three months ago when he had last seen her in the street.

She was the first thing on his mind in the morning and the last thing at night. Everything he did he did for Matilde. The way he spoke to people, the way he dressed, the way he did business, as though she was his silent audience, but still she hadn't replied to his notes, his flowers or his emails and calls.

At times he wondered if he was just trying to prove that he could be patient, when she doubted him so much, but eventually he gave in to his heart and recognised he couldn't find anyone who challenged him or was as self-possessed as Matilde.

He clicked on the article, and the *Telegraph* masthead came onto the screen, and then the headline.

A family affair revealed

His eyes scanned over the images. A lovely photo of Celeste and Matilde, and then a group portrait of Matilde, Celeste, Billie and Elisabeth.

Then he started to read and, as he did, he felt his mouth drop.

Henri Le Marche was Celeste's father, not Robert.

Part of him celebrated at the news of her recently revealed lineage, but he wondered what the secret had cost Matilde.

He read on as Matilde spoke about the scandal.

'We felt that it was time to tell the truth, now that Le Marche is entering a new era. We wanted to be able to be proud about this instead of ashamed; there has been too much shame in this family for too long.'

So Robert must have threatened to release the news and the women took control of the announcement with the exclusive interview themselves, he thought, reading between the lines.

Sibylla was very candid about her father and finding new footing with Celeste as a half sister, not a cousin.

'We're friends, business partners and family. We have boundaries around all three of these separate relationships, but I am glad to not be an only child any more. Having Celeste be that one level closer to me means more than I could have imagined. She has memories of my father that I don't share, and I feel I'm getting to know him even more. Even though he's gone, he lives on in us, so does Daphné, our grandmother, and soon she will live on when my first child is born.'

His eyes scanned for more from Matilde, and then he read.

'I don't have a relationship. I'm not saying I'm not open to one now, but I had to right my relationship with my daughter and niece and sister-in-law first, and, most of all, I had to forgive myself. I think if someone came into my life now, and was happy to accept that I'm a fifty-five-year-old woman with wrinkles and a complicated family, then sure, but they would

have to be a fool to take this on, or love me very much. Age doesn't matter to me. If they're younger, then they better have a great tennis game. I am an excellent serve.'

Was she trying to send him a message? Was she saying age didn't matter? That she was ready for him now?

He had always been brave, but this felt a journey like no other. Everything had always come easily to him, except Matilde, and he knew, if he didn't take this chance, he would regret not knowing for the rest of his life.

He hailed a taxi, and barked out the address to the taxi driver.

This was it, his last chance. God only knew he had waited long enough to find out.

Arriving at Daphné's apartment, he rang the doorbell and waited, his heart beating fast in his chest.

It opened, and there stood Matilde.

'Hello,' she said, in her usual nonchalant manner.

Without speaking, he stepped forward and kissed her. She tasted of coffee and smelled like violets, and he felt her arms wrap around his neck.

When she pulled away, she looked him in the eye. 'You took your time,' she said softly.

'I waited until you were ready,' he answered, as he held her close.

She rested in his arms, and he thought he was a fool for waiting for so long, but it didn't matter now. He was here and she was in his arms.

She looked up at him. 'I assume you know about Celeste,' she said, looking uncertain.

'Yes,' he smiled. 'Are things OK with you all?'

'Yes. Slow but yes, they will be. We just have to deal with Robert. I think he expected a different outcome when he told Billie. He's angry now.'

Dominic walked her to the sofa and they sat, very close, her hand in his.

'Robert will always be angry.' He shrugged.

'I don't want him to take any more from them. He is so destructive.'

He saw the worry on her face and felt her pain and guilt.

Dominic thought for a moment. 'I can talk to him if you like.'

'No, you've done enough. The girls wouldn't be here if it wasn't for your investment.'

He kissed her again, to calm her, and because he needed to. He would never stop kissing her if he could help it.

'Marry me?' he asked, but Matilde laughed.

'I'm too old to be married,' she said, shaking her head.

'Then live with me here,' he said.

'In London?' she said. 'No. I gave up too much for a man once, I won't do it again.'

Dominic was silent. Could he live in Nice? Could he live Matilde's life?

'I don't think I could play tennis every day,' he admitted.

'I played tennis because there was nothing else to do,' she said defensively. 'But I have a job now. I'm modelling for Le Marche again. I will be here, in France, in Japan—they have a whole tour planned for me.'

'Will you have any time for me?' he asked with a smile.

'Don't patronise me,' she snapped.

'I'm not.' But was he? What did he want from Matilde? For her to be there whenever he felt like it? To slot into his life?

He was ashamed to admit it was true and he leaned back on the sofa.

'I just want to be with you,' he said, feeling like a teenage boy with a crush.

'I know,' she said and now she leaned in to kiss him. 'And we will be, but I'm used to being alone and it will take time for me to make room for you.'

'I'm patient,' he said, his hands moving to her waist.

'I know,' she said.

He pulled her to him. 'I need you,' he said, as she moved to his lap.

'I know,' she said.

'You know a lot,' he groaned, as she moved against him.

'I know many things, this is what being with an older woman gives you,' she said.

'A hard-on?' he asked, as he felt her hand on his shoulders, grinding against him.

'If he's lucky,' she said and then with a strength he didn't know he had, he stood up, holding her, her legs wrapped around him.

'Bedroom, now,' he demanded to know.

'Down the hall,' she murmured into his neck, then kissed him.

He moved down the hall and, when he arrived at the side of her bed, he gently laid her down. He slid her skirt from her, then her tights, and traced a finger over her stomach where her shirt had ridden up, exposing her skin.

She lay still as he unbuttoned it, opening the fabric as though revealing something amazing and, to him, the sight of Matilde in her sensible white bra and underpants was amazing. Sexual energy oozed from every pore. He could see she wanted him as her hips rose at the touch of his fingers.

'God, you're beautiful,' he said.

She pulled him to her. 'You need to be inside me or I'm going to explode,' she said, her voice husky with desire.

'I know,' he said, as he started to undo his tie. He took his time with the tie, enjoying watching her squirm on the bed.

'Hurry up.' She pulled at his shirt.

'Be patient,' he admonished her gently. 'We have the rest of our lives.'

'I'm old remember, the clock is ticking.'

Dominic laughed as he pulled his shirt over his head. 'I love you Matilde,' he said.

'I know,' she answered as he lay on top of her, naked.

He felt her open for him, and she sighed with pleasure.

'I love you, Dominic,' she said in the smallest voice, one filled with fear and uncertainty.

'I know,' he said and then he kissed her again, taking away any anxiety she felt.

'I'm not going anywhere, Matilde. We will make this work, I promise you.'

When they eventually left the bed later that morning, Matilde made them jam crêpes, which they ate in the kitchen, while she told him about Celeste's wedding and Billie's baby, and he thought there was nowhere he would rather be than in Daphné Le Marche's old apartment, with his beauty Matilde, listening to kitchen table talk about her world and knowing he was now truly a part of it, for ever and ever.

Chapter 50

Paris, 2017

One year and one day after the reading of the last will and testament of Daphné Le Marche, Celeste and Billie arrived at Lombard Odier in Paris for the opening of the vault.

'God, it's so exciting,' said Billie.

A well-dressed bank employee met them at the door and, with a quietly reverential manner, he asked them to sign the appropriate paperwork before he took them to down to the vault.

As they walked through the tunnel, the women looked at the hundreds of vaults behind bars.

'Imagine the secrets in here,' said Billie.

'And the jewels,' added Celeste, admiring her own engagement ring of pink Burmese rubies and diamonds.

Edward had proposed properly on New Year's Eve, in front of the television at his flat, at exactly midnight, while Celeste was eating popcorn and drinking champagne, and watching the countdown to a new year.

They were to be married on the large terrace at Matilde's

villa in three weeks with a small guest list and food and drink supplied by the tennis club.

Celeste was going to wear a simple Sophia Kokosalaki dress, with Shirley's veil, and she had asked her mother to give her away.

The metal drawer was left on a wooden table that looked as old as the building, and Billie put her hand on the cold steel.

'God I'm nervous,' she muttered.

'I'll open it then,' said Celeste in her usual busy manner. 'If it's something incredible, then we don't want you having a panic attack in the vault.'

Celeste took the code that the bank employee had left them, typed onto a piece of card with the bank's name embossed on the top, and punched it into the electronic lock, and then a green light came on and a click sounded.

'Ready?' asked Celeste, and Billie nodded.

She lifted the lid and found a single envelope inside the red-felt-lined box with the words written across the front—*To be opened according to the instructions in the Last Will and Testament of Daphné Le Marche.*

Celeste picked it up and held it up to the light.

'It might be easier to read if you opened it,' suggested Billie.

'I know, I'm just savouring the moment,' said Celeste, and then she sat on one of the leather chairs, and Billie sat on the other.

'I thought it would be larger, considering it's a formula,' Billie said, peering at the letter-sized envelope.

Celeste carefully opened the envelope, and then slid the

contents from it and left it closed on the desk. Two pages of their grandmother's handwriting.

'Do you want to read it aloud?' she asked Billie.

'If it's in French, then it's best if you do it, besides, I'm too nervous.'

Celeste opened the piece of paper and smoothed it out on the desk.

To whomever reads this note,

My name is Daphné Le Marche, and this letter is to be opened only in the event of my death.

If my beloved grandchildren have opened this, then I am proud of you for getting to this point in the agreement of my last will and testament. One year and a day—I am sure so much has changed for you both.

You are both great women, like me, but I hope you have made better choices than I did.

Celeste looked up at Billie. 'She's very hard on herself, isn't she? Her diaries are filled with self-recriminations like this.'

Billie felt her eyes fill with tears. 'I wish she knew how well we think of her. Everything has her touch on it, even the new products, and the scents we are making for the perfumes are going to be amazing.'

Celeste nodded in agreement and went back to the letter.

If this is Robert reading this, then I hope that you made things right with Celeste and Sibylla before you came back to Le Marche and I hope you can forgive yourself for anything you have done to get here.

Celeste raised her eyebrows. 'God knows he tried to get back here,' she said.

'You still haven't heard from him?' asked Billie gently.

'I invited him to the wedding but he hasn't replied.' Celeste looked down at the letter.

Billie knew that while the revelation of Celeste's biological father changed almost everything, it didn't change the fact that she loved Robert, and there were times of great tenderness and love between them.

'Perhaps try again,' said Billie.

'I will always try, especially when Edward and I have a child,' said Celeste.

She started to read again.

Le Marche created a revolution for skincare, and with that came the responsibility to create something that would change women's skin and the way they felt about themselves. I always created for what I needed in my own life. However, one thing eluded me—how to make a woman glow. How to give her that incandescence that made people wonder what she used on her skin, how to make her look radiant.

'A primer,' said Billie.

'A foundation,' said Celeste in return and then went on reading.

I have only ever had that glow once in my life. It was short-lived through tragedy, but, as I look back on the years, I have discovered that there is a formula to achieve this beauty.

Celeste paused, and looked at Billie, and then turned to the next page and read.

There are three ways to achieve this dernières lueurs.

Celeste looked up at Billie. 'That's like an afterglow, or that last light before the sun sets.'

'God's light,' said Billie and Celeste nodded and went back to reading.

All the skincare in the world cannot conjure that blush and perfection of colour in a woman's face, not even Le Marche products.

The answer lies in this:

1) Fall in love

2) Become with child

3) Success

Any of these are the formula. I am sure this is not the answer you were hoping for, but it is true.

When I look back at my life, I see I only achieved this glow when I was carrying Henri, the business was growing and I was deeply in love with Yves. If time had been kind to me, I would have hoped to have held on to the glow for longer, but that was not my life.

If you have any of these in your life, carry them carefully. Cherish them, and grow them, but don't let them rule your life. You must always remain true to yourself and not fall for the trap of lust, wealth or control as none of these last for ever. The only thing that does is your soul, and it reflects the colours of your world.

Love yourself but don't lose yourself in others or material items. Be brave, be truthful, be kind and be curious and always try to make things right in the family.

I failed at this task and it is my greatest sorrow. I cut myself off until there was nothing and no one left.

Too much sadness took away my glow, but I hope this life will bring it back to the Le Marches.

*This is your legacy to change this family now. Start with
yourself and the rest will follow.*

Deviens lumière,

Signed,

Your grandmother,

Daphné Le Marche

* * *

'*Deviens lumière*. Make of yourself a light,' said Celeste,
looking up at Billie, whose face was strewn with tears.

'That's beautiful,' Billie sobbed.

'It is,' said Celeste quietly.

The women sat in silence, reading and rereading the letter
and then finally Celeste stood up.

'I have to go and find Robert,' she said. 'This drama stops
now. I am going to do everything I can to make sure I honour
her request.'

Billie nodded and wiped her eyes.

Celeste picked up the letter. 'Do you mind if I take this
for a while?'

'Go ahead,' said Billie. She walked to the door then paused
and looked at Celeste. 'I'm happy to be a Le Marche now.'

Celeste smiled at her. 'I'm happy you're one also. I couldn't
do this alone. I need you. You're the other half, perhaps more
than Camille ever was.'

* * *

Celeste was married on the terrace at Matilde's three weeks
later and, when she walked through the house, both Matilde
and Robert stood waiting to walk her to Edward.

'You came,' she said to Robert, feeling her eyes burn with tears.

'I read the letter Maman wrote,' he said. He looked tired and old, and Celeste saw the pain in his face.

'Let's be kind to each other, Papa,' she said, as she felt a tear fall.

Matilde leapt forward and blotted her daughter's face with a tissue. 'If you need to cry, put your head back and tears will roll back inside you,' she insisted.

Celeste laughed and did as she said. 'It works.'

'I know many things about nothing much,' said Matilde.

'You ready?' asked Billie behind them, and they turned to see her in lavender.

The sound of soft guitar music started from the terrace, and Robert stepped forward and lowered the veil over Celeste's beautiful face.

'You're all I have, Celeste. I am so sorry I hurt you.' His eyes filled with tears.

She smiled. 'Put your head back, Papa. It works, I promise.'

Billie walked on the terrace first, making her way to Edward, where he stood with his five brothers in a row behind him, and she smiled at the groom.

Then Celeste stepped out into the light, Matilde and Robert on each side of her. The guests gasped at the sight of them and Celeste paused for a moment, trying to adjust her eyesight.

'Are you OK?' whispered Matilde.

Celeste looked ahead to Edward, bathed in the sunlight and she smiled at her beautiful Mr Badger.

'I'm wonderful, just wonderful.'

Epilogue

Daphné closed the last journal and placed it carefully into the desk drawer with the others. All of the same Smythson black leather, the only difference were the dates on the spines.

There wasn't a journal for each year, that would be indulgent, but there was a decade in them. Only the major events were recorded, but, as she looked at them, she felt betrayed by so much bad luck. Perhaps the next generation would break the Le Marche curse. She closed the drawer and locked it with the small gold key.

Luck had nothing to do with it, she decided. Bad choices, impulsive decisions, instant gratification were always the undoing of her and her progeny.

Edward would be here soon to finish the will, but she hadn't made her choice yet. Loyalty made her sway towards Robert, but she knew he had said something to Henri that made him jump and Robert would never admit it. He was so like his father, she thought.

'Madame Le Marche, it is time for the heart medication,' said the new nurse, who was kinder than the last.

'Thank you,' said Daphné, feeling the breathlessness returning.

The last days she had been connected to an oxygen tank, but she hated it more than the idea of dying.

'We all die in the end,' she had told her doctor.

The nurse placed the small white tablets in a plastic medicine vial with a glass of water on the edge of the desk.

'Give me a few minutes,' said Daphné.

The nurse left, shutting the door behind her, and Daphné picked up the pills and held them in her hand.

She would like to go on but not like this, she thought, and she threw the pills into the wastepaper bin, where they fell, hidden amongst the papers.

Slowly, she rose from the chair, using the desk as support, her vanity and independence refusing a frame on wheels like those people she saw at the hospital.

On opening the door, she saw the nurse, who rushed to her side, but knew better than to lecture Daphné on her illness.

Step by step, she made her way to her bed, now leaning on the nurse, who then helped her into bed, leaving on her satin bed jacket.

'Light me a fire,' ordered Daphné, 'and then call for Mr Badger.'

The nurse did as she asked, and she lay waiting for Edward to arrive.

Everything anyone ever needed to know about her was in those journals. She hadn't lied about the past, escaping responsibility for her actions.

She shouldn't have slept with Giles, and she should have

waited for Yves to come that Christmas—perhaps they would have fallen in love without Giles' influence.

She should have listened to Anna about Robert and Henri.

She should have pushed for Elisabeth to get Henri more help. She should have been a better mother.

Perhaps she would be a better grandmother, she thought.

***

After Edward had left, and the final details were arranged, she lay in the bed. The night nurse was asleep in the other room, and she made her peace with herself and closed her eyes.

And at the end of the bed stood her mother, then Yves, Henri and Anna and at the very back stood Camille, looking exactly as Daphné remembered her.

Was she dreaming or dying? she wondered, as her mother straightened her bedclothes.

'Where am I going?' she asked the room.

'Wherever you want,' said Anna.

'Choose,' said Camille.

Daphné's whole life had been about choices, and yet this one was the easiest.

And when it was over, she looked at Yves sitting by the fire, as she made up her potions at the kitchen sink, a little vase of violets on the windowsill, and the scent of a cherry clafoutis coming from the oven.

'Are you sure?' he asked.

'I am,' she said. 'This was where I was happiest, even if

it was for a moment, it made up for a lifetime of everything else.'

'I love you, Daphné,' Yves said.

'I know,' she said and went back to her work.

Why hadn't she seen this was heaven all along?

It didn't matter now. She was home.

PICTURE PERFECT

Movie stars aren't always picture perfect,
especially when it comes to secrets
from their past…

And in Hollywood, a town built on illusions,
believing you can escape might just be
the biggest deception of all.

Full of sex, secrets and scandal, *Picture Perfect* is ideal
for fans of Paige Toon and Lindsey Kelk.

HARLEQUIN®MIRA®

Bringing you the best voices in fiction
🐦 @Mira_booksUK

40 years of marriage
8 golden charms
One man's journey of discovery

On the anniversary of his wife's death, 69 year-old Arthur Pepper finally musters the courage to go through her possessions, and happens upon a charm bracelet that he has never seen before.

What follows is a surprising adventure that takes Arthur from London to Paris and India in an epic quest to find out the truth about his wife's secret life before they met, a journey that leads him to find healing, self-discovery, and love in the most unexpected of places.

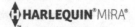

Bringing you the best voices in fiction
🐦 **@Mira_booksUK**

**The ovens are pre-heating, the Prosecco is chilling…
and *The Sunshine and Biscotti Club* is
nearly ready to open its doors.**

But the guests have other things on their minds…

Libby: The Blogger

Life is Instagram-perfect for food blogger Libby…until she catches
her husband cheating just weeks before her Italian cooking club's
grand opening.

Evie: The Mum

Eve's marriage isn't working, but she's not dared admit it until now.
A trip to Italy to help Libby open The Sunshine and Biscotti Club
might be the perfect escape…

Jessica: In Love with her Best Friend

Jessica has thrown herself into her work to shut out the memory of
the man who never loved her back. The same man who's just turned
up in Tuscany…

**Welcome to Tuscany's newest baking school – where your
biscotti is served with a side of love, laughter and ice-cold
limoncello!**

CARINA™

0716_CARINA_SABC

What do you do when you can't find any decent men? You date tried and trusted men, that's what – your friend's exes!

After a series of truly disastrous dating experiences, Marnie is trying something new – dating her friend's exes in an attempt to 'freecycle' love.

At least that's the plan. But through bad dates and good, Marnie and her three best friends Helen, Rosa and Ani begin to realise that while there are advantages to dating pre-screened men, there can also be some serious pitfalls to falling for your friend's ex!

In the chaos of New York, true love
can be hard to find, even when it's
been right under your nose all along...

Love has never been a priority for garden designer
Frankie. After witnessing the fallout of her parents'
divorce, she's seen the devastation an overload of
emotion can cause. The only man she feels comfortable
with is her friend Matt – but that's strictly platonic.

But when Frankie and Matt are thrown into close
quarters working together on a beautiful roof garden
in Park Avenue… will the seeds of friendship grow
into something deeper?

M453_SICP

Bound by blood.
Separated by scandal.

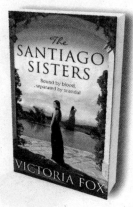

Twins Calida and Terisita Santiago have never known a
world without each other… until Terisita is wrenched
from their Argentinian home to be adopted by world-
famous actress Simone Geddes.

Now, while Terisita is provided with all that money can
buy, Calida must fight her way to the top – her only
chance of reuniting with her twin.

But no-one could have predicted the explosive events
which finally bring the Santiago sisters into the
spotlight together…

M451_TSS